A former meteorologist and EMT, Air Force veteran Larissa Ione now gets her daily dose of excitement from vampires, werewolves, demons and the Four Horsemen of the Apocalypse. She lives in wintery Wisconsin with her US Coast Guard husband, her teenage son, a rescue cat and her hellhound, a King Shepherd named Hexe.

Visit her online:

www.larissaione.com
www.facebook.com/OfficialLarissaIone
www.twitter.com/LarissaIone

D0334749

Essex County Council

3013020388828 3

ALSO BY LARISSA IONE

THE LORDS OF DELIVERANCE SERIES

Eternal Rider
Immortal Rider
Lethal Rider

THE DEMONICA SERIES

Pleasure Unbound
Desire Unchained
Passion Unleashed
Ecstasy Unveiled
Sin Undone

Rogue Rider

Larissa IONE

piatkus

PIATKUS

First published in the US in 2012 by Grand Central Publishing
A division of Hachette Book Group, Inc.
First published in Great Britain as a paperback original in 2012 by Piatkus

Copyright © 2012 Larissa Ione Estell
Excerpt from Pleasure Unbound copyright © 2008 Larissa Ione Estell

The moral right of the author has been asserted.

*All characters and events in this publication, other than those
clearly in the public domain, are fictitious and any resemblance
to real persons, living or dead, is purely coincidental.*

All rights reserved.
No part of this publication may be reproduced, stored in a
retrieval system, or transmitted, in any form or by any means, without
the prior permission in writing of the publisher, nor be otherwise circulated
in any form of binding or cover other than that in which it is published
and without a similar condition including this condition being
imposed on the subsequent purchaser.

A CIP catalogue record for this book
is available from the British Library.

ISBN 978-0-7499-5557-1

Printed and bound in Great Britain by Clays Ltd, St Ives plc

Papers used by Piatkus are from well-managed forests
and other responsible sources.

MIX
Paper from
responsible sources
FSC® C104740
www.fsc.org

Piatkus
An imprint of
Little, Brown Book Group
100 Victoria Embankment
London EC4Y 0DY

An Hachette UK Company
www.hachette.co.uk

www.piatkus.co.uk

For Jillian. Your generosity is absolutely amazing, and truly, you are as beautiful inside as you are on the outside. I think Reseph's heroine lives up to the name. Thanks for everything...including the frying pan!

Acknowledgments

While writing the Lords of Deliverance series, I realized just how important friends and family are. I've needed walks on the beach, house/kid/pet sitters, shoulders to cry on, and drinks...lots and lots of drinks.

Bonnie, you have no idea how much I appreciate you. Thanks for being there. You and Ziva have been lifesavers for me and Hexe.

I also need to thank Nancy Popour, who has been so awesome as well—I don't know what I'd do without you!

Mom and Dude, thank you for being willing to drop everything at a moment's notice to fly out here to help. Because of you, I've been able to attend conferences and go on vacations that have made a big difference in my professional and personal lives.

I also need to send thanks to my father-in-law, Mike, who has been willing to help out when needed, which is a huge relief, since my husband is gone so much.

Thanks also to the amazing ladies who belong to the Book Obsessed Chicks Book Club. I had a blast hanging out with you, so lots of virtual cupcakes to Jennifer, Terry,

Nina, Holly, Penny, Denise, Francesca, and Kimberly Rocha!

And last but certainly not least, thanks to everyone at Grand Central Publishing for all the work you put into making these books the best they can be.

Glossary

The Aegis—Society of human warriors dedicated to protecting the world from evil. See: Guardians, Regent, Sigil.

Agimortus—A trigger for the breaking of a Horseman's Seal. An agimortus can be identified as a symbol engraved or branded upon the host person or object. Three kinds of agimorti have been identified and may take the form of a person, an object, or an event.

Camborian—The human offspring of a parent under the possession of a demon at the time of conception. Camborians may or may not possess supernatural powers that vary in type and strength, depending on the species of demon inhabiting the body of the parent at the time of conception.

Daemonica—The demon bible and basis for dozens of demon religions. Its prophesies regarding the Apocalypse, should they come to pass, will ensure that the Four Horsemen fight on the side of evil.

Fallen Angel—Believed to be evil by most humans, fallen angels can be grouped into two categories: True

Fallen and Unfallen. Unfallen angels have been cast from Heaven and are earthbound, living a life in which they are neither truly good nor truly evil. In this state, they can, rarely, earn their way back into Heaven. Or they can choose to enter Sheoul, the demon realm, in order to complete their fall and become True Fallens, taking their places as demons at Satan's side.

Guardians—Warriors for The Aegis, trained in combat techniques, weapons, and magic. Upon induction into The Aegis, all Guardians are presented with an enchanted piece of jewelry bearing the Aegis shield, which, among other things, allows for night vision and the ability to see through demon invisibility enchantments.

Harrowgate—Vertical portals, invisible to humans, which demons use to travel between locations on Earth and Sheoul. A very few beings can summon their own personal Harrowgates.

Khote—An invisibility spell that allows the caster to move among humans without being seen or, usually, heard.

Marked Sentinel—A human charmed by angels and tasked with protecting a vital artifact. Sentinels are immortal and immune to harm. Only angels (fallen included) can injure or kill a Sentinel. Their existence is a closely guarded secret.

Quantamun—A state of superaccelerated existence on a plane that allows some supernatural beings to travel among humans. Humans, unaware of what moves within their world, appear frozen in time to those inside the quantamun. This differs from the *khote* in that the *khote* operates in real time and is a spell rather than a plane of existence.

Regent—Head(s) of local Aegis cells.

Sheoul—Demon realm. Located deep in the bowels of the Earth, accessible only by Harrowgates and hell-mouths.

Sheoul-gra—A holding tank for demon souls. The place where demon souls go until they can be reborn or kept in torturous limbo.

Sheoulic—Universal demon language spoken by all, although many species also speak their own language.

Sigil—Board of twelve humans known as Elders, who serve as the supreme leaders of The Aegis. Based in Berlin, they oversee all Aegis cells worldwide.

Ter'taceo—Demons who can pass as human, either because their species is naturally human in appearance or because they can shape-shift into human form.

Watchers—Individuals assigned to keep an eye on the Four Horsemen. As part of the agreement forged during the original negotiations between angels and demons that led to Ares, Reseph, Limos, and Thanatos being cursed to spearhead the Apocalypse, one Watcher is an angel, the other is a fallen angel. Neither Watcher may directly assist any Horseman's efforts to either start or stop Armageddon, but they can lend a hand behind the scenes. Doing so, however, may have them walking a fine line that, to cross, could prove worse than fatal.

Rogue Rider

One

It was cold. So fucking cold.

He opened his eyes, but he saw...nothing. Groaning, he shifted, because he seemed to be facedown. Yeah...he was doing a face-plant, all right. But where was he? All he could see was snow. No, that wasn't true, he could see trees laden with snow. And snowbanks laden with snow. And snow laden with more fucking snow.

So he was in a forest...with snow. But where? Why?

And who the hell was he?

Reseph.

The name slurred through his ears as if uttered by a drunken man.

Reseph.

Sounded vaguely familiar, he supposed. Reseph. Okay, he could work with that. Especially since no other names popped into his head.

Weakly, he tried to push himself to his knees, but his

arms wobbled like rubber, and he kept falling on his face. After four tries, he gave up and just lay there, panting and shivering.

Somewhere overhead, an owl hooted, and a few minutes later, a wolf howled into the growing darkness. Reseph took comfort in the sounds, because they meant he wasn't alone. Sure, the owl might fly over and shit on him, and the wolf might eat him alive, but at least he'd have company for a little while.

He didn't know much about himself, but he knew he didn't like to be alone.

He also did *not* like snow.

Curious then, how he'd ended up alone in the snow. Had someone abandoned him here? A tremor of anxiety shook him on the inside as hard as the cold was shaking him on the outside. Surely someone was looking for him.

He held onto that hope as he gradually became aware of a gnawing ache in his bones, accompanied by a stabbing pain in his head. Looked like he was in for a little unconsciousness. Cool. Because right now, he was both freezing and burning up, hurting and numb. Yep, passing out would be a good thing.

Real. Fucking. Good.

Idiot. Dumbass. Meteorological moron.

Jillian Cardiff mentally cursed the meteorologist who screwed the pooch on the timing of this blizzard. She had nothing against weather people; hell, she'd worked with them for years in the FAA. But this...this was ridiculous.

Now she was in a rush to get back to her cabin before

visibility went completely to shit and her draft horse, Sam, got testy.

"Come on, boy." She gave the big sorrel an affectionate slap on the shoulder. "The rest of the firewood can wait."

Sam followed her, not needing to be led by the rope snapped to his halter. He knew the way home and was as eager as she was to get inside a warm, cozy building. The sled carrying a quarter cord of firewood dragged behind him, cutting through the five feet of fresh snow they'd gotten a few days ago. This new storm would probably dump another couple of feet, and by the end of December they'd have more snow than they'd know what to do with.

The wind shrieked like a living thing, and snow blasted her face. Hefting her rifle more securely onto her shoulder, Jillian put her head down and pushed against the gale. Times like this, she really missed Florida. Not that she'd ever go back. Some things you just couldn't forget.

Like being torn apart by demons.

She shivered, but it had nothing to do with the temperature. She was not going there again. The attack was behind her, and as long as she didn't watch TV, get on the Internet, or look at her scars, she never had to think about it.

A long, mournful howl pierced the late afternoon darkness. Had to be close if she could hear it over the wind. Sam snorted and tossed his head, and she slowed to take the lead rope and give him a pat on his white-blazed nose.

"It's okay, buddy. The wolves won't bother us." No, wolves generally left humans alone. If anything, cougars were the big concern. In recent weeks, two area hunters had been found torn to pieces, the carnage blamed on the big cats.

She could handle a cougar. What she couldn't handle was the dark. Demons lurked in the dark.

Abruptly, Sam reared up, a desperate whinny breaking from his big chest. The rope jerked out of Jillian's hand, and she nearly lost her footing in the icy snow as she scrambled to catch it. Sam's front hooves hit the ground and his shoulder rammed her, sending her tumbling down an incline. Her yelp cut off as she slammed into a tree trunk.

Pain spiderwebbed around the right side of her rib cage, and ouch, that was going to be tender tomorrow.

"Dammit, Sam," she muttered, as she crawled back up the snowy slope, pausing to grab the rifle that had been flung into a snowbank.

Sam was snorting, going nuts as he pawed at a snow-drift. Jillian dug ice from places ice shouldn't be as she clomped through the snow, wondering what in the world had startled Sam and now had him so freaked out.

"You'd better be digging up a pot of gold, you mangy—" She broke off with a startled gasp.

A man...a *naked* man...his body facedown and covered in a dusting of snow, lay in a messy sprawl just off the trail.

"Oh, my God." Her hands shook as she stripped off her glove and brushed aside his long, platinum hair to put her fingers to his throat. His skin was icy to the touch, which she expected, but when the steady thump of a pulse bounded against her fingertips, she nearly jumped out of her own skin. He was alive. With a strong pulse. Holy cow, how?

Okay, so...think. She had to get help, but they were in the middle of an intensifying snowstorm, and there was no way off the mountain except by snowmobile. She couldn't risk that in the storm, and it could take hours to get to the nearest town. He could be dead by then.

Shit.

Praying this guy wasn't a serial killer and trying not to think too hard on why he'd be in the mountains, naked, in the winter, she eased Sam up the trail until the sled was alongside the man's body. As quickly as she could, she heaved the firewood to the other side of the path and tucked the ax into the loop on Sam's padded harness.

Rolling the man onto the sled was not as easy as she'd hoped. The guy was heavy as a damned boulder and *huge*. And...handsome. And very, very naked.

"Really?" she muttered to herself. "You're going to notice how hot he is *now*?"

Granted, it was impossible not to notice those things, but she still felt a little guilty as she ran her hands over him, checking for injuries. Aside from being unconscious and as frozen as a fish stick, he appeared to be uninjured.

Interesting horse tattoo on his right forearm, though. When she'd skimmed her fingers over it, she'd felt a dim vibration, as if the henna-colored lines pulsed with a mild electrical current. Too bad warmth didn't ride in on that current, though, because damn, she swore the temperature plummeted twenty degrees in the few minutes it took to check the guy out.

As if Mother Nature had some sort of grudge against her, the biting cold wind picked up even more, and the snow, which she normally loved, became an enemy. It was probably stupid of her, but she stripped off her coat and laid it over the guy, tucking the coat's sleeves carefully beneath him. The shirt layers she was wearing should protect her for a while, as long as they hurried.

"Let's go, Sammy." She urged the gelding to move faster than she'd normally like, but nothing about this situation was normal.

She was freezing and exhausted by the time she smelled the smoke from her wood stove, and her eyelashes were crusted with ice by the time she eased Sam up to the rickety porch. The frigid air burned her lungs with each breath as she dragged the man's dead weight off the sled and then unhitched Sam. She'd remove the harness later. Right now she had to get the man into the house and the horse into the barn.

She ran the thirty yards to the barn and, battling the wind, tugged open the door. Sam trotted inside, but she didn't bother taking him to his stall. He'd find it on his own.

Too bad getting the man to her bedroom wasn't nearly as easy as putting up the horse. As a fitness freak who worked a small farm, Jillian wasn't a wuss, but she thought she might have dislocated something as she dragged Fish Stick across the floor. She spent another ten minutes heaving and straining to lift him onto her bed.

Once he was sprawled out on his back, his broad shoulders taking up an enormous amount of room on the mattress, she cranked the electric blanket to the highest setting and checked his pulse. Still strong. Shouldn't it be sluggish? She'd taken basic CPR classes as well as Search and Rescue training, and from what she remembered, hypothermia caused a slow, weak pulse. Fish Stick's couldn't be more opposite. Steady, surging, and she swore his skin had already pinked up a little.

Leaving the mystery alone for now, she checked the phone, and sure enough, it was dead. Next, she stoked the fire and turned up the electric heat to eighty degrees. She was lucky to have electricity at all, actually. The power kept flickering, and it was probably only a matter of time before it went the way of the phone line.

Ooh, and then she'd be alone, in the dark with no phone, in the middle of nowhere . . . with a stranger.

This was a horror movie setup. She even had the token small animal to prove the situation was serious and make all the women in the audience worry.

Her Bengal cat, Doodle, watched the activity from his bed in front of the wood stove, unconcerned that there was a strange man in the house. But then, nothing really fazed him. As long as he had food and someone to pet him, he didn't bother to get excited about much.

"You're a big help there, buddy." She shot Doodle a dirty look as she changed into dry sweats and slippers. "I'm going to check on the complete stranger in my bed, but don't worry about me, okay?"

Doodle blinked his green eyes at her.

Wishing she had a big dog right about now, Jillian slipped into the bedroom. As she entered, Fish Stick sighed and shifted in the bed, just the smallest movement, but enough to give her a bit of hope.

Then his eyes popped open.

Startled, she leaped back, slapping her hand over her mouth. His eyes . . . God, they were amazing. The lightest shade of blue, and crystal clear, like the edge of a shallow glacier. They bored into her, but there was nothing cold about them. The raw heat in them pierced her all the way to her core.

Feeling silly for her overreaction but with her legs trembling anyway, she returned to the bedside.

"I'm Jillian. I found you in the woods. You're going to be okay." She wasn't sure if he understood or not, but his eyes closed, and his thickly muscled chest began to rise and fall in a deep, regular rhythm. His color was good now, and his full lips, once pale and chapped, were a smooth, dusky rose.

Remarkable.

What now? Maybe she should get something hot into his stomach. Quietly, she started for the door to put some broth on the stove.

"Hey," he rasped, his voice a broken whisper. "Did I... hurt you?"

She inhaled sharply and turned, risking a look at him. Once again, his eyes drilled into her, but this time, they seemed to... glow a little.

"No." She swallowed dryly. "No, you didn't hurt me."

His long, golden lashes fluttered down, as if he was satisfied by her answer. But dear God, why would he think he might have hurt her?

Who the hell had she brought into her house?

Two

❦

Fish Stick didn't wake up again for a full twenty-four hours.

When he did, it was only long enough to drink a cup of hot beef broth. He hadn't said a word, had merely stared at her with those gorgeous blue eyes and then fallen back into a deep sleep, as if he'd been awake for a year.

Jillian had tried to call Stacey, a local sheriff's deputy and her best friend of twenty years, but the phone lines were still down. Figured. The storm seemed to have stalled, and Jillian decided she was going to hunt down that meteorologist and beat him with his own anemometer.

Doodle had taken to the stranger, and if the cat wasn't eating or chasing one of his toys, he was curled up on the bed. The little traitor.

At the forty-six-hour mark, Jillian went to check on Fish Stick, her heart doing a crazy little skip when she saw him sprawled in her queen-sized bed, taking up the

whole thing. For some reason, her thoughts went to what
he'd do with a woman in it. Someone his size needed a
king mattress, especially if he had…company.

Stop it. Why in the world was she thinking like that about
a total stranger whose name she didn't even know? Maybe
because, even in his sleep, he exuded power, an off-the-
charts masculinity that made every female hormone quiver.

Stop. It.

The covers had slipped low on his hips, revealing hard-
cut lower abs and sinewy obliques that disappeared under
the sheet. Just one inch lower, and there would be nothing left to the imagination. She'd gotten a good look when
she'd brought him in, but now that his skin had color in it
again, he was a totally different man. Before, he'd been
like a marble statue, weak as a baby. Now…oh, boy.

His hair, a thick, long mane of white gold, had been
hopelessly matted. A couple of times she caught him growling in his sleep and tearing at it, so she hoped he wouldn't
mind that she'd sort of…cut it.

She'd left it as long as she could, but the shoulder-
length cut was still a good twelve inches shorter than it
had been.

Now it spilled over the red flannel pillowcase like spun
silk, and really, it was so not fair that a man had better hair
than she did. Better hair *and* eyelashes. Dammit, women
paid to get lashes as long and thick as his.

"This is getting ridiculous," she muttered, as she sank
onto the mattress beside him. *He's just a man*. A man who
appeared to be in his late twenties and gifted with a freak-
ishly perfect body.

She palmed his forehead, relieved to find that he was
neither feverish nor cold.

She reached for the covers to tug them up when suddenly, in an impossibly fast movement, he grabbed her, whipped her roughly beneath him, and slammed his forearm across her throat. Fear spiked, sharp and biting. Under his weight, she could barely move, and with his arm on her windpipe, she could barely breathe.

His eyes were shards of winter ice as they bored into her, and she immediately reevaluated her estimate of his age. He might look to be no more than twenty-eight, but his eyes... they were ancient.

"Who are you?" he growled. "Where am I?"

"I—" She coughed, trying to suck air into her burning lungs. He let up on her throat. A little. "I'm Jillian." She gulped a breath. "You're in my house."

His gaze narrowed, and she felt like a deer pinned by a wolf. "Why?"

"I found you," she rasped. "In the snow. You were almost dead."

He frowned. "That's impossible."

"That you were almost dead or that you were in the snow?"

Confusion flashed in his eyes, and he let up on the pressure a little more. "I'm not sure."

"Okay," she said slowly, not wanting to agitate him again. "Let's start with something simple. What's your name?"

"I think... I think it's Reseph."

"You *think*?"

The pressure on her throat lessened to almost nothing, but each breath still burned. "Reseph is the only name that comes to me."

He wasn't sure about his own name? And what an odd

name it was. His deep, resonant voice did have the slightest accent, though. Not that she could identify it. "Do you know where you're from?"

"No idea. I can't remember...anything." He pushed up, his shoulders and biceps flexing with power, and looked down at his naked body. "Did we fuck?"

She nearly choked. "No."

"Why not?" He eased back down on top of her and buried his face in her neck, inhaling deeply. This time she felt the distinct presence of an erection settling against her pelvis. The buzz in the very air around him shifted suddenly from menacing to blatantly erotic, but no less dangerous.

Oh, God. "Because we're complete strangers."

He lifted his head. "So?"

So? This was not going well. "Look, maybe you should, ah, get off me, and we'll discuss everything over dinner."

"Dinner?" He grinned, and good Lord, he was stunning when he wasn't scaring her half to death. "Totally on board with that. I'm starving. Maybe we could fuck first?"

This time she did choke. "Sex is not on the table. But chili is."

"You can have sex on tables," he said, and great, she was now picturing doing things in the kitchen that had nothing to do with eating. At least, not eating food.

"Chili," she croaked. "No sex."

He appeared to consider that, and she nearly passed out from relief when he rolled off her. "Okay, so where's the food?"

"Kitchen." She leaped off the bed, ignoring his amused grin and trying not to look at his erection...his *very* nice erection...which he wasn't making any effort to cover up.

Nope, he lay on his back, legs spread, one arm behind his head as if he was in his house, in his bed, and she was merely the date he'd invited home last night.

Again, she wondered just who she'd brought into her house, because this guy was not flying with a full crew. Definitely not right in the head.

Averting her gaze, she backed toward the door. "I'm going to see if I can find you something to wear. Feel free to use the shower—"

He was already halfway to the tiny master bathroom. Despite her annoyance, she couldn't peel her eyes away from his body as he strode across the wood floor. Every muscle was a fluid work of art as they powered his strides, bunching and rippling. And that ass...sweet Jesus, he had the nicest set of glutes she'd ever seen.

He disappeared into the bathroom, and she swore the last flex of his butt muscles was just for her. Oh, this guy had to go.

While he showered, she headed to the kitchen to stir the Crock-Pot of chili before taking the stairs down to the cellar. Half of the underground space was dedicated to food storage, but the other half was piled high with the remnants of her life in Florida, and with huge Rubbermaid containers of Christmas ornaments and things that had belonged to her parents.

She hadn't been through any of this stuff since she moved here, and she cursed her misty eyes as she pawed through one of the plastic tubs of her parents' clothing. Every shirt brought back a memory, every pair of shoes a story.

Just grab something and get it over with.

Jillian wasn't sure "grabbing something" would be

adequate. Although her father had been a tall man, there was nothing of his that would fit Reseph well. She supposed he'd have to make do with the forest green flannel pajama bottoms and the oversized black sweatshirt.

Glad to be done digging through memories, she trudged back up the stairs and nearly swallowed her tongue when she stepped into the kitchen at the same time that Reseph sauntered in.

Completely naked.

"Um . . . you couldn't find a towel?"

He looked down at himself. "I found a towel. I'm dry."

The man apparently had absolutely no inhibitions. "Right. Silly me." She shoved the clothes at him. "Do you think you hit your head?"

"Might be why my memory is gone," he said, and okay, sure, that might explain the amnesia, but that wasn't what she'd been getting at.

While he dressed . . . reluctantly, it seemed . . . she spooned chili into bowls. As she reached into a drawer for spoons, she sensed a presence behind her. Reseph's warmth engulfed her as he peered over her shoulder.

"Looks good."

So Reseph had no inhibitions *and* no concept of personal space. At least he'd put the clothes on.

"It *is* good," she said, scooting out from under his shadow. "It's my mom's recipe." She placed the bowls on the table—opposite ends.

"I wonder if I have a mom." There was a thread of . . . sadness? . . . fear? . . . worry? . . . in his voice. Maybe it was a mix of all three.

She could only guess at how she'd feel if she woke up in a strange place with no memory of how she got there or who she was. The idea that there was a family out there who might be looking for him—including, maybe, a wife—had to be unsettling.

Especially since he'd wanted sex from a complete stranger. Jillian hoped to hell he wasn't married.

"Let's get some food in you, and we'll see what we can figure out." She opened the fridge. "I have milk, water, orange juice, Sprite—"

"Beer?"

"Sorry. Out of beer." She liked a cold one now and then, but it just wasn't a winter drink.

"Chili without beer is a crime in some places," Reseph said. "Well, it should be. Sprite, please."

She grabbed two cans and two glasses, and when she turned around, Reseph was seated. But he'd moved his bowl to a seat closer to hers. She sighed. Her mom would have said he needed to be house-trained.

"Thank you," he said softly.

"It's just chili."

He shook his head, his wet hair brushing the sweatshirt collar. "For that, and for taking care of me."

As if he were embarrassed, he looked down at the bowl and dug in.

Reseph had never seen a woman as beautiful as Jillian or tasted anything as awesome as her chili. Well, he was pretty sure of the *never* part. With her chin-length dark hair that was clipped shorter at the nape and brilliant green eyes, Jillian drew his gaze as often as his bowl drew his spoon. He was ravenous for both company and food, which made him wonder how long he'd been without either.

He finished off the bowl before Jillian had eaten a quarter of hers.

"I'll get you more." She started to stand, but he gripped her forearm and held her down.

"You've done enough. I can get it." Though he supposed if he let her serve him, he'd be able to watch her fine ass sway in those worn jeans that hugged her perfect curves. Not even the worn black and blue flannel shirt she wore could hide what he suspected was a fantastic body.

No, he'd felt enough of that body when she'd been beneath him on the mattress to *more* than suspect.

She looked a little flustered...from his touch, maybe? He got that, because her warm skin felt so good under his hand, good enough that he wanted to leave it there. And he did, for a few seconds longer than was appropriate.

Because somehow he knew what appropriate was. He just didn't care.

Had he always been like that? He was kind of a dick, wasn't he?

With a mental shrug, he fetched a heaping bowl of chili and returned to the table. "So. Where are we?" When she gave him a startled look, as if he wasn't sure he was in a kitchen, he laughed. "In the world. Where are we in the world?"

"Oh." She smiled in obvious relief. A beautiful smile on a generous mouth and lips the color of a ripe apple. Made him wonder if they'd taste as sweet. "Colorado. We're in the Rockies, near the Wyoming border."

"Why?"

Her sable brows shot up. "Why?"

The spoon clacked as he dug into his bowl. "Why do you live here?" Why was *he* here?

"Um...because it's where I grew up. I inherited the cabin from my parents when they passed away."

He dug deep into his brain, trying to find a memory that involved his own parents, but there was nothing. "What do people do around here?"

"For a living, you mean?" When he nodded, she sipped her drink, as if needing time to come up with an answer. "Well, I guess they mostly work in the ranching, logging, or hunting industries. The nearest town is barely a speck on the map."

"So why would I be here?"

She shook her head, making her hair sweep against her jaw in soft waves. "I have no idea."

"Maybe I was hunting?"

"You were naked. And you didn't have a gun or bow."

Bow. For some reason, having a bow...it sounded familiar. Naked? That sounded familiar, too. But maybe not naked in the snow.

He considered the winter-nudist scenario. "Were there tracks near me? Maybe I was attacked."

"If so, you don't have a mark on you." A soft blush spread across her cheeks, and he grinned.

"Got a good look at me, huh?"

"I was checking for injuries." She cleared her throat. "In any case, you weren't injured, and there weren't any tracks near you, but the blizzard would have covered up any."

He thought about that for a second. "What were you doing out in a blizzard?"

Her spoon clinked against her bowl as she fished for a kidney bean. "I was collecting the last of the firewood I cut yesterday."

"Firewood..." He recalled the trees he'd seen while he was lying in the snowbank. "What's the date?"

"December tenth."

Cool. He might not like snow, but December was his favorite month. "It's Christmas time. Maybe I was out here to get a Christmas tree."

"Naked, with no ax or vehicle? And if you were, you were trespassing on private property."

Reseph finished off his soda and asked, "You found me on your property?"

"Yep."

He watched her stir her chili, her hands delicate but work-roughened. "You live here by yourself?"

"Yep again."

"Why?"

She shrugged, making the embroidered black wolf emblem on the pocket of her shirt dance. "I like being by myself."

Reseph definitely did not like being alone. "Do you have a mate?"

One dark eyebrow climbed up. "Like, a friend?"

"Like a lover. You know, a mate."

"I'd sure like to know where you're from," she muttered. "But no. No...mate."

For some reason, he liked that answer. "Why not? You're pretty. You should have lots of them."

She coughed a little. "Maybe we should concentrate on your situation."

She was probably right, but he wasn't sure where to even start. "Do you have a computer?"

"I do, but the Internet is dial-up, and it's twitchy. Like the electricity."

"What about TV?"

"I have a satellite dish, but it doesn't always work."

Twitchy Internet and electricity, spotty television, and snow. Christ, Jillian lived in hell. "What do you do out here? How do you keep busy?"

"I read a lot. Hike in the woods and hunt mushrooms. It isn't hard to stay busy. The farm takes up a lot of my time."

Hunt mushrooms? Who did that when you could buy them at the store? "Sounds like you're massively tied down."

Annoyance flickered across her face. "I'm not tied down. I love it here."

"But you're alone." He eyed her, thinking she was too beautiful to ever be alone. "And a farm is a lot of responsibility."

"Neither of those things are bad," she said, but Reseph wasn't so sure. Being alone sucked, and *responsibility* was just another way to say *tied down*. "And how did we get back onto me as the topic of conversation?"

"I have a history of a snowbank," he said simply. "And I don't even like snow."

"I'm sorry, Reseph." She dropped the spoon into her half-eaten chili, as if her appetite had gone. "When the storm dies down, we'll take the snowmobile into town if the road isn't clear. I'll take you to the sheriff's office and they'll help you."

Alarm rang through him, stealing his appetite as well. "You can't take me there." His voice was a humiliatingly low rasp.

"I have to," she said, reaching for a napkin. "They'll be able to help more than I can."

His pulse kicked into high gear, and a load of hot adrenaline seared his veins. He wanted to find out who he was, but right now, the only thing he knew was Jillian and her cabin. He couldn't deal with more unknown. He couldn't be abandoned again. Assuming he'd been abandoned in the first place, anyway.

Hastily shoving back from the table, he stood, startling Jillian to her feet.

"What is it?" she asked. "What's wrong?"

"Nothing." Son of a bitch, that wasn't true. He shook his head, which was starting to pound, almost as if there was someone on the inside, tapping on his skull. "Everything. Fuck, I don't know."

She started to move toward him, but he wasn't ready to be touched or to be talked down or to answer questions. Some sort of sensory overload was making his brain tweak out. Or maybe he *had* hit his head. Whatever was freaking him out, he didn't like it.

Before she could get closer, he grabbed his empty bowl and glass and darted to the sink. Then he stood there like a dolt, his palms sweating and his heart pounding.

"Reseph?" Her voice was tentative. Soft. "Are you okay?"

Not even close. "You have a dishwasher."

"It's old, but it works."

He swallowed. "I don't know how to use it."

"Every model is different—"

"No. I don't think I've *ever* used one." It was such a stupid thing, but it made him feel so...lost.

"You have amnesia, Reseph."

"It's not that. I mean, I might not remember anything, but some things are familiar. I knew I liked chili. I know I like sex. I know how to use a computer. But I don't know what to do with a dishwasher."

Her hand came down on his as he held onto his bowl in the sink, and he changed his mind about not wanting to be touched, because her hand soothed him as quickly as a shot of fine tequila. Which was another thing he knew he liked.

"I'll do this," she said gently. "Why don't you get some rest?"

"I've gotten enough rest."

"Then go watch some TV. I have DVDs if the satellite isn't working."

He didn't want to leave her, but he wasn't even sure why. Still, he sensed that she needed some space, and why wouldn't she? He was a stranger in her house, where she was clearly used to living alone. Really, it was a miracle that she'd taken him in. A lot of people would have left him to die.

Wait…how did he know that? If he was right about people leaving him to die, he must have known some real scumbags in his life.

Which didn't speak highly for him. In fact, in the deepest recesses of his brain where the strange tapping was going on, there lurked a nasty suspicion. The suspicion that Reseph himself might be a scumbag.

Or worse.

Three

"How are you doing there, you hot, naked hunk of angel?"

Reaver opened his eyes just long enough to glare at Harvester, a fallen angel who seemed to delight in annoying the shit out of him.

Closing his lids, Reaver settled back against the wall of bone behind him. "I'm an angel trapped in hell, and I'm being slowly digested in the belly of some giant demon. How do you think I am?"

Harvester snapped her fingers in front of his face, startling him into opening his eyes again. She crouched at his feet, her ebony hair cascading all the way to her hips over her black leather and lace minidress, a backpack next to her on the ground. "You *do* regenerate. Quit being dramatic."

He sighed. "It's interesting how your latest torture method is to annoy me to death."

"Annoy?" In a surprising move, she sat down beside

him, back to the wall. "I call it conversation. Would you rather be alone in here?"

"Ah. So you're revealing your softer, gentler side. Sacrificing yourself to keep me company."

"You're so cynical."

"Maybe that's because a year ago, you tricked me, held me captive, cut off my wings, and tried to get me addicted to marrow wine." He shot her a sideways glance. "Clearly, my cynicism is unwarranted."

She shrugged. "Maybe I didn't want to do those things. Maybe I was under orders."

The Horsemen Watcher Council in Sheoul operated much the same as the Council in Heaven, meaning they offered suggestions and passed along information from Those In Power. But ultimately, it was up to the assigned Watcher himself to take responsibility for any action he or she took. Harvester, as the Four Horsemen's evil Watcher, would know that.

"Holding a Watcher captive is a violation of Watcher rules. It doesn't matter if your orders came from the Council or Satan himself. You'll be punished." Probably by both Sheoulic *and* Heavenly forces. Each side was responsible for punishing their own Watcher, but sometimes both sides demanded the right to mete out punishment.

"Eventually." She waved her hand in dismissal. "Right now everyone is too busy putting the human realm back together. Besides, I'll get a slap on the wrist. Maybe have Watcher duty taken away. I'll live."

"That would be a shame."

Though he was being sarcastic, there was a part of him that would prefer she remained alive and kept her job. As the Horsemen's Heavenly Watcher, Reaver had to deal with whoever would replace her, and as fallen angels went, there were a lot worse than Harvester.

He shifted, wincing at the agony of his skin scraping on acid-coated taste buds. "How long have I been here, anyway?"

Time worked differently in some regions of Heaven and in Sheoul-gra, and you never knew if one hour spent in one of those places meant three months in the human realm, or if it meant three seconds. Time shifted as often and as quickly as the wind, with no discernible pattern.

"In the half hour you were here with Reseph, three months passed in the human realm. After you threw him out, time here went the opposite way. You've been here for three months, but only minutes have passed in the human realm." She lifted one slender shoulder in a shrug. "Basically, it all evened out. Three months for both realms."

Which would mean that Reseph would have only recently awakened.

"How do you know I threw Reseph out?"

Harvester rolled her eyes. "You didn't come here to chat with demon souls. No angel would risk coming to Sheoul, let alone Sheoul-*gra*, without a damned good reason. Reseph was your reason." She smirked. "Plus, Hades told me you did something to Reseph to make him disappear."

"That blue-haired bastard," Reaver growled. "As if running demon purgatory doesn't keep him busy enough? He had to rat me out to you?"

"He has to amuse himself somehow, I guess." Harvester tapped the backpack. "I brought you clothes." She raked him with a naughty gaze. "Not that you should put them on, you sexy thing."

Suspicion churned in his gut. "What's the catch?"

"No catch." Standing, she unzipped the pack and tossed a pair of bright pink sweats dotted with kittens into his lap. *There* was the catch...looking stupid. "So where did you send Reseph? I can't sense him at all anymore."

"I'm not telling you."

"I need to know. He's in danger."

Clutching the goofy sweatpants, Reaver popped to his feet. "What do you mean, he's in danger? Reseph's Seal was repaired and he's no longer Pestilence. The *Daemonica*'s prophecy was thwarted."

There had always been two apocalyptic prophecies about the Four Horsemen, one catalogued by a demon holy book, the *Daemonica*, and one accounted for in the human Bible. The differences lay in how their Seals would break and what side the Horsemen would fight on...good or evil. Reaver was relieved that only the "good" prophecy was left, but whatever Harvester was babbling about sent a tremor of alarm through him.

"Fool. You know prophecies can change. Reseph's Seal may not be able to break again until the Bible's prophecy comes to pass, but the events of the last year have caused a disruption in what was originally foreseen. The Horsemen are still predicted to fight on the side of good in the biblical Apocalypse. But..."

Reaver ground his teeth. "But?" he prompted.

"But Reseph's evil side was awakened when he became Pestilence. His demon isn't dead. It's merely locked up."

"I know." And that was actually Reaver's doing. He'd been in possession of Wormwood, the dagger that could have destroyed Pestilence, but it would have killed Reseph, too. Instead of giving it to the other three Horsemen, he'd let them use Deliverance instead, a dagger they'd wrongly believed would kill Pestilence. "That's why I took his memory and sent him away."

"Well, I recently received word from Those In Power that when his memories come back, if he's not strong enough and he's subjected to evil again…"

"Pestilence could return," Reaver said grimly. *Damn.* He supposed he should be grateful to Harvester for delivering the news, seeing how he was cut off from his own Watcher Council.

But he couldn't afford to be grateful for anything Harvester did. She would never forgive a debt.

"He won't have the same powers if he comes back," she said, "and he can't bring about the same kind of destruction on the Earth that he did before; at least, not on the same scale. But he can still spread plague and disease, and it will still mean that he can plot, disrupt lives, raise armies in preparation for the biblical Apocalypse. And it would mean one less Horseman to fight for you Goody Two-shoes in the future."

Through a filter of skepticism, Reaver considered what Harvester was saying. "You're playing me, Fallen. You only want to find him so you can help that evil side of him come out again."

"Trust me," she spat. "I don't want Pestilence to show his bastard face anytime soon. I want to know where he is so I can keep it from happening."

Reaver almost believed her. She hated Pestilence, and he couldn't blame her. Pestilence had hurt her in ways even *she* didn't deserve.

He tugged on the sweatpants. They were ridiculously

tight, no doubt thanks to Harvester's sense of humor. "I can't tell you."

"You do realize you've violated a massive Watcher rule by casting him out of here, right? And by not telling me where he is, you're violating another. I could have you *so* punished."

"No doubt you will," he muttered. "But I can't risk telling you. If what you're saying is true, and anyone else knows he's out in the world, he'll have every evil being in Sheoul after him, all trying to bring Pestilence out. If they even suspect that you know where he is, you'll be tortured for the information."

"Aw, thanks for caring," she said with a flutter of eyelashes. "But I can handle it."

Yeah, he'd seen how well she'd handled it when he found Gethel, the Horsemen's ex-Heavenly Watcher and a black-hearted traitor, working Harvester over with *treclan* spikes. Harvester had been broken.

"Speaking of torture, any news on Gethel?"

Harvester's eyes gleamed. "Rumor has it that she's recovered from your ass-kicking and is on a mission to find Reseph and bring back Pestilence."

"*What?*" Beneath him, the ground shook, the giant digesting demon's reaction to his roar. "You couldn't have started off the conversation with, 'Oh, hey, you didn't kill Gethel, and by the way, she's trying to locate Reseph to turn him back into Pestilence'?"

"Why? It's not as if you can do anything about it."

She had a point, but he wasn't going to tell her that. "How does she know Reseph is out in the world? Did Hades tell her, too?"

Harvester smoothed her hands down her dress, as if the

skintight sheath was wrinkled. "I have no idea. I can only assume that she or Lucifer has spies. But you can bet they won't keep the knowledge a secret. That's why I'm here. I need to find Reseph before they do."

So the choice came down to evil or . . . evil. Awesome.

Reaver wasn't prepared to consider either option. What he needed was more information. And a way to get out of here. Right now, his only hope for either was to play nice with Harvester. Finding common ground was probably his best bet.

"How are the other Horsemen doing? What did Regan and Than name their son?" A pang of regret that he hadn't gone to see the new baby before he'd come to Sheoul-gra ran through him.

"They're all well, and Than and Regan named the baby Logan Thanatos." Harvester smiled, and Reaver nearly fell over. She actually seemed happy for them.

He also realized that this was the first time they'd ever had a civil conversation. It was almost . . . friendly. Weird, since Harvester generally reacted to friendliness with bitchiness.

The scream of a demon in agony echoed from somewhere outside of the gullet of the creature they were standing inside, reminding him that no matter how polite their chat was going, they were still in hell. "What's Logan look like?"

"He has Than's blond hair and Regan's hazel eyes. He smiles a lot." Harvester twirled a strand of hair around her finger as she eyed him. "I'll get you out of here to see him if you tell me where Reseph is."

"No deal."

"Stubborn git." She toyed with the ends of her hair,

brushing them playfully across the deep furrow of her cleavage. "I have one other offer. If you don't take it, you should know that Azagoth has been pressing me to torment you with more than annoying conversation. He's furious that you released Reseph. He had serious plans to make Pestilence pay for torturing his daughter."

And that was one of the reasons Reaver had freed Reseph. Azagoth, Sheoul-gra's gatekeeper, wouldn't care that the male trapped here was Reseph, not Pestilence. Reaver couldn't allow Reseph to suffer for his demon half's deeds.

He narrowed his eyes at his fellow Watcher. "What's the offer?"

Slowly, seductively, Harvester licked her generous lips, and Reaver's gut twisted. "Sex," she said, her voice all silk and sin. "You agree to pleasure me at the time of my choosing."

"What?" He blinked like a dope. "Why? You hate me."

"My reasons are my own." She trailed one slender finger down her throat, continuing lower, until she was caressing her nipple through the sheer fabric at the bodice of her dress. "Well? What's your answer? Give me sex in return for your freedom."

The very idea made him want to hurl. But it wasn't as if he was rolling in options. "When? Where? And for how long?"

"When I wish it. Could be tomorrow, could be in two hundred years. Where? We'll make it fair and say in the human realm so neither of us has a power advantage. How long? Twenty-four human hours."

"And what," he said through clenched teeth, "will you have me do?"

Her eyes sparked with hunger. "Whatever I want you to do. But you should know that I'm into pretty much everything." Her voice became a throaty, honeyed drawl. "And I especially appreciate a talented tongue."

He really was going to throw up. Closing his eyes, he considered her offer and in the end decided that twenty-four hours in Harvester's bed couldn't be worse than an eternity in a Sheoul-gra torture chamber.

Probably.

"Fine," he ground out. "But just you. No threesomes, no spectators, and no commands that aren't directly related to...pleasuring you." He barely managed those last two words.

"Deal." She sauntered up to him and placed her palm over his heart. "A kiss to seal it."

Lifting her face, Harvester slanted her mouth over his. He wasn't sure what he expected from her, but soft lips and a flavor like fresh rose water wasn't it. Neither was the vague sense of familiarity. Had she kissed him before? Maybe when he'd been held captive in her house and under the influence of marrow wine?

Her tongue slid along the seam of his lips, and okay, if she wanted to play, he'd play. She thought she was stealing a kiss from an angel, thought she had the upper hand.

Never. Gripping her shoulders, he spun her into the wall and pinned her with his body. His wings flared high, draping them both in darkness. She grunted as he plunged his tongue into her mouth, taking instead of giving.

"You like it rough then, do you?" she murmured against his lips. "I can do you that way."

A surprisingly pleasant sting sizzled through his mouth, and then Harvester was licking at his lips and tongue. He tasted blood, knew she'd clipped him with a fang. Heat rushed south, stirring his loins.

This wasn't supposed to happen. He hated Harvester. Despised everything about her. And yet...*damn*.

Before she discovered the extent of how much his body was betraying him, he kissed her savagely hard and stepped back, summoning every measure of icy composure he had.

"Deal sealed," he said.

Harvester's eyes were glazed as she dabbed at the blood on her lips with the back of her hand. "Sealed." She smiled, flashing shiny white fangtips. "Now, I'll get you out of here. But remember, angel. When I call, you come running. And make sure you're fully clothed. I want to strip you myself."

Gethel stood atop a rocky outcrop in Scotland, her gaze focused on the castle in the distance, its bottom half shrouded in mist. Her sharp eyesight caught a glimpse of two Aegis Elders, Lance and Omar, as they stood on the south wall smoking cigarettes. She wondered if they were discussing her; she'd given them enough to talk about for a month straight. All lies, of course, meant to trick them into doing her bidding.

Well, the fact that the Horsemen hated The Aegis wasn't a lie, but she might have exaggerated about how many Aegi the Horsemen planned to kill in retaliation for The Aegis's role in trying to kill Thanatos's child.

All the better to scare The Aegis into following her blindly. And why wouldn't they? She was an angel, after all.

Twin wisps of smoke rose from the Elders' cigarettes, dissipating quickly in the brisk breeze. She could almost smell the tobacco, and her mouth watered. Tobacco was a distinctly human and demon pleasure, and as such, most angels turned up their noses at so much as standing down-wind of the smoke. But in her meeting yesterday with Lucifer, she'd been offered a plethora of sinfully decadent drugs, drinks, and foods, and there was no way she could turn down everything. Not when Lucifer, Satan's right-hand man, insisted.

The cigarette had represented yet another step down a path from which she couldn't return, and each step was another knife in her soul.

She'd spent three months denying that helping Pestilence had really been so bad, but with each new sin, each action she took against Heaven, it began to sink in.

Still, she felt like she was straddling the line between good and evil, had yet to jump into either pool with both feet. As proof that she wasn't *all* bad, she hadn't revealed the location of The Aegis's headquarters to the forces of hell...maybe because she'd always supported the demon-slayers' cause. For thousands of years, they had been all that stood between demons and humans, and she respected their awesome sacrifices.

That, and for now, The Aegis had no idea she had taken a few turns at playing for Team Evil. They still believed she was a Heavenly angel, and she supposed that was true enough. None of her angelic brethren had found her, tried her, and ripped her wings from her back before drop-kicking her straight into Sheoul.

Her crimes would not earn her a stop at the halfway point, the human realm, the place most disgraced angels went to make a choice: try to earn their way back to Heaven, or enter hell and become irreversibly evil, a True

Fallen. No, as Reaver had pointed out during their battle three months ago, she was Fallen...she just hadn't lost her wings.

Reaver was such an obnoxious bastard.

This was all his fault. If he'd refused to replace her as the Horsemen's Heavenly Watcher, she wouldn't have grown angry. She wouldn't have plotted against him and the Horsemen by working with Pestilence and Lucifer. What had the Archangels been thinking by appointing him? Reaver, who had once done something so egregious that they'd wiped his past from his memory and that of every angel in existence? Reaver, who had disobeyed too many rules to count and had been stripped of his wings just thirty years ago?

Yes, he'd earned his wings back by saving the world with some idiot incubus, but it had been clear to Gethel even then, when she'd awarded him with his angel status, that little had changed. He was still the same arrogant, defiant fool he'd always been.

He was going to pay for what he'd done to her. For what he'd forced her to do. But first, she needed to find Reseph.

Closing her eyes, she turned her face to the sky and repeated a summoning spell she knew by heart. She'd already made the appropriate sacrifice, even though it had pained her to do it—a human male virgin and a pregnant human female. Now she need only wait for the agent of her summons to appear.

When he did, she barely kept herself from recoiling.

The creature, his oozing flesh hanging off his skeletal frame in jerky-like strips and crawling with maggots, materialized before her. He clacked his sharp teeth, and the sound pierced her eardrums like a blade.

"Beautiful angel." His voice gurgled, as if he was speaking through oil. "What can I give you today?"

"I need *khnives* and Soulshredders."

The creature hissed. "Soulshredders don't do anyone's bidding."

"They will this time." She paused, taking a moment to enjoy the skepticism in the demon's rheumy yellow eyes. "Their master, Pestilence, is somewhere in the world, and they need to find him."

"Lies," the creature rumbled. "Pestilence is dead."

Drawing on a current of Heavenly power, Gethel flared her wings and came off the ground to hover over the demon. "Angels do not lie, you pathetic wretch." Her voice boomed like thunder, and the demon cringed. "Pestilence lives, trapped inside his brother's body, and every Soulshredder in Sheoul needs to be looking for him." The *khnives*, horrid opossum-like creatures, could help as well…they excelled at spywork.

The demon nodded vehemently. "A rescue."

"Exactly." Gethel cut herself off from her Heavenly power source, praying no one had sensed her while she'd been connected, or if they had, that the connection had been too weak or too brief to trace. To be safe, she needed to get away from here. "Off with you," she said, shooing the demon away with a flick of her hand. "Get the word out to the Soulshredder Council. I want Reseph found, and if they have to torture and kill everyone who means something to him to do it, it's a price I'm willing to pay."

Pay? Seeing Reseph's loved ones die would be a bonus.

Four

Jillian took her time cleaning the kitchen, allowing Reseph a chance to unwind. He'd seemed so sad and confused, and while she might not know him very well, her heart had broken for him.

The TV blared from the living room, and when she finally finished in the kitchen, she found Reseph lounging on her couch, feet up on the coffee table, with Doodle purring in his lap. He'd been eyeing the pictures on the wall, skimming over the nature artwork and focusing on the photos of her skydiving and skiing. She used to be good at those things before the demons came.

Jillian nodded at the cat. "He likes you."

She stood there, hesitant to take a seat next to Reseph, but the couch was the only place to sit. She'd moved her father's ratty old recliner down to the cellar a few months ago. Her mom had, for years, complained about the thing, saying it was fit only for the local landfill, and while Jillian agreed, she couldn't bear to part with it. Not yet.

Reseph ran his hand over the cat's spotted brown fur in long, even strokes. "What's his name?"

"Doodle."

"*Doodle*?" He winced. "No wonder he's so friendly. He's begging me to call him something like Fang, or Chaos, or Styx." He patted the empty cushion next to him. "Have a seat. I won't bite." A cocky smile accompanied a waggle of his brows. "Unless you like that kind of thing."

Her cheeks burned at the unbidden image of him nipping at her sensitive spots. "Do *you* like that kind of thing? I mean, do you think you do?"

His voice turned smoky. Rich. Decadent as hell. "I *know* I do." He scratched Doodle's chin. "See, I know some stuff."

Now she was burning all over as she sank onto the couch, putting as much space between them as she could without looking like she was trying. Still, he knew, shooting her an amused glance before turning his attention to the TV.

"So what's going on in the world?" He gestured to the CNN news anchor talking about recovery efforts in Sydney. "What happened in Australia?"

Oh God, he didn't even know about *that*? How could he be a blank slate? Was that even medically possible?

She tucked one leg under her and got comfortable, because this was going to be a very *un*comfortable conversation. "What's the last thing you remember about the world?"

Doodle nudged Reseph's hand, clearly not happy that his new best friend had stopped petting him. "I don't remember anything before the snowbank."

"Okay, what's the last thing you know?" she asked. "Like, do you know who the president is?"

"Of what country?"

"The United States."

He frowned. "I have no idea."

"Who is the last one you remember?"

"Washington." He sounded proud of himself for remembering something, and she hated having to crush him.

"You couldn't remember him," she said faintly. "He's been dead for more than two hundred years."

Throwing his head back, Reseph lowered his lids and concentrated. "I've got other names in my head, but I can't place them. Like Napoléon and Hitler and Azagoth. It's like I have all these puzzle pieces in my head, but I can't fit more than two together." *Azagoth?* He uttered a mild curse and opened his eyes. "I give up. So what's up with the news showing destroyed countries? And why have they been blathering about economic meltdowns and recoveries? And apocalypses."

"Because up until three months ago, the world was under siege by demons." The last word came out as a broken whisper. It still didn't seem real, and all at once, *too* real.

Reseph's hand stilled on Doodle's shoulders. "And now it's not?"

"Thankfully, no. All of a sudden, demons all over the world were burned to ash or disappeared. People are calling it WV-Day, for World Victory Day. Every government is taking credit for the WV-Day, but no one can say why or how it all went down." Conspiracy theories were off the charts, though. There were as many rumors floating around as there were trees on her property.

"All the demons are gone?"

"That's the story." God, she hoped it was true. Sightings were still reported, but authorities claimed that no demon sighting since WV-Day had been substantiated and that most likely people were just seeing things.

He cocked his head at her. "Did you see any demons?"

A chill slithered up her spine at the memory she could never quite get away from no matter how deeply she buried herself in the forest. "Too many."

She started to get up, but Reseph's hand snapped out to circle her wrist. "Is that why you live out here in the middle of nowhere? So demons won't find you?"

Jesus. Had he seen through her so easily? Very deliberately, she peeled his fingers off her arm.

"I have to check on the animals." She practically ran to the door and shoved her feet into her boots. It was dark outside, but as much as she hated the night, she hated the subject matter more.

"Jillian." The soft but commanding tone froze her as she reached for the doorknob. "It's weird, isn't it, how I don't remember anything, and you remember too much."

"I think," she said quietly, "that maybe you got the better deal."

Reseph sat with the cat for a few minutes after Jillian went outside. He was still trying to process what she'd said about the demons. It wasn't that he found it difficult to believe—on the contrary, it felt disturbingly familiar. And almost...casual. As if demons were part of everyday life, but that couldn't be the case, because even with his lost memory, he was certain that most humans hadn't been familiar with demons before their appearance.

And why the hell was he thinking about humans as if he wasn't one of them?

Frustrated at the direction of his thoughts, he gently nudged Fang-Doodle off his lap and headed to the barn to see what Jillian was up to. Didn't matter that he didn't have shoes or a coat. He just went. The cold hit him like a million tiny icicles, but he ignored the sting as he trudged through the snow, following her tracks toward the barn, which was outlined in faint streaks of light that escaped from between the wood slats and tiny windows.

Felt good to get out of the house and into the open. Jillian's cabin was cozy but confining, way too home-and-hearth for him. Which made him wonder how he normally lived.

The crack of gunfire shattered his thoughts. *Jillian*. He sprinted down the path, heart racing as fast as his feet. He skidded around the side of the barn and nearly did a body slam into the fencing surrounding a chicken coop. Jillian stood a few feet away next to a bloody scatter of feathers, a rifle in her hand, staring into the woods.

"What happened?" He came up behind her, his senses on high alert as he focused on the forest around them.

"Marten," she muttered. "Damned thing got one of my chickens." Cursing, she swung around to him, her windblown hair whipping at her cheeks. Her breath, visible in the cold air, blew out like steam when she looked down at his bare feet. "Get back in the house! You nearly froze to death, and now you're out here with no clothes? What are you thinking?"

He snorted. "I have more clothes on than when you found me. Besides—" He broke off as a tingle of awareness skittered over his skin. Something flitted in his peripheral vision, a dark shadow melting between the trees where the marten tracks disappeared.

A nasty growl rumbled as if coming from all around them, the sound of a boulder rolling down the side of a mountain. Without thinking, Reseph tore across the yard, his focus narrowed and honed, his heart pounding, his body hard and primed for battle.

And, he realized as he was running, sex.

Holy shit, he was jacked up, as if he'd just spent half an hour engaged in foreplay and was now on the verge of sinking into a hot, willing female.

Jesus, what kind of sicko was he that gearing up for a possible fight made him horny?

"Reseph!"

Jillian's voice throbbed through him, adding fuel to the burn in his veins, but he couldn't go back to her, not now, when violence and desire were both warring just under the surface of his skin.

The metallic scent of blood slammed into him, and that fast, the violent urges beat down the sexual one.

There. Movement. With a snarl, he ripped a fallen branch off a stump and snatched the beady-eyed creature behind it by the scruff. The demon hissed, its sharp teeth snapping, blood spattered on its fur.

"You little—" Reseph stared. "Marten." Not a demon. The weasel stared back, fear glinting in its dark eyes.

Overreact much?

"Reseph!"

"Shit." He dropped the critter into the snow and watched it scamper off, wondering why the hell he'd sensed danger.

Feeling like a fool, he jogged back the way he'd come. He'd run a good third of a mile in pursuit of the weasel, and for what? Jillian was going to think he was nuts. And she might be right.

At least the maddening lust had eased. But then, humiliation had a way of deflating the dick, didn't it?

She was standing at the edge of the woods, her expression veering from worry to anger when he emerged. "What the hell? Why did you take off like that? You scared me half to death."

His cheeks heated. "Ah, yeah . . . sorry. I saw something."

"What was it?"

Probably not a good idea to admit he thought he'd been chasing a demon. "An animal. Turns out it was the marten."

"You caught up to the marten?" Her gaze dropped to his hands, which were smeared with blood. "You killed it?"

Squatting down, he wiped his palms in the snow. "I let it go. The blood on its fur was probably the chicken's."

"You *released* it? You do realize it's killing my chickens."

Reseph understood Jillian's frustration, but he'd felt sorry for the creature. It had been trapped and afraid, and somewhere inside, Reseph understood *that* even more. "It's just trying to survive."

She shook her head. "Reseph, you can't go running off into the woods like that. Especially not without shoes."

"Shoes are overrated." He headed into the barn, ignoring her curses. If she wanted to get serious about letting the four-letter words fly, she really needed to work on her vocabulary. "Whatcha got in here?"

"Reseph." Behind him, Jillian huffed with annoyance. "I'm serious."

"So am I. I want to know what you keep in the barn." It was warm—relatively. Two single lightbulbs lit the six-stall building, and as he strode through the clean straw, he inhaled the familiar scent of horse. For some reason, his tattoo itched. Was he allergic to horses? Ahead, from the last stall, a big sorrel and white draft horse looked over the divider at him.

"Obviously, I have a horse. I also have goats." Jillian sounded all irritable, which was kind of cute. "They're in the first two stalls."

Sure enough, he peeked inside at the four goats in one, and three in the other. "Milk or meat?"

"Milk. I sell the kids to a local farmer. They also keep my property cleared of brush."

"And the pigs?" He peered over the rails of the third and fourth stalls. One of the black-and-white sows *oink*ed at him.

"Same thing. Well, without the milk."

Reseph eyed Jillian, noting that her hair was still adorably tousled. Damn, she was attractive. He was pretty sure he hadn't ever been drawn to women who didn't wear makeup and who dressed in farm clothes, but something about Jillian's fresh, natural beauty had him wanting to go organic.

Speaking of which . . . "Do you eat any of these things?"

"Some of the chickens," she said with a shrug, "but they're mostly for eggs."

"And the horse?"

"I would never eat a horse." Her voice was laced with a teasing false indignation.

He thought about the tattoo on his arm and shot her a wink. "Do you lick them?"

"Lick?" Confusion put a soft frown on her face for half a heartbeat, and then she rolled her eyes. "No, I don't lick horses *or* tattoos." She gestured to her gelding. "Sammy helps me with heavy hauling and riding the fence line."

Sammy? And Doodle? She was determined to make

all of her animals run away, wasn't she? A horse needed a majestic name, like Conquest or Battle. "How much property do you have?"

"Two hundred acres." Jillian scooped some grain out of a storage bin. "We used to have more, but my parents sold three hundred just before they were killed."

He closed the lid on the grain bin as she walked to Sammy's stall. "By demons?"

"No, thank God." She dumped the food into the horse's hanging grain bucket. "My dad was a pilot. He and my mom were flying their plane around the mountain when he had a heart attack. The plane crashed about twenty miles from here."

"I'm sorry. That must have been hard."

"It was." She glanced down at his feet. "You really need to get back to the house. I didn't save you so you could get frostbite by walking around barefoot in the middle of winter."

"Tell you what," he said. "I'll help you with the animals. Then you'll be done sooner, and I can get back into the house faster."

She slammed the grain scoop into its holder with a little more force than required, and he could practically smell her frustration. "No."

"Come on," he cajoled.

"No means no." Bending, she gave him a nice view as she picked up the rifle she'd propped against the wall.

He swallowed hard, and every drop of blood in his body went south in a hot rush. How long had it been since he'd had loud, sweaty, mind-blowing sex? Hell, when was the last time he'd had any kind of sex? Felt like forever, as if sex was more than a good time for him. This deep-seated primal urge was something that went to his very core. Sounded insane, but he couldn't shake the feeling that sex was a necessity, maybe to his very survival.

He took a slow step toward her, his libido tugging at him as if he was on a leash and Jillian was holding the handle. But at the second step, she stiffened. He halted, though every instinct was screaming at him to keep moving toward her.

"Do I scare you?" he asked roughly.

There was the slightest hesitation as she hung the weapon in a bracket near the first stall. "If you did, I'd have had the police here by now."

She was lying. The police couldn't make it up the mountain through this snow. She'd said as much when she mentioned getting to the nearest town.

An owl hooted somewhere in the night, and Jillian's gaze darted to the darkness outside. For a split second, shadows of fear flitted across her expression, and then, as if she was giving herself a pep talk, she threw back her shoulders and opened a bin of what he thought might be goat food.

"I won't hurt you, Jillian." Sensing she needed a moment to chill—and hell, so did he—he strode toward the door, the straw crunching under his feet. "I promise you."

She said nothing as he stepped out into the snow and headed toward the cabin. Man, he wished she had beer. He could use one right now. Or a margarita. Or a piña colada, or—

He came to a stop so fast that he slipped and nearly landed on his ass.

Something was watching him. Again. This time, though, the feeling of being watched was accompanied by a disturbing internal stirring, as if an inky, oily cloud was billowing up from out of his soul.

Pivoting, he tracked the external sensation, and there, deep in the shadows, red eyes stared at him from out of the trees. It wasn't the marten—these eyes were level with his.

They stared, unblinking, for another second, and then they were gone, taking with them the weird darkness inside him. What the hell? And why the fuck was the skin on his forearm rippling? Startled, he looked down at the horse tattoo peeking out from under his rolled-up sleeve. He'd sworn only one of the front legs had been straight, the other lifted in a stationary prance. Now, both legs were straight, as if the horse had stomped its hoof.

First the thing in the woods and now the horse. Was he losing his mind?

"Reseph?"

He didn't turn to Jillian. What if the crazy he was feeling showed in his face? "Yeah?"

"Why did you really take off into the woods?"

He shrugged. "I thought I heard a growl. I must have been hearing things."

"No, I heard it, too."

"You did?" *Thank God* and *Oh shit* collided. He wasn't going crazy, but there really might be a malevolent presence lurking nearby. "Go inside. There's something dangerous out here."

"I don't think that's necessary."

Finally, he swung around to her. "Why not?"

There was a moment of silence, and then Jillian said something that chilled him to the bone. "Because it was you, Reseph. The growl came from you."

Five

By the time Jillian got back inside the house, she was only a little freaked by what had happened outside. Just as she'd started to think that Reseph was the kind of guy who didn't take much seriously, he'd sensed something in the forest and morphed into what she could only describe as a predator. The scary thing was that the shift had been more than behavioral; it had been physical. From the set of his jaw and the flare of his nostrils to the baring of his teeth and what she swore was a glow in his eyes, he'd become something she'd never want to meet in a dark alley.

Hell, she'd avoid him in a *sunlit* alley.

And that growl. Dear God, the bloodcurdling sound he'd made had lifted every hair on the back of her neck.

And yet, when he'd sauntered into the barn just moments later, all traces of the man who had snarled like a beast, run into the forest, and come back with blood on his hands was gone.

She stared at Reseph's broad back as he stood in front of the wood stove, head bowed. He'd stripped off the sweatshirt, leaving it in a messy pile in the corner. She could hardly be annoyed though, not when being shirtless meant she got a view of the most perfectly sculpted male body she'd ever seen. Before his amnesia episode, he must have spent a lot of time in the gym.

Like, a *lot*.

"Hey." She hung up her coat and stepped out of her boots. "You okay?"

"Yeah." For being okay, Reseph's voice was off, permeated by an underlying scrape of gravel. "Did I scare you?"

"Maybe a little." His shoulders slumped, and his head sank lower. She felt like she'd just kicked a puppy. "Reseph, I wasn't afraid you'd hurt me," she said, realizing it was true. He'd frightened her, but not because she was afraid for herself. She was afraid for anyone who crossed him.

She didn't plan to cross him.

She padded across the hardwood floor, stopping a few inches away. Without thinking, she placed her hand gently on his lower back. Beneath her palm, hard muscles twitched. "What's wrong?"

The fire crackled for a long time before he finally said, "I scared *myself*."

He turned around, catching her hand before she could drop it. His warm hand engulfed hers. He was so much bigger than she was, and she supposed that under normal circumstances she might feel intimidated, but this was not a normal situation, and Reseph was *far* from a normal man.

"Were you afraid you'd hurt me?" she asked.

Reseph stared down at her hand, his thumb making slow sweeps over her fingers. "Not... intentionally." He raised his gaze, his eyes burning into hers. "And that's what scares me. I acted without thinking. I don't know myself. I don't know anything and I think I might be crazy."

Once, while Jillian had been getting ready to come on shift at the air traffic control tower, she'd watched a small private jet crash on the runway and burst into flames. In sickeningly slow motion, she'd seen movement inside the craft as the passengers tried frantically to get out. The helplessness Jillian had felt still haunted her today, and now a similar feeling was squeezing her heart. She had no idea what to say or do to make things right.

"I wish I could help more," she said softly.

"Are you kidding?" Reseph reached up, stroking his warm fingertips over her cheek in a tender caress that startled the hell out of her. "You've done so much already. If I live a thousand years I won't be able to repay you." His thumb traveled along the line of her jaw as he held her with his gaze. She didn't even consider stepping away from him. The hypnotic current running between them held her fast.

How could she be so attracted to a freaking *stranger*? Then again, she'd experienced instant attraction to her ex-fiancé when she'd first met him, albeit nothing like what was going on with Reseph. And then Jason had proved that men could remain strangers even after you'd been in love with them for a year.

The memory was a much-needed splash of cold water, and she stepped back from Reseph.

"You don't need to repay me. I haven't done anything any decent person wouldn't do." She smiled, hoping to lighten the mood a little. Or to at least get her pulse back to normal. "Now, why don't you get some sleep? You can take my bed."

One blond eyebrow popped up. "Will you be in it, too?"

"Ah, no. I'll take the couch."

He shook his head. "If I can't be in the bed with you, I want the couch."

The man was impossible. "You won't fit on the couch. Trust me, I'll be fine there."

"Nope." In a heartbeat, he leaped over the sofa's armrest and sprawled out on the cushions, legs hanging over the edge, hands behind his head. "Mine. You can't move me."

So neener-neener. "You're like a big child, you know that?"

His grin was so disarming that she had to bite back a smile of her own. "There is one thing that can get me to move."

She folded her arms across her chest and summoned every ounce of stubborness. "No. We're not sleeping together."

"I wasn't planning on *sleeping*."

Not only was he impossible, he had no filter, no inhibitions, and no sense of societal boundaries. Maybe he was some sort of overindulged, spoiled prince or wealthy heir. But he hadn't displayed any of the traits she'd expect to go with an indulged lifestyle. He wasn't demanding, snobby, or entitled. He just seemed so unguarded and guileless. It was refreshing, really.

Not refreshing enough, however, to give in to his desire to get her into bed.

"I'll get you some blankets," she said crisply, and headed to the linen closet, the sound of his soft chuckle at her back.

But a chuckle was much better than a growl.

Reseph was a huge pain in the ass. But Jillian enjoyed his quirky personality when she'd thought she'd long ago had enough of intense, oddball personalities in her old job. Air traffic controllers were a breed all their own.

So was Reseph. After she'd given him the blankets and pillow, she'd climbed into bed, but twice she'd gotten up to check on him as if he were a child sick with the flu. Both times she found him standing outside on the porch, looking out into the darkness, a silent sentinel in the night. When she'd asked him what he was doing, he'd said he needed to feel the air and open space.

She'd gotten the impression that he felt trapped in the house. Restless. But she'd also gotten the uneasy feeling that he'd been watching for something. What, she didn't know, and she wasn't sure she wanted to.

This morning, she let him sleep while she made breakfast, and as she put the pancakes, eggs, and bacon on the table, he shuffled in, bare-chested and with his hair sleep-mussed. God, he was gorgeous in the morning. There was just something extra compelling about a big, powerful man looking slightly vulnerable moments after he woke.

Not that the sleepiness took anything away from the lethal air that surrounded Reseph. She knew now that if the situation called for it, he could snap into battle mode in less time than it took for her heart to make a single beat.

In the light of day, the idea was much less disturbing than it had been last night.

"Hey," she said, and he gave her a drowsy smile that made her head swim.

"Hey." He regarded the table, and his eyes lit up. "Sweet. I love bacon. And pancakes. And eggs. All my favorites." His smile grew wider. "You didn't have to go to the trouble, but I'm glad you did."

"It's nice to be able to cook for someone." She took a seat and gestured to Reseph's plate—which she'd placed across the table from hers. He moved it and sat down kitty-corner from her. "My friend Stacey stays over sometimes, so I cook for her, but she's the only one."

"Stacey?" He scooped some eggs onto his plate, and she tried not to get distracted by the way his biceps moved under his smooth, deeply tanned skin. "Is she hot? Like you?"

Heat flushed her cheeks. "You just say whatever you're thinking, don't you?"

"Nope. If I said what I was thinking right now, you'd throw your plate at me."

He was probably right. She eyed his muscular chest and ripped abs, and her body hummed in appreciation. Well, *maybe* he was right.

"So this Stacey," he said, as he loaded his pancakes with butter and syrup. "Do you see her often?"

"Why?"

"Because you shouldn't be alone."

His answer surprised her. "You think I need protection from something?" Like maybe whatever he'd been looking for on the porch. "You think I can't handle myself?"

"Oh, hell, no. I saw you with the rifle." He glanced over at her, and his voice went a notch deeper. "It was fucking hot. I love a badass female."

She laughed. "I love being called a badass." She regarded him with curiosity as he took a huge bite of eggs. "So why shouldn't I be alone?"

"Because you're a good person. You should share that with people who need someone like you in their lives." He reached for his glass of juice. "Like me. Thank you again for everything."

"You're welcome." Her pulse picked up at both the compliment...and from guilt. The road had been cleared this morning, and she was thinking about taking him to the sheriff's station. Why she should feel guilty she had no idea. Maybe it was because a good person would keep him.

Keep him...as if he were a stray dog. Nice. If he were a stray dog, she *would* keep him. But he needed help she couldn't provide.

And she couldn't afford to get attached.

They ate in silence for a minute, which was all it took for him to finish off six pancakes, as many eggs, and half a pound of bacon. Finally, he came up for air.

"Can I use your computer?" he asked. "I want to see if I can find anything that might help me figure out who I am."

Her pancake sat like a paperweight in her gut. "Actually, I'm taking you into town today. I'm hoping we can get some help at the sheriff's station. First, you need some real clothes, so we'll hit Bernard's department store."

"I promise to pay you back when I find out who I am." He lounged back in the chair, looking sated. Content. But no less dangerous. Like a tiger that had just fed. "I must have money somewhere."

"Don't worry about it." She stood. "Now, I'm going to take care of the animals, and we'll go after that. Feel free to use the shower if you want."

A muscle ticked in his jaw, and she prepared herself for a suggestive reply. "I'll help you with the chores tonight, though, okay?"

Well, shit. She'd have preferred one of his overtly sexual suggestions. She offered him a shaky smile, because she wasn't sure he was coming back with her. He didn't belong here, and there was a perfectly good shelter where he could stay in town while the police figured out who he was.

She took care of the critters at the barn and chicken coop, and by the time she'd gathered a dozen eggs to drop off at the Wilsons' place down the road and got her truck warmed up, Reseph was ready. She wished she had shoes for him, but he didn't seem to care. He merely hopped into the pickup's passenger side and played with the radio, settling on a country music station as she drove the thirty miles into town.

"I don't know why," she said, "but I'd have taken you for a rock and roll guy."

"Seems my brain is full of country lyrics. Not so much with the rock." He tapped his fingers on his thighs to the beat of the music and studied the landscape as though he were mapping every tree, every fence post.

"You people know how to decorate," Reseph said, when she turned the truck onto Main Street. "It's like we're at the North Pole." He shifted around in the seat so he was lounging against the door, one leg up on the bench as if he had moved in and belonged right there next to her. Damn, but she could *not* be thinking that way. "You need Christmas decorations in your house. And a tree."

She eased the vehicle around an icy corner. "Seems kind of pointless."

"Don't you like the holidays?"

"I love them. But when it's just me and Doodle, there's not much point in doing all the holiday stuff." Stacey always invited her to her family's place for Thanksgiving and Christmas, so it really did seem like a waste of time to decorate her own place. She pulled up to the department store and shut down the engine. "Why don't you stay here while I run in and get some clothes for you?"

"Nah. I'm good." Reseph climbed out of the truck. Didn't matter that he was shoeless and in pajamas...he ignored the curious stares and walked inside with her. The man didn't have an ounce of self-consciousness. But then, as big as he was, she doubted people messed with him much. And as hot as he was, she'd bet he could get anything he wanted from women.

As soon as they walked through the door, Tanya, one of Jillian's old high school classmates, greeted them. Her gaze lingered long enough on Reseph to make Jillian clear her throat.

"Hi, Tanya. Obviously, we need the men's department."

Tanya pointed toward the back of the store. "You might want to hit the shoe department first. It's against policy to allow bare feet in here." She smiled at Reseph like she was picturing him with a lot less on than shoes. *Ha*. Tanya couldn't even *begin* to imagine the truth of what Reseph looked like without clothes on. He was see-to-believe. "We'll make an exception this time."

Reseph grinned back, and Jillian did not like that. She grabbed his hand and led him to the shoe department, where he picked out a pair of black work boots. Which looked absolutely ridiculous with the too-short pajama bottoms. Still, he didn't seem to notice at all.

Next, they hit the men's department. "Well, what do you like?"

He looked around at the racks of clothes and shrugged. "Pick something out for me."

"Dress you?"

He waggled his blond brows. "Or undress me." Now *there* was the Reseph she was getting used to.

"I think we'd have an audience for that," she said, glancing over at Tanya and two other employees who were not-so-covertly watching Reseph.

Leaning into her, so close his breath fanned over her cheek, he said in a low, silky voice, "That's what dressing rooms are for."

Oh, the images he'd just conjured in her head. She had to clear her throat before she could speak.

"You're impossible, you know that?" Not waiting for a response, she pulled two pairs of distressed jeans off a Big and Tall rack and shoved them into his hands. Next, she wandered through the shirts and settled on a black tee, a light blue thermal Henley, and a flannel charcoal button-down. "Let's see how these fit."

"All three?"

"You need more than one set of clothes." When he opened his mouth, she shook her head. "Don't argue. I don't expect you to pay me back."

He glared, but wisely, he sauntered into the dressing room without a fight. Maybe he was partly house-trained after all.

Tanya sidled up to Jillian the moment Reseph disappeared. "Who *is* that? Is he your boyfriend?"

"No, he's just a..." A what? Friend? Acquaintance? Perfect stranger? "Guest."

"Yeah?" Tanya's eyes were glued to the dressing room door. "I'd love to have a *guest* like that."

"Your divorce is final, huh?"

Tanya nodded. "Now if I can just get that rat bastard to pay child support, the drama would be over."

Jillian wished Tanya luck with that. Her ex had kids with two other women he was supposed to be paying child support to, and apparently, that wasn't happening, either. Men could be such scum, and that was something Jillian knew far too well. They never turned out to be who you thought they were. No doubt Tanya's husband had seemed like a decent guy when she married him. Now he was a cheating bastard who fathered two children outside of their marriage.

"Oh. My. God." Tanya's breathy words brought Jillian's attention back to a man who, as far as she knew, *wasn't* a cheating bastard.

Reseph had emerged from the dressing room, and Jillian's tongue rolled out like a welcome mat. The jeans she'd chosen fit like they'd been tailored for him, hugging his muscular thighs and bunching around his big boots. The Henley, perfectly matching his eyes, stretched across the broad expanse of his chest, emphasizing the hard-cut muscles and flat stomach. This was a man who made normal, everyday clothes into something special. He was a walking fashion ad . . . except that no other man would buy those clothes, because no one could wear them as well.

"What do you think?" he asked, his voice a low, seductive rumble.

"Think?" Tanya whispered to Jillian. "I lost that ability about five seconds ago."

Jillian had, too, and she licked her lips to buy some time for her brain to kick in. "You look great, Reseph."

He stomped his foot and flexed his shoulders. "I don't like them."

"We can look for something else—"

"It's not that. It's clothes in general. I don't like them." He frowned. "Maybe I was a nudist?"

"Sweet mother of hotness," Tanya whispered. "What magical island did you find him on? I'm booking the next flight."

Well, *that* fired Jillian's imagination, and for a moment, she pictured herself lounging at a tropical resort, where all the men had big, muscular bodies...and walked around nude.

And they all looked like Reseph.

"Sadly, we have to wear clothes in our society," she said, resisting the urge to fan herself at the sudden hot flash. "Did all the shirts and jeans fit?"

He gave her that panty-melting smile of his. "Yep. You have a good eye."

The compliment made her ridiculously giddy. "Okay, now socks and underwear."

"I don't wear underwear."

Jillian's throat went so dry she couldn't even swallow. She imagined popping open those jeans and having him right there, ready for her touch.

What the hell? She'd never been so inflamed by a man. Oh, she knew lust, knew how good sex could be, but with Reseph, it was as if the switch for her libido was stuck in the *on* position, and all attempts to shut it off were failing.

Somehow she found her voice, but it was thin and embarrassingly squeaky. "You sure?"

Looking down, he slid his palms over his hips and butt as if feeling for underwear lines, and when his long, tapered fingers brushed his fly, Tanya let out a strained moan.

"Pretty sure," he said, looking up.

"Okay, then." Jillian was on fire, her heart thudding out of control in her chest. Socks. He needed socks. Socks weren't sexy. "We'll grab you some socks and toiletries." She turned to Tanya. "Can he wear the clothes out?"

"Of course." Tanya looked Reseph over like he was a steak and she was starving. "We'll just have to get creative with scanning the tags."

Creative. Uh-huh. They grabbed a package of socks and various toiletries, and at the checkout counter, Tanya definitely took advantage of the fact that Reseph was wearing some of the clothes she needed to scan. Jillian was pretty sure he didn't have a tag down the back of his pants, and after enough of Tanya's fondling, Jillian found the tag herself...on the outside of the waistband.

Reseph was amused by the whole thing, but Jillian had to admit that while Tanya's attention made him grin, it was Jillian's touch that made his eyes darken with heat.

She wasn't sure if that was a good or a bad thing. No, she was sure. He needed help she couldn't give him, so he had to go. Nothing good could come of getting attached to a man with no past.

"Now where to?" he asked, when they climbed into the truck.

"The feed store, and then the sheriff's station."

Going taut, he swallowed, turning his sober gaze on her. "What if they find out I'm someone...bad?"

"They won't." She started the engine.

"You sure?"

No. "Yes."

He said nothing more as they drove to the feed store, and in the two minutes she'd spent paying for eight sacks of grain, he had them stacked neatly in the back of the pickup. He was waiting for her at the tailgate, elbow propped on the top, one booted foot crossed lazily over the other.

"I noticed the floor of your barn storage space gets damp," he said. "I can use some of the fallen logs behind your house to build a platform to keep the grain off the ground when we get back." He gave her a lopsided smile. "I can't run a dishwasher, but for some reason, I think I'm handy with old-fashioned tools."

The way he offered, so casually, as if this whole situation was run-of-the-mill, made her heart constrict. None of this was casual, or run-of-the-mill, or even welcome. She could take care of herself. She didn't need him, didn't want to grow dependent on him, and certainly didn't want to get used to having him around.

The last time she'd let a man into her life, she'd ended up with more than a broken heart; she'd gotten a few broken bones, too.

"Thanks," she said firmly, as she hopped into the truck, "but it won't be necessary. I've got it handled."

He joined her, not bothering to buckle in as she peeled out of the lot. "You don't like accepting help, do you? Why not?"

Sudden anger welled up from out of nowhere, shocking her with its intensity. "Because when you need something the most from someone, they always let you down."

"You didn't let me down when I needed you," he said quietly.

Wincing with guilt, she whipped into the sheriff's parking lot, grabbed the bag of clothes and toiletries, and practically ran into the station.

"Hey, Jillian." Matthew Evans, who had graduated high school two years before she had, stood from behind his desk. "Stacey isn't due in until tonight."

"I'm not here for Stacey." She patted Reseph on the arm. "I have a mystery for you."

"What's going on?"

"This is Reseph. I found him near my house. He has amnesia and we don't know who he is."

Matthew gave her a you-can't-be-serious look. "Is this a joke?"

"Unfortunately, no."

After a moment probably spent trying to decide whether or not to buy into her story, Matthew nodded. "Okay, let's take a report and see where we need to go with this." He gestured to Reseph with his pen. "Do you know anything at all? Where you live? How you got on the mountain ... ?"

"No." Reseph's voice was level and serious, the total opposite of how he'd been with her and Tanya.

"All we have is his first name," Jillian said.

Matthew guided them to a couple of chairs, and they spent the next half hour answering questions and filling out paperwork. When they were finished, Matthew stood, and Jillian and Reseph did the same.

"I'm going to contact the state police and hand this over to them. But first, I'll call the local shelter and get you set up, Reseph." He turned to Jillian. "It was good seeing you." He strode out of the room.

"What does he mean, shelter?" Reseph's crystal eyes searched hers.

Crap. Jillian blew out a long breath. "It's where you'll stay now. Matthew and the social workers will help you find out who you are."

His jaw clenched so hard she heard it pop. "And if that doesn't happen?"

"Then they'll get you the help you need to take care of yourself."

He stepped closer to her, overwhelming her with his size, his presence, his masculine, outdoorsy scent. "I don't want to go to a shelter. I want to stay with you."

"You can't." She backed up, needing to extricate herself from the magnetic pull that seemed to surround him. "You need things I can't give you."

"I don't know these people." He sounded so distraught that she almost reached for him. God, how easily he stirred emotion in her. Another reason he had to go. "I don't want to know them."

She had to get tough. But not for him, for her. "Reseph, I have enough to deal with on my farm. I can't keep an extra stray."

"Stray?" He was on her in a flash—she didn't even have time to be afraid or question his intentions, because his mouth was on hers and his body was a hard wall against her curves. "Does this feel like I'm nothing but a stray?" he murmured against her lips.

Good...God. No, it didn't, but she couldn't risk an emotional attachment, especially with someone who could turn out to be a serial killer or something. Talk about a guy turning out to be something different than you'd thought.

"Reseph, please..."

He renewed the kiss, taking her face in his broad hands, and it didn't occur to her to protest. In fact, when he ran his tongue along the seam of her lips, she opened for him. He took advantage, driving his tongue against hers and then slowing it down to nibble on her lower lip. His masterful possession had her melting bonelessly into him. Her breath grew ragged as she got lost in his kiss and the feel of his body pinning hers to the wall.

Her own body strained to get even closer to him. All sense of time and place became only a hazy niggling in the back of her mind as Reseph's thick thigh separated her legs and his chest pressed against her breasts.

"Take me home, Jillian." His whispered words tickled her kiss-swollen lips. "I promise you'll never think of me as a stray again."

Tempting. So damned tempting.

"What the—?" Matthew's voice cracked in the small room, making her jump. "Get off her, buddy."

Reseph went utterly, dangerously still. Then, very slowly, he turned his head. "Fuck off. *Buddy.*"

Whatever Matthew saw in Reseph's expression made him step back and flex his hand over the pistol at his hip.

Oh, shit. Heart pounding, Jillian slid out from under Reseph's body and put herself between the two men. "It's okay, Matthew. We were just saying good-bye."

Abruptly, the menace surrounding Reseph evaporated and hurt flashed in his eyes. She almost gave in. Almost asked him to come home with her. Instead, she managed a shaky smile.

"Take care, Reseph."

And with that, she got the hell out of there.

Six

Pain lanced Reseph as Jillian walked away, becoming a deep, sharp ache when he heard her truck peel out of the parking lot. She'd left him. She'd really left him. And it hadn't even seemed to be all that hard to do. She hadn't looked back, had run out of the building as if she couldn't wait to be away from him.

But why? He might not remember being with any women, but he knew desire when he saw—and felt it. When he'd kissed Jillian, she'd reacted like a female who needed her male naked. She'd thrown off more heat than her wood stove, and her body had melted into his so fluidly, so easily, that if they'd been alone, he had no doubt he could have been inside her in a matter of minutes.

So why had she abandoned him?

"It's for the best," Matthew, that dick, said. "She's had it bad enough without having to deal with you, too."

Reseph ignored the crack aimed at him. "What's she had to deal with?"

"Nothing you need to concern yourself with." Matthew gestured to the door. "Come on. I'll take you to the shelter."

Having no choice, Reseph grabbed his department store bag and allowed the dick to drive him a mile away, to a building that looked like an old prison. Or prison hospital.

Deputy Dick confirmed his suspicions. "This used to be a sanitarium."

"And now it's a homeless shelter? You have a big problem with homelessness here?"

"We had to reopen it when the demons came. It's not a homeless shelter as much as it is a women's shelter." He gestured to a side yard, where a half-dozen kids were building a snowman near the swing set. "Most of them have homes."

"Then why would they be living here with their kids?"

"A lot of their husbands went off to fight and never came home. These women are afraid to be alone."

"But the demons are gone."

The deputy's expression turned sad. "Not for them."

They went inside, and shit, the shelter was depressing. Someone had tried to dress the place up with colorful paint, construction paper artwork, and cheap Christmas garland on the gray, cracked walls and rusted iron railings, but it was still a *gore-toad* in a kitten suit.

Wait...what the hell was a *gore-toad*? Were things starting to come back to him? God, he hoped so. With Jillian gone, he needed *something* to grab onto.

And dammit, why had she left him?

A gray-haired lady met them at the desk, and Reseph allowed her to lead him to a cell with concrete walls, a cot, and a two-drawer metal filing cabinet that doubled as a dresser.

This was going to be his home.

It was nothing like Jillian's warm, cozy cabin.

The lady, Nancy, handed him a clipboard with paperwork. "I need you to fill out everything you can, and sign where indicated. There's a sheet of rules and a schedule you need to agree to. Everyone chips in to help out, from cleaning to laundry to yard work and cooking. Men's bathroom is down the hall."

She left him alone with his paperwork and a skinny black pen.

He sank down onto the cot with his plastic bag of everything he owned in the world. But even that wasn't his, was it? Jillian had bought the stuff for him.

So what now? He didn't want to be here. Didn't want to be away from Jillian. That kiss... damn, that kiss. He'd been attracted to her before, but there had been some serious chemistry behind the intimacy they'd shared.

Yeah, the earth had moved for her so much that she left you like a mongrel dumped at the pound.

His fingers tightened on the bag. Maybe he'd scared her more than she'd let on. Maybe he'd been too much of a burden.

He considered everything she'd done for him, from hauling him to her house and taking care of him, to cooking for him, buying him clothes, and getting him help. Okay, so he'd been a burden. But he didn't have to be. While he worked on trying to find out who he was he could help out around her house. Earn his keep like he'd be doing here.

"She didn't give you that option, idiot."

Muttering to himself, he looked out the narrow, barred

window at the playground, where a woman was watching over kids engaged in a snowball fight. Every once in a while, she smiled at them, but Reseph recognized her nervousness. Her tense posture was set in fight-or-flight mode, and her gaze kept darting to their surroundings, as if she expected monsters to jump out at her at any time.

These women are afraid to be alone. Matthew's voice rang in Reseph's ears.

These females' demons were still haunting them. Jillian was like that, too. He'd seen it in her eyes when they'd been in the barn the other night. Had Jillian been hurt? Or widowed? She hadn't mentioned a husband, but maybe his loss was too painful to talk about.

Reseph had to find out more. Surely someone knew Jillian well enough to discuss her.

He tossed the clipboard aside and headed to find Nancy. She wasn't at the front desk, but he heard her voice coming from a room down the hall. He slowed as he approached, singling out her voice from the other two females.

"I'm not sure I like having a man staying here," Nancy said. "Especially not one with amnesia. He could be an ax-murderer for all we know."

So... judge-y. Insulted, Reseph bit back a curse. Nancy could be right, but he could also be a world-famous surgeon who donated time and money to orphans in third-world countries.

"Didn't the deputy say they were going to run his fingerprints?" asked a woman whose voice was a two-pack-a-day rasp.

"That'll only help if his fingerprints are in a database," said another woman.

"I don't know about you," Two-packer said, "but given

what happened to the Bjornsen couple, the fact that this Reseph person was found only a mile away from them makes me nervous."

"Bjornsen couple?" Nancy asked.

The woman's smoky voice lowered even more. "The Bjornsens are that weird couple who moved here from California."

"I met them once," Nancy said. "What happened to them?"

"Shh. I don't think this has been made public yet. I only know because I overheard Sheriff Miller talking on his phone at the Purple Plate. He was saying that the Bjornsens had been slaughtered in their own trailer a couple of nights ago. Quite the coincidence that this man shows up with no memory at around the same time."

Reseph's gut twisted. He didn't think he'd have done something like that, but "think" was the key word here, wasn't it? He didn't *know* much of anything. Although he was reasonably certain he wasn't an altruistic world-class surgeon.

"Have the police questioned him about it?"

"I don't know, but from what I hear, the deaths are being blamed on an animal." The woman's voice became a whisper. "Or a demon."

"Don't say that," Nancy said sharply. "The demons are gone."

Reseph scrambled backward away from the door. A killer was on the loose near Jillian, and whether it was a demon or an animal, it didn't matter. He might still be upset and angry that she'd abandoned him, but *he* wouldn't abandon *her*.

But what if it was you who killed those people? It

couldn't have been. Deputy Dick would have questioned him if they'd suspected, right?

Reseph needed to see the scene. Needed to know for certain that he wasn't responsible for slaughtering the Bjornsens.

But first, he needed to make sure Jillian was okay.

The house was so empty without Reseph. Worse, Jillian kept seeing his face when she'd told him she was leaving without him. She'd been deliberately cruel, wanting him to get upset with her, but instead, he'd kissed her. Kissed the breath right out of her.

And still she'd left him.

He didn't know anyone. He had no home, no job, no friends. And she'd left him to be dropped off at a women's shelter.

No doubt Reseph would have as much company as he could stand.

That particular thought annoyed her enough that she stopped worrying about him.

For an hour.

Then she realized how big the living room looked without him to fill it. How lonely the kitchen table was without him to talk to.

And how stupid was she anyway to get so worked up over someone she'd only had in her house for a few days?

But wow, could that someone kiss. Even now, her body heated in remembrance. The way he'd touched her had lit her on fire. There'd been nothing inappropriate about where his hands had been, but there'd been a whole lot of inappropriate in her thoughts.

The phone rang as she was buttoning her coat to do her evening chores. When she picked up, Stacey was on the other end, and she didn't even bother with a hello.

"Why didn't you tell me you had a strange man at your house all weekend?" Stacey snapped. "A strange man with amnesia?"

"Hello to you too, Stacey."

"Well?"

Stacey was nothing if not tenacious. "The phone lines were down, and I don't know smoke signals."

"You realize he could have sliced you up with a chainsaw, and it could have been months before anyone knew?"

Jillian sighed. "You come up here all the time. You'd have found my mangled body in a couple of days."

"That's not the point," Stacey said, "and you know it."

"Well, you're always telling me I need a man around the house."

Stacey cursed, which cracked Jillian up. Her friend had grown up with strict, religious parents, so whenever Stacey used a four-letter word, it would come out as a whisper or as something barely understandable.

"A *man*," Stacey shot back. "Not Freddy Krueger."

"Trust me," Jillian muttered. "Reseph's no hideous slasher movie guy." She braced her shoulder against the door. "You at work tonight?"

"Yeah. That's why I'm calling. I just got off the phone with Nancy Garrett."

A tremor of unease ran up Jillian's spine. "The lady who runs the shelter?"

"Yep. Seems Freddy's gone missing."

Jillian bolted upright. "Missing? When? Did he tell anyone where he was going?"

"Nope. Nancy went to check on him a few minutes ago, and he was gone."

"Shit." Jillian's gaze darted around the room. Keys. Where were her keys? She must have left them in the truck. "You've got to find him. He'll starve or freeze out there."

"I'm sure he'll be fine. He was obviously resourceful enough to weasel his way into your house."

Jillian looked around for her gloves. "He didn't weasel his way anywhere."

"Do you think he might have remembered something?"

"I don't know." She found the gloves on the coffee table and jammed them into her coat pockets. "Look, I'm on my way in. I'll help look for him."

"Jillian, no. He's not your problem anymore. We'll take care of it."

Problem. That was basically what she'd said to him. He was a problem. He had nothing and no one, and she'd dumped him the way some people abandoned pets without a single thought about how afraid and confused they'd be without the only people and home they'd known. An overwhelming sense of shame crushed her.

"I think," Stacey said quietly, "that you should come stay with me for a little while."

"What? Why?"

"I can't talk about it right now, but trust me, okay?"

A chill seeped into her bones. "Is this about Reseph?"

"Not...exactly. I'd just feel better if you weren't out there all alone."

Why did everyone think she shouldn't be alone? She liked alone. When she was alone, she had control of her life.

"We can talk about it later. I'm coming into town to

look for Reseph." She was not going to back down from this. "I'll come by the station."

She hung up before Stacey could argue. Where could Reseph have gone? What if he was injured or lost?

Sick with worry, she hurried outside. Darkness had settled in, but she wasn't going to obsess about what might lurk in the shadows beyond the farm. Reseph could be in trouble, and she had no one to blame but herself.

She'd almost reached the truck when a whisper stopped her in her tracks. No, not a whisper... it was more of a puff of warm air blowing across her cheek and ear. A rank odor made her nostrils burn and a sour taste fill her mouth.

Oh, Jesus. Her knees nearly buckled. The stench was horrifyingly familiar, even after a year. Suddenly she was in the airport parking lot all over again, shrouded in darkness and at the mercy of monsters.

Another hot breath ruffled her hair. A scream welled in her throat, but terror had frozen her ability to let it out.

Please, no. Not again. She'd barely survived the first demon attack. She couldn't live through another.

But she also wouldn't die like a coward.

In a jerky, slow movement, she turned. Nothing. She swayed in relief. There was nothing but empty space. But how could that be? She could still smell the demon's breath lingering in the air.

She was losing it. Losing it badly. Maybe Stacey was right. Maybe she shouldn't be alone right now.

She bolted the remaining distance to the truck, but when she was a few steps away, a shape emerged from the darkness. A demon.

Holy shit, it was a demon.

She glanced around in desperation. The barn and the

house were equal distances away. Firearms in both. But the figure was coming up the drive between them.

Hands shaking, she lunged for the truck's door handle. "Jillian."

Reseph. Oh, thank God. At that moment, Reseph's voice was the most beautiful thing she'd ever heard. Relief sapped her strength, and she sagged against the truck. He materialized from out of the shadows, his huge body throwing a menacing silhouette, his incredible eyes glowing like lasers, the department store bag dangling from one hand.

Even the foul stench of demon breath fizzled away, leaving her to wonder if she'd imagined the whole thing.

"What..." She swallowed against her dry throat, her heart lurching spastically in her chest, her palms sweating. "What are you doing here? How did you get here?"

"Some guy let me ride in the back of his pickup part of the way. I walked the last eight miles."

She pushed away from the truck. "Why?"

He sauntered closer, his shoulders rolling, his gaze holding her frozen. "Because the demons aren't gone, are they, Jillian?"

Her entire body jerked in shock. "You ... you saw it?"

"Saw what?"

Great. He was going to think she was nuts. "Nothing. I ... don't know what demons you're talking about."

"Yeah," he said, "you do." When he got close and it was clear he wasn't going to stop, she stepped backward until her spine slammed against the pickup cab. He dropped the bag at his feet. "And I'm not leaving you alone to deal with them by yourself."

"I've been dealing with them just fine." Until tonight. One hand slapped down on the truck roof to her left.

Thump.

His other hand came down to her right.

Thump.

She was caged in by his arms and his body.

"I'm sure you have. But now you don't have to do it by yourself. We both have demons, Jillian. I just don't know what mine are yet." He dipped his head a little, getting even closer, and her heart beat faster. "I'll earn my keep while I work on finding out who I am. You won't think of me as a stray, I promise."

"I shouldn't have said that," she said, hating herself for the tremor in her voice. "I was upset."

"And now? Are you upset that I'm here?"

She should be. She'd been so careful to carve out an independent life far away from the demons—both literal and figurative—of her past. She didn't want to rely on anyone, didn't want to *need* to rely on anyone. But the truth was that something had just frightened her out of her mind, and whether the demon was real or imagined, Reseph's arrival had sent it scurrying.

"Well?" he prompted. "Are you upset that I'm here?"

"No," she admitted, a little breathlessly.

His smile was pure male triumph. Arrogant. Cocky. Sexy as hell. "I didn't think so."

He brushed his lips over hers, and she didn't even bother with a token protest. She was too glad to see him.

His mouth opened, and she met his kiss boldly, going up on her toes as she clung to his shoulders. He leaned in, pinning her against the vehicle. Her breasts rubbed against his hard chest, becoming suddenly sensitive. The temperature outside had to be below zero, but her body burned with need.

Inhaling a ragged breath, she slid her hands up to his neck, and when she scraped her nails over his skin, he let out a throaty, encouraging growl. His kiss became urgent, possessive. His tongue slipped inside her mouth to meet hers in a fierce, wet tangle.

She'd imagined him to be a playful lover, but right now, she could also picture him being raw and rough, the kind of man who lost all pretense of civility and higher thought as he tore clothes, popped buttons, and fucked his woman against a tree or into the ground.

Yes. She'd been that kind of woman once. Adventurous and intense. Hard-edged and a risk-taker. Something about Reseph made her body remember. Made it crave. Made it feel like it had been deprived of food and was starving.

She arched into him, and he hissed as her hips rolled against the ridge of his erection at the fly of his jeans. No underwear. He didn't wear underwear.

"You are so damned beautiful," he murmured against her lips. "I didn't come here for this, but with every step closer to your house, I imagined kissing you again."

She moaned as he dragged his lips along her jaw to her ear. His hot breath was a caress, his teeth instruments of pleasure as he nipped her earlobe.

"Yes," she breathed, not caring if she sounded desperately horny. She hadn't been with a man in more than a year, and Reseph was like no man she *had* ever been with.

Thinking this was crazy, she slid one hand down his throat, to his chest, intent on going lower...when she realized he'd gone deadly still. So still he didn't even seem to be breathing.

"Reseph?"

"Shh," he whispered into her ear. "Where's your rifle?"

She blinked, her lust-soaked brain not understanding the question. "What?"

"Your rifle. Where is it?"

"In the barn. Why?"

"I want you to get inside the house." His voice was calm, quiet, and so cold it chilled her to her marrow. "Right now. Something is watching us."

Seven

A sense of pure evil vibrated inside Reseph like a tuning fork. Something was out there, lurking in the woods, and it wanted to kill.

Very slowly, he pulled back from Jillian. He expected to see fear, and yeah, that was there in her eyes, but he didn't expect the fierce determination on her face.

"I'm going with you."

"I won't argue this with you, Jillian. Go in the house."

Her smile was sweet as she bent over and picked up the bag of clothes. "Fine."

She'd capitulated way too easily, and male instinct told him to be wary of that, but for now, she'd agreed and that was all that mattered. He eased them slowly toward the front door, and when they were a dozen feet away, he sent her inside as he walked, nonchalantly, to the barn.

He snared the rifle off the wall where it hung and by the light of the full moon, he jogged toward the trees in the direction he'd sensed the feeling of eyes on them. The sinister vibration was gone, but the air was still, the forest too quiet, as if nature was cowering in fear.

Reseph's adrenaline surged as he crept through the snow, between trees, sticking to the shadows thrown by the moon's silvery glow. On his arm, the horse tattoo tickled, as if it were moving beneath his shirt. He ignored it and pressed on.

Ahead, something dark was splashed on the snow, destroying the pristine white landscape. The coppery stench of blood was strong, but it wasn't human.

It's disturbing as shit that you know it's not human blood.

He tamped down his inner voice and made a mental note to not revisit the fact that he could identify human blood by the scent.

Crouching, he crept closer. The scene was saturated with evil, and tracks tore up the snow . . . a battle had taken place here. It must have happened before he'd arrived though, or they would have heard it.

He studied the tracks. One set had been made by a big cat, a cougar most likely. The other . . . Jesus, what had made those? The prints were the size of a large human male's feet, but the four toes were three times as long— and clawed. Whatever it was, it had won the battle and had either eaten the cougar or taken it somewhere. The cat tracks led to the site, but they didn't leave.

Behind him, a twig snapped. He pivoted, rifle trained in the direction of the sound. He saw Jillian before she saw him. She carried a pistol, and dammit, that was why she'd capitulated so easily. She'd gone into the house to get another weapon.

He was both irritated and turned on by her bravery . . . he'd always liked tough chicks. At least, he thought he had.

But she didn't need to see this. She was already battling some kind of trauma, and until he knew what it was, he wasn't going to add to her worries. Quickly, he trampled over the freaky tracks and met her when she was about a dozen yards away.

"I told you to stay in the house."

Her steady gaze met his. "Well, that's the thing. It's *my* house, and no one tells me to do anything on my own property. If you're going to stay here, get that through your head. 'Kay?"

"Feisty." He shot her a wink. "I like it."

She rolled her eyes and then started toward the grisly scene. "What is it?"

"Looks like a cougar got a deer," he said, moving to intercept. "It's gone. Let's head back to the house."

She frowned, and he didn't like her troubled expression. She was too decent to be worried about anything. "There have been a lot of cougar attacks lately."

"On what? Deer? Livestock?"

"People." She holstered her pistol like a pro. "It's strange."

"That is so hot."

"What?" Her head jerked back as if she'd been slapped. "Cougars eating people is hot?"

"No." He grinned. "You. Handling a weapon like that. It's sexy as hell. Hot chicks with guns is, like, fantasy material."

"You," she said sternly, "are a very odd man."

"I'm also a very hungry man," he said, more to distract her than because his stomach was growling. "You got food?"

"Come on," she muttered. "I'll feed you."

She started back toward her house, and he followed on her heels, keeping an eye out for anything that might decide she looked as tasty as he thought she did. But as they caught sight of the house, he couldn't resist grabbing a fistful of snow and hurling a snowball at her. It broke apart on her back, showering her in white stuff.

"You're going to pay for that." Her voice was a singsongy warning that egged him on, and he threw another, this one exploding off her shoulder. "I was a softball pitcher in high school, buddy. Back off."

Right. Now she was just asking for it. He bent to grab another handful of snow, and son of a bitch, she nailed him in the head with a clump the size of his fist. Chunks of snow went down his shirt, and even as he stood to hurl a snowball at her, another smashed into his neck.

"You little—" He broke off to duck at another one she sent hurling at him, catching him in the arm. And then she was off, darting toward the house, her laughter carrying like a bell in the clear night air.

He gave chase, gaining ground easily. She might have great aim, but he was faster, and when he put on a burst of speed, he caught her in a matter of heartbeats. Tossing the rifle carefully aside, he tackled her, twisting so she came down on top of him. He cut off her squeal of delighted outrage with a kiss. For a second she struggled playfully, thumping her fists lightly against his chest, but he rolled her over, using his weight to control her and his mouth to seduce her.

With a sigh, she relaxed, winding her arms around him and shifting so he was between her legs. They couldn't stay like this for long in the cold snow, but he wanted to have this, if only for a minute. She tasted like a lemon-lime soda and smelled like the outdoors, like a clean mountain spring. She was magnificent, and he wanted to drink her in, wrap himself around her and stay that way forever.

"Let's go inside," he said against her silky lips. "I'd much rather be doing this in front of the fire."

Her eyes glimmered in the moonlight. "I don't know how ready I am for anything more than this," she whispered. "I don't know you ... and it's been a long time."

He was ready. He was so ready his balls felt like they might blow all on their own. But he wouldn't push. Jillian was far too important to him already to do anything that might make her uncomfortable. He could go slow. Couldn't he? He frowned, because the whole going slow thing felt really, really alien.

"You call the shots." He shoved to his feet and held out a hand to her. "Food?"

She took his hand and allowed him to lift her to her feet. "You have a one-track mind."

"Nah. Two tracks." He winked. "I'll let you guess what the other is." He bent to pick up the rifle he'd tossed—and the next thing he knew, she'd shoved a handful of snow down the back of his jeans.

"That," she said smartly, "will cool down that other track."

Jillian was so glad Reseph was back. She had no idea how a man she hadn't known for long could so easily thread his way into the fabric of her life and make her feel so comfortable around him, but Reseph had done it.

And he didn't just make her feel comfortable ... he made her feel safe. The way he'd moved through the forest, the way he'd handled himself at the scene of the cougar-deer attack, it all spoke of confidence and familiarity. She'd been spot-on when she'd first thought of him as a warrior. Maybe he'd been in the military?

Then he'd gone from dangerous and intense to playful and mischievous in a matter of seconds, but even when he'd tackled her, he'd been careful, taking the brunt of the fall, rolling her gently to settle his weight against her with the greatest of care.

Of course, she was still dragging clumps of ice out of her hair, thanks to Mr. I Don't Like Snow.

Doodle was as happy to see Reseph as she'd been, as evidenced by the way he practically climbed up Reseph's leg the moment he walked through the door.

"If you'll keep the cat entertained, I'll grab you a sandwich." She stepped out of her boots and shed her jacket. "Is ham and cheese okay?"

Reseph looked up from petting Doodle. "Anything you've got is okay. I'm just happy to be here."

"I probably shouldn't admit this, but I am, too."

His impish grin confirmed that she shouldn't have admitted it, and she shook her head as she headed into the kitchen, glad she'd stopped at the store on her way home after leaving him at the police station. She quickly put together a sandwich and grabbed a cold beer from the fridge.

She found Reseph stretched out on his side on the living room floor, rolling a sponge ball for Doodle.

"My cat is going to love you more than he loves me if you keep that up." She set the plate and bottle on the coffee table, amused when Reseph's eyes lit up. "Yes, I picked up beer. Figured that if I made chili again, I didn't want the beer cops coming for me."

"Smart woman."

"Yeah, well, this smart woman is going to shower and change." She also needed to give Stacey a call. "Help yourself to anything in the fridge."

He leaped to his feet, and lightning quick, he tugged her against him. How did he move like that?

"Thank you." She didn't even have a chance to respond, because he planted a hot kiss, so full of promise, on her lips. And then, as quickly as he'd grabbed her, he released her and sat down with the food.

Slightly dazed, she showered and changed into her favorite pajamas and robe, the ones Stacey had told her to never wear in front of a guy if she wanted to get laid. Somehow, Jillian didn't think the oversized olive-and-brown plaid pjs would deter Reseph, though. Then again, when she stepped out of the bedroom, he turned from where he was looking out the window and winced.

"Those are hideous." One corner of his mouth turned up in a naughty smile. "You should take them off."

"You're impossible, you know that?"

"I prefer . . . persistent." He gestured to his empty plate. "Thank you. It was the best sandwich ever."

"You certainly know how to make a woman feel good." Too late, she realized what she'd said, and the spark in his eyes said he knew it, too. "Don't say it. And don't look at me like that."

"Like what?"

Like you're still hungry. "I don't know."

"Yeah, you do."

"I wonder," she said, "if you were this arrogant before you lost your memory."

Hurt flared in his eyes, but it was gone in an instant, his expression shifting into a light mask of indifference. "Probably."

God, she felt like a heel. "I'm sorry. I didn't mean to rub it in—"

"It's okay."

Tentatively, she put her palm on his biceps. "No, it's not. That was insensitive."

He turned into her, filling her vision with his powerful shoulders. "One thing I know about myself is that I'm not easily offended or hurt."

She might buy the *not easily offended* part, but she'd seen how bothered he'd been when she'd left him at the sheriff's station and now, when she'd brought up his lost memory. She wasn't going to call him on it, though. She knew firsthand how survival could depend on believing the things you told yourself.

"You definitely aren't easily hurt," she said lightly. "Your recovery from nearly freezing to death has been amazing."

"Clearly, I have incredible stamina." His voice had gone low and seductive, and she'd just bet he had stamina worth bragging about. "Outside you said it's been a long time since you had sex."

And there went that lack of a filter thing again. "More than a year."

"Why?"

She hesitated, unsure how ready she was for too much detail. "Because I moved here and haven't wanted to throw myself into the dating pool." She doubted she'd ever dip a toe in that murky water again.

"You don't have to date," he said, as if she was a moron for mentioning it. "Who wants to waste all that time and energy? Just jump straight to the commitment-free sex."

Although she had absolutely no right to be angry with him, his answer, combined with how easily he'd charmed Tanya, irked her. "Is sex really so casual for you?"

He shrugged. "Why shouldn't it be? Humans are so

uptight about it. It's just pleasure. It's what our bodies are made for."

Humans? As if he wasn't one of them? "We're also made for relationships. Emotional connections." She couldn't believe she was arguing for something she'd sworn off.

"Mating for life?" He looked like he'd bitten into something bitter and foul. "That might have been ideal when humans had short life spans, but who wants to be tied down to one person until the end of time?"

Tied down. He'd said that before about her house and farm. "So you're saying you never want to get married? Have kids? Live happily ever after?"

"Jillian," he murmured. "I don't even know my last name. How can I say what I want in the future?"

"Shit." She blew out a breath. "I'm sorry. I don't even know what I was getting worked up about."

He'd touched a raw nerve she hadn't even known was exposed. She certainly had no right to judge his casual outlook on emotional attachments. She hadn't let anyone in since the day she found out her fiancé was married to someone else. Only Stacey had a place in Jillian's inner circle, and that was because she'd been there for twenty years.

Shit. She gave herself a slap on the forehead. "I need to call Stacey. She's out looking for you."

"I'll shower while you do that." He reached out and stroked her cheek. "I'm sorry I upset you."

He strode into the bedroom, leaving her flustered. *She* had owed *him* the apology, not the other way around. Damn, but he had a way of keeping her off balance. As an air traffic controller, she'd prided herself on being calm, cool, collected, even during high-stress periods and hair-raising emergencies. Yet Reseph, with nothing more than a feather-light touch or a few softly spoken words, could throw turbulence right into what was expected to be an uneventful, smooth flight plan.

Get back on course, idiot.

She grabbed the phone and dialed, not giving her friend a chance to even say hello. "Stace. Hey, sorry I didn't call sooner, but Reseph is here. He's fine and I'll call you later—"

"*Wait!*" Stacey's voice cracked over the airwaves. "You said you're with Reseph? When did he get there?"

Jillian glanced at her watch. "An hour and a half ago, maybe."

"How did he get there?"

"He hitched a ride part of the way and walked the rest. Why? What's this about?"

Stacey's pause made Jillian's stomach knot with dread.

"I'm not supposed to talk about this, but a couple of days ago, the Bjornsens up the road from you were killed—"

"Jesus. How?"

"I'll give you the details later. But…damn it, there's no easy way to say this. The Bjornsens weren't the only ones. I'm sorry, Jillian. It's the Wilsons," Stacey said. "They're dead."

A crushing press of denial looped around Jillian's chest and squeezed hard. "That's not possible. I saw them this morning. I dropped off eggs on my way home from town."

"What time was that?"

"Around eleven," Jillian whispered.

Oh, God, this could not be happening. She'd known the Wilsons almost all her life. Maggie Wilson had made her Halloween costumes and had bought tons of Girl Scout cookies. And when Jillian's father had suffered his first heart attack, Joseph Wilson had helped out with the farm for months while her father recovered.

"Jillian?" Stacey's voice pierced the buzz of memories in her head. "You okay?"

"I'm fine," she rasped. "But why would you ask about Reseph? You can't think he had something to do with it."

As if summoned, Reseph came out of the bedroom, hair wet, body glistening. He was wearing only a pair of unbuttoned jeans.

"We think it was an animal, a cougar or bear, but it happened three to five hours ago. If Reseph walked, he'd have gone right by their house. He might have seen something. I need to talk to him. Can I come by?"

Numbly, Jillian nodded, then realized that duh, Stacey couldn't see her. "Yeah," she croaked.

"I'll be there in a little while."

Reseph's arms came around her, and she went willingly into his embrace. "What's wrong?"

"The Wilsons...they were my parents' best friends. I grew up with their daughter. They're dead."

He hugged her tight. "I'm sorry."

"Reseph...you walked by their place. It's the house five miles down the hill, with the wagon wheel at the entrance to the driveway. Did you see anything?"

"Like what?"

"A cougar, maybe? Or a bear? Even tracks in the snow?"

For some reason, he went taut, just a subtle stiffening before he relaxed. "Do the police think that's what killed them?" When she nodded, he ran his hand up and down her spine in a soothing gesture. "I didn't see any cougars, bears, or anything else."

She knew what *anything else* could be. Just as she knew that not seeing *anything else* didn't mean there was nothing there.

Some demons were invisible.

Eight

Jillian's friend Stacey was a hardass. Reseph had decided within thirty seconds that he didn't like her. He did, however, approve of her as a friend for Jillian. Reseph was sure the cop had clawed her way out of some bitter acid pit in hell, but he couldn't fault her protectiveness of her friend.

She'd walked into Jillian's house like she owned it, gave Reseph the evil eye, and then interrogated him as if he were the prime suspect in a plot to assassinate the president. Whoever the president was. Not Washington, apparently.

It wouldn't have surprised Reseph if Stacey had broken out a bamboo cane and a pair of pliers for the next level of questioning. When he told her as much, she'd been less than amused.

No sense of humor, that one.

He'd left Jillian and Stacey alone for a few minutes to talk while he rummaged through the kitchen. When he went back into the living room where Jillian and Stacey were seated on the couch, it was with a cup of hot tea. Crouching at her knee, he put the mug in Jillian's hand.

"You're shivering," he said softly. "Drink."

Her startled eyes snapped up to his, and he was glad to see that at least they'd lost the stunned glaze. The Wilsons' deaths had hit her hard, and he'd seen how difficult listening to Stacey question him had been.

"Thank you." Jillian graced him with a smile that made his pulse kick up a notch before she turned to her friend. "Stace, why are you handling all of this? Shouldn't the state police be in charge of the investigation?"

Stacey shifted and averted her gaze, and yeah, that chick was hiding something. "The state police are passing on this," Stacey finally said. She paused for a few taut seconds before she continued in a low, conspiratorial voice. "We're supposed to keep this under wraps, but there are paranormal investigators coming to look into the killings."

Jillian's hand shook so hard that tea sloshed over the rim. "I thought you said animals were responsible."

"From what I understand, it's just a precaution." Stacey eyed Reseph as he grabbed a napkin and mopped tea off Jillian's arm. "I haven't seen either crime scene, but I'd feel better if you came into town and stayed with me."

"I can't leave the animals," Jillian said.

Reseph took the cup from her before she spilled more. "Maybe you should go with Stacey. I can take care of the farm."

"No!" Jillian's voice was little more than a snarl. "I will *not* live in fear again. Do you understand that? That... *thing*... will not win. You can both go to hell if you think I'm running away—"

"Hey." Reseph took her hand, and when she jerked out

of his grip, he took it again, more firmly. "It's okay. No one is forcing you to run anywhere." He slid Stacey a *give me a nod of agreement right now* look, and she did. "If you want to stay, I'll stay with you."

Jillian's face flushed, and he had a feeling she was a little embarrassed by her outburst. She didn't need to be. She clearly was harboring a trauma that was simmering hot. The release of steam could only be a good thing.

Stacey pushed to her feet. "I need to get back, but Jill, you know if you need anything . . ." She left the rest unsaid, the bond between the two friends needing nothing further.

"Thanks." Jillian gave her friend a fragile smile. "I'll be fine."

Stacey grabbed her parka and shot Reseph a meaningful stare. "Care to walk me to my car?"

It wasn't a question. It was an order full of *do it or I'll shoot you* subtext. The women in this part of the country loved their guns, didn't they? Sexy as hell.

Jillian huffed. "Stacey—"

"It's okay," Reseph said, heading off any tension. "I'll be right back."

He followed Stacey out to her police cruiser, where she rounded on him, a bundle of brunette fury.

"Listen up, whoever you are. Jillian has been through hell, and it's only been in the last couple of months that she's come out of her shell. She doesn't need you hanging around here like some mangy tomcat carrying God-knows-what kind of baggage."

Mangy? And he really wanted to know what kind of hell Stacey was talking about in regards to Jillian. "It was a demon, wasn't it?"

"That killed the Bjornsens and Wilsons? I don't know."

"No. That put Jillian through the hell you just mentioned."

Stacey's expression went utterly flat. "That's none of your business. I want you out of here by morning. With you gone, maybe she'll come stay with me."

Fat snowflakes began to fall in lazy swirls as he casually reached out and braced his hip against the roof of her car.

"Yeah, see, that won't happen. You have a point about the baggage. And it's cool that she has a buddy like you to look after her. But she also has me to do that. We both know she's not leaving her farm, and as long as there's something out here killing people, I'm not leaving her alone. I won't let anything, or anyone, threaten her."

Her chin came up. "What if you're the threat? Can you honestly say that you aren't? What if you wake up tomorrow and remember that you're a serial rapist? Or a drug lord? Or slave trafficker?"

Stacey the Hardass had just tapped into Reseph's own fears, but her examples didn't even come close to where his thoughts had gone. He couldn't explain it, but he got the feeling that if he was going to be a scumbag, he'd make a drug lord look like a playful kitten.

Not that he'd tell Stacey that. "If I were any of those things, I think the last place I'd be is in the middle of nowhere. I'm guessing you don't have a huge drug or slave problem in your one-stoplight town."

"Two," she snapped. "There are two stoplights."

"Oh, well, then, I'll see if I can get the slave trade going in your thriving metropolis."

She narrowed her eyes at him, which just made him grin. "Just keep in mind that if you hurt her, I'll come after you with everything I have."

She shoved his arm out of the way, got in the vehicle, and took off. The slight fishtail from hitting the gas too hard probably pissed her off, but it amused the hell out of him.

At least, he was amused until he felt a presence. He listened to the fading sound of Stacey's vehicle, and then he listened to the forest. An owl's hoot pierced the night, but other than that...nothing. But he felt like he was being watched. The odd thing was that this time he didn't get a danger vibe. The opposite happened, in fact. There was something comforting about the feeling he got.

"Whoever you are," he said quietly, "I'd like to see you. Because right now, I'm thinking I might be a little touched in the head."

No one popped out of thin air or stepped out of the woods. Naturally.

"Come on, you damned voyeur. Throw me a bone." He did a three-sixty, looking in every possible direction. "I don't suppose you can tell me who I am. No? Well, fuck you."

He waited another minute, and the sensation faded, leaving behind only an awareness that he was outside in the cold, in the dark, and Jillian, who was warm and light, was inside.

Frustrated, he went back into the cabin, alarm spiking when he didn't see her. He checked the kitchen, and then found her in the unlit bedroom, sitting on the edge of the bed.

"Did Stacey read you the riot act?" Her voice was gravelly, with a note of tears.

"Little bit. I think she wanted to shove that nightstick up my ass. And not in a fun way."

She looked down at her feet. "I'm sorry about that."

"Don't be. She's a good friend." He climbed onto the mattress and stretched out, wrapping his arms around her to pull her down beside him. "You okay? Is there anything I can do?"

"This is perfect." She snuggled into the crook of his arm. "Too perfect, I think."

"How can anything be too perfect?"

"Because," she whispered. "That's when everything falls apart."

Reaver was happy to see that Reseph was doing well. The Horseman seemed to have adjusted to life in the human world, and he certainly hadn't looked any worse for wear when Reaver had spied on him and the female deputy from the cover of the *Khote*.

The same couldn't be said of Reaver.

Harvester had gotten him out of Sheoul-gra as promised, but he was still bearing the wounds he'd gotten from the demon that had been eating him slowly for the last three months. And Harvester, the bitch, hadn't even offered to heal him. Not that he'd have taken her up on it. But still.

As an angel, Reaver healed quickly... unless the damage had been inflicted in Sheoul or by a particularly powerful angel. Then all bets were off and he got to look like he'd spent some time in a meat grinder.

So as he strode down the pristine white walls of the Archangel Multiplex, his bruises and raw skin added a much-needed splash of color. He had, at least, taken the time to stop by his residence to shower and change out of Harvester's pajamas and into jeans and a blue T-shirt. In

Heaven and a few places on Earth, angels could snap their fingers to clean up and change, but he'd opted to enjoy the feel of hot water sluicing over his aching body. His time spent as a fallen angel had given him a taste for simple pleasures, and he really didn't give a damn if his fellow angels looked down their perfect noses at him for that.

Ahead, crystal arches marked the entrance to the compound's Watcher headquarters, where teams kept track of the goings-on of beings all over the world. This was where Reaver's bosses worked, as well as the bosses for other classes of overseer angels, such as Memitim.

Reaver took a hard right at the second archway, passing through a sparkling membrane that acted as a sound barrier. Inside the seemingly endless room, angels flipped through books and perused scrolls, monitored screens that hung in the air like holograms, and chatted among themselves like office workers around a water cooler.

Angels liked to think they were so much better than humans, but Reaver hadn't seen much evidence of that.

With nothing more than a thought, he created a stage in the center of the space, leaped up on it, and made sure his voice carried—again, all it took was a thought.

"Hey! Fellow angels." Yeah, so not protocol, and Darnella, a snooty ginger-haired angel who took extreme pride in wings that matched her hair color perfectly, called him on it.

"Reaver. Have you no shame?"

"I'm standing here in jeans and a T-shirt, with a split lip, broken nose, and black eyes. Do I look like I have shame?" He could have dressed appropriately formal—or at least business casual—for this, but screw it. He was feeling rebellious today. He looked out at the two dozen annoyed angels. "I don't suppose anyone has seen Gethel?"

Blank stares were his only answer.

"Okay, let's try this. Does anyone know what she's done?"

Modran, a dark-haired male wearing a ridiculous jeweled silver robe, stepped forward. "She's no longer part of our department. Why would we have seen her or know of her activities?"

Reaver had no idea where she'd been reassigned after Reaver had taken over for her as the Horsemen's Heavenly Watcher, and he didn't care. He also didn't have access to high-ranking angels who might know, but some of these idiots did.

"I just thought you'd like to know that she's gone bad. Really bad. She colluded with Pestilence to kill Thanatos's child and start the Apocalypse."

There was much scoffing. And skeptical expressions. And flat-out calls of "liar." Fools. Problem was, he didn't have a lot of credibility. It didn't matter that as a fallen angel he'd helped save the freaking world a few years ago; the only thing these morons focused on was the fact that he'd been fallen in the first place. They were going to flip their halos when they learned about his newest stunt. Tossing Reseph into the human realm wasn't going to go over well.

Especially since Gethel knew Reseph was out there and was trying to find him.

Darnella arched an eyebrow. "And you have proof of this?"

"I have witnesses. Thanatos among them." He explained what had happened, and gradually, shock, sadness, and fury replaced the skepticism.

"More than three months have passed in the human realm," Darnella said. "Why did you wait so long to bring this to us?"

"I was stuck in Sheoul." Reaver braced himself for the rest of the confession, but before he could speak, a blond male Reaver didn't recognize moved forward, dressed from head to toe in white.

"I'll speak with the Archangels to determine if an investigation is needed and if Gethel will be required to hand over her *sheoulghul.*"

"*If?*" Reaver snorted in disgust. And Gethel was in possession of an artifact that allowed for recharging angelic powers in Sheoul? Most *battle* angels didn't have access to *sheoulghuls*, and battle angels were the ones who needed them most. "I'm telling you that she's gone bad. She's sided with the bad guys—you remember them—the demons? Even now she's plotting to bring Pestilence back."

"And how, exactly, does she plan to do that?" Modran asked, skepticism dripping from his deep voice. "Pestilence is dead."

Reaver winced. "Not...exactly. Thanatos used the wrong dagger. Reseph was sent to Sheoul-gra with Pestilence locked away inside him."

Murmurs resonated through the crowd, and Darnella spoke up. "That's unexpected, but good news. We stand a better chance of winning the future biblical Apocalypse with an extra Horseman on our side. We calculated the odds of success without him, and they were, sad to say, not encouraging."

"Not encouraging?" Reaver was always amazed at his brethrens' capacity for understatement. "You are aware of the theory that Reseph's death could unravel history?

Overnight, every reference to four Horsemen would be erased, including those from the Bible, and everything Reseph ever affected in any way would take a new course. If he'd died, we could all have woken up to a very different world."

It was something that had happened before, when the Horsemen, before their curses, had started a war. Angels had stepped in and changed human history and memories with little consequence. But Reseph had been around for five thousand years and had affected countless lives and events.

Darnella smiled coldly. "Speculation. And irrelevant, since he's not dead. Hopefully he's suffering a million deaths right now."

Everyone nodded in agreement, and Reaver prepared himself for a flaying that just might be physical as well as verbal.

"He's not in Sheoul-gra," he said abruptly. Rip the bandage off quickly and all that. "I wiped his memory and turned him over to the human realm."

Stunned silence. And then furious roars and a few screeches of, "You did *what*?" Calls for Reaver's wings to be severed followed next, along with too many offers to do it right now.

Reaver held up his hand, but the cacophony only died down a little. "It gets worse. Yeah, that's right; save your insults and demands for my expulsion from Heaven for later." He looked out over the furious crowd and wondered how long it was going to take for his Watcher duty to be taken away from him. Or worse. "Gethel knows Reseph is free, which probably means every key player in Sheoul does, too. As I said, she's trying to bring Pestilence back, and if she finds him, she could do it if she subjects him to evil again."

"How do you know this?" Modran asked—through clenched teeth.

"Harvester told me—"

"*Harvester*?" The jewel-robed guy practically screamed her name. "You trust the word of a fallen angel?"

"Not normally," Reaver said. "But she has reasons to speak the truth about this. And her Watcher Council has known about Reseph's release from Sheoul-gra for months, thanks to loose-lipped demons. Now that you know, you can confirm everything I've said." He hopped down from the stage, letting it poof away. "I have an angel to hunt. I suggest you put the wheels in motion for others to be on the lookout for Gethel as well."

"You're going to be punished for what you've done," Modran swore, as if Reaver had been at all unsure about that.

Reaver ignored Modran and strode toward the exit. He'd do everything in his power to find Gethel, but first he had to check in on the Horsemen.

And given that he'd missed a birth, a wedding, and who knew what else, he had a feeling that explaining his absence to them was going to be a lot more difficult than explaining it to angels.

Nine

Jillian woke to the smell of burned pancakes and charred bacon. She sat up, blinking, the events of last night as fuzzy as her eyes. She'd crashed, and crashed hard. She remembered waking at one point in the night, and although she couldn't recall why she'd woken, she did know that Reseph had been holding her, and his chest had been wet with her tears.

He hadn't said a word. He'd just handed her tissues and kept her close, his strong arms banded around her. And now, it seemed, he was trying to burn down her house.

She made a quick trip to the bathroom and donned her robe before hurrying to the kitchen, where Reseph, wearing only jeans, was dousing a fire.

Smoke drifted out of the sink, billowing up around a stream of rushing water. "Oh, uh...hi." Reseph shot her a sheepish grin over his shoulder. "I tried to make you breakfast."

"I can see that." She peered into the sink, where the remains of paper towels and pancakes were an ashy mush. "I think, in the future, you should leave the cooking to me."

He frowned down at the mess. "It's like I've never cooked in my life. How could I not have cooked?"

"Maybe you only ate out?"

"Maybe I'm rich and have servants," he suggested. "That would be cool."

She turned off the gas burner that was heating the empty cast iron frying pan. "I don't think I'd like being that rich."

He pivoted around and propped his hip on the counter, giving her a tantalizing view of his sculpted chest. "So there's nothing you'd want to change around here? No place you'd like to travel?"

The magical island full of hunks like Reseph came to mind. "Maybe I'd get a new truck and expand the barn, and a tropical vacation would be nice, but no, I like my life the way it is."

"Huh." He rubbed his sternum and worked his way up to his shoulder, getting out the morning kinks, and Jillian could barely tear her eyes away to open the fridge. "How are you feeling?"

"I'm better," she said, as she fetched the bowl where she kept her fresh eggs.

"Do you want to talk about it?"

"Nope." She didn't think she'd ever want to talk about her neighbors' deaths, or the fact that she'd freaked out last night. "But thank you. And thanks for getting the fire going."

"I also fed the animals and shoveled the path to the barn."

"You didn't have to do that."

He shrugged. "Couldn't sleep. I hope it's okay, but I spent some time on the Internet."

A twinge of anxiety shot through her. "Did you find anything? About yourself?"

"No, but I scanned my horse tattoo and uploaded it to a skin art forum to see if anyone recognized the work. Nothing so far. I also caught up on what happened over the last year. Sparked my memory on a lot of stuff. I remember who the president is now." He ran his hand through his hair, and her fingers itched to do it for him. "It's weird, though, because I swear I actually remember Washington." He shook his head. "But the really fucked-up thing is that I've got bits and pieces of memory and knowledge up until around the time everything started. Then nothing after that."

Placing the bowl next to the sink, she thought about her own month in a coma. When she'd awakened in a hospital bed, confused and alone, she didn't remember what had landed her there. It was only weeks later that it all came back, and in many ways, she wished it hadn't.

"Maybe you were injured. In a coma or something."

His expression was troubled. "Maybe. But that still doesn't explain how I got onto your property, naked and half-frozen. And what if the explanation for why I have no memory is something worse than an accident or coma?"

"Like what? Like something terrible happened, and you're blocking it out? Some sort of post-traumatic stress disorder?"

"I don't know." He pushed off the counter and began to pace. "It's like there's a wall in my brain that surrounds my past, and if I could just break through it, I could remember.

It's right there...I can almost touch it." He shook his head. "But then I think that maybe I don't want to."

"I get that," she murmured. "I so get that."

"What happened?" Reseph brought his hands down on her shoulders, and her breath caught. He was so careful, so gentle with his strength. "You cried out in your sleep last night."

She suppressed a groan. "I was upset about the Wilsons."

"Bullshit." The harsh word was spoken softly. "It was a nightmare, and you have them a lot."

"You can't know that," she blurted, too defensively.

Reseph dropped his hands, but he didn't move away. "When I slept on the couch, I heard you."

She couldn't outrun his accusation, but she could get away from him, and she crossed to the other side of the kitchen and busied herself with wiping the counter. "Everyone has nightmares."

"But you don't have to wake up from them alone."

The way he said it, so weighted with emotion, wrapped around her heart. A strange tension sprouted between them, as if they were both uncomfortable with the way their relationship was progressing. Which was way too fast, for Jillian, at least. She didn't *want* a relationship, but she couldn't help how she felt, either. And the more time she spent with Reseph, the more she liked him. The more she found herself craving the way he made her feel.

Lighten it up. Fast. She jammed her hands on her hips and rolled her eyes in mock disgust. "You will turn anything into an opportunity to get into bed, won't you?"

A slow smile spread over his face. "Jilly, you know me so well."

Wince. No one had called her Jilly since she was in

diapers. She grabbed the frying pan off the stove. "Call me Jilly again, and I'll nail you with this."

"Looks heavy."

She hefted it higher. "Cast iron."

"You wouldn't really hit me, would you...Jilly?"

She spoke through clenched teeth. "Yes."

Reseph sauntered over, and her heart pounded faster with each step. He stopped when they were almost touching and leaned in so close his lips grazed her ear. "You know I love a woman who can handle a weapon."

"Yeah? You know what you can *do* with the handle?"

Laughing, he raised his hands in defeat and stepped back. "I'm going to check on the animals."

"Didn't you already feed them?"

"Yeah, but there's something out there."

The reminder put a damper on the light mood. "Be careful."

"Yup. If I had a middle name, careful would be it." He waggled his brows. "I think."

"Somehow, I doubt that."

He shrugged, making all those luscious muscles play under his skin. "You're probably right."

Reseph tugged on a T-shirt and stepped out into the cold, grateful for the icy breeze. For once, it wasn't the sexy play that had gotten him sweaty. It was the talk of Jillian's nightmares. He hadn't been exactly...forthcoming. Yes, she'd whimpered in her sleep, cried out at times, and she tossed and turned like she was a kernel of corn in a popcorn popper.

But so did he.

This morning, what had driven him from bed had been nightmares that played like movies every time he closed his eyes.

He'd seen monsters...horrific creatures of all sizes and shapes. The worst ones had been the beasts who, at first, looked human, but who then morphed into things that fell upon actual humans and...did things to them. There'd also been plagues, so many people suffering.

The worst part of all was that in the nightmares, Reseph sensed that he was supposed to enjoy the horrors. The blood. The death.

Maybe he shouldn't have spent so much time researching the shit that had gone down over the last year. He'd watched news reports, read up on official statements released by governments worldwide, seen pictures so disturbing he'd grown nauseous.

It had all been so familiar.

He needed to know why. He needed answers, answers the Internet couldn't provide.

Glancing back over his shoulder, he made sure Jillian was still in the house and started down her driveway. He trudged to the main road and made a left, heading up the mountain in the direction he assumed the Bjornsens had lived. He wasn't sure how long he walked, but he knew when he found the right driveway.

Even if the grim, sinister vibration hadn't grabbed him, the sight of the tire-chewed driveway would have. Out here, in the middle of nowhere, there had been a lot of traffic turning onto the crude gravel drive.

Cautiously, he followed the tire tracks, his eyes and ears alerted to danger. The drive twisted for a good half a mile. As he rounded an uphill bend, he spotted a rusted-out trailer house ringed by police tape. There were no cars save the ancient Jeep wagon parked in front of the detached garage.

The sense of evil became more concentrated as he ducked under the police tape, and with it, his pulse kicked into high gear. Again, the familiarity was tapping at the inside of his skull. His hand trembled as he reached for the door handle.

The unlocked door swung open, and the stench of death slammed into him. The rank odor of blood and bowels was also accompanied by an odd smokiness, like a combination of sulphur and brimstone.

Brimstone? How would he know what brimstone smelled like? Hell, how did he know what death smelled like?

Fuck. This couldn't be good.

Reseph stepped inside, careful to avoid messing up any of the police evidence marks, tags, and photos that had been pinned all over the place. Dried blood created gruesome art on the walls and furniture, and pools of still-damp blood sat like muddy gel on the linoleum floor and orange shag carpet.

His boots crunched on broken glass in the kitchen, remnants of shattered dishes and a window. Crouching, he studied the claw marks that raked the cabinets. They were deep, some completely piercing the flimsy particleboard. Bloody footprints littered the place...some human, and some...not.

He hovered his palm over one of the *nots*. The print was longer than his hand, and wider, very similar to the ones he'd seen in the snow near the cougar tracks.

This was definitely not a cougar, and if the cops

suspected a bear, they were morons. At least they'd been smart enough to call in experts.

I'm responsible for this.

The thought came out of nowhere, a stab in the brain that rocked him on his heels. He couldn't be responsible. He'd been frozen in the snow.

Unless I killed them and then wandered through the woods until I collapsed.

A breath shuddered out of him. He was so sick of doubting himself. Almost idly, he dragged his finger through a scatter of salt from a broken shaker. Some demon-proof-your-house advice website had claimed that certain supernatural creatures couldn't cross a line of salt. Sounded stupid to him, but hell, anything was worth a try if it would keep Jillian safe.

The sound of an engine had him leaving behind ideas about stealing road salt trucks. He leaped to his feet and scanned for a back door. It wouldn't be cool for the cops to catch him here. Especially if the cop was Stacey, who already wanted to string him up by his balls. Shit.

Ducking low, he eased to the kitchen window to peek out, and his heart stopped. It wasn't the police. It was Jillian on a snowmobile.

Double shit. He'd almost rather Stacey found him. Dressed in black ski pants, snow boots, and a green parka, she climbed off the machine, eyeing his footprints as she walked toward the door, where he met her.

And she. Was. Pissed.

Expression set in fury, she clenched her gloved hands at her sides. "What the hell are you doing? This is a crime scene. Why didn't you tell me you were taking off? That was an ass move—" She broke off, her gaze glued to the scene behind him. The fire that had been snapping in her eyes snuffed out, and her skin lost so much color he prepared to catch her if she passed out.

Before he could step out and close the door, she bulldozed her way past him.

"Jillian," he said, taking her arm, "you shouldn't see this."

"Oh, but it's okay for you to see it?" She jerked out of his grip. "I'm not a child."

"You're the one who pointed out that it's a crime scene."

She glared. At least she wasn't carrying a frying pan.

The moment she stepped into the kitchen and saw the claw marks in the cabinets, she went even paler.

"I don't know much about police procedure," Reseph said, "but it seems odd to tape pictures of the victims and the evidence at the scene."

She swallowed sickly a few times. "I don't think it's standard procedure for normal crime scenes. A while ago, Stacey mentioned that when paranormal specialists are called in, they require the police to leave pictures of the victims and evidence since the specialists don't work closely with law enforcement."

Swallowing harder, she peered at one of the pictures, and Reseph held his breath. Of all the photos, that was the most graphic, revealing a pattern of claw marks on a woman's torso.

The photo was of just her torso, since her legs, arms, and head were missing.

Jillian slapped her hand over her mouth and ran for the door. He chased after her, found her around the side of the house next to the woodpile, trying desperately not to throw up.

Helplessness was a lump in his gut, so he did the only thing he could. He rubbed her back, small, gentle circles over her coat. "I'm sorry. Did you know these people well?"

She shook her head. "They've only been here for a few months. Honestly, they were jerks. He shot one of my goats for wandering onto their property, and his wife didn't care at all. But I didn't wish...this on them." She shivered. "That was no wild animal, Reseph. We both know that."

His heart nearly stopped, and even in this cold, his palms began to sweat. "Do you know what it was?"

"Yes." Her green eyes came up to cling to his. With shaking hands, she unzipped her coat and lifted her sweatshirt.

On her belly were scars. Scars scratched into her skin in the exact same pattern as the claw marks on the dead woman.

Ten

⌐

"What happened?" Reseph's voice was low, deadly, and this time, Jillian knew she wasn't going to get away with deflecting or telling him she didn't want to talk about it.

"I'll tell you everything." She looked around and shivered. "But I want to go home first. This place is giving me the creeps."

Reseph gave a decisive nod and headed to the snowmobile. "I'll drive. You look like you're about to pass out."

"Do you know how to operate one of those?"

"Strangely, yes. I can drive a car, too. Pretty sure I'm good at horse-drawn buggy." He hopped on and held out his hand, which she took, and settled herself so her body was flush against his, wrapping her arms tightly around his waist. "Lower."

"What?"

"Move your hands lower."

Inhaling the warm, earthy scent of his silky hair, she

obeyed, and then punched him in the shoulder. "You and your one-track mind."

"Can't blame a guy for trying." He started the engine, the roar cutting off any hope of a smart comeback. Which was, no doubt, the reason for his convenient timing.

He gunned it, turning them around in the circular drive. As they started down the long, winding driveway, headlights flashed between the trees, coming at them. Reseph stopped the machine.

"Who is that?"

She tightened her arms around him. "Could be the police. Or the special investigators."

"Who are they, anyway?"

"Demon hunters." She'd never seen any, but talk of them was all over the news.

Reseph went taut, the muscles in his back turning to cement against her chest. "Is there another way back to your place?"

"Why?"

"I don't know. I just have a bad feeling."

"About them?"

"No," he said roughly. "About me." His entire body went even stiffer as the vehicle got closer. "I can't explain it. We just need to go."

Unease licked at her, but Reseph hadn't steered her wrong yet. She pointed toward a thin grouping of trees. "That way. There's a meadow we can cut through."

Reseph didn't waste time. He hit the gas and tore through the forest. Jillian held on for dear life, although she had to admit that he drove the snowmobile like he'd been doing it professionally for years.

"You're good," she yelled into his ear.

"I know."

"Arrogant ass," she muttered, and she swore he chuckled.

He ripped across the field, keeping close to the tree line, as if he didn't want to get caught out in the open. Ahead, a deer bounded over a log and into the trees, turning to look at them as they sped through the snow. Reseph saluted the creature and turned the machine into the forest at the trail Jillian gestured toward.

They arrived at her house in one piece, which almost seemed like a miracle. Reseph drove well, but he drove like a maniac.

As soon as they were inside, he stripped off his shirt and socks, leaving him only in jeans. She might think his hatred of clothes was strange, but she certainly didn't mind looking at his bare body.

"Now," he said, crossing his arms over that magnificent chest. "What happened?"

"I don't even get a chance to relax?" She headed into the bedroom, and he followed.

"You had time to relax on the way here."

She shot him a dirty look. "If you think being on the back of a snowmobile with you is relaxing, you're crazy."

"That's highly likely." He propped himself in the doorway. "So."

"So." The dark memories of her past rose up. Delay. She needed to delay even for just a minute. "Why don't you go first and tell me what about the demon investigators made you nervous?"

"I don't know," he murmured. She measured him for the truth, studying his body language right down to the twitch in his straight, strong jaw and the glint in his eyes, but it dawned on her that it was a waste of time. She was batting zero when it came to judging men. "I guess I had a witch hunt freak-out. You know how zealots see what they want to see? What if they took a gander at my situation and decided I should burn at the stake? Look what happened during the Salem witch trials. No one put on trial was actually a witch. One was a demon, but no witches." He paused. "How do I know that?"

"Maybe you saw it when you were online. But yes, I can see how running into demon police types could be a little unsettling," she admitted.

"Exactly. Now," he said, in a deep voice that dripped with command, "tell me what happened to you."

Dammit. He definitely wasn't letting this go, but she couldn't blame him. She'd invited the discussion the moment she showed him her scars. God, she wasn't even sure what had possessed her to do that. She hadn't even let Stacey see them.

"It happened a year ago." She sank down on the bed and pulled a pillow onto her lap. "I was leaving work at the Orlando air traffic control tower after a swing shift, so it was almost midnight. The parking lot was well-lit, but all of a sudden, the lights dimmed."

"A year ago. That's about when all the demon stuff happened, right?"

"Sort of. Apparently, it had been happening for a few months, but the general public didn't really know until then. That's when the shit hit the fan and just kept getting worse." Until three months ago, when everything just… stopped. "So yeah, there were rumors and stuff, and it was getting scary, but world leaders were trying to downplay everything." A shudder rattled her. "I wasn't as cautious as I should have been, but I was supposed to be meeting my fiancé in the parking lot—"

"Fiancé?" Somehow, Reseph's voice went even deeper.

"Yes, but, I mean...it's over. We're not together anymore. Obviously. Or I wouldn't be here." Good God, could she have babbled more? And why did she feel the need to explain? "Anyway, I was in the lot, and when the lights went out, I should have run back inside the building. Instead, like an idiot, I went to my car."

"You couldn't have known," he said. "And weren't you at an airport? Isn't the control tower in a secure area?"

"Yes, which is probably why I had a false sense of security." She inhaled, bracing herself for the rest. "When I was almost to my car, I saw blood. A lot of it, leaking out from under the truck parked next to mine. At the time, I thought it was oil."

"Because it was dark."

"Exactly." She winced. "But I remember the smell. I should have known. It was so stupid." She didn't give him a chance to offer comforting, useless words. "I walked around the back of my car, and that's when I saw Sandy. She was the electronic technician who monitored the weather instruments in the field. She was being...attacked...by some kind of monsters." The things had been sexually assaulting her, even as they ripped at her body with their massive teeth. "She was dead...God, I hope she was dead."

"What did you do?"

"I ran. Tried to run, anyway. One of them had me on the ground before I made it ten feet." She looked up at Reseph, who was watching her with concern, but, thankfully, not pity. "The strangest thing is that I don't remember the pain. I know it was cutting at me with its claws, and I was terrified, but I don't remember it hurting." The fear though...she'd never forget that.

"What else do you remember?"

"Its breath." She shuddered again, this time hard enough to shake the bed. "It was like rotting eggs and meat mixed with feces." She realized she'd been rubbing her belly, running her palm over the scars, and she pulled her hand back. "And then there was the man."

Reseph shoved off the door frame in a slow, sinuous motion. "Man?"

She nodded. "In the shadows. I didn't see him, but I... felt him. It was like he was a big furnace, only instead of giving off heat, he was radiating evil." She gave a nervous laugh. "Sounds crazy, doesn't it?"

"We're talking about demons," Reseph said, as he moved in front of her. "So nothing sounds crazy. Or maybe all of it does."

"I think it all does."

He kneeled at her feet and put his hands over hers. "Then what?"

"I don't know." It was a lie, but she wasn't ready to relive the gory details. She doubted she'd ever be ready. "I remember the sound of flapping wings, though. It was so odd. There were all these growls and snarls...and through them, I heard the whisper-soft flap of wings." A few seconds passed in silence, and when she spoke again, her lips were numb from pressing them together. "I woke up in the hospital a month later. The doctor said airport police had found me during a routine patrol. I didn't remember anything for a few weeks, and by the time I did, I was discharged from the hospital. I couldn't go back to work, so I quit my job and came here."

"And your...fiancé?" Reseph's last word came out as a low growl.

"I never saw him again."

A vicious smile curved Reseph's mouth. "Did the demons eat him?"

"I wish," she muttered. "A day after I woke up in the hospital, I had my first visitor—his wife." Apparently, Jason had confessed everything to his wife, saying that he'd intended to leave her, but the circumstances around the world had made him see the light, blah, blah. That was why he hadn't met Jillian in the parking lot like he was supposed to. He'd changed his mind about her and his marriage. His wife had been the one to come to the hospital and tell Jillian that the relationship was over.

"You were engaged to a married man?"

Humiliation spread like wildfire over her cheeks. "I didn't know he was married. He told me he was divorced."

"Bastard," Reseph snapped.

"Can't argue that one."

Reseph studied her, and once again she got the impression that he was far, far older than he appeared. "Stacey knows what happened, doesn't she?"

"Yeah. She's the only one. Until you." She squeezed his hands, grateful for his presence. "I was doing really well, and now...shit." She closed her eyes, but it didn't shut out what she'd seen in the neighbors' trailer. "The same kind of demon butchered my neighbors, didn't it? God, what if it was because of me? What if it's here to finish what it started? Reseph, what if it's coming after me next?"

"Then I'll kill it," he said, his eyes blazing. "I swear to you, Jillian, no monster will ever touch you again."

A lot of men had made a lot of promises to her in

her life, and she'd learned not to believe them. But she believed Reseph. She didn't know why, but she did. Now she just had to hope that when he finally remembered who he was, he wouldn't forget the things he'd promised.

Kynan Morgan climbed out of his rented SUV, his boots crunching in snow torn up by vehicles, including at least one snowmobile. He'd seen a flash of red metal through the trees as he'd driven up, but whoever had been here was gone, the fresh tracks leading off into the forest.

"Who do you think that was?" Arik Wagner, Ky's partner and relative-by-marriage, stared off into the distance.

Ky peeled off his sunglasses. "Local, maybe?"

"Wanna follow the tracks?"

"Feel free, if you have snowshoes in your pocket."

Arik snorted. "Ass." He headed toward the house, halting at the door.

Neither one of them liked going into scenes like this, and the one they'd just come from down the mountain had been horrific enough that Kynan's mind was still going back to it. Not to mention the fact that sometimes demons lurked near the scenes of their attacks, reliving the kill, feeding on the horror and fear of the humans who visited the scene. Kynan, at least, didn't have anything to fear; thanks to Heofon, the amulet around his neck, and the charm that came with it, he was immune to harm from anything but fallen angels.

"Go, man."

Arik opened the door. The odors common to death-by-demon scenes slapped Ky in the face, and he could only be thankful that it was winter in the north and that the house hadn't been cooking in humid summer heat in Louisiana or some shit.

"Fuck," Arik muttered. "Fucking hate demons." He didn't mean it...not about all demons, seeing how his sister was a werewolf mated to a demon, and Arik himself was married to one of the Four Horsemen of the Apocalypse.

Then again, Arik had spent a month in hell—literally, hell—being tortured. So he pretty much despised any demon he wasn't related to or having sex with.

Ky combed the house, taking note of the footprints, the claw marks, and the injuries on the victims. "Soulshredder. Just like the last scene."

"So that makes two families in the area, plus a couple of hunters." Arik drove his hands through his hair. "How many demons are we talking about, do you think?"

Kynan blew out a breath. "Definitely just one at each scene, but that doesn't mean we don't have a pair or even an entire pack hanging out in the area. The weird thing about it is how they're killing."

Soulshredders didn't usually kill everyone at a scene. They liked to leave one person alive so they could torture them over time, coming back to the person every once in a while for years, driving them crazy, haunting them.

"And why here?"

"The demon or demons must be drawn here for some reason. Maybe to a person."

"So we have to find the person." Arik cursed. "I was really hoping for a quick in and out on this case."

Ky cocked an eyebrow. "Limos keeping you busy?"

"You have no idea."

"Oh, I have an idea. Gem wants another baby, and when they decide they want one..."

"They don't think about anything else." Arik nodded. "Yeah, I know. And Limos is . . . insistent."

Kynan laughed. Yeah, Limos was definitely one to get what she wanted, when she wanted. And after five thousand years of celibacy, she had a lot of catching up to do. Not that Arik complained. Much. But the boy was always dragging ass. Sure, he dragged ass with a smile, but still.

"Okay, so let's chart all the kills and see if we can get a bead on commonalities. Whoever the Soulshredder is drawn to will probably be inside the kill circle."

Arik sighed. "I can't believe we've been reduced to supernatural CSIs."

"Someone needs to do it."

"It used to be The Aegis's job," Arik muttered.

Bitterness coated Kynan's tongue. The Aegis had been—and still was—the oldest and most major anti-demon force in the world, and Arik and Ky had been part of it. Hell, they'd run it. But the organization had broken apart three months ago, and Kynan, along with Val, Arik, Decker, Tayla, and Regan, and a few others, had been forced out.

Now Ky and the rest of the outcasts were working to build an agency that operated on the principles that had gotten them kicked out, but it hadn't been easy. Most Aegis members preferred the "old ways," which pretty much involved killing all demons, vampires, and shifters on sight. The Aegis didn't believe in "good" demons.

But the new offshoot, the Demonic Activity Response Team, headed by Ky and the others, had recruited a few members, enough to form two bases, one in New York and one in Madrid. They were planning another DART office in Los Angeles. Unfortunately, The Aegis wasn't being a good sport, and they'd been causing trouble where they could, when they could.

Kynan pried a piece of broken claw out of a cabinet. Sometimes DNA could be used to locate its owner. "The Aegis never really worked like this, though."

Nope, The Aegis had been an uber-secret agency that mainly operated with its ear to the ground, taking care of problems as they heard about them through police and news reports and rumors. Now they were out of the closet and were so busy putting down demon rebellions around the world that they didn't have time for small local issues like this one.

Which was where DART came in, filling a void that needed to be filled. They'd made themselves known and available to law enforcement agencies, and shit, they'd been kept busy. Most demons had gone back to Sheoul when Pestilence had been destroyed, but some had remained behind, preferring the human realm over the demon one— and honestly, Ky couldn't blame them. Sheoul sucked.

"What if we're dealing with a summoner?" Arik asked.

"If someone has been summoning this demon, we kill them, too."

"And if it's an unintentional summoner?"

Ky ground his teeth. This was where the job got tough. An unintentional summoner was someone who'd been marked by a demon for some reason... to be used as a breeder or as food or as an energy draw. In any case, the person would be a magnet for all demons of that species, which meant that killing a single demon wouldn't solve the problem.

"We do what we always do," Ky said. "We take them out."

Eleven

Reseph rarely got angry. He might not remember who he was, but he knew that about himself. And he knew that the kind of fury he was feeling now was unusual. Something had hurt Jillian, had nearly killed her, and yet, she'd survived, coming back strong in a way he doubted many people did. And now she was afraid again.

Something was out there, hunting her neighbors and killing wild animals. He'd thought he was seeing things, but now he knew that a demon had been within sight of Jillian's cabin. If it was the last thing he did, he'd take it out and mount its head on a pole to warn others. *Don't fuck with my woman.*

His woman? And shit, where had he gotten the idea that it would be a good idea to mount a demon head on a pole? Whatever. He'd do it if it would keep Jillian safe. As for her being his woman, well, it would probably be best to get his memory back before he went all, *you're mine.*

Especially since the nagging feeling that he wasn't a Boy Scout was growing stronger with every passing hour. He had too many weird thoughts, knew too many fucked-up things.

Maybe he'd been a demon hunter, like the people investigating the Bjornsen and Wilson killings. That might not be so bad. Might be kind of cool, actually. He'd hunt down the demon lurking here in the mountains, and then he'd track the ones who had hurt Jillian at the airport and make them feel everything they had done to her. Right after that, the ex-fiancé asshole would have to go.

Another burst of rage made his blood sizzle. Nothing would hurt her again. Nothing.

"Reseph?"

He blinked, realized he'd been lost in his own mind like some kind of head case. "Yeah?"

"You were growling." She was looking at him like she thought he was some kind of head case, too.

"Shit." He brought one of her hands to his mouth and pressed a kiss to the silky skin. "Sorry. I just feel so damned helpless. I want to kill the thing that attacked you, and I want to protect you from everything else, but what if..." He trailed off, not wanting to voice his darkest fears.

"What if...what?" She hooked one finger under his chin and forced his gaze to hers. "Reseph? Don't shut down on me. I just shared with you. Your turn."

Yeah, it wasn't fair for him to not spill his guts after she just had, but there was a big difference here. What she'd told him had made him feel even more for her, had plucked at every tender, protective gene he had. But what he held inside could only do the opposite to her.

"What if it's me I have to protect you from?"

"I'm not afraid of you, Reseph." Her level gaze was unwavering.

"But you don't know who I am."

"I know you're cocky and funny. You're protective and sweet. You're not afraid of hard work. You're strong, but gentle. You can't cook worth a shit."

"I think I'm offended."

"But you *really* can't cook," she grumbled.

"I was talking about the 'sweet' part."

Her full lips quirked in an impish smile. "Sweet."

This wasn't going well, not when she wasn't taking his concerns seriously. "Jillian, maybe that's who I am now. But what if we find out I'm a sick bastard. What if—"

"Stop." When he would have argued, she tugged him up onto the bed with her so they were both lying across the mattress. Her dark hair framed her face in messy wisps, softening the stubborn light in her eyes. "Look, I'm not going to lie and say I'm not worried about who you were before. I've dated a lot of guys who ended up being total dicks, and Jason was the icing on the cake. It's hard for me to trust a guy not to turn on me."

"Who were the guys?"

"What?" She propped herself up on one elbow so she could look down at him. "You want to know about the morons I dated?"

Yep. Including addresses. "What did they do to you?" God, this possessive, murderous side of him could not be good.

"Let's see... well, one cheated on me, one had a gambling problem, one was an accountant who failed to tell me that he was a cokehead." She sighed. "And I already told you about Jason."

"I think," he growled, "that I must have been an assassin before I lost my memory, because I really want to hunt down those guys and put a crossbow bolt between their eyes." It didn't even bother him that he'd do it and not feel an ounce of remorse. She'd taken so many blows in her life, and yet, she was still standing. She was so strong, and his admiration for her swelled.

"I'm not sure if I should be flattered or extremely freaked out."

"Go with flattered." He pushed himself up on one arm so he could face her. So he could feel her heat mingle with his. "If you aren't afraid of me, then why did you leave me in town?"

He hated the shame that settled into her expression, the little frown he wanted to kiss until she smiled again. "Because I don't trust myself."

"You don't trust yourself to what?" He reached out and trailed a finger along her jaw. "To not let me strip you naked and lick every inch of your body?"

A delicate smudge of pink spread across her cheekbone. "As...interesting...as that sounds, no. I don't trust my judgment, and I don't trust myself to not get attached."

It was on the tip of his tongue to say, "Then don't," because it seemed like the obvious solution, but then he'd be a hypocrite, because he was definitely developing feelings for her that he wasn't sure how to handle. It was almost as if now should be the time he started running for the hills. Was that what he'd done before? Why? He loved how he felt when he was with Jillian, so why wouldn't he have wanted that before now?

So many questions, and the only thing he knew was that he was growing close to Jillian, and he wasn't going to fight it. She, obviously, was. And frankly, the more he thought about it, the angrier he got, even if he understood her reluctance. He had no past, and because of that, a questionable future. So he understood it, but he didn't like it.

Stung by her rejection, he leaned forward, forcing her back. "Then don't get attached. Because let's face it. I've wanted to fuck you since the moment I woke in your bed, surrounded by your scent." Her eyes flared with surprise, and he pressed the issue, getting right in her face. "And I know damned good and well you would have let me take you right there in the sheriff's station if we'd been alone. So let's screw around, no emotional commitment. That way, we'll both have protected our delicate little hearts if we find out I was some kind of asshole scumbag in the past."

Huh. Guess they didn't need to wait to find out if he was an asshole. He'd just taken that on-ramp.

Jillian's lips parted in shock before she pressed them together and her eyes hardened with a cold inner resolve. "Fine. You're right." She palmed his chest. "Wanna have sex?" She dragged her hand down his abs to his waistband, and he nearly stopped breathing, but his cock jumped, all, *hell, yeah*.

Then he stunned the hell out of himself when he grabbed her hand and stopped her from unbuttoning his jeans. "Are you sure?"

What the fuck. Why wasn't he taking what she was offering, no questions asked? This was so...foreign. Like he'd never in his life questioned or turned down sex.

"After all your chasing, *now* you're backing off?" She nipped his fingers hard enough to make him let go and dropped her hand back down on his fly. "Yes, I'm sure.

I used to like sex. I miss it. Commitment-free sex, you say? Sure. Why not? My delicate little heart will be just fine." Their eyes met, hers glinting with determination that sucked the breath right out of his lungs. "So are you gonna follow through on your offer, or do I have to take a cold shower?"

Her palm cupped him through his jeans, massaging and squeezing, and his decision was made. Reaching up, he tangled his fingers through her hair and brought her lips to his. Kissing her, he pulled her down on top of him, loving the weight of her on his body. What he didn't love was how this was going down. Maybe in the past, meaningless sex would have been fine. But with Jillian he wanted more. Stupid of him, no doubt, but clearly, he wasn't a male who operated on logic. He was all about instinct and impulse, and right now, both were leading him to Jillian.

Jillian couldn't believe she was doing this. Commitment-free sex? She'd never tried that, had always gone into relationships thinking they'd lead somewhere. Yes, she'd been adventurous and bold in bed...but only after she'd given herself permission to love the man she was with.

And hadn't *that* worked out? Not so much.

Maybe Reseph was right. Obviously, she'd been an idiot before, so hey, why not try something new. Sex without emotional attachment. She could do it. She could. She *had* to.

He was so warm beneath her, the hard planes of his body molding perfectly to hers. She kissed him as she ran her hands through his hair, reveling in the silky texture. He had the kind of hair women would kill for.

Stroking her back, he shifted so his thigh came up between hers and his arousal prodded her hip. He skimmed his hands over her ribs, down her spine, to the curve of her rear, and pressed her against him as he rolled his pelvis. The slow undulation practically undid her right there.

Pulling back, she kissed a trail along the sharp angle of his jaw, stopping now and then to scrape her teeth over his smooth skin. Each time she did that, he moaned, and each time he moaned, she felt a pleasant tug in her pelvis. She loved the sounds he made, from the small hitches in his breath, to the soft rumbles in his chest.

His hands slipped under her sweatshirt, and in single second, he'd unclasped her bra.

"I need to see you," he said, his voice husky and low. "Let me look at you."

She'd never been self-conscious... until the attack. She hesitated, nervous butterflies flitting around in her gut. For a brief moment she considered leaping off the bed and running... to where? The middle of nowhere? She was already living there. She was already as far from the place where she'd been attacked as she could get.

She wouldn't let herself be cornered again. Taking a deep, steadying breath, she pushed herself up onto her knees and let him strip her. His hungry gaze fell immediately to her belly and the ugly white marks. He reached out and drew one finger over the longest scar, the one that went from between her breasts to her hip bone.

"Is this uncomfortable for you?"

"Letting you see them?" When he nodded, she bit her lip. "They're hideous."

His gaze snapped up to hers. "Wrong." Gripping her waist, he lifted her easily and flipped them so he was on top of her and he was kissing her belly. "You're a warrior, Jillian. Your scars are as beautiful as you are."

Flustered, she had no idea what to say...not that she could speak if she wanted to. His tongue darted out to lick the long scar, starting where it disappeared under her waistband and all the way up. When he reached the ragged crest, he kissed her there, his lips lingering, warm, perfect.

His hands came up to cup her breasts as he dragged his mouth to one nipple, his breath a wave of sensation on her skin. She arched into him, seeking more, which he gave her when he sucked at her breast, gently rolling the swollen nipple between his lips.

"More," she gasped, reaching low to push his jeans off.

He chuckled and scrambled off the bed, and in two seconds flat, he had her stripped of her pants, though he left her in her panties. Then, in slow, torturous motion, he peeled open his fly, releasing his erection. It sprang free, a long, thick column of dusky brown skin and dark, pulsing veins that twined from the thick base to the smooth plum head.

She'd had a handful of sexual partners, but never had she been so entranced by the sight of a fully aroused male, and she'd definitely not felt the searing need that was making her shake with anticipation.

Reseph seemed to know, and he leveled a lopsided grin at her as he pushed down his jeans and stepped out of them. Completely naked, he was a luscious work of art, a lean, toned thing of beauty she could worship all day—and night—long.

Never looking away from him, she popped open the bedside table drawer and fumbled around for the box of condoms Stacey had bought her as a joke—and a hint.

When she tossed them onto the tabletop, Reseph barely gave them a glance.

Leaning forward, he gripped her ankles, using his thumbs to rub light circles on the sensitive flesh just under the inner ankle bone. His lips came down on her thigh, and she wondered where he was going with this. Not that she'd stop him from doing whatever he wanted, but she was rapidly learning that with him, there was very little chance of keeping one move ahead of him.

He nuzzled her thigh, working his way up her leg with his mouth and up her calves with his hands. The sensual massage made her squirm with pleasure, and the things he did with his mouth, even just on her freaking thigh, made her moan.

She thrust her hands through his hair as he kissed and licked, massaged and stroked. And when she felt the lightest brush against the cotton material covering her center, she let out an appreciative hum of approval.

"You like this," he murmured, his lips tickling the crease between her leg and her sex. "You like where I'm headed, don't you?"

She dug her nails into his scalp. "Dumb question, Reseph."

She felt his smile, then she felt his mouth open over her core. Oh...damn. He licked at her through the fabric, using his tongue to push in, teasing her through the barrier. The friction from the damp material sent a sizzle of erotic sensation shooting all the way to her breasts.

He slid his palms under her hips and lifted her to his mouth, forcing her legs to spread wider and exposing her to his onslaught. He blew on her core, and the sudden cool air on her heated flesh made her whimper with need. Before she could come down from it, he covered her with his mouth again, licking and nibbling as if the panties weren't there. God, no one had ever done this, and she could only wonder why not. It was an amazing kind of tease, so effective and yet, so maddening.

He stoked her arousal so easily, taking her higher with every expert stroke of his tongue. "You're making me insane," she murmured.

"Then we're even." He slipped his tongue under the elastic, and she cried out as he licked deep. "Fuck, you taste good." He went at her with even more enthusiasm, never removing her panties...instead, he nuzzled them aside, kissing and licking around them, over them, under them. The combination of right there and almost there nearly brought tears to her eyes, tears of ecstasy and of impatience.

His wet tongue stroked her, plunging into her core and then sliding up to the sensitive knot that craved the most attention. Finally...God, finally...he growled and tore her panties away. He dove at her as if he were starving, and she couldn't take it anymore. Closing her eyes, she let the waves of pleasure crash over her, peaking when he latched onto her clit and sucked hard while humming in the back of his throat.

She came with a cry, bucking and thrashing as he worked her out until she became too sensitive for even the lightest flick of his tongue.

"You're good at this," she rasped breathlessly. "I think...I think you've had lots of practice."

"I think you're right." His voice was guttural, a reso-nant growl that vibrated her to her marrow. He prowled up her body, the muscles in his thick shoulders and arms bunching and flexing, his gaze bright and predatory. "But this feels like the first time."

He kissed her as he reached for a condom and settled between her thighs. His mouth assaulted hers, his tongue swirling and his teeth nipping sharply. The little stings of pleasure-pain streaked all the way to her sex. He paused to sheathe himself with a faint curse and a muttered, "Shit, it's like I've never done this in my life."

She was ready, so ready when she felt the head of him prod at her entrance.

But then he froze up. His muscles locked, and he lifted his head to stare down at her.

"What is it?" She framed his face in her palms and stroked his cheekbones with her thumbs, brushing the hair out of his face. His lips, slightly parted, glistened with their kisses. "Are you okay?"

"Oh, yeah," he murmured. "There are so many things I want to do to you. So many ways I want to do them. It's like I have an encyclopedia of sex in my head. But I feel like a damned virgin, and I want this first time to be about more than positions and multiple orgasm contests."

She swallowed. "The multiple orgasm contest thing doesn't sound too bad."

His grin was panty-melting. Or, it would be, if he hadn't already melted them off. "Oh, we'll get to that. There's time for fucking on the hood of your truck or going down on you while you're bent over the deck rail or fingering you to climax under the table at a restaurant. But right now, I just want to make it last."

Holy... oh, my. Truck hoods and deck rails and restaurant tables. And all commitment-free. She had no idea why that last thought was tinged with bitterness, but when

Reseph rocked his shaft through her folds, the dizzying sensation jolted her right back into the lust.

"Yes," she choked out.

"To what?"

"All of it."

He was so free with his smiles, and he graced her with yet another one as he entered her in excruciatingly slow increments. And as the pleasure began to build again, she wondered how long this thing between them could last, because if her dating experience had taught her anything, it was that men like Reseph were meant to be enjoyed.

Not kept.

Twelve

Reseph was in heaven. Jillian's soft, panting breaths as he slid into her were the most erotic sounds he'd ever heard, and he could still taste her passion on his tongue, mingled with the flavor of her skin. As her hot core clamped around him, it was as if he were drowning in sex, losing himself in a fantasy.

He forced himself to go slow, to revel in the magic of Jillian's body. It was strange how he had all this knowledge, and yet, this was all so new to him. The sex wasn't new...it was the way it was happening that was so foreign. He didn't think he'd ever done it slowly, and with so much...care. And reverence. And emotion...which he shouldn't be feeling.

Jillian undulated beneath him, her eyes closed, her bottom lip caught between her teeth. A sexy flush tinged her skin, bringing a sunset glow to her cheeks. She brought her hands up to grip his shoulders, her strong, short nails digging in with the perfect amount of erotic pressure.

Tight…she was so fucking tight as he moved inside her. Praying for control, he forced himself to take his time with each stroke, pulling back until he was almost free of her, and then inching forward again until his balls rubbed against her. Her slick passage rippled and contracted, squeezing his length with every thrust.

He held himself above her on extended arms so he could watch her expression, see her body move, and get a view of their joining. Each time he looked down to see her feminine cleft swallow his cock, his release nudged closer. The graphic sight made him burn and revved him up more than he thought could be possible.

"Jillian," he rasped. "Ah…damn. I'm close. So close. Too…soon." He slowed down, rolling his hips instead of thrusting.

Her hand came up to massage the back of his neck before sliding into his hair. With a low growl, she guided his head down until his mouth met hers. She was so sweet, not just her taste, but her. There was something so pure about her that made him feel clean, like the new snow outside. He supposed that he did have a fresh start, and she was part of that, as much as his memory loss was. In a way, maybe his amnesia was a good thing, because something told him that the man he'd been before didn't deserve a woman like Jillian.

"Reseph," she breathed against his lips. "Faster." She lifted her hips, taking him deeper, and his control snapped.

He lunged, pounding into her with such force that she reached behind and braced her hands on the headboard.

"Yes," she moaned. "Oh, yes…yes…*Reseph*!"

Her slick, velvety walls contracted around him. She

arched, pressing her full breasts into his chest and clench-
ing her thighs hard around his hips as she came. His own
release rolled through him in a scorching wave of pleasure, and before it finished, another one blasted through
him, and then another, until he was wrung dry, trembling,
and couldn't hold his own weight anymore.

He collapsed on top of Jillian and buried his face in her
hair. "Holy ... fuck," he breathed.

"What you said." Her fingers trailed lightly up and
down his back, and one foot rubbed his calf. "Did you
have more than one?"

"Mmm-hmm."

"I didn't think men could do that."

Didn't feel strange to him, but he was still pretty sure
that was the best sex ever. "Maybe it's a side-effect of
whatever caused my amnesia. Awesome trade-off."

He rolled to the side, hating to pull out of her heat,
but he was squishing her. Scrounging up the strength to
swing his legs off the bed, he headed to the bathroom to
clean up. As he tossed the condom, he wondered if Jillian
had noticed his awkwardness when he'd put the thing on.
He knew he wasn't a stranger to sex, knew what a condom was and what to do with it, but wearing one had felt
utterly wrong. Maybe he got tested a lot. Or was sterile.
Or maybe he was a big, fat jerk who didn't give a shit.

He didn't like any of those thoughts. And wait ... why
was he bothered by the idea that he might be sterile? The
niggling sense that parenthood was something he'd never
wanted to experience made him twitch. Why wouldn't he
have wanted to be a father in his old life? Because even as
messed up as he was now, he could still envision a good
life with Jillian that included kids.

Er . . . a little premature, don't you think, given how she doesn't want to get attached?

Yeah. Dumbass.

With a mental shift in thinking, he hopped back into bed with Jillian.

Her delicate yawn made him smile as she rolled into him so her forehead was braced against his shoulder. Shifting onto his side, he traced the strong line of her jaw as she lay beside him, taking immense pleasure in the smooth texture of her skin. She closed her eyes, and as her breathing settled into a slow, even rhythm, he thought about her scars, wondering if the ones he couldn't see were as bad as the ones visible on her belly and thighs. Were they even worse?

And how bad would his scars be when—and if—he got his memory back?

It was highly unusual for Jillian to take naps, but Reseph had worn her out. Worn himself out, too, if his snoring had been any indication.

She'd dozed for an hour and then taken a shower, her mind replaying over and over what they'd done. He was *such* a good lover. She'd suspected he'd be great in bed, but he'd gone beyond great and right into out-of-this-world phenomenal. What she hadn't expected—or wanted— had been the connection she'd felt between them. She had no doubt he could keep himself emotionally detached . . . hadn't he been the one to say that there was no need to date? *Hey, just have sex! Screw the relationship crap!*

She'd seen how restless he was, how often he needed to get out of the house, how distasteful he found the idea of being tied down. Yep, she had to stay strong. Had to keep her heart locked up tight and protected. Any day now he could get his memory back and take off for the life he had before. She had to be ready.

By the time she was dressed, Reseph was up, looking out the bedroom window. Nude, of course.

He swung around to her, and she wondered if she'd ever stop being fascinated by the effortless way he moved, the play of muscles under his bronzed skin, the sweep of his thick hair around his shoulders. "I was hoping to catch you in the shower."

"Somehow, I don't think we'd have gotten a lot of showering done," she said wryly.

He sauntered over to her, his smoldering gaze making her heart flutter. "Not true," he said, as he planted a kiss on her neck. "There are all kinds of fun things we could do with soap."

"No doubt." She looked down at him. "I'm going to grab a pair of my dad's sweatpants for you. Running around in only jeans...or naked...can't be that comfortable."

"Naked is very comfortable."

"Maybe, but it's also very distracting."

He grinned. "I distract you?"

"I'm not answering that. Your ego has no need of more stroking." She arched an eyebrow at him. "And don't tell me you have something else I can stroke. I've been around enough men to have heard it all."

A low, rattling sound pumped out of his chest. "I'm not like other men."

"No shit," she muttered, as she headed down to the cellar.

Reseph, naturally, followed her. Thankfully, he threw

on jeans first. "What is all of this?" he asked, when he hit the bottom step.

"My parents' belongings, mostly. And a few things from high school."

He ran his hand over a dusty box labeled THROW RUGS. "Why do you keep all this stuff?"

She shrugged. "I dunno."

When he picked up a jewelry box sitting by itself on a shelf, she snatched it out of his hand before he could open it. "That's nothing."

"Nothing?" He eyed the box. "You're pretty concerned over nothing."

She shrugged again and returned it to the shelf. This time, when Reseph picked it up, she didn't protest. He opened it and drew a sharp breath.

"It's an engagement ring."

It was a symbol of her stupidity. "Very astute."

He cocked an eyebrow. "Yours?"

"Yep."

"The married bastard?"

"Yes."

"So why do you keep the ring? He hurt you. You should have shoved it so far up his ass he could use it as a tooth filling."

That image made her laugh, even though she was pretty sure Reseph wasn't kidding. "Maybe I'm still hoping to do that."

He studied her, his icicle-blue eyes piercing so deep inside she felt a chill. "No. You're holding on because you can't let things go. That's why you don't want to get attached, isn't it? Because you hold on so tight."

Damn him. How could he know that? His observation

left her off balance, wobbling on her mental axle, and she had to fumble for the calm reserve she'd prided herself on cultivating for her air traffic control job.

"I guess," she said, but there was no *guessing* about it. She'd never been able to let go of things that reminded her of strong bonds, to the point where holding on could be paralyzing.

It had taken her a full year to finally grieve for her parents, because she'd felt that as long as she had their things, she didn't have to let them go.

Reseph put the box back on the shelf. "Seems strange to me. When things are gone, they're gone."

"Does that include people?" She knew the answer before he said it, and her stomach clenched.

"Yeah." He glanced up the stairs as if suddenly uncomfortable with the conversation. "I should probably shower." As if his feet were on fire, he shot up the steps, taking them three at a time.

Okaaay. So it was easy for him to cut someone loose, but he didn't like talking about it. Or, probably, facing it. She wondered if he was one of those guys who broke up with their girlfriends in text messages.

Son of a bitch. Leave it to her to get involved with someone like that.

No, not involved. They were *not* involved.

Yup, because if you repeated it twice, that made it true. *Moron.*

The sound of an engine cut through her dismal musings. She wasn't expecting any deliveries, but Stacey sometimes—okay, often—popped in unannounced. She mounted the stairs and got to the front door just as the doorbell rang.

For a split second, she hesitated, the scene she'd witnessed at the neighbors' house flicking through her brain. She doubted, however, that the monster that butchered them had rung their doorbell. Still, her pulse picked up a little as she opened the door.

Two men stood on her porch, both tall and dark-haired, but the one with the denim-blue eyes looked like he'd had his throat chewed on by an alligator. When he spoke, his gravelly voice doubled her alligator suspicion.

"Ms. Cardiff? My name is Kynan Morgan, and this—" he jerked his thumb at the man to his right "—is Arik Wagner. We're special investigators, and we'd like to ask you a few questions." He smiled, but she was anything but reassured. "May we come in?"

Special investigators. Her first thought was that they might be here for Reseph. Yes, she knew that more likely, the police would be the ones to show up with any news about who he was, but she suddenly had a bad feeling, as if these were not people she wanted to give too much information to.

"I'm sorry, but I'm not in the habit of bringing strangers into my home." *Unless I find them naked in snowbanks.* "I'm sure you understand." She stepped out and pulled the door closed behind her. The one named Arik frowned and tried to peek inside, but she tugged until the door clicked.

"Of course," Kynan said politely. "Are you alone?"

She smiled just as politely and made a point of not answering his question. "What can I help you with?"

Kynan tugged off his gloves with brisk, purposeful movements. "I assume you're aware that your neighbors on both sides of you were killed, as well as a couple of local hunters."

"I'm well aware."

"We'd like to know if you saw or heard anything." He tucked both gloves into one pocket and rested his right hand casually inside his other pocket.

A weapon. I'll bet he's got a weapon in there. "Not a thing."

Kynan studied her as if trying to see through her, and it was unnerving as hell. "Have you ever seen a demon, Jillian?"

"Ms. Cardiff. And no."

He gave her a tolerant smile, and Jillian got the same instant jolt of *oh-shit* she used to get when two planes were on a collision course. Somehow, Kynan knew she was lying. "Have you ever been attacked by a demon, Ms. Cardiff?"

Okay, now she was getting pissed. Especially because the other guy, Arik, was wandering around her deck, taking covert peeks through her window.

"If I had been attacked by a demon, then I'd have seen one, isn't that right?"

"Not necessarily," Kynan said. "Some are invisible."

She smiled tightly. "Why don't you tell me what special investigative unit you're from."

"We work for the Demonic Activity Response Team."

DART. She'd read about them on the Internet. "I'll assume that you've been in touch with local law enforcement?"

"Both the county sheriff's office and the state police."

"Then if you want anything more from me, I suggest you bring one of the officers with you, because I'm done with your questions." She jerked her chin at the SUV in the driveway. "Now get off my property before I exercise my rights as a homeowner dealing with trespassers."

Kynan cocked an eyebrow at her as she spun around

and stormed into the house. She closed the door behind her, locked it, and fell back against the wood, her heart pounding crazily. She allowed herself two calming breaths, and then she grabbed the phone and dialed Stacey.

"Hey, Stace." She didn't even give her friend time to say hello. "I need to know what those guys from DART know about me."

Stacey took a sip of something, probably coffee, on the other end of the line. "What are you talking about?"

"They were just here, asking me questions about demons."

"Well, they're investigating the attacks, and you're the closest neighbor. It makes sense."

"But do they know about my attack?"

"Well, I certainly didn't tell them. They came in last night, and we briefed them on the situation, and then they were headed to the scenes. They haven't been back."

"Did you tell them about Reseph?"

"No. Why? Is everything okay?"

"It's fine." She heard the truck outside start up. "Look, I gotta go. I'll call later."

"Jill—"

Jillian hung up as Reseph came out of the bedroom, dressed as usual in jeans and nothing else. His gaze focused like a laser on the window.

"Who are they?" As he watched, his entire demeanor changed, going from carefree and loose to...well, she could only describe it as deadly. And yet, he still appeared to be relaxed. But there was a new intensity in his expression and a subtle tightening of his muscles.

"They're the demon investigators."

His voice went low. "Did they follow us here?"

"I don't think so. They just wanted to know if I've seen

anything strange." Confusion flitted across his expression. "Reseph? Are you okay? Do you recognize them?"

As the truck drove away, the lethal vibe radiating from him scaled back, but his jaw was still tight, his hands still clenched. "No. But there was something...shit, I don't know. It's like I felt I should know them, but if I did, they'd want to kill me."

"Kill you?" She put down the phone, hoping he didn't notice that her hand was shaking. "I think that's a little extreme. They deal with demons. Not humans."

"Yeah, you're right." He smiled, but it didn't match the worry she saw in his eyes. "I'm sure you're right."

Thirteen

Reaver's first stop after trying to convince his Heavenly brethren of Gethel's betrayal was Ares's manor. Somehow, he wasn't surprised to find all of the Horsemen—save Reseph—on the beach. Ares and Thanatos were manning a barbecue grill while Cara and Regan played with Rath, Cara and Ares's adopted Ramreel demon toddler. Limos was holding a baby, who Reaver instantly knew was Logan, Than and Regan's son. Circling at her feet was a pitch-black hellhound puppy the size of a Labrador retriever that kept looking up at the infant. It didn't take a genius to figure out that the pup had bonded to the baby and would forever be a faithful bodyguard.

Reaver kicked off his shoes and walked on bare feet toward the group.

Limos saw him first, but then, she usually did. Her grin was blinding, and he knew that if she hadn't been holding

Logan, she'd have thrown herself into his arms, again, as she usually did.

The rest of the gang was more measured with their greetings, and Reaver braced himself. Thanatos, his bare upper body encased in layers of tattoos, crossed to Limos and took the baby, and with Regan at his side, they waited for Reaver to walk up to them.

"He's beautiful," Reaver said, his voice shakier than he'd expected. He liked babies, but this one was special, and it wasn't just because his birth had saved the world. This was the first Horseman offspring, and Reaver felt like a proud uncle.

"Yes," Than said coolly, "he is. You missed his birth."

And...it started. "I was fighting Gethel."

"For three months?"

"I'm sorry, Thanatos." He nodded to Regan. "If I could have come sooner, I would have."

Ares approached, reddish-brown hair glinting in the sunlight, but Cara remained back with Rath. The little demon darted to the surf to play in the waves, his hooved feet kicking up ivory foam. "What happened? Where's Gethel?"

"So you haven't seen her, then?" Damn. Reaver was hoping she'd shown her traitorous face...not because Reaver wanted her messing with his Horsemen, but because anything she said might reveal her hand.

The blond braids at Thanatos's temples slapped his cheeks as he shook his head. "Last we saw her was with you."

He looked past Reaver, and a tingle on the back of Reaver's neck said that Harvester had arrived. Excellent, because Reaver really needed another complication.

She eased up next to him, and he nearly groaned when

he saw what she was wearing. Or, more accurately, what she wasn't wearing.

Her long black hair hung over one shoulder, cascading over breasts barely covered by a skimpy knit swimsuit top. He suspected that her matching yellow bikini bottom was a thong, but she'd at least tied a sheer black cover-up around her waist. Not that the cover-up did anything to hide a body made for sin. Literally. And Reaver, who had always appreciated a female who dressed provocatively, had to tear his gaze away before *his* body started reacting to Harvester the way it had when they'd kissed in Sheoul-gra.

"How are my lovely Horsemen today?" she chirped, all sunshine and rainbows. Something was up. She was never happy-happy.

"We're waiting for Reaver to tell us what happened with Gethel," Than said.

This time when Reaver held back a groan, it was because he was expecting Harvester to spill the beans, and Reaver wasn't ready to tell them what he'd done with Reseph. If he could destroy Gethel before she found Reseph, Reaver might be able to salvage some of his plan to keep the Horseman safe in the human realm while his mind healed. Of course, if Gethel had told anyone at all that Reseph was free, the plan might be all shot to hell.

"Gethel and I fought, but the chamber filled with demons, and she escaped."

"And where have you been since?" Than's question wasn't a challenge. There was too much hurt in his tone.

"I was trapped in Sheoul," Reaver said. It wasn't a lie, but wasn't the complete truth.

"How?" Limos's violet eyes flashed.

Shit, now Reaver either had to lie or exercise his

authority and tell them he was under no obligation to answer, according to Watcher law. But yeah, *that* would go over like a lead balloon.

"It was my fault," Harvester blurted, stunning the shit out of Reaver. "I was pissed that my team got their asses kicked, so I locked him in Pestilence's chamber for a while." She shrugged. "Broke another Watcher rule. Whatever. It was worth it."

Limos growled. "You're such a bitch."

"Hey," Reaver said in an attempt to divert the conversation from unexplained fibs and undeserved insults. Harvester might be a bitch, but in this case, it wasn't true. "Is this a party? Because no one has offered me a hot dog yet." He eyed the little blond squirming bundle. "And no one has introduced me to that adorable kid yet, either."

Harvester's "deed" forgotten, Limos flounced away to the ice chest while Ares headed back to the grill. Than and Regan, grinning like the proud parents they were, held the baby out. "Reaver, this is Logan Thanatos."

Very gently, Reaver smoothed a finger over the baby's velvety cheek. "Nice to meet you, Logan."

"You can hold him," Than said, but Reaver stepped back. He'd held a lot of infants, had even delivered a few when he worked at Underworld General, but for some reason, the idea of taking this particular child in his arms sent anxiety tripping through him.

"I shouldn't—"

"Of course you should." Regan took the baby from Than and placed him carefully against Reaver's chest, leaving him no choice but to cradle Logan in his arms.

The moment the baby locked eyes with him, Reaver melted, and warmth danced in his heart. Abruptly, he knew where the reluctance to hold Logan had come from. The baby was a reminder that Reaver was missing a huge chunk of his life...a chunk that might contain children. Did he have any? Had their memories been wiped the way his had? He'd never been granted an audience with the Archangels to ask, but maybe it was about time that he stopped requesting and started demanding.

"I can sense the angel in him," he said softly. "It's powerful, almost as intense as if he was half angel instead of just a quarter."

"The Force is strong with this one," Thanatos said in a damned impressive Darth Vader voice, and Reaver had to catch himself before his jaw dropped. Thanatos had never been easygoing or playful, and this new side of him was good to see.

"Yes, it is." Logan's tiny fingers wrapped around Reaver's thumb. "He exhibited battle angel powers while he was still in the womb, which is rare for any infant who isn't fully angel, but now his powers feel even stronger." Reaver glanced down at the hellhound pup, who was drooling on his toes. "What's his name?"

"Cujo," Regan said.

Reaver arched an eyebrow. "You named your son's pet after a rabid monster dog?"

"No," Thanatos growled. "Wraith did. Bastard taught the pup to respond to Cujo, and we couldn't get him to respond to anything else after that."

Reaver laughed. Sounded exactly like something the Seminus demon would do.

Harvester eased closer, the merest hint of a smile curving her lips as she gazed at Logan. "Can I hold him?"

"Not a chance," Thanatos said.

"But Reaver, who didn't even want to take the baby, gets to hold him?" The devastation in Harvester's expression kicked Reaver right in the gut.

"Than," he said softly, "I don't think it would hurt to let her take him for just a minute."

Thanatos's pale yellow eyes glittered with anger. "She was playing for the team that wanted my son dead. I don't want her anywhere near him."

"I swear I didn't want Logan to die." Harvester's voice was as close to a plea as Reaver had ever heard from her. "Never. There were other ways for Pestilence to get what he wanted."

"I said no." Thanatos carefully took Logan from Reaver, as if he were worried that Harvester might snatch the child. "Reaver, I'm glad you're back. Stay as long as you want."

The Horseman shot Harvester a glance that said she wasn't welcome before he and Regan headed back to the group, Cujo on their heels until they walked past the grill. Then the mutt took a detour to grab a package of hot dogs off the cooler. Ares gave chase, but when Hal joined in, the hot dogs were lost between two snapping hellhound jaws.

Harvester turned away, her wings drooping. "Good thing I didn't want to stay anyway."

"Wait." Reaver snagged her by the wrist and turned her back to him. "I don't know why you lied for me, but thank you."

Harvester snorted. "I didn't do it for you. I did it because I have a reputation to uphold. And I certainly didn't want to hold the brat."

"Then why did you ask?"

She shrugged. "I wanted to see what Thanatos would say."

She was lying, but why? Her behavior lately had been

completely baffling. Even now, she was stealing glances at Logan, and with every covert look, her expression softened.

Definitely baffling.

"Are you . . . okay?"

Harvester's head snapped back so violently he might as well have punched her. "Of course I am, you haloed fool." She spread her wings, blotting out the sun and throwing a massive shadow. "Look at me. My blood runs with power. Do I seem weak or pathetic in any way?"

"Never mind," he muttered. Her defensiveness made it so difficult to deal with her sometimes. "I spoke with my supervisors about Gethel. None of them know where she is. Have you had a chance to talk with your colleagues?"

"Talk?" Her lip curled. "We don't talk. They dictate. I tell them to fuck off."

She. Was. Impossible. "Okay then. Did they dictate to you before you told them to screw themselves?"

"Yes. They said to leave it alone. I'm guessing they know more about Gethel than they're saying, but they won't tell me anything." She finally tucked her wings away. "Are you ready to tell me where Reseph is?"

"No."

"You sure? Maybe I could pleasure the information out of you."

"Yes," he gritted out from between clenched teeth, "I'm sure."

"Fine, fine. Don't get your pinfeathers all prickly." She slid a glance at where the Horsemen were gathered around a tub of iced drinks, their laughter carrying on the ocean breeze. "I got something for Logan. Do you think Thanatos and Regan will accept it?"

This just kept getting stranger and stranger. "Probably depends on what it is."

"It's not a poisonous viper or a razor-wire mobile," she snapped. "Go to hell, Reaver. Oh, wait, I just rescued you from there. Go *back* to hell."

She flashed off the beach, leaving Reaver staring at empty air and feeling like he'd been spun like a top. Harvester had always been volatile, but these mood swings were extreme even for her.

"Reavie-weavie!" Limos called out from next to the picnic table. "Food!"

Food. A cookout. A beach, kids, and pets. All so normal when just three months ago the world had been on the verge of apocalypse and this family had been embroiled in a hellish war that could have put the Horsemen on the wrong side of the battle.

Reaver was happy for them. Even Reseph seemed to be at peace. But Reaver couldn't shake the feeling that things were not as they seemed.

The danger to the world might have been averted, but the trouble had just begun.

Harvester materialized inside her residence and was instantly thankful that her werewolf slave, Whine, wasn't there to greet her. She didn't want anyone, even her slave, to see her like this.

Tears spilled from her eyes, burning, stinging. Which pissed her off, because she never cried. Ever. She'd long ago allowed evil to encase her heart in a diamond-hard shell—a necessity if one was to survive Sheoul.

But the Horsemen had always been her weakness, and

she'd never been able to completely detach herself from them emotionally. She'd tried, oh, how she'd tried. And now that the Apocalypse was over, she'd let her guard down even more, hoping that they had done the same.

Time was running out for her, and all she'd wanted was to hold Logan before the ticking clock in her head, the impending sense of doom, became a reality. And to maybe be invited to stay for the get-together. But she couldn't blame Thanatos for his attitude toward her, and that was the problem. Up until now, Harvester had owned her choices. Had owned her fall from Heaven.

But now she found herself wishing... what? That she could go back in time and not fall? No, that had to happen. What was done was done.

Cursing herself for weakness, she dashed away her tears with the back of her hand.

And realized something was terribly wrong.

The stench of blood tinged the air, and her skin prickled with a sudden sense of malevolence. She whirled around and snarled at the male standing in her living room doorway, his lips wet with blood.

"Lucifer," she hissed. "How dare you enter without permission."

Dead, ebony eyes gleamed, and his tongue made a slow, taunting sweep over his lower lip. "I did more than enter."

She now understood why Whine hadn't greeted her. Lucifer had done something to him, but now wasn't the time to show either concern or fear.

And yet both were making her quake on the inside.

"Get out." She flared her wings, and he returned the defiant gesture, his black, leathery wings scraping her ceiling. "Unless you're here to bestow some great honor on me, get the fuck out of my home."

"Great honor?" His laughter rattled the Bedim demon artwork gracing her walls. The sensual paintings depicting the romantic rituals of dozens of demon species always reminded Harvester that love was a weakness even for the lowliest of demons. "Because of you, we lost our bid for an Apocalypse."

Her gut twisted, and her lungs seized. How much blame were he and Satan going to lay at her feet? The clock in her head picked up its pace.

"What's the matter, Harvester?" His voice was low, smooth, and laden with poison. "You look a little frightened."

She scoffed, even though he'd struck the bull's-eye. "I have nothing to be afraid of. As Watcher, my job was not to help our team. It was to keep an eye on the Horsemen and dole out information as it was given to me."

"Oh," Lucifer said silkily, "I think you did far more than that."

"If this is about some broken Watcher rule, punish me already. Or leave me the hell alone."

Lucifer's toothy smile sent a chill slithering up her spine. "Broken Watcher rules are the least of your worries, *Fallen*."

"Come, Lucifer, games aren't your style." She hoped the underlying tremor in her voice was audible only to her. "Why don't you put that forked tongue to good use and tell me what you're dancing around?"

"Ask your werewolf." With that, Lucifer flashed out of there.

Shit. Harvester's shaky legs barely supported her

as she lurched toward her bedroom, where the smell of blood grew stronger. As soon as she entered, she saw why.

Poor Whine was curled up on his pallet on the floor, his body a mass of bruises and cuts and wrong angles. The moment he opened his one functional eye and saw her, he tried to get up.

"Whine, no." Harvester kneeled next to him and pushed him down. "Stay still."

The werewolf shuddered and closed his eye. "Sorry... mistress."

"Shh." Mentally cursing Lucifer, she stroked Whine's hair. She'd gained ownership of the warg thirty years ago after she'd killed his cruel owner, and since then, she'd sworn to protect him. Granted, she hadn't been particularly kind to him, but that had been to keep them both safe. Kindness in Sheoul got you killed.

"What did Lucifer want?" she asked, and Whine shuddered again.

"He demanded the... malador."

Harvester's breath shot out of her lungs. "Did you tell him where it is?" *Please say no.* The tiny item was her one ace, the only card she had to save herself.

Or to save someone else.

"No," Whine rasped. "Never. But—"

"But what?"

"He... he told me you were going to suffer a traitor's death."

Her hand froze mid-stroke. A traitor's death. The death part was misleading, because in Sheoul, traitors were kept alive, in agony, for eternity. Often, after centuries of torture, they were... peeled... and encased in wax to suffer endlessly on display like dead body art.

So what did Lucifer suspect her of? And where was he getting his information? Not that it mattered. She wasn't going to go meekly to anyone's torture chamber. She could run, and if worse came to worst, she'd find an angel to kill her—

"He also said..." Whine inhaled a ragged breath. "If you try to escape, he'll destroy everyone you care about."

Damn him. She'd been so careful to not show affection to anyone for this exact reason.

Closing her eyes, she sank down on the floor beside Whine. In her head the ticking clock sped up even more, the hands moving so fast that the individual ticking sounds were barely distinguishable. Very soon, the alarm was going to go off, and Harvester's time would be up.

Fourteen

It took Reseph a full forty-eight hours to get the hinky feeling out of his gut. Something had triggered his internal alarm when he'd seen the demon investigators, and he still didn't know why. Except he got the distinct impression that they were a danger to him. But why the hell would he be of any interest to them?

The sense of danger was growing, and some of it was coming from within himself. It was as if *he* was dangerous, a bomb fuse waiting for a spark, and he was terrified that Jillian would be the one to take shrapnel.

He and Jillian had spent two days bouncing between town, where they scoured the library and the Internet trying to figure out who he was, and her farm, where he did shit Jillian needed done. He'd repaired a hole in the siding of her barn, strung barbed wire along a section of droopy fence, cleaned stalls and the chicken coop, and he'd even folded laundry.

Folding laundry was the worst. Matching up socks was

like some sort of monotonous torture. Give him heavy lifting any day.

But Jillian made it all worthwhile with her cooking, her hot cocoa, and best of all, her stamina in the sack.

Smiling at the memory of what they'd done in the shower and then again in bed, he rolled over on the mattress and tucked her against him, her back to his chest. She snored delicately, and while the erection probing her backside made it tempting to wake her up, he let her sleep. She worked so hard during the day, and he kept her busy well into the night, so yeah, she needed the rest.

It was strange, though, how he really didn't need sleep. A couple of hours of shut-eye, and he was good to go. Sometimes he'd get up and prowl the property like some sort of animal surveying its territory, or he'd hit the computer to see if he could find out anything more about himself, but other times, like now, he'd lay in bed with Jillian, just to be with her.

He wondered if he had been so sappy before.

He'd even, during the nights when he'd hung outside in the crisp silence, fashioned her a gift. It wasn't much, and he wasn't even sure where he'd gotten the talent to take a knife to wood, but every discovery about himself was a clue.

And it was awesome when the discovery wasn't something horrible, like finding out he didn't know how to use a condom or could recognize human blood by its odor.

Closing his eyes, he buried his face in Jillian's hair, taking in the fresh scent of her fruity shampoo, which never seemed to wash away the underlying scent of crisp mountain air. She always smelled like the outdoors, like sparkling streams and green trees. He liked that so much better than the cloying perfume the women in the department store had worn. Besides, he somehow knew that perfume tasted bad on the skin. Jillian's skin tasted clean, with a tang of spice when she was aroused.

His cock jerked, appreciating the direction of his thoughts. Yup, he needed to get out of bed and get away from Jillian before he did what he swore not to do and woke her with his mouth between her legs.

Groaning silently, he rolled onto his back and started to swing his legs over the side of the mattress, but in a flash of motion, Jillian flipped over and took his shaft in her hand.

"Where do you think you're going?" Her voice was husky, drowsy, and so fucking sexy he damned near came in her palm right then and there.

He fell back into the pillow and hissed at the slow pump of her fist. "You're insatiable."

"You're the one with the hard-on."

He slid his hand between her thighs and spread her open. "You're the one who's wet." He eased his finger inside her, testing her readiness, because he was *so* ready to mount her. She was silky and hot, and yeah, she was ready.

Shifting to give him more access, she dropped her hand to cup his balls. Her fingers worked him aggressively, massaging, pinching. He loved how sometimes she was sensual and tender in bed, but at other times she liked it rough and raunchy.

Right now it was rough and raunchy, and he didn't hesitate to give her what she wanted.

He dipped another finger inside her and pumped them hard and fast. "What do you think? Another sixty-nine?" He brushed his thumb over her swollen clit, and she bucked. "Nah, we did that earlier. You on top, facing away from me? I loved that." He arched up and tongued her nipple, enjoying how it made her gasp. "No, I'm going to take you from behind this time. First, while you're on your hands and knees I'll lick you there, fill you with my tongue and fingers. Then I'm going to fuck you so hard you won't sit in a saddle for a week."

"Yes," she breathed, pushing against his hand.

"But I'm not going to come that way." Reaching up, he twined his fingers in her hair and brought her mouth to his, but he didn't kiss her. He teased with his tongue and teeth, nipping and licking. "I'm going to lay you on your belly and pin your legs tight together while I'm inside you. Ever done that? Makes my thrusts shallow, just teasing your entrance. Only the head of my cock will be fucking you, and you'll be begging for more, isn't that right?"

She was panting now, on the edge, and truth be told, so was he. The graphic, raw words meant to work her up had taken their toll on him, and he was close to spilling in her hand.

Time for action. Rolling, he grabbed her and flipped her onto her hands and knees. He used his own knee to nudge her legs roughly apart, opening her completely to him. She was glistening and swollen, and he was so diving into that. He didn't waste time with teasing or being subtle. He palmed her ass with both hands and used his thumbs to spread her wide. His mouth watered, and he was about to get down to it when something wrenched on his insides.

He jerked, his body having a hard time shifting from the all-encompassing lust to the focused, sharp prod of danger.

"Reseph?" Jillian's arousal-sodden voice buzzed in his ears alongside the sudden bleat of goats.

Then came the horse's screams and the pained squeal of the pigs. He flung himself off the bed and swept his jeans off the floor.

"Stay here!" He didn't wait for Jillian's response. He hastily threw on his jeans and tore out of the house. Icy air stung his face and the crusted snow cut into his feet as he ran toward the sounds of terrified animals.

A goat stumbled out of the open barn door, its fur matted with blood. Unable to stop, Reseph leaped over it and landed at the doorway threshold. Heart pounding, he flicked on the light.

And came face to face with a nightmare on legs.

The thing standing in front of him, its crimson eyes level with Reseph's as it stood on two thick, black-veined legs, let out a bear-like roar and dropped the body of the goat it had been shredding with its serrated claws.

For several tense heartbeats, the demon stared at Reseph, making no aggressive moves. It seemed almost as if it was expecting something from him. What, Reseph had no idea. A chat? Praise? A date?

What it was going to get was dead.

Master?

The word was a raspy whisper in Reseph's brain. A memory? Or was the thing speaking? *Master.*

What the fuck ...

Master. Master. Master! Gripping his head, Reseph stumbled backward, as if he could escape the voice in his skull.

"Do you know me?" he shouted. "Do you know me, you son of a bitch?"

Master.

Demons filled Reseph's vision, even behind closed eyelids. They surrounded Reseph, handing him offerings of body parts and wriggling, suffering creatures. Deep inside Reseph, there was a purr of pleasure, as if he'd been split in two and only part of him was horrified at the scene playing out in his head.

Frantic to stop whatever horrific memory seemed to be shaking itself loose, Reseph spun, grabbed the pitchfork from against the wall behind him, and buried it in the demon's skeletal chest before it even had a chance to flinch. The thing snarled as it stumbled backward, clutching at the handle. Reseph dropped and kicked a leg out, catching the demon behind its knee, sending it crashing to the ground.

Screeching, the demon ripped the pitchfork from its chest and hurled it aside, narrowly missing clocking Reseph's skull. It leaped to its feet and swung at him with those huge-ass claws. Reseph ducked and struck out, punching the thing in the snout. There was a satisfying crunch as its head snapped back and blood spurted from its mouth and nose.

The demon recovered quickly with a lightning-fast lunge. Reseph wheeled out of the way, snared the pitchfork, and forked the fucker again. The demon threw its body sideways, catching Reseph in the shoulder. Reseph slammed into one of the stalls, his spine taking the painful brunt of the impact. The horse went nuts, but Reseph couldn't afford to calm the animal. The demon came at Reseph, its jaws gaping and dripping saliva.

Just as it dove for his throat, a shot rang out. Blood and bone sprayed from a tear in its side. It screamed and changed course, hurtling toward Jillian, who stood in the doorway, pistol raised, a skinny tendril of smoke rising from the barrel.

Reseph tackled the creature, slamming it to the ground and driving the tines of the pitchfork deeper into its body. The wooden handle snapped, flipping into the air. Reseph caught it and in one smooth motion, drove it between the creature's eyes.

The thing grunted and seized, flopping like a dying fish as Reseph climbed off it, going for the machete hanging on the wall. When he turned back around, the thing appeared to have died, but he wasn't taking any chances.

Here's your master, you ugly piece of shit.

He brought the blade down on its neck, severing its head.

Damn, that felt good. It also felt familiar, like he'd done it before. A lot.

He looked over at Jillian, who was staring at the body. "That…" She swallowed. "That's the thing that attacked me. It looked just like that."

Reseph leveled a vicious kick at the corpse. "I should have made it suffer."

Her startled gaze lifted to his. For a moment, he thought she was going to chastise him, but after the initial surprise, she nodded.

"You should have." Carefully, she flipped the safety on the pistol and laid it on one of the barrels before squatting down next to a dead pig. "That monster." She moved to the goat that had been disemboweled. "Definitely should have made it suffer."

The image of himself surrounded by demons flashed through Reseph's head again, bringing with it a streak of pain at his temples. Ruthlessly, he shoved it away, hoping like hell it wasn't truly a memory. Maybe it was a remnant of a nightmare he'd had.

Keep telling yourself that, asshole.

Jillian was looking at him like she was trying to figure him out, probably because he was standing there like some delicate princess with the vapors. Fuck. He needed to get his head out of his ass.

"If you check the animals in here, I'll see if I can find

the goat that ran out." Reseph gripped the machete tight and headed outside. He'd check on the goat, but he was also going to patrol the area for more of the fuckers.

He found the goat a dozen yards away, trembling in the snow behind a tree. He performed a rapid exam, feeling for broken bones and bleeding, but all of the blood on the animal seemed to have come from its barnyard pals.

The goat didn't struggle as he hefted it into his arms and carried it back to the barn, where Jillian was doing her best to calm the surviving animals with treats and soothing caresses.

"This one seems fine." He settled the little doe in one of the empty stalls and stepped out in time to see the dead demon on the floor fold in on itself and disappear before his eyes. "The demon's gone."

Jillian popped her head up from inside Sam's stall. "Gone?"

"Disintegrated. Guess that explains why the general population didn't know demons existed until a year ago."

"No dead bodies to study." She slipped out of the horse's stall and joined Reseph, wrapping her arm around his waist. He absorbed her weight, drawing her against him. He'd hold her like this all night if she wanted him to. Hell, he'd do it anyway. The confrontation with the demon had rattled him to his bones. "I'm glad you were here, Reseph. I don't think I could have dealt with that... thing... on my own."

"Bullshit." He ran his palm up and down her arm, noting the slight quiver under her skin. "You were a badass with that gun. No hesitation."

"Because it was attacking you. If you hadn't been here—"

"Hey." He gripped her shoulders and turned her to

face him. "You were amazing and brave. If I weren't here you would have done what you had to do to protect your animals and yourself. One of those things might have attacked you, but it definitely didn't destroy you."

Her smile was shaky. "What doesn't kill you makes you stronger, right?"

"Right."

Except that was a lie, wasn't it? Too often, what didn't kill you came back to finish the job. He had no idea how he knew that, and honestly, he didn't want to know. All this time he'd been longing for his memories, scouring the Internet, searching his brain—hell, he'd called out to the empty air for help.

Now he was afraid he'd get exactly what he was looking for.

"You *bitch*." Reaver stared at Gethel from inside the *quantanum*, the plane of existence that was invisible to humans but allowed some beings, such as angels, to travel at accelerated speeds. He'd been hunting Gethel, tracking blips of her signature that he could sense when she channeled Heavenly power. Oh, she'd been smart about it, using it only in short bursts and weak doses, but Reaver had been patient, knowing she'd eventually use a little too much for a little too long.

Today, as she held court with two Soulshredders and a bald fallen angel near a hellgate deep inside the Nicaraguan Masaya volcano, she'd made the mistake Reaver had been waiting for.

She spun around, simultaneously hurling a massive ball of lightning. The crackling sphere filled the tunnel, giving Reaver no room to run. If he flashed out, he'd lose her.

He threw up an elemental shield, which borrowed properties from the area around it. The surrounding volcanic rock absorbed the lightning's impact, but the force knocked Reaver a dozen yards down the tunnel. He crashed into a stone pillar and crumpled to the ground.

Damn, that hurt.

Gethel's cackle echoed off the walls. "You can't hope to defeat me on your own, Reaver."

Reaver shoved to his feet. "I don't have to defeat you. Not yet. I just have to stop you from finding Reseph."

Her smile was cold. "Time's on my side. From what I hear, it'll take decades, probably centuries, for his mind to heal."

"If you've got all this time, why are you and Lucifer striking now?"

"Please," she said. "You're not that dense, are you?"

Apparently, he was.

"Humiliation." A miniature lightning ball popped out of her hand and bounced between her fingers. "Satan is extremely embarrassed by his defeat. He's ordered that everyone who played a role be either destroyed or get involved in restoring Pestilence and neutralizing the other Horsemen."

Too bad Gethel hadn't been lumped in the destroy category. Reaver strode toward her, keeping his power skating along the surface of his skin, ready to go in a split-second. "What happened to you, Gethel?"

"I told you. The Horsemen—"

"Yeah, yeah, they couldn't find it in their hearts to say good-bye when your Watcher duty was taken away. Big deal. You're either a big whiny baby, or there's more to the story." He was pretty sure there was some mental instability written between the lines of that story as well.

Behind her, the Soulshredders hissed and snarled with every step Reaver took. The fallen angel just watched, his dead shark eyes glued to Reaver.

"Who are you?" Reaver called out to the fallen angel, who seemed to be a big fan of black leather.

The male bared his teeth. "You'll find out soon enough."

"Ah, cryptic. That's so original." Reaver rounded on Gethel. "So, which is it? Big whiny baby or more to the story?"

"Fuck you, Reaver," she spat. "You know nothing. I loved them."

"I know, but...oh, wait." Reaver was nearly blinded by the lightbulb that went off in his brain. "You didn't just love them. You *loved* them." He smirked. "Which one, Gethel? Ares? Thanatos?" He cocked an eyebrow. "Limos?"

She threw the lightning ball, and he easily swatted it away. "Did I touch a nerve?" With a snap of his fingers, he sent a boomerang of angelfire at her, aiming for her head, but when she dove aside and it merely scraped her shoulder, he wasn't surprised. She wasn't going to just roll over and die, after all. "Let's see if I can figure this out," he mused, as she doused flames in her clothing. "You didn't seem to be causing much trouble for Ares. At least, not that I know of. But Limos, you did send *khnives* after her husband."

Cursing, she launched herself at him. He met her midair in the tunnel, and the collision rumbled the very mountain.

"You think you know everything, don't you?" she screeched as she slammed her fist into his jaw. It was like being hit with a sledgehammer, and Reaver grunted, blinking to the tune of cartoon birds circling around his head. "You think you're so superior."

He pounded his fist into her chest, a quick double-tap before backhanding her in the face so hard she fell out of the air and landed awkwardly on her neck and shoulder.

"I *am* superior," he growled.

She rolled to her feet and blasted him with her favorite weapon, a storm of sparks that burrowed through living flesh. He leaped to the ceiling of the cave, avoiding most of them, but a handful cut into his leg, and agony drilled into him in the form of fine-bore holes.

"You know nothing! I have secrets you can't even begin to touch, you worm."

"So bitter," he ground out. "Just when did that happen?"

"When?" She beckoned the Soulshredders, and they lumbered to her. "When the Aegi whore took Thanatos's virginity." Red-hot hatred spewed from every one of Gethel's pores. "I was supposed to be the one to break his Seal."

What a bitch. "It must have killed you when his Seal didn't break and Regan got pregnant." He inhaled sharply. Of course. That was why Gethel had been so eager to see Logan dead. It wasn't as much to start the Apocalypse as it was to destroy the physical proof that Regan had taken what Gethel wanted.

Hell hath no fury like a jealous angel with emotional instability and a mental defect.

"Get him," Gethel snarled.

The Soulshredders leaped at him at the same time that she peppered him with spears of lava. Fire scorched his skin and Soulshredder claws tore at his muscles. He could win this battle with the demons, but even as he summoned a shear-whip, Gethel and the fallen angel vanished.

Damn.

He cut the demons down, slicing one horizontally in half,

and then he flashed out of there himself. Despite his burns and various injuries, and the fact that he hadn't caught or killed Gethel, he was pretty satisfied with the encounter.

As he materialized inside his Heavenly residence, his fingers found the little treasure in his pocket that he'd lifted off Gethel. He opened his palm, amazed that the tiny crimson stone could channel so much power within the depths of hell.

He closed his fist around the *sheoulghul* and smiled. He didn't have use for it yet, but he had no doubt that someday, it would come in very, very handy.

Jillian and Reseph had spent the next two hours in the barn, cleaning up the mess. She'd watched in awe as Reseph dug in to help, working tirelessly even when she started to flag. He was amazing, making everything he did seem so effort-less. Even the way he'd killed that demon, so efficiently, as if he knew exactly what he was doing, had been incredible. There'd been no fear, no panic. He'd moved like a phantom, so fast she'd been sure she was seeing things at times.

One thing was certain; he knew how to fight and how to kill. Maybe, given how comfortable he'd been fighting the demon, he belonged with the people who had recently come to light as ancient demon-slaying warriors. The Aegis, she thought it was called.

Whatever training had given him the skills to take down a demon so easily, she was grateful for it. She'd been very honest when she'd said she didn't think she could have dealt with it on her own. Seeing the thing, identi-cal to the demons that had attacked her, had frozen her solidly in place. Reseph must not know that she'd stood in the doorway, paralyzed with fear, for what seemed like hours before she'd finally fired the pistol.

No, she wasn't a badass or brave. She'd moved here from Florida thinking that her decision to live in the middle of nowhere by herself had been a fearless, bold move, but what if it was the opposite? What if she'd been trying to escape her fears?

Epic fail. She'd run right into them. And seized like an overheated engine.

Shame had fueled her as she'd hauled blood-soiled straw out of the barn while Reseph repaired the door, and then they'd showered—together, but neither one of them had been in a sexual frame of mind. He'd washed her with the greatest of care, taking his time to massage the tension out of her shoulders and back. As the morning sun came up, he'd tucked her into bed and lain with her until she fell into an uneasy sleep.

Nightmares had plagued her. Nightmares of demons and dying animals, of the attack in the parking lot, and worse, of Reseph leaving her.

Any day now, he was going to find out who he was and leave.

Irritated by her obsession with Reseph's probable departure, Jillian slammed the lid on the grain barrel as the barn door opened and he entered wearing jeans and the blue Henley that matched his eyes. In his hand was a steaming mug.

"Brought you something to warm you up." He gave her a lopsided smile. "I can't cook, but I can make a mean cup of hot cocoa."

"Doesn't take much to boil water and open a packet." Even as the words fell from her lips she regretted them, and God, she kicked herself hard at the flicker of hurt in his eyes. "I'm sorry, Reseph. I didn't mean that." No, what she'd meant was, "Stop being so wonderful, because I'm falling for you, and I'll be devastated when your memory comes back and you take off."

He shrugged and handed her the cup, which made her feel even smaller. "It's true."

The rich chocolate aroma filled her lungs and soothed her mood. "You were being nice, and I was an ungrateful bitch."

"Will this help?" He dug into his pocket. "I made this for you." Very gently, he took her hand and placed a wooden carving in her palm.

Jillian stared at the tiny bird, its fine features perfectly etched across its graceful lines and curves. The wings, outspread in flight, were so thin and delicate that she was afraid to close her hand.

"Reseph, this is amazing. How long did this take you?"

One big shoulder rolled in a casual shrug. "Few days. Ah . . . you might want to sharpen your nice paring knife."

"I think I can manage that." She stroked her finger over the smooth beak. "Why a bird?"

Another shrug. "They're free, you know? They can go anywhere they want, whenever they want. They can just spread their wings and go."

Naturally, Reseph would gravitate toward an animal that wasn't tied down. She wondered if he felt at all caged in here. No, she didn't have to wonder. She knew. He was like a panther in a zoo, always pacing the fence line.

He plopped down on the barrel and stretched his long legs out in front of him, crossing his booted feet at the ankles. "What's wrong?"

She hesitated, carefully balancing the little bird on a railing and taking a sip of the cocoa to buy some time. She didn't know how to explain, partly because she didn't even know why she felt the way she did.

"Cocoa is good," she murmured. "Thank you."

"You're welcome. And you're stalling."

Leave it to him to call her out. Still, she sipped again, maybe a little defiantly. Guess she was still feeling bitchy.

Finally, she cupped the mug in her cold hands and looked down at the swirling froth. "I'm afraid, Reseph." There. She'd said it. "I hate being afraid. It goes against everything I've ever lived for. My parents taught me to be strong, and growing up, I was tough. I played sports and got jobs on farms instead of working at fast-food joints like my friends. When I went away to college, I made sure I was the best in all my classes. I never let fear get in the way." She swallowed. "But now I'm afraid and I don't know how to handle it."

"You don't have to," he said softly. "I'm here. I won't let another demon near you. I've been researching ways to construct a demon-proof perimeter, and I swear, you'll be safe."

Sweet Jesus, he was too good to be true. "It's not that. It's not the demons. I mean, they're scary, but…" She trailed off, the hot cocoa curdling in her belly.

"But what?"

"It's you," she whispered. "I know you need to find out who you are, but some small part of me is afraid you will. I know it's selfish of me, but I like who you are now."

"I'll still be the same man, Jillian. I'll still be me." He rose and started prowling around the barn, and she got the feeling he was working off frustrated energy. "And you never know…I may never remember my past."

She watched him straighten the bridles and harnesses hanging on the walls, as if he needed something to do. "You might not get your memory back, but even if we only find out who you are, it could change things. What if you're something we didn't expect?"

He swung around to face her. "You said you didn't believe I was a serial killer or something."

"I still don't believe that. But what if you've got a family? You said you're sure you don't have a wife, but what if you're wrong? Or what if you're a politician or big media mogul? Or maybe you're the king of Oompa-Loompa Land. Just knowing where you belong will change things. And you'll have to go."

"Oompa-Loompa Land?" He shook his head. "No way. Orange people give me the creeps. I don't even like fake tans. I'd never be their king."

She laughed, but sobered quickly. His humor was one of the things she'd miss after he found out who he was and left her. God, her chest hurt already.

The stray wisps of straw on the concrete floor crunched under his boots as he walked toward her. He took the mug out of her hand and set it on a shelf, and when he swung back around to her, he took her hands. She couldn't help but notice how small her hands looked in his.

"I can't promise that you'll like who I was before you found me. But I can promise that my feelings for you won't change." He palmed her cheek, his touch tender, and in that moment, he might as well have reached inside her and stroked her heart instead of her skin. "I know we agreed on no emotional attachments, but I can't help it; I'm falling for you, Jillian. It's scaring the shit out of me, because it feels so damned new." While she stared in stunned silence, he glanced up at the rafters. "It's strange, because some things feel familiar, like sex and using a computer. And killing that demon. It's like when you watch a movie and there's an actor you recognize but can't place. You know you've seen him before, but you can't remember where." He returned his gaze to her, his eyes glittering with intensity. "But what I feel for you is so different. It's like I've never seen the actor before. Hell, I haven't even heard of the damned movie."

Every word was a prick to the heart. He was falling for her? She should be happy, because like it or not, she was falling for him, too. But this was going to end badly. She'd never been a pessimist, but she'd danced this dance before. Not with an amnesia guy, but with every other guy she'd dated.

"You can't promise your feelings won't change," she rasped. "You could love someone else."

"That's what I'm trying to tell you. I don't. I know I don't. What I feel for you is too foreign. I'd know if I'd felt it before."

She wanted to believe him, but there just wasn't enough for her to go on. He didn't remember his past, so maybe he didn't remember emotions, either.

"Jillian, if I could guarantee that my feelings wouldn't change and that I'd stay here no matter what, would that be a good thing?"

"You can't—" His finger came down on her mouth, shutting her up.

"Hypothetically."

Reaching up, she wrapped her hand around his and pulled it away. "Hypothetically, yes. It would be a good thing. I'm falling for you, too."

In a smooth surge, he backed her against a stall and kissed her. Kissed her hard. "Jillian," he murmured against her mouth. His voice was pained, urgent, and she knew exactly how he felt.

"Shh. I don't want to hear promises you can't keep or hollow assurances that everything will be okay. Let's just make the best of the time we have." She needed a distraction. A rough, fun escape. And Reseph could give her that. "Remember what you said a few days ago, the first time we had sex? That there would be time for fucking on the hood of my truck or...other things?"

"Oh, yeah. I remember."

"Good." She dragged her hand down his chest to his fly, behind which a pronounced bulge already indicated that he was game. "I think it's time."

"Yeah?" A wicked smile ruffled his mouth as he leaned into her and put his lips to her ear. "How long has it been since you came so hot, so furious, so *fucking intense*, that you forgot your own name?"

Oh, God. She'd just forgotten it. "Never," she whispered. "You?"

"I can't remember," he murmured huskily, "but ask me in a few minutes and I'll have an answer." He tugged her against him and kissed her. His lips were firm but soft as they melded with hers. She opened to him immediately, but he teased her, taking her bottom lip in his teeth in a gentle show of dominance. A shiver of pleasure skated over her skin. He was an explosive combination of playful but aggressive, tender but strong, commanding but caring...and so very, very male.

Reaching up, she cupped his jaw, savoring the feel of his warm skin under her palm as he kissed his way down her neck. He nuzzled her throat, and with a moan, she rocked her head to the side, granting him more access for that talented mouth. One of his hands remained tamely around her waist, holding her against him, but the other slid beneath her shirt. When his fingers came into contact with her bare belly, she hissed in pleasure.

"I love the sounds you make." His voice was a smoky drawl. "I'm going to wring them from you until you're out of breath."

Her heart pounded so hard it hurt, as if it were trying to get to his hand, which was sliding torturously slowly up her rib cage. He nipped her shoulder blade as his fingertips brushed the underside of her breast, creating an electric sizzle that shot from his mouth to his hand. Sensation rippled through her, stealing her thoughts, her breath, the moisture in her mouth.

With another moan, she palmed his thigh, digging her fingers into his hard muscles to steady herself. There was the slightest hitch in his breath at the contact. He eased his hand up to cup her breast, and they both groaned.

"You're so beautiful." His voice was muffled against her shoulder. "I want to feel more of you."

Oh, yes. If he wanted more, he could have it.

Fifteen

Jillian was a dream come true. Cliché, maybe, but clichés existed for a reason, and Jillian was a prime example. She massaged him through his pants, and he was ready for her in about two seconds flat. Hell, he was always ready for her.

Her fingers teased, and with a nimble flick of her wrist, his fly popped open and his cock was in her hand. He hissed in pleasure and then hissed in surprise when she dropped to her knees and jerked his pants down to mid-thigh. Her hands gripped his legs, which twitched under her warm palms as she massaged her way up.

"You have the most incredible birthmark here." She pressed her lips to his inner thigh, and he sucked air through clenched teeth. "It looks just like an angel's wing." Her tongue smoothed over the surface of the mark, and holy hell, erotic fire shot from her mouth to his cock. Major erogenous zone.

"Can we not talk about angels while we're—" He broke off with a strangled cry as she took him in her mouth. She stroked him with one hand and gripped his hip with the other, her nails digging into his skin.

"Damn," he said hoarsely. "You're serious."

"Mmm-hmm." The humming vibration around his shaft nearly had him coming right then and there.

He knew what she was doing, using sex to purge emotions and erase reality for a little while. That was fine with him, especially when her tongue flicked over the sensitive head as she moved her lips up and down, swallowing when he was deep.

Pleasure was a hot wave that crashed over him with every nibble, suck, and swipe of Jillian's tongue on his cock. Needing to touch her, he drove his hands into her lush hair and watched as his shaft disappeared into her eager mouth.

"Ah…damn," he whispered. "Holy…*yeah*." He groaned, bucked when she dropped one hand to cup his balls.

Man, she was good at this. Too good, and he wasn't going to last another ten seconds.

Harnessing his libido—barely—he hauled Jillian to her feet, ripped open her jeans, and jerked them down to where they tangled around her boots. He didn't need her completely free to move around. Sometimes, a little bondage was a good thing.

He straightened, let out a low growl when he reached the apex of her thighs, and gave her a deep, slow lick on the way up. Her eyes darkened, her pupils swallowing the smoldering green of her irises, and her lip twitched in a naughty smile.

He spun her, catching her around the waist so his shaft

was cradled by the soft seam of her ass, and held her that way as he kissed and nipped her ear and neck. She pushed back against him, but no, this was his show. She'd started it, but he'd finish it.

"Not giving you what you want yet, my girl," he said roughly, and then he pushed her forward and bent her over the saddle draped on a nearby sawhorse.

He went down on his heels behind her and used his thumbs to spread her succulent flesh. The tangle of her jeans around her ankles kept access to a minimum, but that was ideal for teasing.

And Reseph *loved* to tease.

Her breathing became ragged when he flicked his tongue around the rim of her opening. She tasted like a sparkling mineral spring and her own rich essence, and he was definitely going to drink his fill later.

She wiggled her ass, her impatience becoming clear, the greedy minx. He appreciated how demanding she was, how absolutely uninhibited. He gave her what she wanted, pushing inside her and thrusting, fucking her core with his tongue.

"Yes," she breathed. "Oh . . . yes."

Her climax was coming, but he denied her, instead slowing things down, giving her several slow, shallow licks before diving deep again, licking and sucking and pumping until she cried out in release. He didn't bring her down slowly the way he usually did. Instead, he surged to his feet, dug into his pocket for a condom, and sheathed himself.

"Aren't you the Boy Scout," she rasped.

"I want to be ready to take you anytime, anywhere," he said on a shallow breath, and entered her in one smooth thrust.

The jeans around her ankles didn't allow for deep penetration, but this position delivered different sensations, more skin on skin and a tighter fit. He pounded into her, his hips pistoning back and forth in an unrelenting rhythm.

"Is this what you wanted?"

"Yes." She moaned, pushing back against him, meeting every thrust. She was still trying to take control. Not happening.

He pulled out, and she whined in disappointment. Dropping to his heels again, he ripped off one of her boots and jerked her foot out of the jeans. He gave her another lick between the legs on the way back up, and then he lifted her onto the saddle draped over the sawhorse, forcing her to straddle it backward. The saddle, which she'd had specially made to allow for easy mounting and dismounting while Sam was hauling farm supplies, featured an almost nonexistent cantle and pommel, which would prove handy for what Reseph had planned.

"What are you doing?" She watched him with curiosity, her gaze heavy-lidded and smoky.

He didn't respond. Roughly, he straddled the sawhorse, keeping his feet planted firmly on the floor as he gripped Jillian's knees and forced them up so she had no leverage and was leaning back against the saddle's shallow pommel. Moving forward, he entered her again. She gripped his shoulders and squeezed his waist between her knees as he drove into her. The position was awkward and unsteady, forcing him to lean forward and take shallow thrusts, but he relished the unique sensation, and if her soft cries were any indication, she was loving it, too.

Pleasure washed over him, euphoria that inflamed his

entire body. He didn't last, and the moment she cried out at her peak, he went with her, agonizing ecstasy shooting through his balls and shaft, going on and on, and as the first orgasm waned, another started up. Jillian came with him again on his third, his name breaking from her lips.

Gradually, the sexual storm passed, and he fell forward, arms and legs trembling, to catch himself on the sawhorse. Jillian's mouth found his, and her slow, tender kiss made him tremble for a different reason.

He hadn't been lying when he'd said he was falling for her. With every passing day, she became more and more the air he breathed. When she wasn't around, he felt empty, restless. When she was there, he calmed and found a sense of peace that was just...right. And now that the demon was dead, he could tell himself that the vision and whispered voice in his head was imagined.

"Thank you," she said against his lips.

He pulled back a little. "Are you crazy? I should be thanking *you*."

"You know how you can thank me?"

"How?" Lick her until she screamed? Caress every inch of her body until she begged him to stop?

"You can dig the second snowmobile out of the garage and gas it up."

He blinked. He could lick her on a snowmobile, he supposed. "You have plans?"

"We're going to go have fun. Snowmobiling and snowmobile-cooking." He must have looked confused as hell, because she laughed and said, "You put meat and veggies in a foil wrapper and pop it under the sled's hood next to the exhaust pipe. When you get tired of riding, you stop and your food is cooked."

"Babe, you keep surprising me." He eyed her with a whole new appreciation for her sense of adventure. "Let's go."

Lance McKinney sat with two fellow Elders at his desk at Aegis headquarters in Scotland. Juan and Delia were both nursing cold cups of coffee, which had more to do with the fact that the castle was always freezing than anything else.

"Have the outposts in Australia and Japan been reestablished?" He glanced at Delia, their newest Elder. The stout, dark-haired woman had been with The Aegis for twenty years and had been Regent at one of the Barcelona cells before almost everyone who worked under her was killed by Pestilence's minions.

She nodded. "We've only got enough Guardians for one cell in Japan." She handed him a report from the Tokyo Regent. "We're barely at half-staff in the Sydney cell, but that'll change as more evacuees make their way back."

Fuck, there was a lot of rebuilding to be done. The near-Apocalypse had just about destroyed several countries and had killed millions of people. Now, three months later, disease and starvation were wracking some of the worst-hit areas. The fools at DART insisted that the infections and starvation were a natural result of disaster, but The Aegis wasn't convinced. Pestilence was rumored to be dead, but what if he was still killing people through his diseases? And then there was Famine, or *Limos*, as her sympathizers called her. She could be causing the mass starvation.

Man, Lance fucking hated Horsemen. He hated even more that humans needed them. The evil Apocalypse, which would have put the Horsemen on the demons' side of the fight, had been averted, but there was still a Biblical Apocalypse in mankind's future. This time, when their Seals broke, the Horsemen were supposed to ally themselves with humans and battle demons right alongside The Aegis.

Except that the Horsemen hated The Aegis, and Lance had no doubt that if those bastards ever learned the location of Aegis headquarters, Aegi would become an extinct species.

There was a tap at the door, and Omar, one of the original twelve Elders, strode in, his expression grim. "You aren't going to like this." He flexed his hands at his sides. "Aaron has been monitoring reports of possible demon activity in the American Rocky Mountains. Nothing overly unusual, but DART has reported to investigate."

Lance yawned. "And? Those pussies will probably capture the demon and try to rehabilitate it or some shit. Why do we care?"

"That's what I thought at first. Then yesterday Aaron noticed an usual surge in Internet searches related to demons coming from a town called Bardsley. The interesting thing is that a lot of the searches have to do with the name Reseph."

Lance sat up a little straighter. "Reseph is Pestilence's human name."

"Yes, but the name is also linked to historical places and gods, so Aaron yellow-flagged it to keep an eye out, but the name didn't go red flag." Omar's lips thinned into a slash of disapproval. "Until today."

Juan swung around in his chair. "What happened?"

"Aaron got hold of a police report. At around the same time the demon attacks started in Bardsley, a stranger showed up in town. He claims to have no memory except of his name. Says it's Reseph."

Lance's stomach turned over, spilling acid into his bloodstream. "Description?"

"Six-nine. Platinum blond hair. Horse tattoo on his right forearm."

"Jesus Christ," Lance breathed. Juan and Delia had gone ashen. "It's him, isn't it?"

"That would be my guess." Omar scrubbed his palm over his face. "It could also be why DART is there."

Delia frowned. "Wait...Pestilence was destroyed. So how could this be him?"

"Think about it," Lance said. "We didn't *see* anyone destroy him. We got a fucking phone call from Kynan." A rude-ass phone call full of threats and lies. Kynan had tried to convince Lance that the angel who had been helping them, Gethel, had gone bad. If that were true, she wouldn't have spent the last month helping The Aegis develop a potential containment weapon against the Horsemen. "What if he was wrong, or what if this is some kind of Horseman deception?"

The mug in Delia's hands shook, sloshing coffee over the rim. "So do you think DART is in Bardsley to neutralize Reseph? Or Pestilence? Oh my God, what if the Horseman is still evil?"

"There's no *still* about it," Lance said. "The Horsemen are half demon, and anything demon is always evil." When Pestilence's Seal broke, he'd simply gone *more* evil. "We need to get to Bardsley. No way are we letting those asshole upstarts take control of this situation."

"So we'll be testing out our new weapon?"

"Yes," Lance said slowly. "We will. And if all goes

right, we'll finally have a way to lock up the Horsemen and hold them until the Biblical prophecy requires their presence."

"What about their families?"

"We imprison the ones who can't be harmed and kill the rest."

"And Thanatos's kid?" Delia asked. "Won't killing him break the Horseman's Seal?"

Yeah, that was a nasty bit of business. The Aegis had been led to believe that killing the child would save the world, but in truth, it had been the opposite. Because of that clusterfuck, The Aegis had made enemies out of the Horsemen, which was why it was so important to neutralize them. According to Gethel, the Horsemen were planning to murder every Guardian on the planet.

"Kynan said nothing we can do will break their Seals now. Gethel hasn't confirmed or denied, and we haven't seen her in a month. So we take the kid. Raise it. Make it loyal to us. He could be our greatest weapon in the fight against demons, and our best protector against the Horsemen if they manage to escape our captivity."

"So we're doing this?"

Lance grinned. "Pack for winter. We're going to catch us a Horseman."

Sixteen

Kynan and Arik hadn't found a damned thing. They'd studied the area, questioned whoever would talk to them, and chased down leads. And still ended up with nothing.

It was time to bring in the local cops, because something niggled at Kynan, something about Ms. Cardiff. She knew more than she was saying, and if it took getting an officer to the house to get her to talk, that's what he'd do.

At least, that's what he'd do as a first step. He'd play nice... for now.

Ky glanced over at Arik as they climbed out of their SUV and started across the parking lot to the sheriff station's entrance. "How did Reaver seem to you when you saw him?"

An arctic blast kicked up snow all around them, and Arik had to speak through chattering teeth. "I only saw him for a second. I was getting to the beach party as he was leaving. Seemed fine, though, for a guy who spent three months in hell." Arik's own stint in Sheoul had given him a unique perspective on the horrors to be found in the demon realm. "Limos said Harvester admitted to trapping Reaver there, but then Reaver defended Harvester to Thanatos and Regan."

Halting at the station door, Kynan stared at his friend. "You're kidding, right? Was your wife drunk?"

"Nope. Limos laid off the alcohol. She wants to be all healthy while we're trying for a baby." Arik stomped his boots on the welcome mat. "I'll never understand angels."

Neither would Kynan, and he even had an angel in his family tree.

Warm air welcomed them as they walked into the station and were greeted by a deputy who introduced himself as Dennis Waltham.

"I'll be right with you folks," Waltham said. He grabbed some paperwork and disappeared into a room down the hall.

Ky stared after him. "Gotta love small towns."

"Ky?" Arik's voice was strangled. "Oh, holy fuck. Holy *fuck*."

Kynan wheeled around to Arik, who was staring at the bulletin board. "What?" Arik just stood there, his face the color of chalk. "Jesus, you're scaring the shit out of me." He strode over to his partner. "What are you—" He broke off, his throat closing like his neck had been caught in a wire noose.

It couldn't be. The picture on the wall could *not* be Pestilence. Even as Ky's brain scrambled for an explanation, his eyes locked on the information scrawled below the photograph.

First name: Reseph. Last name: Unknown. He'd been

brought in by Jillian Cardiff one week ago. He was suffering from apparent total amnesia.

Jesus.

Waltham came back, and Kynan and Arik both rushed over to him so fast they nearly tripped over each other.

"That man on the wall," Arik blurted. "Where is he?"

"Why?" The deputy looked at Arik and Ky like they'd lost their minds. "What's this about?"

Arik slammed his fist on the counter. "Tell me, dammit!"

Waltham glared. "You might be some kind of demon experts, but I don't answer to you, so why don't you try being a little nicer?"

"Excuse us, deputy." Kynan moderated his voice to counter Arik's freak-out, but inside, he was screaming. Outside, he was sweating ice cubes. "But this is important. Do you have a file on this guy?"

"We don't have a lot." Waltham took his sweet time digging a file out of a drawer and tossed it to Kynan. "We haven't been able to find out anything about him. What's in that file is all we have. Is Jillian in trouble? Do I need to get out there?"

So this guy was staying with Ms. Cardiff. Wow, so not a shock. "No," Ky said calmly. "I overreacted. It's not the guy we're looking for. Thanks anyway."

The deputy shot them a dubious glance, but Kynan didn't give him the opportunity to get nosy. Ky dragged Arik out of there at breakneck speed. At the SUV, Arik stopped, his entire body a churning cauldron of hate. Kynan had never seen Arik like this before. He was usually level. Very little could rattle him.

Right now, Arik was rattling like a baby's toy.

"That was fucking Pestilence. How the fuck is he here? He's supposed to be dead, Ky. I was there. I saw it happen. What if he's still evil? He can't start an apocalypse, but he'd still be like a lion in a sheep pen. He could kill millions with plagues alone...holy shit...how the fuck are we going to take him down?" Arik paused in his tirade to take a breath and slammed his fist into the vehicle's hood, denting the cold metal. "We'll break into Aegis HQ and grab some *qeres*—"

"Arik—"

"I'm not letting that fucker near Limos—"

"Arik." Kynan grabbed the other man by the shoulders and shook him hard. "Listen to me. If it's really Reseph, we have to be smart about this."

"*If*? I'd know that son of a bitch if he was wearing a spacesuit and covered by a motherfucking burka. He blackmailed my wife, nearly broke me in half, and forced me to drink his blood. He owns my soul, Ky. He *owns my goddamned soul.*"

Yeah, Kynan wouldn't be overly calm right now if he were Arik, either. Releasing his friend, Kynan dug his cell phone out of his pocket and speed-dialed Ares.

"What's up, human?" Ares said.

Kynan kept a watchful eye on Arik, because the dude looked ready to launch into orbit. "I need you to get everyone to your place. Arik and I'll be there in half an hour." He disconnected before the Horseman could ask questions. This place was too public, and Arik was too...well, fucked up.

"C'mon, buddy," Kynan said. "Let's hit the Harrowgate. Your in-laws will know what to do."

"What if they don't? That fucker can't be allowed to

roam the earth, Ky. We thought he was gone. We were moving on with our lives. What now?"

Kynan wished like hell he could answer that.

Reaver strode into Ares's Greek manor and wasn't even a little surprised to find Limos mixing margaritas behind the bar. Now that the Apocalypse had been averted, every day was a party for her. What he was surprised about was that she handed out the drinks to everyone, including Reaver, but didn't take one for herself.

Then again, she'd been busy lately, drawn to the starvation epidemics around the world. She'd always said that when others were going hungry, she couldn't keep food down.

"Hey, Reaver." Ares, who was pinned to the couch by a young hellhound lying on his lap, downed his drink and wiped his mouth with the back of his hand. "Don't suppose you know what this is about."

"What... what's about?"

Thanatos, sitting on the arm of the chair Regan was perched in, looked up from the cradle he was rocking with one foot. "Kynan called. Said to gather everyone here."

"Looks like I have good timing." Reaver moved over to the cradle, where Logan was sound asleep and Cujo was sitting, one shoulder propped against the frame. "I hope The Aegis isn't causing trouble. What have he and Arik been working on?"

"Some rogue demon tearing up a town somewhere," Limos said in a bored tone. No, a single demon wouldn't even make the Horsemen blink. At five thousand years old, they'd learned to separate the big problems from the small ones, and it took a lot for them to consider anything a big problem.

"How's everything else?"

Ares scratched the inky black lap hound behind the ear, and the thing made a guttural sound Reaver could only hope was a happy noise. "I'm not sure. There have been some odd rumors floating around Sheoul, rumblings about Pestilence's old buddies trying to regroup. And Cara is worried about the hellhounds. A bunch have gone missing, and more disappear every day. She won't let Hal out of her sight."

Odd. Only someone very powerful would mess with hellhounds. Reaver made a mental note to check with Eidolon, head of Underworld General Hospital, to see if he was aware of a fatal hellhound virus running amok.

Kynan and Arik burst through the front door. Arik went immediately, wordlessly, to Limos and folded her against him.

"Arik." Her voice was muffled against his chest. "What is wrong with you?"

"Let me cut to the chase." Kynan peeled off his leather jacket and tossed it over the back of one of the chairs. "Your brother is back."

Reaver's lungs seized, and oh-shit adrenaline flashed like fire through his veins. His secret was about to become not-so-secret, and not in the way he'd wanted.

Ares came to his feet, dumping the hellhound on the ground. "That can't be. He was destroyed. We saw it."

"How can you be sure?" Than asked Kynan, and Reaver didn't miss how he'd angled himself closer to the cradle, as if expecting Pestilence to pop out of thin air and grab his son.

Arik kept his arm around Limos. "We were hunting a Soulshredder in Colorado. We found what we believed to be the epicenter of the attacks, a woman living in a cabin in the middle of nowhere. Then we discovered that a stranger appeared around the time the attacks started, a male named Reseph. We saw his picture. It's him."

Kynan nodded. "We believe he's staying with the woman."

Limos swallowed sickly. "Staying, or holding her hostage? Is he Pestilence, or is he Reseph?"

"We don't know," Arik said, "but the fact that there's a Soulshredder killing people around him doesn't look good for him being Reseph."

"Soulshredders were Pestilence's favorite demon to use to terrorize humans," Limos breathed. "Oh, God. If he's Pestilence—"

"He's Reseph," Reaver muttered, and all eyes turned on him.

"You knew about this?" Ares asked, his voice going low. "You knew he was alive and walking around with humans and you didn't tell us? How long have you known?"

Reaver hated that Reseph's existence had been revealed this way, but he had no one to blame but himself. "I've known since the day Thanatos stabbed him in the heart with Deliverance. I'm the one who got him out of Sheoul-gra."

Stunned faces stared back at him. Finally, Arik broke the silence. "I hope to fuck you have a good explanation for this, because angel or not, I want to kick your ass right now."

"You're out of line, human," Reaver said, maybe a little too defensively. "I don't do anything without a good reason." He just hoped his reason was good enough. "I went to Sheoul-gra to make sure Reseph's soul was secure. He still has a part to play when the Final Days come. The *Daemonica*'s prophecy may have failed, but there's still one more to play out."

"We know that," Thanatos ground out. "Get to the part where you turned him loose."

"Patience," Reaver snapped. "I'm not one of your servants." He calmly rolled up his sleeves, giving himself a chance to find the right words. "I went to Sheoul-gra. But I didn't expect to find Reseph the way he was. He wasn't... a soul. He was himself."

"Himself?" Ares asked. "As who? Pestilence or Reseph?"

"Reseph. But he was broken."

Limos pulled away from Arik. "What do you mean, broken?"

"He was Reseph. But he remembered everything he did as Pestilence."

"Oh, God," Limos whispered. "How awful."

Kynan cursed. "I don't understand what the deal is. So he has to take responsibility for murdering millions of people. Why is this a problem?"

"I'm wondering the same thing, myself," Arik said. "So what if he remembers what he did?"

"You didn't know Reseph," Limos said. "Neither of you did. You only knew him as an evil monster. But before his Seal broke, he was fun, happy, and he never intentionally hurt anyone. If he knows all of the things that happened at his hand, it'll kill him."

"And that's what he was doing," Reaver said. "He was harming himself. I've never seen such self-torture in my life." Well, what he could remember of his life, anyway. "His mind was fractured."

"I don't care." Arik snapped. "The fucker deserves every drop of misery he experiences."

"*Pestilence* does," Reaver said. "*Reseph* doesn't. But that's not why I did what I did."

"What, exactly," Ares ground out, "did you do?"

"I erased his memory and dropped him in the human world."

"Why?"

"To give him time to heal. We need him whole when the Biblical Apocalypse starts. Even if it doesn't happen for another thousand years, we need all the time we can get to heal him. He needs to reintegrate his good side, because Pestilence is still in there. His power is diminished and he can't bring about the end of days anymore, but he could still wreak havoc on Earth and in Sheoul."

Regan shoved to her feet. "Put him back in Sheoul-gra."

Reaver closed his eyes. "Regan, I understand your concern for Logan—"

"Respectfully, Reaver, I don't think you do," Regan said. "Pestilence wants Logan dead. He tried to kill us both, so I don't think you get it. You don't have kids, so you can't possibly understand."

Thanatos slung his arm over her shoulder and tugged her against him. "I'm with Regan. I want him taken back."

"So you want your brother, who you loved for thousands of years, to suffer unimaginable pain?"

Ares, who rarely let emotions interfere with his battle-wise thinking, didn't make an exception now. "The pain is regrettable, but it's what's best for everyone."

"I drove a blade through his heart," Thanatos said flatly. "He's dead to me." Than scowled, his brow slamming down over his yellow eyes. "And wait, why didn't Deliverance destroy him?"

Reaver braced himself for this next part. "Deliverance wasn't the blade you needed to kill Pestilence."

The sudden silence in the room was broken only by Than's low growl. "Reaver…"

The souls of those Thanatos had killed, the ones who got sucked into his armor, began to billow around his feet as Than's anger mounted. Regan lay a comforting hand on his arm, and though the souls eased off the frenzied swirling, the fact that they were still there wasn't good.

"What's going on?" The bright orange flower in Limos's ebony hair wilted, as though it sensed her mood. "What are you not telling us?"

"Remember how Pestilence was trying to find Wormwood?"

Kynan nodded. "He tore apart Aegis headquarters and killed dozens for the dagger."

"Well, he got it. He knew Wormwood was the dagger that would kill him." Reaver looked Than in the eye. "You'd been searching for a way to repair Reseph's Seal, but what you didn't know was that Deliverance was the answer. You had it all along."

"*A blade his Deliverance*," Than murmured. "Okay, so that part of my prophecy was about saving Reseph. But *The Doom Star cometh if the cry fails*? We thought the Doom Star was Halley's Comet."

Reaver shook his head. "The Doom Star was Wormwood. Gethel and Pestilence figured it out."

"So if we'd failed to stab Pestilence with Deliverance

at the moment of Logan's first cry, we could have killed Pestilence at any time with Wormwood?"

"Exactly."

Thanatos's furious curse made the hellhounds in the room leap to their feet and look for a threat. "I could have killed him. I could have ended this and you didn't tell me? All this time we were living with a false sense of security? My son could still be in danger and you thought it was best to not tell us?"

The accusing glares of everyone in the room shriveled Reaver's heart. There were very few people Reaver cared about disappointing, and those here happened to be the few. "I didn't know about Wormwood until just before Logan's birth. I only had a few moments to make a choice about giving it to you, and I chose Reseph's life. He isn't a threat to you. His memory is gone."

"Damn you, Reaver," Thanatos croaked, the rare emotion in his voice shredding Reaver's insides. He hated to see any of these warriors hurt, and knowing he was at least in part responsible only made it worse. "Damn you."

Ares swore in disgust. "Take him back to Sheoul-gra."

Reaver understood Ares's anger, but dammit, Reaver had made a decision, and he had to stand by what he believed was best. "A, you don't order your Watcher, or any angel, around. B, we need him whole. He won't heal if I send him back."

Limos cast a worried glance at Arik. "What does this mean for Arik's soul? We thought that with Pestilence dead, it had reverted to Arik. Can Reseph give it back?"

"No." It had been a long time since Reaver had willingly taken a drink of anything stronger than wine, but right now he could use a gallon-sized shot of tequila.

"Only Pestilence can release his soul, and if he takes over again, he could release it into Sheoul out of spite."

"Meaning?" That from Arik, who looked a little green around the gills.

"Meaning that when you do die, you're doomed to Sheoul."

"Oh, good," Arik said. "Because I didn't get enough torture the first time around."

"This is so fucked up," Thanatos snarled. "We have to move on this. We can't just sit around and wait for Reseph to get better in a thousand years."

Arik cleared his throat. "Um...you need to do something." He was staring at his cell phone. "I just got a message from Decker. He's got a spy inside The Aegis, and it looks like they're onto us. They're sending a team to Bardsley."

"Fuck." Limos hurled a juiced lime into the garbage so hard it bounced back out. "That can only end badly."

Arik shoved the phone in his BDU pants pocket. "We've got to get Reseph before they do."

"Typical day with the Horsemen." Kynan scrubbed his hands over his face. "Things with you guys only go from bad to worse."

"No," Reaver said softly. "I don't think we've begun to see worse yet. Not even close."

"What does that mean?" Limos asked.

Closing his eyes, Reaver braced himself. When he lifted his lids, hard eyes stared back at him. "Gethel knows he's free. She's got Soulshredders hunting for him."

"And if she finds him..." Arik prompted.

"If she finds him, she can bring out Pestilence," Reaver said. "And if you think he was angry before, imagine how pissed off he's going to be this time around."

Seventeen

"Jillian Cardiff. It's about time you got out of that lonely cabin."

She looked up and nearly groaned at the sight of the dark-haired man standing next to her chair. Figured that out of all the country music bars in Bardsley, she and Reseph would come to the one Trey Yates and his thugs were haunting tonight.

"Good to see you, Trey. It's been a while." Not long enough. He'd dated Stacey for a couple of months and then dumped her for a newly single cougar on the prowl. "Still seeing Charlene?"

The live band got the dance floor moving with a Garth Brooks song as Trey chugged his beer. "Nah. She was wanting a new daddy for her brats."

Well, yeah. A blind man could have seen *that* coming. "How's the ranching business?" she asked, but only to be polite. Mostly, she kept her eye on Reseph, who had gone up to the bar for a couple of beers. Seemed like there was a sudden rush of women who just happened to need fresh drinks as well. "Last I heard, you were venturing into bison."

He burped. Didn't excuse himself. "Didn't work out. I'm back to sheep."

No doubt sheep were easier for him to bully. He'd been a total ass in high school, and according to Stacey, not a lot had changed. Why Stace had dated him for as long as she had, Jillian had no idea. Then again, he'd apparently put on a good front and the best of appearances for a while. It wasn't until shortly before he dumped her that his true colors began to show.

Trey jerked his chin toward the stage. "What do you think of the band?"

"They're okay. Why?"

His grin was so damned smug that she wanted to smack him. Funny how, when Reseph got cocky, it worked. On Trey it only looked sad and pathetic.

"I hang out with them," Trey said. "Belt out a song now and then. You should stick around, and maybe I'll sing something just for you."

Same old braggart he'd always been. Some things never changed. "I doubt we'll be here long, but thanks."

Trey never had taken rejection well, and his mouth twisted as he tipped his bottle toward Reseph. "I hear he's new in town. Has some sort of mental problems. Why would you shack up with someone like that?"

She gave him a tight smile. "That's none of your business."

His belligerent snort told her what he thought of her answer. "Is he your boyfriend?"

"Yes," came the deep, rumbling voice from behind her, and Jesus, how had he moved away from the bar so fast? "I'm hers." Reseph's tone, his words, made her all shivery inside.

Trey made a point of sizing up Reseph, dragging his gaze from his face to his feet and back again. "I'm Trey. And you are...?"

"Intolerant of jackasses who fuck with my female."

Trey had been in the middle of guzzling his beer, and now he slowly lowered the bottle from his mouth. "I don't think you know who you're talking to, Amnesia Boy."

Oh, shit. Jillian shoved to her feet and stepped between the two men. Trey looked ready to throw a punch, but Reseph merely looked amused.

"Enough," she said. "Trey, go back to your buddies."

Trey jabbed a finger at Reseph. "You better watch yourself, asshole. Small town like this, word gets around, and we know how to cull the herd." He glanced at Jillian. "Teach your stray some manners."

What. An. Ass. Pissed, Jillian started after Trey, but Reseph pulled her back.

"He's not worth it," Reseph said. "Let me guess; his family has money or some shit?"

"Exactly." She shot Trey one last glare before turning back to Reseph. "His family owns half the town. He has a sheep ranch just north of town, but he'd be flailing if not for his family money and all their connections."

"Well," he said, putting his mouth to her ear. "Let's give him the attention he deserves."

"Which is?"

"None." He got a very naughty twinkle in his eye. "In fact, let's take it all away from him."

She huffed. "I know you aren't thinking of doing something outrageous. Right?"

"Me?"

She poked him in the chest with one finger. "You. I'm going to the ladies' room. Be good while I'm gone."

Reseph's smile was all charm and innocence, which made her instantly suspicious. "I'll be so good you won't know what hit you."

"Reseph..." She narrowed her eyes at him. "What are you up to?"

"I just thought of a way to thank you for bringing me here and for buying the drinks tonight." He lifted his hand to her hair and sifted through it until he was cupping her cheek. "I don't know much about myself, but I'm pretty sure I don't deserve you."

Funny, she thought the same thing about herself. That she didn't deserve him. Or at least, that she couldn't believe her luck, because truly, if she'd given a genie a wish for the perfect man, Reseph would have been the guy who showed up on her doorstep.

Or in a snowdrift.

"Knock it off," she said, leaning in to steal a kiss. "You totally deserve me. Just consider the drinks payment for all your help around the house." He'd done so much, so this afternoon, after she'd taken him to the library for more research, she'd brought him here for a night out. He'd been so distracted at the library, his research half-hearted, and she'd hoped to cheer him up.

He shook his head. "I need to get a job or something. I can't keep mooching off you."

The implied permanence of what he'd just said both raised her hopes and unsettled her. She liked how things were now, and while the logical side of her knew they couldn't stay like this forever, she wasn't ready to start talking about him leaving, getting a job, finding a place of his own.

"We'll figure it out. Once we find out who you are, everything will fall into place." She hoped. God, she hoped.

She hurried to the bathroom, afraid to leave Reseph for long. The roguish glint in his eyes was the most predictable thing about him. It always signaled that he was going to do something utterly *un*predictable.

Sure enough, before she even got back to the table she knew something was up. The fact that Reseph wasn't there was the first clue. The second clue was that there was no music playing. The third was that everyone in the bar was staring at the stage, including Trey, whose expression was pure, red-faced hatred.

Almost afraid to look, Jillian swiveled around in her seat and gasped when she saw Reseph standing behind the microphone, his bright gaze burning a hole right through her. His smile stopped her heart. And then the band started playing. No . . . he wasn't . . . was he?

Reseph brought the mic to his lips, and George Strait's "I Cross My Heart" suddenly became Jillian's favorite song. Reseph . . . could *sing*. And he sang it to her, his gaze never leaving her face.

When he finished, the entire bar erupted in applause that only died down when Reseph moved on to Alan Jackson's "It's Five O'clock Somewhere." That one brought people out on the dance floor, and they stayed for Reseph's incredibly deep rendition of Big and Rich's "Save a Horse, Ride a Cowboy."

When the last note played, the bar crowd once more

exploded in cheers. Jillian, too breathless to cheer, had been so mesmerized by Reseph's performance that she didn't remember standing up. And when Reseph's gaze locked on to her as he leaped gracefully off the stage, she moved to meet him. The people on the dance floor parted to allow him through, his shoulders rolling, his predatory intent clear.

She held her breath as he approached, and when he was inches away, his heat searing her skin, he grabbed her around the waist, tugged her against his hard body, and bent his head to her ear.

"How was that for taking the attention away from Trey?"

"Trey who?" she breathed. "God, you were amazing up there." She'd never in her life been the type of woman to swoon for musicians, but she'd just become a Reseph groupie. "Ride a cowboy? Baby, saddle up."

His teeth grazed her earlobe. "Home," he said roughly. "I need to make you mine. Now."

She shivered at his words, at the erotic undertone. And at the sheer, raw possession. She could tell him she already was his, but she wasn't about to ruin his fun. Or hers.

"Do you think we can make it to the house?" she said, just as roughly. "My truck has a big cab, you know."

She swore flames flared in his eyes, but were quickly doused. "Another time. I'm going to do this right."

Okay, then. She wasted no time grabbing her jacket and paying the tab. Reseph waited by the door, but his eyes never left her, and as she walked toward him, his gaze grew more heated with every step. For fun, she slowed down as she neared him, and even from several feet away and with the music blaring, she heard his impatient growl.

Sweat bloomed on her skin and her blood raced through her veins, and that was enough teasing. She had never been more ready for bed in her life. When she reached him, he very carefully pushed her against the wall and kissed her, a punishing, sensual kiss that probably didn't last longer than five seconds, but that left her dizzy, needy, and so on fire that the ten-degree night air didn't feel nearly cold enough when they stepped out in it.

And seriously, why did she park so far away?

She glanced up at Reseph as he walked beside her, which was a huge mistake. The way he was looking at her made her want to drop into the snow and let him have his way with her right there in the parking lot.

"Hey, dickhead!"

Jillian groaned at Trey's shout, and as they turned around, Trey and five of his lackeys formed a semicircle around them.

"You showoff punk," Trey said. "You think you can come into my town and make me look like an ass?"

"You don't need me to do that," Reseph drawled. "You're doing a bang-up job of it all on your own."

Trey's face mottled with rage. "I'm going to fuck you up, Amnesia Boy. Maybe *that'll* be something you remember."

"Look, man." Reseph's voice was calm, his grip on Jillian's hand firm but gentle. "You want to back off. You and your buddies need to turn around and go back inside. You can tell everyone you beat me up and I ran away crying. I won't say any different. But trust me on this one... you *want* to back off."

"What a pussy." Trey's friend, whose name she thought

was Darren, laughed. "Pussy wants to run off with his tail between his legs."

"Shut up, Darren." Jillian tugged on Reseph's hand, hoping to get the hell out of there before things deteriorated. She didn't doubt Reseph's ability to fight, not after what she'd seen him do to the demon in her barn, but they were badly outnumbered. "Let's go."

Trey and two of his buddies moved to block them. "You aren't going anywhere."

"Last chance," Reseph said. "Go back inside the bar."

"Fuck you."

Reseph sighed. "Okay, then." He shoved Jillian behind him. "Get back."

"But—"

"Get. Back." Deadly menace all but leaked from his pores, and suddenly, she revised her earlier thought. Reseph wasn't outnumbered. Trey and his buddies were.

"Reseph…"

He looked at her from over his shoulder and lowered his voice. "You need to stay out of their reach, because if one of them touches you, I'll kill him."

Jesus. He was serious. The way he'd said it, as if he was going to take out the garbage on just another ho-hum night…just, *Jesus*.

He swung back around to the idiots just in time for Darren to throw a punch.

It never landed. Reseph blocked Darren's swing and took the other man down with a powerful right hook before spinning around to nail Trey in the gut with a kick that sent the jerk airborne. Trey slammed into his own pickup's tailgate. Before he even hit the ground, Reseph put two more of Trey's friends on their backs, one with a clearly broken arm.

A big red-headed guy rushed Reseph. Almost as if Reseph were bored, he jammed the heel of his hand into Red's face, breaking his nose with an audible crunch. Blood sprayed as Red shouted in pain and lurched toward the bar's back door.

The remaining guy backed off, hands up.

Dear Lord, Reseph had taken out five men and he wasn't even breathing hard. The guys on the ground scrambled awkwardly out of his way as he strode over to Trey, who was holding his ribs and struggling to get to his feet. Reseph grabbed him by the throat and lifted him off the ground as if Trey weighed no more than a jug of milk. With a nasty snarl Jillian could only describe as inhuman, Reseph rammed Trey into the driver's side door, the impact crumpling the metal.

"I warned you," Reseph said, his voice so bereft of emotion she shivered. "And now I'm warning you again. You fuck with me or Jillian, you so much as look at either of us with anything less than respect—nah, let's go with awe—and I'll dismantle you. If you survive, I promise you'll spend the rest of your life pissing yourself every time you hear Jillian's name. You feel me?"

At Trey's frenzied nod, Reseph grinned coldly and looked down. "Looks like you got a head start on the pissing thing." He dropped Trey and wheeled around to Jillian. "You ready to go?"

All she could do was bob her head in answer as Trey and his buddies limped and shuffled their way back inside the bar.

Reseph took her hand and guided her toward the truck. "You okay?"

Aside from adrenaline scouring her veins like Drano,

yes, she was. A huge sense of relief was tripping through her. Something told her that Reseph had held back with those guys. A lot. He'd been level-headed, efficient, and restrained.

It had been kind of . . . hot.

"I'm fine." She twined her fingers in his. "And you?"

"I'm on fire." He jerked her to a halt just shy of the truck and tugged her against him. Even in the shadows of the parking lot, his eyes glowed with a primitive, elemental need that called to a part of her she didn't understand. All she knew was that her body felt both electrically charged and pliant as rubber, and liquid desire bloomed between her thighs. "I can't explain it, but I need to be inside you more than ever."

Her breath stuttered. "Yes," she whispered.

Normally, now would be when Reseph gave her one of those cocky grins, but not this time. This time he was a single-minded predator, locked on target, and she was in his crosshairs. God, she loved this side of him. She never in a million years thought she'd be the type of woman to like the caveman type, but Reseph managed to not overwhelm. If anything, she couldn't wait to feel him unleash his inner Neanderthal on her.

His hand dipped into her jacket pocket and withdrew her keys. Before she could protest, he unlocked the truck and opened the passenger side door.

"I'll drive," she said, but he lifted her into the seat.

"I have to drive, Jillian."

"Why?"

His low, throaty growl triggered another rush of wetness. "Because if my hands aren't on the wheel, they'll be on you."

She damned near moaned. "And that's a bad thing?"

"It is when you're driving." He tugged the seat belt across her, and as he clicked it into place, he pressed a hot, velvet kiss to her throat.

"I can pull over," she squeaked.

His nostrils flared, and she swore she saw flames in his eyes. "I'm on the very edge right now." His voice throbbed with raw lust. "I want you under me. I want to claim you, get myself all over you. And as much as I'd love to mount you right here in public, right now—and I think in my past, I would have—I never want anyone to see you like that but me."

Oh, damn. Her heart was pounding out of her chest. She wanted it now, and who cared who saw or heard what. "I'll park somewhere dark." She fisted his T-shirt, not even ashamed of her desperation. "Out of the way—"

"Tempting…so…fucking…tempting." He gently peeled her hand away, slammed the door, and got in on the driver's side. Then he turned to her, the harsh planes of his face in the shadows creating a savage expression that stuck her tongue to the roof of her mouth. "I need you in bed tonight, Jillian. I need more than a fuck. I need to make love to you until neither one of us can move, because after tonight, I don't want there to be even the slightest doubt that you're mine."

Eighteen

God, Reseph was lit up. Lit like a torch, burning so hot he was afraid he'd melt the steering wheel as he whipped Jillian's pickup into the driveway. The drive had been silent, tense, the air in the cab so charged with sex that he felt it on his skin, as if a single touch could put him over the edge.

If Jillian's spicy scent was any indication, she felt the same way. Her arousal had been powerful enough that twice he damned near pulled the truck over and did exactly what he'd said he wouldn't do.

Thank God they were at her place. He slammed the truck into park and was out in a flash. Before Jillian could even get fully out of her seat, he had her in his arms and was carrying her through the front door. He kissed her as he kicked the door shut, his heart going mad with want. He needed her like he needed air, and until he had her under him, her arms and legs holding him tight, he felt like he might suffocate.

He laid her on the bed a lot less roughly than he could have—would have, if this had been any other night. But he'd experienced a shift today, a one-two punch of reality and emotion. He'd faced the fact that he wasn't going to find out who he was, and the Amnesia Boy bullshit had driven that home. It was time to stop worrying about the past and make new memories.

With Jillian.

Jillian, who had saved his life, taken care of him, made him laugh, given him an anchor when he should have been drifting.

Reseph stripped off his shirt and joined her on the bed, and when she sat up to meet him, he pushed her back down and covered her body with his. Their gazes locked, and Reseph's pulse thundered in his ears. When Jillian's palm came up to his chest, the heat of her touch spread through him, sizzling over his skin.

Lowering his mouth to hers, he kissed her, somehow taking it slow and leisurely, as if they weren't both ready to go into orbit. He undressed her, breaking off the kiss only when he pulled off her shirt or shoved down her jeans. When they were both naked, skin on skin, he kept his hands to rated PG parts of her body, stroking her shoulders, her neck, her arms.

She didn't play like that. No, Jillian's nails scored his back before dropping to his ass, where she dug her fingers into his cheeks as she rocked against him, grinding her mound against his erection. They both groaned at that, but he wasn't ready yet.

Well, he was ready physically, but not mentally. He needed to be thorough, attentive, possessive.

Jillian was his, and she was going to know it when he was done.

Tangling his fingers in her hair, he let his other hand drift up her rib cage. He stroked the curve of her breast, feeling the skin tighten beneath his palm. His thumb circled her nipple, and the impassioned whimper breaking from her throat said she liked it.

"I need you to believe me," he murmured against her lips, "trust me when I say that I've never made love to a woman. Not like this." The knowledge was soul-deep, not even a question, and he needed Jillian to understand.

"I believe you. And I've never had a man make me feel so special." She arched under him, hooking one ankle over his leg and rubbing her foot seductively along his calf.

He looked into her eyes, determined to make sure she understood what he was about to say. "You're more than special. I love you, Jillian. I love you, and I want this to be the start of something new."

Her foot stilled on his leg. "What do you mean?"

"I mean that I don't care who or what I was in the past." The vision he'd had in the barn tunneled up from where he'd buried it in his mind, but he ruthlessly slammed it back into its dark hole. Whatever he'd been before had no place in his new life. "I don't want to know anymore. I'm going to stop looking."

Both hands came up to frame his face. "Oh, Reseph, I can't ask you to do that."

"You didn't ask." He rubbed his cheek against her palm, thinking he'd never felt anything so soft as her skin. "I'm doing it. I love this life, I love you, and I want to start our lives together now."

"You're . . . serious."

"Can you handle not knowing who I was?" He nipped the sensitive skin between her thumb and forefinger before laving it with his tongue. "Can you deal with the man I am now?"

"Yes," she whispered in a husky rasp. "Oh, yes."

"Good," he said, lowering his mouth to her throat. "Because the man I am now is who I want to be. Forever."

At Reseph's admission, Jillian's heart thundered against what remained of the wall that surrounded it. Since the day Reseph had arrived, the wall had been cracking, and each passing day saw the fissures deepen. Now this wonderful man had committed himself to her, leaving behind his past and making her his future. No man had ever given up anything for her, and as her heartbeat knocked down the last shard of barrier that stood between her and surrender, she thanked her good fortune.

Before Reseph, the independent woman in her would have railed against any man telling her she was his, but with him it seemed natural, respectful.

And oh, so sexy.

And speaking of sexy, Reseph concentrated kisses on her throat, each one moving a fraction of an inch lower, his lips following her jugular to the base of her neck. Desire spiraled through her, growing more and more out of control with every passing second. Yet Reseph still wasn't touching her where she needed to be touched.

The man was a sadist. A master of torture. His erection sat heavily against her sex, but no matter how much she writhed, he didn't make a move to enter her. She ached, burned, *wanted*.

"So impatient," he murmured against her clavicle.

"I'm not *impatient*." She thrust her hands into his gorgeous, silky hair to guide his mouth lower, which totally made her a liar. "You've been teasing me since the bar. I'm *ready*."

His husky chuckle accompanied his hand dipping between her legs and finding her slick wetness. "Oh, yeah, you're ready." His lips trailed over the mound of her breast, and his tongue came out to taste her nipple. "I love how you respond to me. Only me." That last bit came out as a carnal growl, and a rush of liquid lust dampened her core. He growled again, slipping two fingers inside her.

Lost to pleasure, she threw her head back and concentrated on breathing as his fingers worked their magic. He covered her breast with his mouth, drawing against her nipple, his warm tongue swirling and caressing. The combination of his fingers thrusting inside her and his mouth suckling her breast was intoxicating. She felt drunk with sensation, almost overwhelmed, because all of this was so much more than physical.

Reseph was pouring emotion into every slow caress, every smoldering kiss, every honeyed, reverent endearment he whispered against her skin. *Beautiful. Amazing. Mine.* There were even a few words mixed in that she didn't recognize but understood anyway. He was taking her. Marking her. Even if, afterward, she didn't have a single scratch, bite, or ache, he'd have left his mark indelibly in her mind and heart.

His fingers pumped faster, taking her higher. "That's it," he rasped against her breast. "God, I love the way you move."

He feathered his thumb over her clit, just skimming the crest. She cried out with both pleasure and frustration. He did it again, this time with more pressure, and her cry was louder.

"Please," she gasped. "Now."

A rattling purr erupted from his chest as he shifted to nudge her thighs wide with his legs. He looked down, watching his hand working her, and that purr went deeper. He twisted his fingers and stroked his thumb through her slit, pressing lightly on her knot of nerves... pressing, not moving, and oh, God, *yes*...

She shouted in total abandon, bucking into his touch, riding the climax he'd coaxed out of her with teasing touches, hot talk, and sweet pledges. The orgasm seemed to go on and on, and even before the throbbing fire had completely waned, Reseph was on his knees between her legs, his erection curved into his abs as he reached for a condom. His fingers still caressed her sex, but with delicate, indirect strokes.

His gaze smoldered, never leaving her face. He tore the condom wrapper open with his teeth, and in a smooth feat of one-handed dexterity, he removed the condom and rolled it over his straining length. His muscles flexed as he prowled forward over her body, covering her, putting the tip of his cock at her entrance.

Still keeping eye contact, he slid inside her. "I love you," he said on a breathy moan.

"I love you, too," she whispered.

A smile ruffled his mouth, and then he closed his eyes and thrust his hips slowly. So damned slowly. How did he have such control? She'd already come once, taking the edge off, but she was still worked up enough to want to get things moving.

Pulling up her legs, she wrapped them around his waist, clinging to him fiercely. His pace picked up, the hot friction sparking bolts of ecstasy deep inside her. She clenched around him and he groaned, moving faster. His entire body undulated over her, every muscle tense and rippling, the tendons in his neck standing out starkly.

She was almost there, her body craving another peak. She panted at the upward momentum, the heat between them, the raw, animal lust. Her heart hammered violently, and her breaths came in short, choppy bursts.

"Jillian," he gasped. "You feel...so...good..." He threw his head back, baring his teeth, pounding into her. "I feel you...coming."

She went over the edge with him, his shout mingling with hers. A firestorm of pleasure seared her from the inside out.

"My...God," he groaned, his hips still pumping in spastic twitches. His eyes were mere slits as he sagged on top of her, burying his face in her neck. His breaths were harsh against her skin, but his hands were gentle as he stroked her face, her hair, her shoulders.

Every muscle in her body had turned to Jell-O, but she held him tight, tapping strength from some hidden reserve.

"Thank you," she said into his hair. "You've given me so much."

With a grunt, he rolled off her, but he didn't get out of bed. He tucked her against him, twining his legs with hers. "I haven't given you nearly enough." He kissed her forehead. "But I'll start working on that."

Her chest swelled with happiness. "And tomorrow...I guess today, really, let's go get a Christmas tree. I haven't celebrated a proper holiday since my parents died. So let's start off our new life with Christmas."

He smiled. "It'll be sort of like my first."

"Mine too," she whispered. "Mine too."

Nineteen

Reseph woke to the sound of a scream. He bolted upright, reaching for Jillian, but her side of the bed was empty. Hoping to God he'd been dreaming, he scrambled out of bed and tugged on his jeans. And then...another scream. Jillian's scream.

Instant, bone-chilling terror and panic ripped through him. Barefoot, he charged through the house and tore open the front door with such force that it snapped the hinges.

Jillian was standing on the porch, face pale, eyes wide. A few yards away, Ares, Thanatos, and Limos were lined up, armored, and mounted on their horses.

"My brothers!" Grinning like a fool, his heart bounding with sudden excitement, he started for them. "Limos!"

"Reseph?" Jillian's voice was shaken.

"It's okay," he said, giving her arm a rub as he walked past. "It's my family. I can't wait for you to meet them. Come on."

"You...you remember?"

"Yup." Freaky, but yeah, it was all coming back to him.

He took the steps down in two strides, but even as he hit the snowy ground below, he realized something was wrong. No one looked happy to see him. In fact, their expressions ranged from wary distrust, to downright hate in Thanatos's case. What the hell—

A memory struck him like one of Jillian's frying pans...Thanatos, holding him down, jamming Deliverance into his chest as nearby, a baby cried. But why...?

More memories came at him, rapid-fire, like bullets from an automatic weapon. His head snapped back as a wall of horror blindsided him. He stumbled, his equilibrium thrown off by the weight of the sudden recollections.

Blood. Screams. Hate...so much hate. The world spun, the ground giving way beneath him, and he crashed to his knees, clutching his head. Hands came down on his back...Jillian's. She was speaking, asking if he was okay. Asking what was wrong, but he couldn't speak. More screams...the screams of those he'd hurt. Countless numbers of them. Oh... *God.*

"No," he rasped. "Oh...please, no."

His stomach turned over, and he lurched, half-crawled, half-stumbled away from her and to the nearest tree, where everything he'd eaten in the last week, month, maybe year, came up. He lost it. Lost everything. Including, possibly, his mind.

What was happening?

Jillian stood in the snow, unable to process any of this. The strange, armored people on their horses watched Reseph break away from Jillian, curiously detached. Until he screamed and threw himself against the tree, slamming his head into the trunk over and over.

"Reseph!" She darted toward him, but before she'd gone five steps, arms came around her and she was held tightly by the huge man with blond braids at his temples and yellow hawk eyes. "Let me go!" She kicked and punched, but she might as well have been beating on an elephant. "Release me, you bastard!"

A godawful roar shook the very air, and Reseph spun, his face dripping blood, his teeth bared. Fury blazed in his crimson eyes as they locked onto the man holding her. He charged, but in a blur she couldn't comprehend until it was over, the guy in leather armor was off his horse and tackling Reseph. Leather Man jammed something that looked like an EpiPen into his throat, and Reseph went completely, utterly still.

"What did you do?" she screamed. "*Reseph!*"

"He's okay, female." The man holding her palmed her forehead. "I'll make this all go away."

"No!" The black-haired woman rushed toward them, her armor, samurai in appearance, collecting snow in the joints as she ran. "Thanatos, don't. You can't go back far enough. Let her remember this."

The man samurai called Thanatos tugged Jillian even closer, until she could feel the chill coming off his white armor. What was it made of, anyway? Bone?

"We can rearrange this, Limos," Thanatos said. "Make her believe Reseph walked out on her."

The woman named Limos shook her head. "I promised Arik I wouldn't mess with anyone's memories again."

Memories? These people could mess with memories? Erase things? What was going on?

Thanatos rolled his eyes. "The things you do for that human."

Behind Limos, the big man in leather armor spoke, and the stallion he'd been riding poofed into smoke and shot into his gauntlet.

Jillian was seeing things. None of this was real. It couldn't be. But it seemed very real when the man threw Reseph over his shoulder, took a couple of steps, and disappeared into thin air.

"No," Jillian whispered. "No. Bring him back." She struggled uselessly against her captor's hold. "Bring him back, you son of a bitch!"

"Let her go, Than," the woman said. "Go help Ares with Reseph. I'll take care of this."

Take care of this? Terror burst through Jillian. Was the woman going to kill her?

Thanatos released Jillian, and the sudden lack of support sent her sprawling in the snow. "Sorry, female," he said gruffly, and offered his hand.

As if. Jillian scrambled backward in an uncoordinated tangle of limbs until she hit the base of the steps and used them to get to her feet. She stood there, panting and freaking out, as Thanatos muttered something and his horse... oh, Jesus, really? His horse dissolved into smoke like the first one and shot into his gauntlet.

Jillian swayed, her head spinning, her heart pounding impossibly fast. *Don't pass out. Do not pass out in front of these people.* She reached out and clutched the railing as hard as she could, praying hard that she'd stay conscious.

Thanatos took a step and disappeared as quickly as the other man had, leaving her alone with the woman and her black stallion. At least, Jillian thought it might be a horse. But she'd never seen a horse with razor-sharp teeth, red eyes, and hooves that created steam in the snow.

Terror was a cold fist around her heart, squeezing so hard and fast that her blood felt like it might explode from her veins. This was a nightmare. She was stuck in a horrible nightmare and reality was sliding right out from under her feet. She must have been speaking her thoughts out loud, because the other woman shook her head.

"This isn't a nightmare. It's all real. My name is Limos. What's yours?"

Jillian swallowed. "J-Jillian. Who...are you?"

"I'm Reseph's sister. Thanatos and Ares are his brothers." Limos glanced around, her sharp, amethyst eyes seeming to take in everything. "Nice place. Look, Reseph has been missing for a few months. We didn't even know he was alive until last night. Where did you find him?"

"In a snowbank," she said hoarsely. "He...he didn't remember anything but his name."

Limos nodded. "Yeah, that's what we were told. Looks like you took good care of him. Thank you."

Thank you? Something about Limos's gratitude struck Jillian as ridiculous, given that they'd knocked out Reseph and then kidnapped him. Sudden anger replaced her fear, and she released the post to get up in Limos's face.

"Where did your brothers take him? Why did he freak out like that? What the hell is going on?"

"They took him home." Limos's voice was calm despite the fact that Jillian was practically shouting now. "As for the rest...it's not important. We'll take care of him." She pivoted around. "You shouldn't have any more demon trouble, either. Thanks again."

"Wait—"

"Trust me," Limos said softly. "This is for the best."

Limos and her horse disappeared, leaving Jillian terrified, confused, and so alone it hurt.

Twenty

Reaver had been prepared to see Reseph in a state of shock, but when Ares brought him back to Greece, slung over his shoulder, Reaver hadn't been prepared for all the blood.

"What happened? Did he fight you?"

"No." Ares's voice was gruff as he strode toward the bedroom they'd prepared. "He went a couple of rounds with a tree. Tree won."

"Damn," Reaver whispered. Reseph had done the same thing in Sheoul...thrown himself against a wall over and over, as if he could beat the demon out of himself.

"He seemed to remember everything once he saw us. I used the last of the *qeres* on him," Ares said. "When this wears off, we'll have no way to neutralize him."

Reaver followed Ares to a guest room, where he set Reseph on the bed. "Summon Harvester," Reaver said. "She has a particular talent when it comes to restraints."

Reaver knew that firsthand, and the memory made his bones ache.

"Nothing can hold us," Ares said, as he grabbed a towel from the connected bathroom. "You know that."

"Harvester's restraints are made from the victim's own bones, chains grown out of the skin and attached like part of the body. He can break free, but doing so would be so excruciating that he'll think twice. He might stay put just to avoid the agony." Then again, Reseph might welcome the misery.

"Interesting." Ares wiped Reseph's face more gently than Reaver would have expected. "Sounds like you know something about this."

"Too well." He regarded Reseph, a dull ache throbbing in his gut at the sight of the once happy, carefree male looking so tortured, even while unconscious. "How did he seem before he remembered?"

"He was happy," Ares murmured. "He seemed like his old self."

"Maybe he'll be able to remember that through the rest."

"I hope you're right." Ares whistled, and a hellhound came from out of nowhere. Reaver moved aside, giving the beast plenty of room. They might be lapdogs around Ares and Cara, but they were the same vicious, people-eating demons they'd always been to everyone else, and they especially hated angels. In fact, the buffalo-sized creature snarled at Reaver as he passed, and it took a huge amount of restraint to not strike out at the thing with a punishing heavenly weapon.

Cara would kill Reaver for that, and the look Ares gave Reaver said he knew exactly what Reaver was thinking.

"I'm behaving," Reaver muttered. "As long as Rin Tin Tin minds his manners, we'll be fine."

"His name is Eddie."

Reaver rolled his eyes. "I can't believe you name them." He gestured to the thing, which was eyeing Reseph like he wanted to dismember him. Understandable, given how Pestilence had put a bounty on their heads. "Pestilence was immune to hellhound venom. Reseph might be as well."

"I know. But Eddie can warn us when Reseph wakes up."

Reaver wasn't so sure that leaving a pissed-off hell-hound with a helpless enemy was a good idea, but Ares didn't have the same concern, and he strode out of the bedroom without a word. Reaver sighed and accompanied Ares to the great room, where a clearly worried Cara was holding a squirming toddler Ramreel demon.

"I don't like having him here, Ares," she said.

"We discussed this." Ares's voice softened as he pulled her against him. "We can't take him to Than's place because of the baby, and we don't want him at Limos's house in such close proximity to Arik. Until we know he's got nothing left of Pestilence in him, we can't risk him being anywhere but here."

If Harvester hadn't smashed Reseph's mountain cave in retaliation for Pestilence's violence against her last year, it would have been a perfect place to keep him. She'd screwed them with her angry actions, but Reaver couldn't blame her.

"Where are Limos and Thanatos?"

Ares stroked the baby Ramreel's furry back. "I don't know. I left them with the human female."

"Her name is Jillian," Reaver said.

Ares's head whipped around. "You know her? Another secret you were keeping from us?"

"I have no obligation to explain myself, Ares. We've been through this. She suffered a demon attack. I thought they could heal each other."

"Forgive me if I don't want him healed," Cara snapped, pulling away from Ares. "I want him dead." She stormed out of the house with the little demon, and Reaver couldn't fault her.

Ares cursed and went after her, opening the door just as Harvester strode in, looking like a damned high-class hooker. She was dressed in leather, including a skimpy bra top. At least she had on a long duster. Maybe she should button it up, though.

Her lips, painted as black as her outfit, quirked in a wicked smile. "Hello, lover."

"I'm not your lover," he ground out.

"Not yet." Every long-legged stride popped her leather miniskirted hips out in exaggerated supermodel style. High-heeled thigh-high boots cracked on the marble floor. Toned bare flesh flexed between the top of the boots and the bottom of the obscenely short skirt, and Reaver cursed the slow curl of lust that stirred his insides. "But you will be."

"Do you have any idea how badly I want to strangle you?"

She flipped her long hair over her shoulder. "You're into asphyxiation play? Nice." She jerked her thumb toward the door. "Why did Ares summon me?"

Voices outside carried; Thanatos and Limos had arrived and appeared to be trying to calm Cara. Reaver wished them luck.

"We have Reseph," he told Harvester.

Instantly, her entire demeanor changed, her posture stiffening, her eyes going icy. "Where?"

"In one of the bedrooms. We were hoping you could use your fun bone-chains to restrain him."

"Gladly."

He was about to tell her to cool it, that this was Reseph, not Pestilence, when he heard a howl followed by a blood-curdling scream and a series of crashes.

He and Harvester ran to Reseph's bedroom, where they were greeted by the sight of destroyed furniture. The hellhound was unharmed, standing in the corner with his hackles raised, baring his teeth at Reseph, who had clearly hurled himself around the room. Now he was sitting on the floor, back to the wall, and rocking, the heels of his palms pressed into his eyes. Every once in a while he threw his head back into the wall hard enough to put cracks in the plaster and, likely, his skull.

Next to Reaver, Harvester began to shake, her rage billowing off her in a cloud that scorched his skin. Reseph, as if sensing their presence, slowly lifted his head. For a long moment, he stared as if confused, and then horror flooded his expression.

"Harvester...oh, Jesus, I...I'm sorry, oh, fuckoh-fuckohfuck—"

In a flurry of motion and wings she was on top of Reseph, screaming, her fists pounding his face. Reseph did nothing to protect himself.

"You fucking bastard! You piece of shit son of a bitch!" Her words fell like weapons, sharp, nonstop, just like her fists. Blood sprayed the walls, her face, and dripped from her hands.

"Harvester!" Reaver hauled her, kicking and screaming, off Reseph.

"Let me go! *I'll kill him.*" Snarling, she bit Reaver's hand, and she nearly slipped out of his grasp before he was able to drag her from the room.

"What's going on?" Thanatos and Limos ran toward them, swords drawn.

"Nothing." Reaver jerked his head back to avoid a blow from Harvester's fist. "Check on Reseph."

The two Horsemen darted into the bedroom while Reaver struggled to get Harvester out of the house. Once they were outside, he released her, expecting her to make another dash inside. Instead, she dropped to her knees and screamed, a sound so full of pain that Reaver felt it as a physical manifestation, as if his wings were wet and weighing him down. Worse, he had no idea what to do.

Had this been anyone else, he'd gather them in his arms and simply hold them. But this was Harvester, and she wouldn't welcome comfort. Still, he moved closer. It didn't matter that she was evil and that he hated her. Pestilence had abused her, and while Reaver wasn't certain of everything that had happened, he could guess.

"I hate him." Tears streamed down her cheeks, leaving trails in the blood smeared across her face. "I hate him so much."

Warily, Reaver crouched as close as he thought he could risk before she could strike out in defense, either physically or verbally. She didn't tolerate kindness well.

"This is Reseph," he said reminded her. "Not Pestilence."

"I don't care!" she screamed. "I want him strung up

on hooks and peeled. I want him castrated and raped and tortured for the next century."

"Listen to me, Harvester." He kept his voice low, soothing, although it didn't seem to be doing much good. "You're his Watcher. You can hate him, but you can't arrange for him to be harmed. Get yourself together or you'll be pulled from duty. Is that what you want?"

"Isn't that what you want?" she snapped. "How nice for you to be rid of me."

"You might not be my favorite person in the world, but I'd rather deal with you than a replacement." A replacement who might be worse.

"Better the enemy you know, right?" Harvester smiled. Just a little, but it was better than the snarls.

"Right."

She met his gaze, and he inhaled sharply, knocked off balance by the naked emotion in her eyes. He'd seen vulnerability in her before, most notably when he'd found her being tortured by Gethel, and now, when she'd been crying. But this was different. This wasn't pain. It was… gratitude? Affection? What the hell was it?

An uncomfortable stirring skated around inside his chest as they locked gazes and the island around them fell away. In the background, he heard the waves crashing on the beach, but it felt as though they were crashing into him. He was being buffeted by the oddest feelings of tenderness.

He cleared his throat of its sudden dryness. "Look, ah, if you can't help with Reseph right now, everyone will understand—"

Harvester exploded to her feet. The anger returned to her expression, only this time it was directed at Reaver.

That was what he got for being kind to a dark-hearted fallen angel, he supposed.

"Understand? I don't need understanding from the likes of you. What do you take me for? A weakling victim? Fuck you and the air current you rode in on." With that, she stormed back inside the manor, leaving Reaver trying to recover from whiplash.

What he didn't think he'd recover from were the feelings she'd ignited in him. Oh, he hadn't fallen in love with her or some crap. What he'd felt had seemed more like an echo, as if he and Harvester had shared a moment of affection before.

He racked his memory, wondering if the time he'd spent as her prisoner, his brain soaked in addictive marrow wine, had anything to do with the déjà vu. Nothing specific came to mind, but then he'd been delirious most of the time.

Still, that had to be it. Because no way had he ever liked her. And even if he had, it wouldn't matter. Because someday, somehow, he was going to kill her.

Twenty-one

Hell was neverending pain. It was a fog the color of blood. It was a set of sharp claws that ripped into the brain and shredded it like pulled pork. With every dig of the claws came a new memory, and with each new memory, Reseph screamed.

Sometimes the claws stopped digging; instead they recycled memories he'd already been through but that were juicy enough to relive over and over, bringing non-stop regret and the pain that went with it.

The things he'd done as Pestilence clanged around inside his skull in a maddeningly loud screech, filling his vision so completely that only rarely did he see his surroundings or his siblings when they came. Reseph wasn't even sure why they came. Limos tried to clean him up with wet, warm cloths, and Ares tried to get him to eat, but Reseph didn't deserve any of it. He did, however, deserve the knockout punch he'd gotten from Arik before Limos dragged the human away.

He also didn't understand why he was here. Thanatos had killed him, so how was it that he was alive?

Then there were the other memories, the ones he wasn't sure were real.

Jillian.

He blinked, slowly becoming aware that he was lying in a fetal position on the floor. He never knew where he'd find himself when he came to or how broken his body would be. And he wasn't sure if the periods of lucidity were better than the periods of driving memories that took him out of the present. At least when he was being tortured by the memories of what he'd done, he didn't have to come face to face with the people he'd done them to.

He'd tried to apologize to them, but after Harvester's beating and Arik's punch to the face, not to mention Thanatos's scorching glares of pure hatred, Reseph had given up. "I'm sorry" was beyond lame, an insult, even, given the gravity of his sins.

And Jillian...had those days spent with her, making love and being at peace, been a figment of his imagination? A dream that made the nightmares seem all the worse? Maybe his conscience was playing tricks on him, because the days with Jillian might well be a dream, but *she* was real.

"Kill me," he whispered through a throat that was raw from his screams. "Someone...kill me."

But there was no one around to hear. Even Harvester, who delighted in his agony, had left after fitting him with restraints. He didn't care about the shackles. He wasn't going anywhere anyway. Besides, sometimes he jerked on the chains just to feel the soul-deep knifing agony that shot through his bones.

How long had it been since she'd chained him, anyway? He remembered a couple of nights, a couple of dawns.

Suffer, you bastard. Suffer as no one has suffered before, she'd whispered, before licking at a trail of blood that ran from his face to his ear. *If you care at all, you should know that you aren't free of Pestilence. Only a sliver of evil could turn you back into him. Oh, not in an apocalyptic sense, but you could revert back to the disgusting creature you were if evil taps into the demon half that was awakened when your Seal broke. You think you're miserable now? Turn back into Pestilence and watch your brothers and sister hunt you into the ground.*

Harvester's words rang in his ears over and over as he fell back into the pit of memories, so soaked in horror.

"End me," he whispered.

But no one heard.

Twenty-two

Limos stood in Ares's great room for the sixth day in a row, biting her lime-colored nails and staring down the hallway toward Reseph's bedroom, where his screams had grown louder over the last hour. They should peak soon, and then he'd fall into a period of soft whimpers as he rocked himself back and forth, staring blankly into space.

"He's not getting any better." She turned to her brothers, husband, and Kynan. "We can't let him suffer like this."

Ares closed his eyes for a second, face tilted to the ceiling. "No one wants Reseph to suffer, Limos."

"Really? You could have fooled me. Thanatos stares daggers at him every time we go in the room."

Than, who was pacing the length of the great room, paused. "It's not that I want him suffering. It's that I can't get what he's done out of my head."

"But that's not Pestilence in there," Limos insisted. "It's Reseph. We need to do something to help him."

"What do you suggest?" Ares asked. "He won't listen to any of us. He won't eat, he won't drink, and when I tried to drag him into the shower today he just dropped to the tiles and screamed. Like he didn't deserve to be clean. I've seen a lot of trauma in my life, but this is beyond anything I know how to deal with."

Arik looked up from playing tug-of-war with Hal. "What about what you did for me? When I was all out of it after escaping from Sheoul."

Limos thought about that for a second. "I stimulated you."

Arik winked. "And you did a damned fine job of it."

"Christ," Kynan muttered. "Get a room."

Ares shrugged. "It can't hurt to try something new. Limos, the woman Reseph was with…he's been calling for her. Do you think they had something going on?"

Jillian's devastation had definitely been real. "I didn't talk to her for long, but if I had to guess, I'd say they had some sort of relationship. Which, for Reseph, would be a first."

"Bring her here." Ares spoke as if he was a general giving a soldier orders, but for once, Limos didn't call him on it or take it personally. Deep down, he was as worried about Reseph as she was. "The human may be the only person who can help him right now."

"I'm on it." She just hoped that Jillian would want to come.

Finding out that the male you had been sleeping with was not only half demon, but that he had almost brought about the End of Days wouldn't be a selling point.

"You might want to hurry." Reaver's voice came from out of nowhere. Limos spun to where he stood near the fireplace, his sapphire eyes bright with concern.

"Why? What is it?"

"I've just come from the Watcher Council. Their fear that Pestilence will return is urgent."

Ares strode forward, a lock of his reddish-brown hair falling over his eyes. "You said exposure to evil could do that. We're keeping him isolated."

"That's good, but in the state he's in, his mind is weakened. This same thing would have happened if I'd left him in Sheoul-gra." Reaver sounded a little relieved that what he'd done had actually been the right choice. "His mind is full of cracks that Pestilence could slip through. He needs to heal, and it needs to happen now. Even then, he's going to spend his entire life fighting to keep Pestilence at bay."

Thanatos cursed. "Then we're screwed. Reseph has always been one to ship out when things get rough."

"We've got to let him try," Limos said fiercely. "I'll get Jillian. Maybe she'll give him a reason to fight."

"And if she doesn't give him a reason to keep Pestilence locked down?" Ares asked.

"Then I give you Wormwood." Reaver spoke in a low, grave tone. "And you put both Reseph and Pestilence out of their misery."

It had been almost a week since Reseph had gone. Six days that Jillian had spent in a desperate search to find him. Or, at least, find out what, exactly, had happened. How the hell did three people pop in and out of thin air? Well, four, counting Reseph.

Jillian had spent the first day crying, curled up in the sheets that still smelled like him, thinking that maybe she was crazy. But then she'd reminded herself that she'd seen demons with her own eyes, so things once thought impossible were now very, very real.

She'd spent the next two days scouring the Internet, getting millions of hits on people who could do what she'd seen. Unfortunately, there was too much information to wade through. Aliens. Angels. Demons. Superheroes.

She had, at least, gotten hits when she typed in the names Reseph, Ares, Limos, and Thanatos. Individually, she got lots of mythical references. But together, she got one very, very interesting return.

The Four Horsemen of the Apocalypse.

At that point, she'd been too overwhelmed to continue doing anything but stare at the computer screen, until she fell asleep on the keyboard. She'd needed solid answers that made sense, so she'd called an agency that seemed to be everywhere.

The Aegis.

They knocked on her door the next day. Five minutes later, she regretted the call.

Two men had introduced themselves as Lance and Juan, representatives of The Aegis, and they'd had a lot of questions about Reseph and his whereabouts.

Where did you find him? A snowbank. *He said his name was Reseph?* Yes. *Did he tell you who he was?* He didn't know who he was. He had amnesia.

Then came the more invasive questions, and Jillian had gotten testy. *Were you intimate with him?* None of your business. *Did he talk about his brothers and sister?* Did you miss the part about the amnesia? *Where is he now?* I don't know. *How can you not know?* Because he disappeared into thin air, you asshole.

She'd tried asking questions of her own, like why they were interested in Reseph and who he really was, but they'd refused to answer. By the time they'd gone, her head had been spinning and she'd been pissed off. She could use a friend to talk to—not that she was sure what to say—but Stacey had left a week ago for her brother's wedding in Arizona and wouldn't be back until tomorrow.

Damn it. She held the little bird Reseph had carved, staring at it as if it could morph into a carrier pigeon and take Reseph a message. Maybe she could take it to a psychic to see if the psychic could glean any information from Reseph's vibes.

Dear God, she was losing it, wasn't she? She was so desperate to find him that she was actually considering going to a psychic. Hell, she'd even flipped through the phone book a time or twelve, but it seemed as though psychics didn't advertise in her town's Yellow Pages.

A knock on the door nearly made her jump out of her skin, and she prayed it wasn't the Aegis guys again. Hastily, she grabbed her phone and peeked out the window. No vehicle.

Heart pounding at the thought that it might be Reseph outside—you know, after popping onto her deck from thin air—she opened the door and sucked in a harsh breath. The woman who had helped take Reseph away stood there, looking very out of place in a bright yellow and green sundress.

Jillian didn't bother with hello. "Where's Reseph? What have you done with him?"

"Chill. He's why I'm here." Limos strolled inside like

she owned the place, her flip-flops slapping on the wood floor.

"Yes, please," Jillian muttered. "Come in."

"Thanks," Limos said brightly. She regarded the room for a moment before turning to Jillian. "Small place. Looks larger from the outside."

"Unsolicited criticism aside, what are you doing here?"

Limos looked down at her bright lime nails. "Did you and Reseph have a relationship?"

Weird question. "Ah ... yeah."

"Was it just sex?"

"Excuse me? That's none of your business." What was it with people wanting to know how intimate she and Reseph had been?

Limos's dark eyebrows shot up, as if she was surprised to be challenged. "It kind of is. I mean, I don't want to know the dirty details, 'cuz, gross. But we need your help, so I need to know how involved you were. Did you fall in love with him?"

"Look, I'm really not comfortable with this—"

"I'll take that as a yes. The real question is just how attached to you he was."

I love you, Jillian. I love you, and I want this to be the start of something new. Fresh pain squeezed her heart. She missed Reseph so much. How could things have gone from being so perfect to being so awful in a matter of hours?

"Jillian?" Limos's voice was quiet, as if she knew how hard this was.

"He said he loved me," Jillian murmured.

"He *what*?"

Jillian crossed her arms over her chest, suddenly feeling

defensive, and maybe a little foolish. "Is that so hard to believe?"

"Let me put it this way," Limos said. "In five thousand years, he's never fallen for a female."

She gaped at Limos in disbelief. "Five thousand years. You want me to believe he's five thousand years old."

"Yep." Limos went back to studying her fingernails. "I guess we didn't tell you. Brace yourself. My brothers and I are the Four Horsemen of the Apocalypse. You probably heard about us in Sunday school."

"I got kicked out of Sunday school before they got to that story," she said with a calm she didn't feel. "But yes, I'm familiar with the Four Horsemen. You're saying that Reseph, the man I saved from a blizzard, is a biblical monster."

"Well, no. I mean, the biblical prophecy is just one of two. We're not all evil and creepy like you see on TV and the movies." She frowned. "Mostly, we're not. Anyhoo, you really didn't save Reseph from a blizzard. He's immortal. He would have survived."

She thought back to his miraculous recovery after being frozen nearly solid. "Okay, so let's say I believe you. Did the hypothermia affect his memory? Was that why he had amnesia?"

Limos winced. "This is where it gets tricky."

As if the rest of it was all normal and easy? "I'm listening."

Limos reached down her shirt and pulled out a gold chain with a circular pendant. "This is a Seal. As long as it's whole, my brothers and I are neither good nor evil. There have always been two Horsemen prophecies ... one human, one demon. The human prophecy, when it comes to pass, will put us fighting on the side of humans. The demon one would turn us evil."

Jillian really didn't like where this seemed to be going. "And the tricky part?"

"The demon prophecy was kicked off a little over a year ago. Reseph's Seal broke."

It took a few heartbeats for Jillian's brain to work through what Limos had said, and when it all came together, her chest constricted.

"So...wait. All the turmoil the Earth went through, the demons, the plagues...all of it...it happened because of Reseph, didn't it?"

"Yes. He turned into an evil bastard named Pestilence. He spent a year trying to break our Seals." She chewed her bottom lip for a second. "There's time for the gritty details later. Right now I need to ask you to help us."

Jillian should have been a lot more horrified than she was, but she suspected that everything she'd just learned was too big to process. No doubt she'd freak out later.

"You haven't answered my question about Reseph's memory."

"We stopped Pestilence. Thanatos drove a dagger through his heart and killed him. Sort of. It took away his power, anyway, and it stopped the Apocalypse. That's why all of a sudden, everything went back to normal. Reseph went to a place called Sheoul-gra. It's sort of a holding tank for demon souls. The problem was that, as Reseph, he remembered everything Pestilence had done. And it was bad. Really bad. Reseph went crazy, and our Watcher, an angel named Reaver, zapped his memory and sent him here to heal."

Okay, now it was starting to process, and Jillian sank

onto the couch, her legs unable to support not only her body, but the weight of everything she'd just heard. "This is unbelievable."

"Yeah, well, believe it." Limos plopped down on the coffee table across from her. "It looks like everything was going well until Reseph's name hit the wrong channels. We had to get to him before someone who wants him evil again found him or before The Aegis showed up."

"The Aegis," Jillian murmured, her voice sounding foreign to her own ears. "They've been here."

"I'm sure they have. They want him imprisoned."

"Why?"

"Because they're extremist assholes," Limos snapped. "They don't listen to reason, and anything they don't understand, they prefer to destroy."

Jillian nearly bolted out of her seat, as if she could somehow attack whoever was threatening Reseph. "They could destroy him?"

"No, but they think that if they can imprison him, or, probably, any of us, they can prevent death and destruction and crap."

"Is that true?"

Limos hesitated, and Jillian's pulse thudded in her ears. "Maybe, in Reseph's case. Pestilence could be extremely dangerous if he returns. That's why I'm here. Now that Reseph's memory is back, he remembers all the shit he did. He's going crazy. Hurting himself. It's leaving him vulnerable to Pestilence. We need to bring him back, but we're not getting through to him. We were hoping you could help."

Overwhelmed by the massive scope of the information she'd just been given, Jillian wrapped her arms around herself, as if the body hug would contain it and help her make sense of it all.

"I don't know what *I* can do. I'm just a…human." A terrified human who had fallen in love with a biblical legend. The thought almost made her hyperventilate.

"Talk to him. Be with him. I don't know. None of us know. This is uncharted territory. But when my husband was trapped inside his head after being tortured in hell, it took me to get him out."

"Your husband was…tortured? In hell? Actual *hell*?"

"We call it Sheoul, but yep. Arik was there for a month. And he rocked it." Limos grinned, fierce pride settling into her expression. "You met him when he was here with Kynan."

Both of those men had come across as confident, efficient, and a little…scary. Now she wondered just how scary Arik truly was to have survived a month in hell.

Closing her eyes, Jillian took a deep breath, hoping for some time to let all of this settle. But if Reseph was in pain, there was no time. She had to help.

"You okay?"

Jillian lifted her lids. "No." Not at all. She felt as if she was teetering on the very edge of hysteria, and all it would take was one more revelation from Limos, and Jillian would tip over. She eyed the female Horseman, needing an anchor to reality, but even her hairstyle seemed inconsistent with who she said she was. Who she'd been when she'd sat astride her stallion-thing, armed and armored like a warrior right out of, well, legend. "Why do you have a flower in your hair?"

"What, it's not very Horseman-like?"

"It's not what I would have expected, no."

Limos huffed. "It's a poison-spitting iris that dissolves flesh on contact."

Jillian edged backward. "Seriously?"

"No." Limos grinned. "I just like pretty flowers. I could remove your flesh myself. I'm great with a blade."

Flesh removal? Oh, God. The reality of the situation was starting to sink in now. "And this…" Jillian swallowed sickly. "This is how you convince me to go with you?"

"Sorry. I probably need to work on my sales pitch." Limos propped her elbows on her knees and leaned closer to Jillian, all business. "So… will you help?"

"Where…" Jillian blew out a breath in a rush. "Where will we go? Um… hell?"

"Greece. Trust me, none of us live in creepy places. Well, Reseph used to, but his cave was destroyed."

Cave? He'd felt confined in her cabin and he'd lived in a cave? "Okay, I'll do it. Take me to him. Beam me up or whatever it is you do."

Limos bounded to her feet. "You're handling this really well. You should have seen how Ares's wife reacted when she first got introduced to our world and who we are."

Yeah, well, Jillian had been given a painful introduction to the supernatural world when demons had attacked her in that airport parking lot. Reseph might be a Horseman, but in comparison, he was a kitten. Abruptly, she recalled the fight at the bar and the battle with the barn demon, and she revised that last thought. Kitten, no. Lion, yes.

She followed Limos outside. "Ares is married to a human?"

Limos bobbed her head. "Cara. She's sort of a hell-hound whisperer."

Jillian stopped so suddenly she slipped on the icy

porch and would have gone down if Limos hadn't grabbed her, lightning fast, and lifted her upright.

"Hellhounds?" Jillian rasped. "D-demons?"

"Ah...yeah." Limos took Jillian's arm and dragged her off the porch. "Come on. Harrowgate is waiting."

Traveling via the thing Limos called a Harrowgate was an unnerving experience, especially when Limos said that the Horsemen were the only beings who could take a conscious human through a portable gate without the human coming out on the other side...dead.

She stepped out with Limos, inside a circle marked by little flags outside a huge Greek-style mansion. Olive trees rose between huge Greek-style pillars and snow-white statues of Greek gods.

"I guess this is Greece?" *Oh, Jillian, you're a rocket scientist, you are.*

"Yep."

"Why are there little flags around us?"

"It's the designated Harrowgate landing. At our houses we keep them marked off so people know not to enter. When a gate opens, it'll slice into any living thing it touches."

Jillian missed a step. Then she missed another—God, Limos must think she was drunk—when she noticed that there were a lot of people and...*not* humans...gathered around the mansion.

"Um..."

Limos waved her hand in dismissal and started walking toward the crowd. "Don't worry about the females. They're here for Reseph."

Females? All those things were *females*? With some it was hard to tell. "What...what are they?" *Please don't say demons, please don't say demons...*

"Demons."

Jillian's throat closed up so hard she actually reached up to loosen the noose that seemed to be around it. *Demons. Holy shit, demons.*

"Hey." Limos's voice cut through the panic that buzzed in Jillian's ears. "They won't hurt you. I promise. Jillian? Stay with me. Reseph needs you."

Jillian squeezed her eyes closed. With the world shut out beyond her eyelids, she could picture Reseph's smile, the hard set of his jaw when they made love, and she could hear him telling her how strong she was. He'd brought her back into the world she'd been hiding from and had given her a precious gift. She would give him the same. Somehow she'd survive this, and she'd help him.

She opened her eyes but kept them glued to Limos. "I'm okay. Let's go."

The throng made a path for Limos, and Jillian followed until one of the creatures, who appeared human-ish except for her gray skin and hair, black horns, and clawed feet, blocked their path.

"Why are you taking this...*human*...when we have to wait out here?"

Jillian didn't even have time to blink before Limos had the demon by the throat, lifting the thing off the ground. "You do *not* question a Horseman of the Apocalypse. Speak like that again, and you'll be lucky if I only take your tongue."

The demon in Limos's grip nodded—as much as she could—and every demon around them backed up, widening the circle. Jillian wondered how close Limos had been to doing the same to Jillian back at her house, because she'd been nothing *but* questions.

Limos released the demon, who fell to the ground and stayed there, gasping for air.

"Anyone else want to piss me off?" When no one came forward, Limos smiled. "Good. Come on, Jilly."

Yeah, Jillian would let that one pass. Good God, she'd threatened a Horseman of the Apocalypse with a frying pan. Reseph could have squashed her with his thumb.

Instead, he'd done amazing, wonderful things with that thumb. The thought that she'd *made love* to one of the Horsemen of the Apocalypse made her dizzy.

"Why are all these, um, women, here? Do they think they can help Reseph?"

"They heard he's back, but they don't know his condition. They just want to get laid."

Abruptly, Jillian felt sick. "These are his...girlfriends?"

Limos snorted. "Hardly. They were just his fuck and party buddies." She snapped her mouth shut with a wince. "Ah, sorry. Look, you should know...he's a bit of a, well, he *was* a playboy. He's never attached himself to one female, but I think it's different with you. That's why you're here."

"You *think* it's different," she murmured, her heart aching as she looked back at all the females gathered around.

There had to be a hundred, and they were all, even the freakiest of them, attractive in some way. Some were downright gorgeous, to the point that it hurt to look at them.

Sympathy dripped from Limos's voice. "Keep in mind," she said gently, "that Reseph is five thousand years old, and demons are long-lived, if not immortal. That's a lot of time to build up a body count."

Jillian struggled to keep her hopes up. She supposed that what Limos said was true, but it didn't help a lot. Applying logic to a hurtful situation rarely worked until there was some distance, and Jillian doubted she'd have distance for a long time. Not when the way she felt about Reseph was different and more powerful than anything she'd felt for a man before.

Did these females feel the same way about him? The thought made her ill.

"Let's go," she muttered.

They entered the mansion, which opened up into a huge room where Thanatos and Ares were talking with a brown-haired woman and Arik. Arik nodded in greeting, the woman smiled, and Thanatos and Ares just stared.

"Oh, for God's sake, boys," the woman said. "She's not an enemy. Stop glaring." She moved forward, and with her came a black dog-like creature the size of a bull. "I'm Cara, Ares's wife. Can I get you anything? Something to drink, maybe?"

I could use a bottle of vodka and a Xanax. The dog-thing bared its sharklike teeth. *Make that a dozen Xanax.* "Thank you. I'm fine." Jillian wasn't sure what she had expected, but a relatively normal, domestic family wasn't it.

Thanatos gestured at her. "Come on. Reseph's this way."

Jillian glanced at Limos, who gave her a reassuring nod. "Thanatos doesn't bite." She shot Thanatos a glare. "Don't bite."

"Ha. Ha." He started down the hall, leaving Jillian no choice but to follow. When they reached a door, he stopped. "Did Limos explain the situation to you?"

"You mean that his Seal broke and he turned evil and nearly brought about the end of world? Yeah, I got the CliffsNotes."

Thanatos arched a tawny brow. "In that case, thank you for doing this, human. I doubt many would. But I was talking about his condition."

"She said he was hurting himself."

"Something like that." His mouth formed a grim line. "I don't know how he'll react to you, but don't expect the man you once knew." He opened the door. "Scream if you need anything."

Scream. Great. That didn't sound reassuring at all. Still, she *knew* Reseph. She wouldn't let these people frighten her. She was strong. She wouldn't fall apart.

She stepped inside the bedroom.

And promptly fell apart.

Twenty-three

~

"Oh, Reseph," Jillian whispered. "What have they done to you?" Thanatos and Limos had warned her, but this went beyond anything she could have imagined.

Reseph sat with his back against the wall, his body a mass of wounds in various stages of healing. His arms were wrapped around his bent knees, his head hung loosely on his shoulders, his hair obscured his face. Wearing nothing but sweatshorts, he rocked back and forth, soft moans breaking from his chest.

From his ankles, seeming to come directly from his skin, were thick, ivory chains that attached to the wall like a root system. They were long, giving him the freedom to move around the room and bathroom, but not long enough to go through the door.

"Reseph?" All of her apprehension fled, and she rushed to him, fell to her knees at his side. "Hey, it's me. It's Jillian."

When he didn't respond, just kept rocking, she very slowly reached out to brush his hair back. She fought a gasp at the sight of his blackened eyes and deeply gouged cheeks. Dear God, it looked like he'd clawed at himself.

"Reseph." This time she spoke louder, with more force, and he jerked.

In a series of choppy motions, Reseph lifted his head and fixed his glassy gaze on hers. For a few agonizing heartbeats, Jillian wasn't sure he recognized her.

"Jillian?" His voice was gravelly and raw. "You look like my Jillian."

My Jillian. The words brought fresh emotion to the surface, and she had to swallow before she could speak. "It's me. I'm here."

His hand shook as he reached for her, but an inch from her face, he stopped.

"Go ahead," she whispered. "I'm real."

His fingertip brushed her cheek, and then his palm, and then, so suddenly she gasped, he threw his arms around her and hauled her against him.

"I can't believe it," he rasped into her ear. "Can't. Oh, fuck. How long? Jillian, how long has it been?"

"A few days."

"No, can't be. Months, it's been months."

How horrible must his torment have been to make him think he'd been stuck in this room for months? "It doesn't matter. I'm here now."

He pulled back just enough to kiss her, and yes, it had felt like months. "I've missed you. I've been...I've been..."

"I know." She traced his lower lip with the pad of

her finger, skimming lightly over a freshly healed cut. "When's the last time you ate?"

He frowned. "Dinner. That night with you."

"You haven't eaten in over a week? Shit. Okay, hold on." She started to stand, but he gripped her wrist.

"Don't...don't leave me." His plea skinned her alive.

"I won't be out of your sight."

He didn't look convinced, but he nodded. She hurried to the door and shouted for Limos, who came running.

"You okay?"

"I need food and something to drink. I think I can get him to eat."

Limos's raven brows shot up. "Seriously? You got it. One sec."

Jillian went back to Reseph, who took her hand the moment she was within reach. "I'm sorry you have to see me like this." He looked down at himself. "I should shower."

"Let me help you."

For once, he didn't make a joke of it with something suggestive, which only emphasized how serious this situation was.

"You don't have to help." Sluggishly, he pushed to his feet. "But...could you stay in the bathroom with me?"

"Of course. But I'm not going anywhere, okay?"

He nodded and moved to the bathroom, wobbly at first, but his strength returned with every step. His body had been terribly abused, but its grace and power had in no way been diminished. She sat on the toilet while he showered and brushed his teeth, the infernal chains clanking with every movement.

There was a light tap on the door. "That's the food.

I'll get it." When she opened the door, Ares stood there with a tray. There were three sandwiches piled high with meat and cheese, two plates of cake, and two bottles of water.

, "See if you can get him to drink all of the water. There's a sedative in it. It won't make him go to sleep, but it should help him relax."

"Thanks."

"Also, fair warning. The sedative might have a mild aphrodisiac effect."

"Aphrodisiac?"

"Thanks to our mother's side of the family, when we have side-effects, they're usually of a sexual nature."

Huh. Well, if someone had to have a side-effect from a medication, she supposed arousal would be better than dry mouth, nausea, stroke, or heart attack.

She thanked Ares again, but just as it occurred to her to ask why their mother's side would influence medical side-effects, he walked away. Well, she could ask later.

When she turned around, Reseph was sitting in the corner, naked, his back to the wall.

"I just realized you must have cut my hair when you found me." His gaze was downcast, his face partially concealed by said hair.

"It was too tangled to brush," she explained, hoping he wasn't upset that she'd taken scissors to his long mane before he'd thawed from his snowbank ordeal. "I'm sorry."

He looked up, smiling a little. "I like it. Kind of cuts away some of ... what I was."

Whew. "We don't need to sit on the floor," she said. "There's a perfectly good bed."

He eyed it sadly. "I don't belong there." His gaze fell to the floor again. "I belong in hell, Jillian."

"Don't say that." She crossed the room and sank to her knees next to him. "From what I understand, you aren't responsible for the things that happened."

"Pestilence is part of me," he rasped. "Even now, I can feel his ugliness. I felt it at your farm, but I didn't know what it was." He shuddered, and she took his hand as if that one lame gesture could fix everything. "It's . . . it's like an abscess on my soul."

Her throat squeezed closed, clogged with emotion. "I'm so sorry. I can't even imagine how that must feel." She pulled the tray closer. "Please eat. It might not help your soul, but it'll help your stomach."

He looked at the food as if it were poison. "I can't."

"If your stomach's upset, try some water."

"Can't, Jillian."

"You don't think you don't deserve it, do you?" Her heart broke wide open. "Don't punish yourself like this. Please, Reseph. Do it for me." When he made no move for the tray, she unscrewed the cap from one of the bottles and put it to his lips. "Please. I hate seeing you like this."

Closing his eyes, he whispered, "For you, love. For you."

Jillian had changed Reseph's life. First, she'd given him sanctuary and showed him that it wasn't necessary to fill every moment with people and parties. For the first time in five thousand years, he'd been content. Happy. And now she was giving him a distraction from the prison inside his head. He didn't deserve her. He didn't deserve any of this—water, food, a room in Ares's house, kindness—not after all the things he'd done.

Hell, if his siblings and their mates wanted to string him up and torture the everliving fuck out of him for years on end, he'd deserve it. He certainly wouldn't fight it. Instead, they were trying to help him. He couldn't believe they'd even brought Jillian.

Jillian, who didn't belong with the likes of him. But he was just selfish enough to be glad she was here, coaxing him to eat and talking to him in a low, soothing voice as she told him about things back at home. When his mind would suddenly jump back into his horrific deeds, she knew, and she'd tap his cheek and force him back to the present.

"You're done with the first sandwich. Faster than I expected."

He glanced down at the crumbs on the plate. "It isn't your chili," he said, "but it's not bad. Ares has always had good cooks on staff."

"You're saying you miss my chili," she teased.

"Yeah." He missed her chili, her house . . . he missed *her*.

Holy shit, he was pathetic, wasn't he? He'd fallen for her so hard. His brothers and sister must be laughing their asses off at him after all his blustering about how he'd never fall in love or even limit himself to one female. But he wanted Jillian and only Jillian. That fact had been made real clear when Than and Ares had tried bringing in a few of his regular bedmates in an attempt to entice him out of what they had termed his "delirium."

The females had distracted him, all right, but only long enough for him to kick them out. Their touch had actually disgusted him and made him invoke Jillian's name like a ward or some shit.

Yep, his sibs had to be choking on their laughter.

"How are you feeling?" Jillian looked at him like a doctor might look at a patient, and he wondered if he looked as beat up as he felt. He had no idea. He'd broken all of the mirrors in the bedroom and bathroom a while ago.

"Better," he said. "But I think it's more because of you than because of the food." He paused. "Thank you for coming. Most people wouldn't."

"Then most people are assholes." She said it so forcefully that he smiled.

"I wouldn't dare argue with you when you're riled."

"Very wise, Horseman." She shook her head, making her dark hair sweep against her jaw. He'd missed the feel of her silky bob on his skin, and he reached out to rub a stray lock between his thumb and forefinger. "I'm still kind of reeling about the Horseman thing."

"You're taking it well," he said, pride swelling in his chest. His Jillian was strong, but he'd known that. "Humans tend to have bad reactions. Usually the human-realm dwellers do, too."

"Human-realm dwellers?"

He shrugged. "Vampires, werewolves, some shape-shifters. Anyone who resides exclusively in the human world instead of in Sheoul. They're usually a little more grounded in the human world than the demon one."

"Vampires and werewolves are real?" She blinked. "Guess it makes sense if demons and Horsemen exist, but wow. It's crazy finding out that legends are real. You said people in the human realm have bad reactions to finding out Horsemen exist, but what about the beings in Sheoul?"

"Demons are pretty much raised on stories about us. You know, 'Be a good demonling and eat your veggies, and someday the Horsemen might want you at their sides during the Apocalypse.' "

"Wow." Her hands, so capable on the farm, fluttered awkwardly up to the collar of her button-up Henley. God, he hated seeing her so out of her element. "So all those... females... outside? Where do they come from?"

"There are females outside?"

"A lot. I didn't count, but it wouldn't be a stretch to say there's easily a hundred."

Oh, damn. He'd give anything for Jillian not to have seen that.

"Yeah," he croaked. "To underworlders, my siblings and I are like movie stars. We have groupies. They even classify themselves according to which Horseman they like best. Ares has War Mongers. Than has Reapers. Limos never really had any who were open about it, though, since she was engaged to Satan, and no one wanted to fuck with her. Literally."

"Satan?" Jillian's voice was strangled. He'd have smiled if this whole thing wasn't so screwed up.

"The very demon."

"I'm glad I'm sitting," she muttered. "What about you? What are your groupies called?"

Aw, shit, he should have seen that question coming, and the last thing he wanted to do was hurt Jillian.

"Hey." Her soft voice, so full of strength, humbled him. "You can tell me. You can tell me anything."

How had he been lucky enough to have *her* be the one to find him in a snowbank? He owed her so much, and that included the truth.

"Reseph's Riders," he said miserably. "My groupies are called Reseph's Riders." He hung his head, staring into his lap, and he was suddenly ashamed of his entire life. "Jillian, I was a total whore."

"When your Seal was broken?" She sounded hopeful, as if there would be a way to forgive that.

He laughed, but it wasn't a happy laugh. "Yeah, then too. Only it was...different." He shuddered and tried to drag himself out of the pit of those particular sick and twisted memories.

"Reseph? It's okay. Take a breath."

Shit, he was hyperventilating.

"Listen to me." She took his hands and squeezed hard. "It doesn't matter what you were like before. I didn't know that man. The one I know didn't so much as look at other women." She gave him a sultry smile. "And besides, after everything we've done, I guess I can call myself a Reseph Rider, too."

He was on her so fast he didn't realize he'd moved until he was on top of her, kissing her with everything he had. She kissed him back, wrapping her arms around his neck and bringing her legs up to cradle his hips.

"You're so perfect," he said, as he kissed a trail along her jaw. "How did I not find you before?"

"I guess you weren't looking."

No, he wasn't. "I promise you, Jillian, I'll never look again."

Twenty-four

Jillian shouldn't be turned on. She knew it, and yet, Reseph's touch set her on fire so easily. Even now, despite the horror she knew he'd inflicted upon so many, including himself, she wanted him. Right here on the floor of a strange house full of strange people and strange creatures.

Reseph tore at her clothes with an urgency that bordered on desperate. She was right there with him, and when he entered her, it was as if all was right with the world. She clutched at his shoulders with matching desperation, almost terrified that if she didn't have hold of him, he'd disappear from her life again.

Lunging, he thrust into her urgently, slamming into her as if his life depended on the coming orgasm. She clung tighter, letting him take what he needed. It wasn't much of a sacrifice, not when her own fervor mounted with every wild pump of his hips.

Reseph churned on top of her, his hands tangled in her

hair, his teeth closing on the curve between her neck and shoulder. Pleasure roared in furious and fast, shattering her, and she bit down on her hand to muffle her cries of ultimate bliss. She felt him swell inside her, and then he climaxed in a frenzied rush, his hot flow filling her, her core milking it all.

As they came down, he shuddered and sank against her, shifting to the side so he wouldn't squash her.

"Fuck," he breathed. "I'm sorry. Are you okay?"

"More than." And then she sucked in a sharp breath. "Oh, damn. Condom."

He nuzzled her shoulder. "S'okay. I can't catch or transmit disease. And I take an herb to prevent pregnancy—" He broke off. "Wait...I stopped taking it when my Seal broke—" He broke off again, but this time with a strangled rush of air. "Jillian. Oh, God, Jillian. I...I..."

"Shh." She pushed up on one elbow and stroked his cheek with the backs of her fingers—fingers that shook, because damn, what if what they'd just done had gotten her pregnant? "It's okay. You need to get some rest."

He nodded and stretched out next to her, his lids droopy. The water Ares had brought seemed to finally be working. The sedative part of it, anyway. The sexual side-effect seemed to have already kicked in.

"Jillian?" His voice was groggy, almost inaudible.

"Yeah?"

"I love you. No matter what happens, remember that." Soft snores drifted to her within two heartbeats, and she settled against him, fighting a losing battle with her own exhaustion. She had so many questions and needed so many answers, but right now she needed rest more.

Most of all, she needed Reseph.

Jillian woke, stiff and sore, partly from sleeping on the hard floor and partly from Reseph's lovemaking. Not that she was complaining, but it made trying to quietly get dressed a little more difficult when she kept hissing at the stabs of pain. Her ribs, shoulders, and hip bones had never fully recovered from the demon attack, and sometimes she had to eat ibuprofen like candy. Today would be one of those days.

Reseph was sleeping peacefully, so she snuck out of the bedroom and wasn't surprised to find that the massive living room was packed. In addition to Ares, Thanatos, Limos, and Cara, there was also a woman holding a baby, who she assumed were Thanatos's wife and child, given how he was hovering. At their feet was a smaller version of the hellhound that lay on the couch over Cara's lap.

And at the entrance to the kitchen was a huge being with ram-like horns. What in the world was it?

"It's not polite to stare," Limos said.

Jillian jumped. "I'm sorry. I just..."

Limos punched her in the shoulder, startling her again. "I'm kidding! Everyone stares at Ramreels." Said Ramreel gave Limos the finger, and she returned the gesture. "You love me and you know it," she called to it, and the Ramreel snorted.

Seriously, Jillian felt like she was in the Twilight Zone. Had she dreamed up a million scenarios of what she thought life for the Four Horsemen and demons would be like...this would not have been one of them.

Ares moved over to them. "How is Reseph?"

"I'm curious about that as well." A beautiful, raven-haired

woman with matching wings appeared from out of nowhere, and Jillian damned near screamed.

"That's Harvester," Thanatos explained. "Fallen angel."

"I'm really not in Kansas anymore," Jillian breathed.

"Well?" Harvester said. "My time and my patience are in short supply."

Adrenaline was still skittering through Jillian's body after being scared half to death, and before she could consider how she should speak to a fallen angel, she blurted, "Is common courtesy also in short supply?"

Limos barked out a laugh. "Oh my God, I love this human."

"Sorry," Jillian said, hoping the fallen angel wouldn't zap her with lightning or something, "but Reseph is miserable, and my nerves are a little frayed. I'm worried about him. I got him to eat and drink, and to clean up. He's sleeping now, but he's just so...not right."

A sudden roar pierced the air, and instantly, they all tore off toward Reseph's bedroom. Jillian got there first. Reseph was tugging at his hair, throwing himself against the wall.

"Reseph!" She ran to him, and although he quieted the moment she gripped his wrist, he still bashed his head into the wall. "Please, Reseph. You've got to stop."

He ignored her, and behind him cracks spiderwebbed up the wall, joining the already existing faults. Plaster fell in small chunks, coating them both in white dust.

"Do something!" She wrenched around to the Horsemen and the fallen angel, desperate for this to stop. "Please. There's got to be something you can do."

"That's why we brought you," Ares said. "We're out of ideas."

"You could take him back to Sheoul-gra," Harvester suggested, with enough relish that Jillian realized the angel was not fond of Reseph. "It won't make him better, but at least you don't have to watch his misery."

"That was so helpful," Thanatos said dryly.

Harvester's cold smile dropped the temperature in the room. "I live to serve."

"You hate him," Limos said. "Why are you even here?"

"It's my job to be here."

Ares swung around to the fallen angel. "Yeah, here's the thing. Your job is to watch over us. You can't do that effectively if you hate one of us. So maybe I go to your boss and have you fired."

Harvester hissed, her huge fangs glinting, and Jillian pressed closer to Reseph. "You're threatening me?"

"It's not a threat. It's a promise." Ares's voice was calm, reminding Jillian of Reseph when he'd been dealing with those jerks in the bar parking lot. If Ares was anything like his brother, that fallen angel had better watch out. "You know me well enough to know I do what I have to do to win a battle. This is a battle. Reseph is fighting for his sanity. If you can't help, you can go."

"Did you make the same demands of Reaver?" Harvester asked. "Help or go?"

Ares's hands fisted at his sides, and Jillian braced for a fight that would, no doubt, make a mockery of the fight in the parking lot. "Reaver tried to help by erasing Reseph's memory."

"Then maybe he can do it again," Harvester said with an arrogant huff.

"No!" Jillian's heart squeezed painfully at the thought

of Reseph losing himself again. "There's got to be something you can do. Please. I'll do anything."

For a long time, Harvester stared at her. Finally, she got a wicked gleam in her eye. "There is something I can do, but it'll require a sacrifice from you."

Thanatos scowled. "What kind of sacrifice? And why didn't you say something sooner?"

"Because what I need can't come from any of you."

Jillian came to her feet, both hope and fear pinging through her. Reseph moaned, but at least he'd stopped banging his head against the wall. "What is it you need?"

"Your mind." Harvester smiled. "I need your mind."

"Explain," Ares barked, and Jillian jumped again. The guy had missed his calling as a drill sergeant.

"I can use Jillian's mind to repair Reseph's. It won't be a total fix, but I can essentially take a piece of Jillian's mind from her and give it to Reseph. Her mind is uncluttered by the kind of horrors in Reseph's head. Essentially, he'll have the ability to not think about everything Pestilence did if he doesn't want to. He'll still be able to access the memories, but at least he won't be a blubbering puddle of insanity."

"What about me?" Jillian swallowed. "Will I lose any of my memories?" Losing the airport attack might not be a bad thing.

As if he knew they were talking about him, Reseph threw himself against the wall with a hoarse cry. Before Jillian could do anything, Thanatos tackled his brother, restraining him the best he could, but Reseph was strong, and he only struggled harder.

Sickened, her stomach churning, Jillian addressed Harvester impatiently. "Well?"

"You won't lose any memories," Harvester said.

Limos folded her arms over her chest and voiced what Jillian was thinking. "Then what's the catch? There's always a catch."

"Of course there is." Harvester's wings flared, stirring the air. "Nothing comes without a price."

"Especially not when you're buying from evil," Thanatos muttered.

Harvester rolled her eyes. "Pestilence is still inside Reseph, and he's getting off on Reseph's memories. He likes to relive all his cruelty, and doing so will chip away at the bond I'll use to attach your mind to Reseph's. So the price, Jillian, is that you and Reseph will have to be connected for life. At least once a year, you must reestablish your connection." At what must have been Jillian's confused expression, Harvester sighed. "Sex. You will have to screw your little brains out. If you don't, his memories will become yours, and you'll go mad and die."

Jillian blushed fiercely at the mention of sex in front of all these people. Heat seared her cheeks, followed by a sudden chill. "Die?"

"Die." Harvester glanced at Reseph and sneered. "You'll have to trust him to come to you once a year."

"Fuck." Ares scrubbed his hand over his face. "Jillian, we'll swear to drag him to you if needed."

Drag him? Why would they have to drag him? "I don't understand."

"He's not the most . . . reliable . . . person on the planet." Limos's gaze was once again brimming with sympathy. "Don't get me wrong, he was a good guy before his Seal broke. But he didn't keep schedules or sit down for more than two seconds, you know?"

Yeah, Jillian did, and her stomach clenched. She'd seen

the signs on her farm, the way he'd prowl around as if he were caged, the way he'd feel the need to get out of the confines of the house, his cavalier attitude about relationships and sex. She'd believed he could change, had convinced herself that when he said he wanted a life with her, he could put his restlessness aside.

But could anyone change what they'd been for five thousand years?

"Wait," she said, thinking about something Limos had told her at the house. "You said Reseph has never fallen in love before me."

Limos nodded. "That's why this could work. Were-leopards *can* change their spots."

Were-leopards? Don't ask. Jillian turned to Harvester. "What will happen to Reseph if I die?"

"He'll return to what he is now." Harvester cocked an eyebrow. "Do you agree?"

She looked over at Reseph, who was lying on the floor, motionless. Thanatos had released him, but the big Horseman stood nearby, ready to restrain Reseph again. What a horrible existence for all of them. How long could they continue like this? Centuries, she supposed.

She turned back to Harvester. "Let's do it."

"Humans surprise me sometimes," Harvester murmured. "Go to him."

"No, Jillian." Reseph's voice, sounding as if it had been dragged right out of hell, had them all turning to him. "Don't do it."

"Reseph—"

A godawful snarl shook the air in the room, and then Reseph was on his feet, his eyes blazing with little red sparks. "Let me show you what you'd be sacrificing for."

Twenty-five

"Reseph?" Shock flooded Jillian's face. Reseph's first instinct was to take her in his arms and soothe her, apologize, make everything better.

But he was going to do the exact opposite. She would not sacrifice *anything* for him.

She moved toward him, but he backed up, knowing that if she touched him, it would be Game Over. He didn't have the kind of strength she had, and he'd end up taking whatever comfort she offered.

"I can help you." She held out her hand, and his fingers twitched with the desire to reach out to her. "I want to help you."

"After what you went through at the hands of demons, I can't let you help another one."

"Help a demon?" She frowned. "I'm helping *you*."

"Ah . . . sorry, Jillian," Limos said sheepishly. "I forgot to mention that our father is an angel and our mother is a

sex demon. The latter is why all our side-effects and shit
are sexual in nature. Long story. I'll lend you the book."

Jillian's eyes went wide. "I...Oh my God, you're a...
demon?" Her hands flew to her belly, and he knew she
was remembering the attack that had put the scars there.

He remembered her attack, too. But...how? Yes, she'd
told him about it, but now that he had his memory back,
he could *see* it. There was a parking lot. He was standing
in shadows, the sound of jet engines all around them. A
woman was screaming. He was...laughing. Laughing as
two Soulshredders tortured her. She was...oh, dear God.
Jillian.

He blinked, hoping the visions would go away, but
they didn't. They got worse. He saw Jillian, screaming,
naked, torn up. Soulshredders were assaulting her, toying
with her. And he was standing in the shadows. Watching.
Touching himself.

He was the figure she'd sensed as she was being attacked.
He was the fucking evil bastard who had set the demons on
her, and for no other reason than the fact that she'd stumbled
upon what he and the demons had been doing to her
coworker. A coworker who had held a secret second job—
she'd been an Aegis Guardian, and Pestilence had made it a
personal mission to take out every one of the bastards.

Jillian's screams lashed at him. He'd been there, he'd witnessed her being attacked, and he'd laughed. He'd fucking
laughed. One of the demons had looked up at him, blood
dripping from its teeth. *You like, Master? You want her now?*

Master. Oh, holy shit, the demon in the barn had called
him Master. It hadn't been in his head. The thing had been
speaking to him as if it had known him...because it *had*.

Sweat broke out over his body. The demons had worked

Jillian over on his command, for his entertainment. Holy hell, he was directly responsible for Jillian's brutal attack. Reaver had to have known—it was too much of a coincidence that Reseph would have ended up in her care. Why would the angel have sent Reseph to be rescued by his own victim?

The screams turned to moans. Jillian's, his—they blended together.

"Reseph! Dammit, what's wrong with you?" Something struck his face hard enough to snap his head back. Limos.

He grabbed her. "Get Jillian out of here," he croaked.

"I'm not leaving." Jillian crossed her arms over her chest and squared her shoulders, digging in for a fight. Wasn't going to happen.

Shoving Limos aside, he dug in just as hard as Jillian. "I was there when you were attacked." His voice was hoarse, and his heart was pounding against his rib cage so hard the bones felt like they might crack. "I ordered it."

She shook her head. "You're confused, Reseph. You wouldn't have—"

"I was the man you saw standing in the shadows."

This time, she shook her head violently. "No. That man's eyes were red. The things I told you are getting jumbled up in your memories."

"You didn't tell me about how one of the Soulshredders put the tip of one claw under your left eye and let you think he was going to blind you. You begged him not to. Remember that? He was going to, but Pestilence—I— told him to do it last, because if you were blinded, you couldn't see the things they did to you."

Jillian lost all the color in her face. "No…you're…I must have talked in my sleep."

Reseph pressed on, relentless. "He dragged his claw

across your face, drawing blood all the way to your ear. He tore out your earring and shoved it in your mouth."

"Stop," Jillian whispered. "Harvester, we need to hurry…"

Dammit, she was still set on whatever bullshit Harvester had planned. Reseph swallowed his disgust. "Do you want me to go on? Do you want me to tell you that if the demons hadn't been interrupted, I'd have watched them——"

"Reseph!" Thanatos's voice was harsh. "That's enough."

"I'm not done." In a flash, he spun Jillian around and shoved her roughly against the wall, every cell in his body shriveling up at the devastation in her expression. "I would have fucked you, then gutted you, then fucked you again. You want a visual on that?" He steeled himself against the tears welling in her eyes. "Because I can get really detailed on how it would go down. Tell her, Harvester. Tell her what I did to you."

"I said *enough*!" Thanatos's furious roar accompanied a brutal slam of his fist into Reseph's shoulder. Well-deserved pain sliced down his arm as he was yanked away from Jillian and Harvester flashed out of the room. Reseph didn't fight. All he could do was watch Jillian flee, sobbing.

Jillian couldn't breathe. Couldn't think. Blindly, she stumbled into the great room, where Harvester stood, eyes averted, her slender body trembling as hard as Jillian's.

Cara caught Jillian's arm and led her to the sofa, but although Jillian's muscles had turned to rubber, her joints had frozen, and she couldn't sit. Couldn't do anything but stand there and choke on her own tears. That person in there, that wasn't Reseph. That wasn't the man she'd found in a snowdrift and nursed back to consciousness. That wasn't the man who made her laugh, love, and feel safe.

She'd been looking at a total stranger.

"My...God." She inhaled on a ragged sob, and finally, her knees went liquid and she sank onto the couch. Cara sat with her and handed her a tissue.

"Jillian?" Limos walked over. "Are you okay?"

Jillian rubbed her arms and tried desperately to stop crying. "The man I love was pretty much the most evil being to have ever walked the earth."

"We told you that," Limos said softly.

Yeah, they had. But Jillian hadn't listened. She'd convinced herself that things hadn't been as bad as everyone claimed. Or at least that Reseph—Pestilence—had been more of a figurehead or man behind the desk than an active participant. But he'd been right there in the front, leading the charge.

"He was there when I was attacked." His eyes...God, his eyes. They haunted her dreams, always growing brighter with the sound of his evil laughter. "He's the *reason* I was attacked."

"It wasn't him, Jillian."

She knew that, but hearing him describe the things that had happened in the parking lot had been crushing. She'd known he'd been evil, but only when he'd gone into horrific detail while showing no emotion had it truly sunk in.

Jillian hugged herself, because if she didn't she'd come apart. "You don't sound convinced."

Limos sank down on the arm of the couch as though her legs had given out. "Yeah. I know. Deep inside, I know Reseph wasn't responsible for what Pestilence did."

"But?"

"But sometimes when I look at Reseph, I don't remember him as the brother who used to pester me to go to movies with him or who used to make us all decorate for Christmas and dress up for Halloween. I look at him and see the son of a bitch who blackmailed me, ruined my wedding day, kidnapped Cara, stole my husband's soul, and tried to kill my baby nephew." Limos was staring at her feet, her shoulders slumped, and it occurred to Jillian that what Limos and her brothers had gone through was far worse than anything Jillian had endured.

"I'm so sorry," she whispered. "It must have been hard to see him change like that."

Limos swallowed. "It felt like I'd lost a limb. And it caused a lot of problems between me and my brothers. Thanatos and Ares were always fighting, and I was keeping secrets, and all around us the world was breaking apart." She looked up. "Do you want me to take away your memories? I can't go all the way back to your time with Reseph at your cabin, but I can get rid of your time in Greece."

The discussion between Limos and Thanatos on the day they'd taken Reseph away came back to Jillian. "I thought you told your husband you wouldn't do that."

"I think he'd understand."

The days and nights Jillian had spent with Reseph replayed like a movie in her head, making this all so much worse. She'd been terrified to find out who he was, afraid he wouldn't be the man she'd fallen in love with. Turned out she had been worried for a damned good reason, because what Reseph was couldn't have been any worse.

She felt so hollow, as if her chest had been scooped out and her heart trampled. It was so tempting to take Limos up on her offer, to be rid of the pain of knowing who Reseph truly was and what he'd done. But she'd been miserable not knowing, too. The mystery of where his brothers and sister had taken him, the worry about him, had eaten her alive.

"Thank you, Limos, but no," Jillian murmured, wondering if she'd regret this decision. "The whole thing just...sucks."

"It does." Limos stood. "Let me take you home."

"No." Jillian dashed the tears from her eyes and turned to the fallen angel. "Harvester, let's do the ritual."

Harvester blinked. "After what he's done, you still want to help him? Why?"

Jillian flushed with sudden, white-hot anger. She'd been helpless in that parking lot, but this was something she could do to fight back.

"Because Pestilence is a fucking monster," she said, "and if I can do something to keep him from coming back, I'll do it."

Limos took Jillian by the hand and pulled her to her feet. "You're awesome."

"Indeed." Harvester murmured so quietly Jillian wasn't sure she spoke at all.

They started toward the bedroom, but Jillian pulled to a sudden halt. "Wait." She gazed out the window at the scores of demons roaming around. Demons Reseph had slept with. Demons who were waiting for him to come back. Screw that. Jillian wasn't going to help him get his mind back just so he could walk outside and have an orgy. "Can I ask a favor?"

"Shoot."

"Can you get rid of all those female demons outside?"

Limos grinned. "You got it. Smitey-smite-smite."

Wondering if Limos was going to *actually* smite them, Jillian and Harvester went into the bedroom, where

Reseph had regressed again and was bashing himself against the wall. And it *was* Reseph. Jillian feared she'd see Pestilence when she looked at him, but this was definitely not the evil being from the parking lot.

Harvester gestured to Reseph with a jerky wave of her hand. "Touch him."

Jillian kneeled in front of him, taking his face in her palms. He calmed instantly, although his eyes were wild and his teeth clenched against panting breaths.

Palming both Jillian's and Reseph's foreheads, Harvester began to chant in a strange, guttural language. Heat spiraled through Jillian from where Harvester was touching her, and her skin tingled. An intense vibration followed, and Reseph fell to the floor, unconscious.

"What happened?" Jillian reared back, but Harvester caught her.

"It's okay," Harvester assured her. "We're almost done." She scored her palm with her fang and jammed her hand to the center of Jillian's chest. A stinging, hot sensation dug into her skin, almost as if she were being branded.

"What," she gasped, "what are you doing?"

Harvester pulled away. "Finishing." For some reason, Harvester smiled, and it was an almost...sad...smile. As if she wasn't happy about what she'd done, but knew it was for the best. "Be well," she murmured. "Be well, and be...forgiving."

With that, Harvester spun around and fled the room, her wings flaring out as if she couldn't wait to take flight.

Jillian, for her part, couldn't have fled if she'd wanted to. Her muscles turned to gel, and before she knew it she was on the floor next to Reseph, and consciousness was... nonexistent.

Twenty-six

Harvester couldn't get out of Ares's house fast enough. She all but ran down the hall, knocked over Ares's servants in the great room, and slammed Reaver out of the way as she darted through the front door.

"Harvester!" Reaver's booming voice followed her as she hit the steps off the porch. "*Fallen!*"

She paused as the spark required to flash out of there skimmed over her skin. "What?" she snarled. She didn't even know why she'd answered. But, she thought, maybe it was because this would be the last time she saw him.

"What's going on in there?" Reaver strode over and stood imperiously before her.

"I just made sure Reseph and Jillian will be taken care of."

"Taken care of?"

"Fuck off, Reaver," she sighed. "I'm tired of your

constant needling. Just give me sixty seconds of peace. Can you do that?"

"*My* needling?"

A breeze spun up, bringing with it the fresh scent of the sea, the sand, the olive groves that dotted the island. It was the scent of freedom and life. She inhaled. Exhaled. Inhaled. Exhaled. She wanted to remember this forever.

"Harvester?" Reaver grabbed her shoulders and spun her around. "What is wrong with you?"

She wrenched free of his grasp. "Nothing. Leave me alone. Can't you take a hint? Or, you know, a direct command?"

Reaver stiffened at her not-so-veiled reference to his inability to follow orders, a character flaw that had gotten him booted from Heaven several years ago. "Something's going on. Does it have to do with the Horsemen?"

"No, it has nothing to do with them." She sniffed. "Which means you have no right to question me."

The sapphire glints in Reaver's eyes hardened into crystal shards. "You've done a lot of things to me that you had no right doing, so you might not want to go there."

She spread her wings, letting the breeze ruffle the sensitive tips. This would be the last time she felt the wind on her skin, in her hair. This would be the last time the sun touched her body. The dark vibration she'd felt in her soul over the last couple of days grew stronger, more urgent. She had to go. Punishment was always worse if someone had to be sent to drag you back.

She inhaled again, recording all the scents to memory. Including the spice that was uniquely Reaver. She eyed him, wondering if she had time to cash in on the day of pleasure he owed her. What a perfect way to go out—with a bang.

The vibration inside her grew more insistent, as if someone had stomped on the gas pedal and the engine responsible was revving at the edge of burnout.

So much for good-bye sex.

"Take care of them, Reaver. Keep their children safe." She wished she could have held Logan just once. Yeah, it was stupid of her to allow sentimentality to soften her now, when she needed to be tougher than ever, but it was just so unfair that the baby boy was here because of her, and she couldn't even rock the child in her arms for a moment.

Then again, she'd accomplished everything she'd set out to do. At this point, whatever happened was out of her hands.

She sparked the energy she needed to flash herself to Sheoul, but in the split second it took to open the connection, Reaver grabbed her again.

"Stop!" He got up in her face, his jaw set in stubborn determination. He had always been magnificent in his anger. "If you tell me what's going on—"

"What? You'll help?" She shoved him, maybe not with as much force as she could have, but with enough that he stumbled backward. "As if I'd believe that. And even if I did, I don't need it."

Reaver threw up his hands. "I give up. Go be bitter somewhere else." He spun on his heel and stalked toward the house.

The breeze kicked up again, and so did the dark vibration, this time to a paralyzing level. No, oh...*no*.

She wheeled around to face two massive angelgoths— fallen angels who had been mutated into skeletal monsters. At one time, they'd been like her...until they'd done something that got them punished with eternal ugliness, slavery, and misery.

Harvester would be *lucky* to merely share their fate. Hers was going to be so much worse.

"I was just going," she said, but they didn't allow her to flash. One sank his clawed hands into her skull, hooking her as if she were a fish. Pain and blood exploded, and all she could hear were her screams and the crunch of bone.

And then she was lifted by her head and flashed into the dark depths of hell.

Straight into Satan's living room.

An indescribable wave of terror shredded her insides as the king of all demons rose slowly from his throne of bones, his massive wings extending all the way to the thirty-foot ceiling. Punching up through his luxurious mane of black hair, two razor-sharp horns swiveled like tiny radar dishes. His clawlike fingernails scraped the arm of his chair, and another wave of terror slithered over her skin.

"Harvester." His voice was cold, like a long-dead corpse.

Trembling so hard her teeth rattled, Harvester doubled over in a deep bow. "Hello, Father."

Harvester's screams were still ringing in Reaver's ears as he blasted the remaining angelgoth's chest with a stream of what amounted to supercharged napalm. The evil bastard burst into flames and screeched loud enough to make Reaver's eardrums ache.

The creature somehow doused the flames and returned fire, snapping a long, whiplike rope of electricity. Reaver dove out of the way, hitting the ground in a roll and popping to his feet. He summoned an elemental sword and swung. The blade, capable of utilizing the natural elements around it, took on the power of the sea and bashed the evil being with the force of a tidal wave.

The angelgoth's body hurled backward and crashed into an ornamental pillar, shattering the thing into a million pieces and a shower of dust.

The sound of running footsteps joined the sound of the angelgoth's groans, and then Ares, Than, and Limos were there.

"What the fuck?" Ares said, but Reaver didn't give the warrior a chance to ask more questions. He grabbed the evil angelgoth by the throat and slammed him hard against another pillar.

"What did you do with Harvester?"

The thing smiled, its rotting lips pulling away from blackened teeth. "She . . . will . . . suffer."

"Explain." When the former angel said nothing, Reaver slammed him into the pillar again. "Where is she?"

The angelgoth shuddered, and in Reaver's fist, he turned to ash. A ripple of sensation skittered over the back of Reaver's neck, and he wheeled around to the source of the malevolent vibe.

The huge male fallen angel Reaver had seen with Gethel materialized, dressed from head to toe in black leather, his bald head glinting in the sun. His wings, black and leathery, were spread wide, with sharp bone tips at the ends. Pointedly ignoring Reaver, he strode toward the manor, his spiked boots thumping on the stone pavers.

Thanatos moved to intercept the newcomer. "Who the fuck are you?"

"Hello, Horseman. I'm Revenant." The male's icy smile would flash-freeze a human. "I'm your new Watcher."

Twenty-seven

Reseph came awake in a bed, and it took him a minute to realize he wasn't at Jillian's house, waking up to the sound of roosters crowing and goats bleating. Instead, the sea waves crashing on a beach were familiar noises.

Ares's Greek paradise.

He frowned. He'd been here for a while, hadn't he? But he'd been crazed, so why was he feeling so...good? So normal. What was going on? And where was Jillian? Had she been here, or had he hallucinated her?

He eased out of bed and touched the crescent-shaped scar on his neck to armor up, since he couldn't find any clothes. Despite the fact that he'd been suiting up in his armor for thousands of years, this time the cold metal felt strange against his skin after so long without it.

He slipped out of the room and found his brothers and sister outside with Reaver and a strange fallen angel.

"Who is this?" Everyone except the stranger watched him warily, as if he were a live grenade.

"Apparently," Ares said, "this is Harvester's replacement. Revenant."

Oh, fuck. "Did she quit?" After what Pestilence had done to her, he couldn't blame her.

The male moved forward. "She was fired."

"For what?" Reseph demanded. "Breaking Watcher rules?"

"Worse. Don't expect to see her again." Revenant looked Reseph up and down. "You look well for having lost your piddly little mind."

Reseph smiled. "You look well for someone who is going to lose his head in about two seconds."

Reaver stepped forward, placing himself between Reseph and the asshole. "Reseph, how are you feeling?"

All eyes focused on him, and yeah, this was uncomfortable. He had a lot of groveling to do now that he wasn't going mad with memories. And why was that, anyway?

"I feel . . . almost whole. Why am I not a drooling mess on the floor?"

Limos fiddled with the flower in her hair. "Harvester did some Sheoul voodoo thing and patched your mind with a piece of Jillian's. So now—"

"She *what*?" Reseph's chest tightened. It was all coming back now. He'd hurt Jillian badly, both as Pestilence, and then here, when he'd told her what he'd done. He'd been determined to keep her from sacrificing anything for him. "Is it permanent? Will it hurt her?"

"Yes to both, if you don't hold up your end of the bargain," Ares said, his no-nonsense, no-bullshit words cutting right through Reseph.

"My end of the bargain? I didn't agree to any bargain. Reverse it." Reseph's head snapped back and forth between the two Watchers. "Make it go away, dammit. I don't care if I'm back to being a head case. Fix this!"

· "No can do, Horseman," Revenant said. "Only Harvester can reverse it, and she's . . . gone."

Fear for Jillian sent Reseph's pulse—and temper—into orbit. "Get her back," Reseph snarled.

Revenant's pupils expanded, turning his eyes oily black. "I see that your Watchers have allowed you too many liberties." He lashed out with his fist, but instead of a taking a physical blow, Reseph was knocked backward by a searing snap of power.

Rage shattered Reseph's control, and he lunged at the same time that his siblings did, all of them going after the new Watcher, but Revenant flashed out of the way and materialized behind them.

"How dare you strike out for so minor an offense." Reaver's wings flared, a sign of his fury. "And what weapon did you use against him?"

Revenant's smirk reeked of self-satisfaction. "Watcher upgrade, you heavenly puke. Maybe if you checked in with your bosses, you'd know about it." His smirk grew wider as he took in Reseph and his siblings, one by one. "It's been decided that we needed a stronger form of punishment to keep you in line. That was just a taste. If I'd wanted, I could have blown you up inside that armor and poured you out like a liquid. You will not harm one of us again."

So this *was* about Harvester. Reseph felt ill. "Get out of here," he growled. "Get the fuck out of my sight."

"You don't give the orders, Horseman. Seems you haven't learned your lesson." He raised his hand, but before he could lash out again, Reaver hit him like a train, and the two angels turned into a whirlwind of fists, wings, and blood.

Then the two were gone, and Reseph was left looking at an empty space.

"Fuck," he breathed.

"I hate the new guy," Limos said. "Wasn't fond of Harvester, but compared to Revenant, she was awesome-sauce."

"It's my fault." Reseph turned to his siblings, ready to get this over with. "Whatever she's being punished for, it has to be because of Pestilence." He reached for his armor scar to remove his shielding before remembering he was naked underneath the metal plates. While he normally didn't give a fuck who saw him nude, he didn't want the extreme vulnerability right now. Not when he was facing the people he'd done so much damage to. "Look, I don't even know where to start."

"Then maybe it's best that you don't start at all," Thanatos said. "I don't want to hear it."

"Than!" Limos dropped her own armor and jammed her hands on her sundress-draped hips. "You were the one who held on the longest, insisting that Reseph wasn't responsible for Pestilence's actions."

"That was before Pestilence tried to kill my wife and son." Nothing Than said was unfair, nor was it unexpected. In many ways, being Death fit him, because while Than tended to hang onto loyalty for a long time, when he was finally done with someone, he was *done*. Reseph was dead to Than. The brotherly bond between them had been severed, and Reseph didn't know how long it would take to repair it, or if it even could be repaired.

"I'm sorry." Reseph looked out over the olive groves,

remembering how much he'd hated how quiet they were. Now he'd give anything to walk among the gnarled trees with Jillian, the only person who had ever given him a moment's peace. "I know it doesn't help. I was there, inside this body, but I wasn't strong enough to defeat Pestilence. I'll never forgive myself."

"I know you tried." Limos dragged her big toe through the sand. "You came through sometimes. Pestilence played it off like he'd been tricking me, but he wasn't, was he? It was you."

"Yeah," he croaked. Man, he'd tried. He'd begged his sister to kill him, had even told her where to find Deliverance. And when Thanatos had driven the blade through his heart, he'd thanked his brother.

Ares came forward. "We know it wasn't you, bro. But Pestilence fucked with us hard. I don't need to tell you that. And Reaver and Harvester both told us he could come back."

Reseph's head snapped up. He remembered Harvester saying something about that, but he'd been so out of his mind that it hadn't truly registered. "How? My Seal—"

"It's whole. It won't break again. Not until the biblical Apocalypse. Which, by the way, is supposed to be ushered in by our father. We discovered evidence that suggests he'll be the one to break our Seals next time."

Whoa. Okay, he hadn't seen that one coming. He'd have to ask more about that later. Right now he was more concerned about his demon half.

"So how could Pestilence come back? You drove Deliverance through his heart."

Thanatos shook his head. "Deliverance wasn't the right blade to kill Pestilence. We needed Wormwood."

Wormwood...Reseph cursed. How could he have forgotten? Pestilence had been desperate to get his hands on that blade, had gone through Aegis headquarters like a blender, killing, torturing, but he'd left empty-handed.

"I—Pestilence—eventually got it from Gethel. She tricked The Aegis into giving it to her. Pestilence knew it was the only blade that could kill him."

Than nodded. "Deliverance imprisoned Pestilence, but he's still part of you. He might have been banished, but the barrier is weaker than before. Reaver said it's like gluing a ceramic vase back together. The vase may still hold water, but it'll never be as strong as it was, and it could leak. Your container is cracked, and Pestilence can seep through." Thanatos scrubbed his hand over his face. "It gets worse. While you were pulping yourself on the bedroom walls, the rest of us did some recon in Sheoul. Lucifer, Gethel, Lilith, and about a dozen other bigshots are planning to do whatever it takes to bring Pestilence back, including hurting our families. And according to Arik and Kynan, Gethel has been working with The Aegis on some super anti-Horseman weapon or some shit. We think the sudden disappearance of hundreds of hellhounds might have something to do with it."

Fuck, this was bad. "Reaver should have left me in Sheoul. He should have left me to suffer."

Closing his eyes, he sought out the memories that tortured him. It wasn't right that he wasn't suffering. Oh, he was miserable, knowing his relationship with his brothers and sister and their families was likely damaged beyond repair, and he was sick at the knowledge of what he'd done to the world and its inhabitants.

But for some reason, the memories felt distant, fuzzy,

like he was watching a film instead of being an active participant in them.

Peeling his lids open, he turned to Limos. "Where's Jillian?"

"She was unconscious after the mind-meld thingie. I took her home and put her in bed. I left a book of our history and our phone numbers on the bedside table in case she ever needs anything."

"She was unconscious? Is she okay? I have to go to her."

"Reseph, wait—"

He didn't listen. All he could think about was Jillian.

Jillian woke up with a scream, heart racing, skin damp with sweat. Demons. She'd been surrounded by demons. Reseph, his eyes glowing, was laughing as claws dug into her flesh.

"Jillian!"

She screamed again as Reseph, fully armored and impossibly huge, burst into her bedroom, a sword in his gauntleted fist. He skidded to a stop short of the bed, but she scrambled backward on the mattress until her spine hit the headboard.

"Hey," he said softly. "It's me. Reseph. Not... Pestilence." The sword in his hand disappeared, but it hardly mattered; he himself was a weapon.

She had no idea what to say or do. So much had happened in the last few hours and so many conflicting emotions were coursing through her body. The one thing she was certain of was that Reseph was still the most handsome man she'd ever seen, and in full, shiny armor, he was like a knight from a fairy tale.

Or, as Pestilence, he was the fable's monster.

Reseph inched toward her. "I was worried about you. Are you okay?"

"I don't know." She came to her feet on the side of the bed opposite Reseph. She needed a barrier between them, even if it was something as ineffective as a mattress.

Reseph didn't take those ancient, knowing eyes off her. "You shouldn't have done what you did. Especially after I told you the truth about your attack."

Irrational anger sparked at his utter lack of gratitude. "That's one hell of a way to thank me."

"Dammit, Jillian." His deep voice went even deeper. "I should have had a say in it. You took the choice away from me."

"Because you would have chosen to suffer," she shot back. "That's stupid. And selfish."

"How is that selfish?"

Reseph tracked her as she paced the length of the bed, doing her best to gather her jumbled thoughts. Three men existed in that magnificent body: Pestilence, the Reseph she'd fallen for, and the Reseph who was a complete stranger. At this point, she didn't know any of them.

"It's selfish because everyone who loves you was suffering with you. Not to mention the fact that it was leaving the door open for Pestilence."

A guttural word fell from Reseph's lips. She didn't know the language, but she understood the sentiment. "I still don't like it. We're linked forever now. You know that, right?"

"Of course I know that."

"You knew, and you still chained yourself to me in some mysterious goddamned bond?" He cursed, and this time she understood the word very well. "Talk about being tied down."

She wheeled around so fast she banged her knee on the bedframe. "Ouch! Son of a bitch." Pain fueled the anger and hurt building in her chest. She was dealing with the stranger Reseph, wasn't she? *"That's* why you're upset? You don't want to be tied down? Oh my God, it's going to kill you to show up once a year and have to fuck me, isn't it?"

Maybe his siblings had been spot-on in their warnings about Reseph. What a fool she'd been.

Reseph had started toward her when she hit her knee, but now he stopped dead. "What?"

"Oh, no one told you the terms of the deal?" She strode up to him and poked him in the chest. Not that he probably felt it through the armor. "Yeah, that's right. Sex. Once a year. If it doesn't happen, I lose my mind and die, and you go back to being a drooling head case."

"No," he rasped. "Oh, no." The sheer horror in his expression was like a bullet between the eyes. Not only did the man she'd loved not want to be tied to her, but he didn't even want to have sex with her once a fucking year.

"You...you'll screw demons...things with hooves and horns and tails, but the thought of being with me is repulsive to you?" She shoved at his breastplate with as much strength as she could muster. He didn't budge an inch. "You *bastard!*"

"It's not that. God, Jillian, it's not that." He wrapped his hand around hers the way he had so many times, and her heart bled in remembrance. "Pestilence is my demon half, and he still lives. He could still come back, and I will *not* put you at risk."

"I'm calling bullshit on that excuse." She jerked out of his grip. "Don't you think he would have come back when those guys attacked us outside the bar? Or when we found the demon in the barn?"

"The demon in the barn was there because of me." He tapped his breastplate, and the noise sounded so hollow. "I put you in danger. Don't you get it?"

"No, I don't," she snapped. Her Reseph would want to be here to kill the demons. Not make up lame excuses to stay away. "What are you going to do between yearly visits, Reseph? Are you going to just hang out by yourself because you're afraid of hurting someone? You're seriously going to take an oath of celibacy?"

He closed his eyes, and she snorted. "You know what? Don't answer that." She stalked out of the bedroom and to the front door. "Get out." When he didn't move, she shook her head. "You're the lucky one in all of this. You have so many girlfriends that you won't have to explain to anyone why once a year you have to sleep with yet another one. But me? I'm thinking that anyone I'm with isn't going to understand why I have to fuck another guy—"

Reseph was on her in a flash, his eyes snapping blue fire and his teeth bared as he pushed her against the doorjamb. "*I will kill any male who touches you.*"

"Really?" Her voice was as flat as it was quiet. "You expect me to sit around and wait for those few minutes once a year when you show up? *If* you show up? Go to hell, Reseph. Go back to where you came from."

He blinked, and the murderous light snuffed out of his eyes. Very gently, he moved her aside to open the door, and then, without a word, he took off, disappearing into thin air when he hit the bottom of the porch.

Twenty-eight

Reseph gated himself to Ares's beach, where he stood, hands fisted, staring out at the sea as he tried to control his emotions. Cutting Jillian loose was the hardest thing he'd ever done. The thought of her being with another male gutted him, but she'd been right...how could he expect her to go the rest of her life without company while she waited for his yearly visit? And how was he going to survive those visits?

He heard Ares approach, and fuck; Reseph was not in the mood to talk, which was odd given how, pre-Pestilence, Reseph had never shut up.

"What happened with Jillian?" Ares's voice rumbled over the sound of the waves lapping at the beach.

"It's over."

"She couldn't handle it all?"

"Actually, I think maybe she could," Reseph murmured. "But I don't want her to have to."

"Ah." Ares picked up a shell and chucked it into the surf. "So how are you doing?"

"I'm fine."

"And I'm a fairy princess," Ares drawled.

The old Reseph would have shot a witty comeback at his brother, but that Reseph had been carefree and shallow, always sweeping bad shit under the rug. The male he was now would never do that again.

"Things would have been better for everyone if Deliverance had killed me."

Ares blew out a long breath. "Yes, they would have."

Ever the commander, Ares didn't mince words or try to placate with false sentiments. He called it like he saw it, something that had annoyed the old Reseph. Yep, the old Reseph had been all about keeping everyone happy and the party going.

"I've got to fix things."

"With who?" Ares crossed his arms over his chest. "With Jillian? With us? With the world? You can't fix what Pestilence broke."

"You're saying the damage he's done is irreparable?"

Ares's gaze pierced Reseph like a crossbow bolt. "Some of it. Probably most of it."

Reseph squeezed his eyes shut, so ashamed of everything he'd done. "What about the damage to my family? Is that irreparable?"

"We know it wasn't you who did those things to us."

Taking a deep, bracing breath, Reseph met Ares's midnight eyes. "But?"

Ares swore, and Reseph knew he wasn't going to like the answer. "But Pestilence could come back, and what will you do to stop him?"

"I won't let that happen," Reseph said fiercely, but Ares's doubt was as strong as Reseph's.

"Really? You let it happen before. You let him torture and nearly rape and kill Cara. You worked with Lilith and Lucifer and the most powerful demons in Sheoul in order to destroy us all. Where were you? Did you even try to stop him?" Ares slammed his palm into Reseph's shoulder. "Did you?"

Reseph couldn't fault Ares for anything he'd just said. Reseph had tried to rear up and take back possession of his body, but Pestilence had been far too powerful.

"Well?" Ares shouted. All around, hellhounds were closing in, sensing Ares's anger and preparing to rip Reseph to shreds.

"Do you honestly think I don't go over every minute in my head, trying to figure out what cracks I should have exploited? That I wonder what else I could have done to stop him? I tried, Ares."

"You didn't try hard enough!"

Anger at the situation, at himself, at Pestilence, all boiled over, and Reseph snarled. "I know that! And I hate myself for it."

"Dammit, Reseph." Ares rounded on him. "It isn't just that. You've never fought for anything. At the first sign of conflict or commitment or emotion, you check out. You've always taken the damned easy road, and it pisses me off."

"Easy? You think any of this is easy? I've changed, Ares."

"Yeah? You fell in love for the first time in your life, and when the time came to fight for Jillian, did you? Or did you take the easy path and let her go because you don't want to do the hard thing and control Pestilence?" Ares got in Reseph's face, so close their noses almost touched. "Or did you let her go because you're afraid to commit? Life's too good with millions of hot females out there to fuck, isn't it? How easy was it to walk away from the one female who has ever loved you enough to sacrifice a piece of her goddamned mind so you could turn around and go back to being the self-absorbed whore you always were? Do you care about Jillian at all?"

With a roar, Reseph slammed his fist into Ares's jaw. His brother wheeled backward, and before he could regain his balance, Reseph tackled him. They went down in a tangle of punches and snarls.

"I love her!" Reseph shouted.

Ares had about twenty pounds on Reseph, and he used his weight to pin Reseph to the ground. "And I love Cara, but that didn't matter to you when you tried to rape her!"

Oh…God. Reseph sucked in a harsh breath and sagged bonelessly into the sand. "Fuck. Ah…fuck, Ares. I'm sorry."

Ares shoved to his feet and jammed his hand through his hair over and over, swearing constantly. "Logically, we all know it wasn't you. But the wounds are deep. We get it. We love you. But we can't trust you."

Reseph's stomach plummeted. "What are you saying?"

"I'm saying we'll help you as best we can. But you need to go somewhere else. We can't risk Pestilence returning and hurting our families."

"He won't." But even as the words came, Reseph knew they were hollow. He wanted to believe he could control Pestilence, but the evidence said otherwise. He couldn't blame his siblings for being concerned, but he wondered if the old Reseph would have. Now that Reseph had found

Jillian, he understood how powerful the need to protect someone was. Even if that protection was from yourself. Ares was wrong about the easy path shit. There was nothing easy about staying away from Jillian.

Still, Ares's rejection stung. Bad. Even now, the hurt was welling up, threatening to overflow and morph into something that had been so familiar when his Seal was broken; horrific anger. Deep inside, Pestilence stirred.

Fuck.

"Reseph?"

"What?" His voice was hell-deep and warped. He had to get out of here before he proved Ares right and let Pestilence too close to the surface. But he'd use this rage, and he'd use it well.

"You need to level out, bro…"

Reseph ignored Ares and smiled as he opened a Harrowgate, because while he might not be able to repair the damage he'd caused to his family, he could take some measure of revenge for them.

It was time to give Pestilence a taste of his own medicine.

Twenty-nine

Underworld General Hospital, staffed by vampires, were-creatures, and demons, came to a screeching halt when Reseph entered through the ER doors with a werewolf cub in his arms.

Probably because three months ago, Pestilence had gone on a rampage inside the hospital, butchering hundreds of patients and employees before grabbing an ex-angel staff member to torture. His rampage was still evident in the cracked walls, smashed equipment, and the dented furniture.

Laughter clanged inside Reseph's skull; Pestilence's satisfaction at what he'd done. Reseph had been battling the bastard all day, engaging in an internal struggle to keep the demon from clawing his way too close to the surface. Most of the time, maintaining control wasn't difficult...the problems came when Reseph's temper surfaced. Pestilence provided an extra shot of adrenaline, more juice to fuel Reseph's strength—both physical and mental. Things Reseph would never have been capable of before, like torture, were now far too easily considered.

But for the first time, Reseph could see the mental container he'd been kept in while Pestilence had been in charge. Now Pestilence was imprisoned inside, and Reaver's assessment was accurate...the vessel was cracked, oozing Pestilence's essence. How the hell was Reseph supposed to repair it?

"You son of a bitch." Eidolon, head doctor and founder of UG, dropped the charts he'd been going over and came at Reseph like a bull, his eyes glowing with crimson fury. "How dare you set foot in my hospital."

Waves of both fear and hatred radiated off of every person in the emergency department. Reseph felt their stares like lashes on his skin. He recognized some of them as Pestilence's surviving victims, and there were far too many to count.

"I'm not here to cause trouble," Reseph said, cradling the squirming toddler against his chest. "This cub needs medical attention."

"What did you do to him?" Eidolon growled.

"I rescued him from a slave trader." And damn, that had felt good. Reseph had gone through Sheoul like a blade through butter, slaughtering dozens of demons who had served Pestilence. Taking out the slave trader, a Neethul who had been Pestilence's right hand, had been the most satisfying.

So far.

Since being relegated back to Sheoul after the Apocalypse had been averted, the Neethul, Silth, had gone back to his first love—slave trading. Reseph had found him beating a werewolf cub who had been sold into slavery by his own parents.

Reseph, who had never possessed a cruel streak, had almost welcomed the cold stir of Pestilence deep inside, because it had allowed him to toy with Silth for a while. He'd relished questioning him about plans to bring Pestilence back, but the demon hadn't known anything. No worries though, because Reseph had several more people to visit.

"Does he have a family?" Eidolon spoke through clenched teeth, his voice distorted with rage.

"His family sold him to the slaver in the first place."

Eidolon took the child, handling him carefully despite the anger that had the doctor visibly shaking. The demon would welcome the chance to get in just one punch if he could. Reseph might let him someday.

"We'll take care of him." Eidolon gestured toward the emergency department's Harrowgate. "Now get out."

Gladly. Reseph got his unwelcome ass out of there and gated himself to Sheoul, where his next self-appointed mission was waiting. He'd gotten as close as he could get to his target without going in on foot—a lot of demons restricted the use of Harrowgates near their homes. No one wanted a surprise attack.

"Conquest, out."

The tattoo on his arm writhed, turning to smoke before materializing as a white stallion next to him. Reseph didn't waste time in leaping onto the horse and riding across the surrounding rocky plains. Smoke rose up from the ground, and a variety of creatures skittered out of the way of the warhorse's hooves as Conquest galloped along a familiar trail deep in the exclusive Fangorg region.

Soon, a massive black mansion rose ominously out of the craggy side of a hill, the knotted trees surrounding it adding an extra layer of security. Those trees were carniverous, their sap running with acid that dissolved the flesh of anyone careless enough to touch the leaves or bark. The vines that crawled—literally—up the stone walls were just as dangerous, and remnants of their unlucky victims lay scattered on the ground, airy husks that blew around Conquest's hooves as Reseph pulled the stallion to a halt at the entrance. He got a kick out of Pestilence's frantic stirrings—this time, the demon wasn't eager to kill.

This time, the target meant something to Pestilence.

Aw, Pestilence actually *cared* about someone. Good. This was going to make revenge so much sweeter.

Reseph dismounted, fed Conquest a sugar cube, and patted him on the neck. "Pestilence didn't give you these, did he? I owe you a year's worth." Conquest pawed the ground, sensing Reseph's mounting anger. Time to play. "To me."

Conquest dissolved into a wisp of smoke and slid under Reseph's gauntlet to settle on his arm. With the horse firmly in place, Reseph stalked into the residence. The guards didn't stop him, although they stumbled all over themselves in confused chaos. Pestilence was supposed to be dead.

In a few minutes, the guards were going to *wish* their idol was dead.

The halls, decorated in the owner's own paintings and sketches, were quiet, but ahead, in the gym-sized room, the sounds of both misery and pleasure grew louder with every step.

Reseph shoved open the massive double doors and walked into a den of lust. Pestilence had played here often, and Reseph's mouth stung with bile. The whipping post had been a favorite, and so had the St. Andrew's cross, where he'd cuffed his sexual partners and used a variety of the sexual and torture toys hanging from every inch of wall space.

Some of his partners had been willing to let him do what he wanted...even if it meant their deaths. But beyond the blood-filled pool in which a dozen people were currently involved in an orgy, unwilling victims languished in cages. They could be purchased for use, but Pestilence had gotten them for free.

Yes, you should be terrified. But also honored that I chose you for my pleasure today. There are those who beg to feel pain and pleasure at my hands and at the tip of my cock. So scream, cry, plead for your life. But know that many of these people will look on in jealousy.

The memory of Pestilence's lecture to one of the victims boosted Reseph's resolve. Not that he'd been wavering about this. But it would be so much easier now.

As he strode across the room, all gazes latched onto him. Even those who had been on the verge of climax stopped to see what was going on. They'd know soon enough.

He was going to kill them all.

His target wasn't in the room, which meant she was probably in her private quarters. Unimpeded by her guards, he threw open the door and there she was, wearing only high heels and getting it on with a female Trillah and a male Ramreel.

Smiling, he drew his sword. "Hello, Mother. Did you miss me?"

Thirty

"My son." Lilith came smoothly, seductively, to her feet, and Reseph felt Pestilence purr. With a wave of her hand, she dismissed the two demons, both of whom gave Reseph a wide berth as they slunk away. "You were rumored to be dead. I've missed you."

No doubt she had. Pestilence had brought her notoriety and attention. "Cover yourself."

She narrowed her violet eyes, so like Limos's. "Who are you?"

"Mother, I'm hurt." He feigned a pout. "You don't recognize your own son?"

She hissed and stepped back so fast she wobbled on her blood-red stilettos.

"Reseph." She spat his name as if it were poison. "Where is Pestilence? I can sense him inside you."

Moving forward, he put pressure on Lilith, using his height and size to keep her on edge. Unlike Ares and

Than, Reseph had used his physical stature to intimidate others only a handful of times. This was the best of all of them, and he savored Lilith's discomfort.

"Thanatos drove Deliverance through Pestilence's fucking heart," he said. "He's trapped, and he's not coming back."

"Then why are you here?" She eyed his sword, and for the first time he saw a glimmer of fear in her eyes.

"I want to know who my father is."

She looked at him like he was daft. "Yenrieth. The name is in all the legends."

"I know that," he ground out. "But there is no Yenrieth serving in Heaven. So he's either dead or is fallen and took a new name. Which is it?"

"I have no idea. Why would I have kept track of him?"

"Maybe because he knocked you up."

She snorted. "So?"

"So what did he say when you told him he was going to be a father?"

It was a question he'd never thought to ask, because truthfully, he hadn't given a shit about the male who had sired him. Giving a shit meant dwelling on questions like this, and Reseph had been all about *not* dwelling. But his time as Pestilence and his relationship with Jillian had given him a new appreciation for family.

"Who the hell cares? I hid all of you from him anyway."

"*Hid* us? You gave us away," he growled.

"Except for Limos." She sighed dramatically. "And what a disappointment she turned out to be."

A burst of hatred went through him, but he forced himself to not give in to it. Yet. "So you know nothing of our father."

"Why does it matter? If he wanted you, he'd have come forward, and if he's dead, he's...dead."

"We don't believe he's dead. There's evidence that suggests he'll be the one to break our Seals in the biblical version of the Apocalypse."

Lilith's eyebrows shot up. "Really." She moved to a painting she had done herself, a gruesome depiction of an orgy, and shifted it aside to reveal a recess in the wall. She reached inside and withdrew a parchment. "I drew this picture of Yenrieth so I wouldn't forget a single detail. He was so beautiful. A perfect, sketchable specimen."

He snatched it from her and sidestepped when she tried to rub up against him. His own mother. Disgusting. Turning away, he looked down at the drawing. In an instant, all bodily functions came to a violent stop. His breath caught, his heart seized, and his synapses stopped firing. Holy hell.

"This...isn't possible." His voice was a trembly rasp.

Lilith plucked a jagged-edged dagger from the wall, the one she favored for genital mutilations. "He has the same wing-shaped mark on his inner thigh that you have. Verify it yourself, if you can find him."

He glanced at his reflection in the mirror behind Lilith's bed. Jesus, the resemblances were there, plain as day. "Why did you give us up?" He returned his gaze to his mother, ignoring Pestilence's hungry growls. "Why did you leave me with a woman who spent more time brushing her hair than she did with me?"

It was stupid to ask anything of Lilith, and he wasn't even sure why he was bothering. The shit had gone down five thousand years ago, and none of it mattered now.

"I gave you up to ensure your survival. I knew you'd be powerful someday, though I couldn't have predicted how powerful." She dragged the blade across the palm of her hand and studied the wet crimson streak that bloomed. "As for the human who raised you?" Lilith shrugged. "She kept you fed and clothed. Stop whining, you ungrateful brat."

"Fed and clothed? She fucking *abandoned* me for days on end while she was off fucking around. I nearly died in a fire because she left me alone. Clearly, your adoption screening process needs some tweaks."

She laughed, a cackling, grating sound that had him gnashing his teeth. "I despise you, Reseph. I'm looking forward to seeing Pestilence again."

Reseph lunged, slamming her against the wall with his forearm across her throat. "What do you know about Gethel's plans to bring him out?"

"Nothing."

Reseph increased the pressure on her neck. "Lie. Try again."

A strangled cough fell from her lush lips. "I know Harvester has been tortured for an item in her possession. Gethel and Lucifer want to expose you to it. They're certain it'll bring out Pestilence."

"Did they get it?"

"I don't know. I swear."

With a shove, Reseph pushed away from Lilith. Damn. It wasn't going to be easy locating either Gethel or Lucifer.

Lilith cleared her throat, gathering her composure before she gestured to the door with the tip of the knife. "Now, be a good boy and fetch one of the females in the cages. You can fuck her while I make her scream. Then we'll kill her together. It'll be like old times."

Pestilence writhed excitedly inside him. Disgusting

memories boiled up, turning Reseph's stomach, and he was done with this conversation.

"You. Are. Vile." In a smooth, fast arc, he brought his own blade down between Lilith's neck and shoulder.

Lilith shrieked as he cleaved through her body. That was the thing about succubi—they tended to be more fragile than other species of demons, and sure enough, he ended her pathetic life with another strike that took her head from her shoulders.

The infamous bitch was dead.

He didn't stop with Lilith. His rage had taken on a life of its own, and he turned her sex den into a bloodbath. His armor, which grew stronger when it absorbed blood, fed well, and when he was done, only the prisoners in the cages were alive. He released them and then gated himself out of there.

He had an appointment with his father.

Reseph went to Jillian's place first, knowing he shouldn't, knowing that seeing her was going to turn him inside out. But he had to make sure she was okay after the way they'd left things.

Reseph wrapped himself in a *khote* spell and strode, in absolute invisibility, into the barn. The lights were on, and the animals were carrying on the way they did when food was coming.

Jillian was inside, but instead of feeding them, she was sitting on a bale of hay, tears streaking her cheeks. Reseph's skin shrank in self-loathing.

"I'm so sorry, baby," he whispered.

Jillian sniffed and looked up. Looked right at him. Son of a bitch. She couldn't see him, but clearly, she'd sensed him. He remained motionless, as if doing so would make him even more invisible. *Idiot.*

At least Pestilence wasn't causing any trouble. The demon was currently in so much agony at losing Lilith that Reseph could feel it in dull pulses in his gut.

Good. The bastard deserved to suffer.

Eventually, Jillian dashed away her tears with her coat sleeve and got to work with the animals. She moved more slowly than usual, and she looked like she could use a week's worth of sleep. He wished he could do something for her, but he was pretty sure he was the last person she wanted to see right now.

Reluctantly, he backed out of the barn and opened a gate to Ares's place, but according to one of Ares's Ramreel servants, he, Cara, and Rath had gone to Limos's. He gated himself there, and great; as if seeing Jillian hadn't been torture enough, he felt an instant hurt at the scent of grilled meat and the sound of Maroon 5 blaring on the sound system. Apparently, everyone had gathered for a party, and Reseph hadn't been invited.

Didn't matter that Reseph understood their reluctance to embrace him as if nothing had happened. It still stung.

He found his siblings and their families hanging out in front of the house, and they weren't alone. It looked as if half the Underworld General staff was there, too. Kids were everywhere, playing on the beach with a couple of hellhounds chasing after them, and Limos was running the portable bar.

One of the hounds, Hal, saw him and turned into a black, sharp-toothed bullet. Shit. Reseph couldn't risk a battle with the thing, not when he needed to prove he wasn't an evil bastard. Pestilence had killed enough hellhounds as it was. He threw a gate, but before he could step through, Cara's command stopped Hal in his tracks.

Still, the canine snarled, his eyes glowing red, and one of the other hounds began a slow crawl toward Reseph as well.

Cara called them both back. Reluctantly they obeyed, although they put themselves between Reseph and Cara and the kids.

Limos put down the margarita blender, and suddenly the music went off and all went silent.

"Well, this is awkward." Reseph strode across the stretch of beach he'd spent so many happy hours on in the past. "I didn't mean to crash the party."

"It isn't what it looks like," Limos said, and Reseph didn't miss the way his brothers moved closer to their wives. Arik casually set down his drink and settled his hand at his hip, where he was no doubt concealing a weapon. The hatred in that man's eyes could burn a hole through titanium.

"You don't have to explain," Reseph said, hating himself for the tremor in his voice.

Ares spoke up. "We were planning on getting together to find you a place to live, since Harvester destroyed your cave. And then Regan suggested inviting over the UG staff as a way of thanking them for everything they did during the hell the Apocalypse brought down on us."

"It was an impromptu get-together," Limos explained.

"Stop." Reseph held up his hand. "You don't owe me an explanation." He approached, pretending not to notice how tense people became with every step he took. "I have news. Lilith is dead."

"What?" Thanatos sounded strangled. "How do you know?"

"Because I'm the one who killed her."

"Oh my God." Limos grabbed the margarita pitcher and drank straight from it. When she was through, she wiped her mouth with the back of her hand. "Do you know what you've done? She was on Satan's council. Lucifer relied on her for the intel she got from the demons she screwed. Jesus, Reseph. There's going to be retaliation. Big retaliation."

"Good. I'll have more people to kill." Reseph walked toward Reaver, who was leaning against a tree trunk, legs crossed at the ankles. "Where is Revenant?"

"Nursing his wounds. Why?"

Reseph moved in a flash, grabbing Reaver by the throat and slamming him into the tree. "Because I found our father," he bit out. "And I want to know how much our Watchers knew."

Limos was there in an instant, Ares and Thanatos providing backup. She laid her hand on Reseph's arm and squeezed. "You found him? How?"

"Lilith drew a picture of the angel who knocked her up, and she was kind enough to give it to me."

Reseph leaned into the angel, getting nose to nose. "Tell them, Reaver."

"I don't know what you want me to tell them," Reaver growled.

"Bullshit. Why have you kept it from us? Thanatos spent centuries trying to find our father, so why the fuck did you not tell him the truth?"

Reaver's voice went deep and low, carrying an edge of calm that was dangerous. "And what truth is that?"

Reseph released Reaver and shoved the parchment into his hands. "That *you* are our father."

Thirty-one

Reaver stared at the sketch in his hand, his head spinning. He heard voices around him, but everything was jumbled together and he couldn't pick out anything specific. Finally, he looked up. Reseph was glaring at him in anger, and the others in confusion.

"Why didn't you tell us?" Reseph demanded. "You've been our Watcher for what, three years now, and not once did you chime in with, 'Hey, I was your sperm donor.' Where the fuck have you been for five thousand years? You let Lilith abandon us, and you let her corrupt the hell out of Limos."

Reaver glanced back down at the drawing. "This has to be a mistake."

"Are you denying that's you?"

Reaver looked up from the parchment at Reseph and everyone else who had crowded around.

"Obviously, the drawing is of me." He cleared his throat. "But I didn't...I don't think I would have slept with Lilith."

"What do you mean you don't think you would have?" Limos asked. "Isn't that something you'd know?"

Reaver blew out a long breath. There were things he "knew," but this wasn't one of them. "I told you my memory was taken away from me almost thirty years ago. No one else remembers me, either. I doubt Lilith would have remembered if she hadn't drawn a picture."

"So you could have slept with her, then."

"No. Impossible." Reaver's throat squeezed shut, the protest sounding hollow. He couldn't imagine getting intimate with someone as vile as Lilith, but he also knew he had a rebellious streak, and if someone had said not to ·bed the succubus, he might have out of spite.

"I can prove it." Reseph's tone had softened now that he realized Reaver hadn't been keeping this massive secret. "I have a birthmark in the shape of a single wing on the inside of my left thigh. Lilith said our father, the angel in that drawing, has a matching one."

Reaver froze. Locked up so hard he couldn't even hyperventilate.

"Well?" Anticipation radiated from Ares, who rarely got worked up about anything. "Do you have this mark, Reaver?"

A mixture of terror and joy tripped through him as he looked each Horseman in the eye. And then he nodded. Now he knew why he'd felt such a close connection with these four. Why he'd risked spending an eternity trapped in Sheoul-gra when he'd cast Reseph out of there. And why, right now, his eyes stung.

"Yes. It..." He cleared his throat of its hoarseness. "It appears that I'm...your father."

Limos threw herself at him, wrapping herself around

him and squeezing so hard he could barely breathe. "I knew it," she whispered. "I knew there was a reason I loved you from the beginning."

"Damn, Reaver," Eidolon said. "You're full of surprises."

Shade, one of Eidolon's brothers, snorted. "The only way you can top this one is to tell us you're a Shadow Angel."

It was Reaver's turn to snort. Only one Shadow Angel, a being who had access to both Sheoul and Heaven and could utilize the powers of both, had ever existed at any given time, and there hadn't been one alive in centuries.

Wraith, blond brother to Shade and Eidolon, clapped Reaver on the back. "Be glad you missed the potty-training stage." He gestured to the Horsemen. "I'll bet these assholes could blow out diapers made of Kevlar."

Thanatos beaned Wraith with a corn chip. Thanatos... Reaver's *son.*

Reaver was a father.

But how? And who in Heaven knew? Had he been given Watcher duty by someone who was aware that the Horsemen were his offspring?

Reaver suddenly had a lot of questions... and an uncomfortable feeling that he wasn't going to like the answers.

Thirty-two

Reseph was so out of there. On the beach Reseph had practically called home, he felt like a stranger.

Hell, the people from Underworld General were more a part of his siblings' families than he was.

No one to blame but yourself, asshole.

Well, Pestilence could shoulder a lot of the blame, too.

Cursing, he strode up the beach to find a safe place to throw a Harrowgate.

"Reseph, wait!" Limos caught up to him and took him by the elbow. "Are you okay?"

He shrugged, putting on his best old-Reseph face. "Yep. I'm just going to go get myself a place to live and then maybe hit the Four Horsemen." Lie. Huge fucking lie.

Yes, he needed a place to live, but he was never again stepping foot in the underworld pub where he'd spent countless hours doing countless females. He only wanted

Jillian, so more than likely he was going to go hang out in her barn like some sort of creepy invisible Peeping Tom.

"Don't give me that crap," Limos said softly. "I know you too well. You miss Jillian, don't you?"

Sure his voice would crack like a pubescent teenage boy's, Reseph merely nodded.

"Then get her back." Limos looked down at the sand for a moment, as if gathering her thoughts. "If you're worried about Pestilence, maybe you should consider the way you came out of your torment when she was around. Maybe she can help keep you level and in control."

He shook his head. "Even if that was true, she'll never forgive me for what happened to her."

Limos stomped her foot. "Bullshit. That human gave you her freaking mind in order to help you, and she did it after learning that Pestilence hurt her. She loves you."

He swore he heard Pestilence laugh, and the memory of her attack started to spread through his brain like spilled mead. Where had Reseph been? Why hadn't he fought to stop what had happened to Jillian? Reseph was just as responsible as Pestilence was.

"I know what you're thinking, but *Pestilence* hurt her," Limos said. "Not you. And I realize I sound like a hypocrite, but you have to remember that Pestilence tormented us almost daily for a year." She glanced back at the group, where pretty much everyone was watching them. "He killed Torrent, who Ares loved like a son. He hung my staff from trees. He stole Arik's soul. Worst of all, he tried to kill Logan. These aren't things we're going to get past easily, even if we know it wasn't you who did them."

He closed his eyes, fighting to keep the memory of preparing to slaughter the newborn at bay, but what he couldn't stop was the nausea. In a clumsy rush, he stumbled to the surf and threw up. Tremors racked his body so violently that he could no longer hold himself up, and he crashed to his knees in the waves.

He didn't know how long he stayed like that, head bowed, water lapping at his legs, when arms came around him and lifted him to his feet. Reaver. Reaver was holding him upright.

"I'm sorry, Reaver," he began, and then paused, because was he supposed to call him Father now? "What I did to you in Harvester's lair—"

"Stop." Reaver gripped Reseph's shoulders firmly and gave him a little shake. "None of us need apologies. We need you to put yourself back together."

Easier said than done. Tormenting your family and killing millions of people wasn't an easy thing to put behind you. Although he had to admit that Harvester's "Sheoul voodoo," as Limos called it, had gone a long way toward making that happen. But why had she done it? She hated him, and with good reason.

"Reaver…do you know why Harvester was fired as our Watcher?"

"No, but maybe you can shed some light on that. Did she help Pestilence in any way?"

He nodded. "It was her idea to trick The Aegis into taking Thanatos's virginity so his Seal would break. She wrote the document that made them think a baby was the key to averting the Apocalypse."

Turned out, the baby *had* been that key. He'd also been the key to breaking Than's Seal and starting the Apocalypse. Logan had come into the world with a lot of weight on his tiny shoulders.

Reaver frowned. "Were you aware that Regan can sense emotion when she touches ink on skin or parchment?"

"No, why?"

"Because she confirmed that whoever penned the note believed every word they wrote. So if what you're saying is true, Harvester knew all along that Than's virginity wasn't his *agimortus*."

Reseph sucked in a harsh breath. "So she knew the baby was." He rubbed his temples, trying to get a grip on this new information. If she'd known, why hadn't she told Pestilence? He hadn't figured it out until later. Something wasn't adding up.

"Whether she'd known or not, it's clear she was helping Pestilence, which is a broken Watcher rule," Reaver said.

"Maybe that's why she got taken off Watcher duty and replaced by the douchebag."

Reaver looked troubled. "Maybe. But it seems like overkill to have her dragged to hell for the punishment."

"She's being tortured," he said. "Lilith said Lucifer wants something from her. Something with the power to draw out Pestilence. Do you know what it could be?"

Reaver's frown deepened. "No idea."

The party music started up again, Reseph's cue to get out of there. A year ago he'd have joined in, started up a game of volleyball or some sort of drinking challenge. Now he wanted to join in, but he wanted Jillian with him. He'd take her out in the waves to surf, and maybe he'd mess with her a little underwater, where no one but she would know what his hands were doing. Later, when everyone was gone, he'd make love to her on the beach with all the reverence she deserved.

A pang of loneliness and loss ripped through him.

"Thank you," he said to Reaver. "Thanks for giving me Jillian for a little while." He regarded his father, wishing he'd known the truth sooner. Like—when he'd been a child would have been good. "It was you, wasn't it? The night she was attacked, she said she heard wings. You were there."

"Yes." He touched Reseph's hair with surprising fondness. "It was hard to keep track of Pestilence, since he was so often in Sheoul. But that night—"

"That night he was hunting Aegi," Reseph said, remembering the dozen Guardians who'd lost their lives over the course of a couple of hours.

Reaver nodded. "I was finally able to catch up with him. I'm the reason Pestilence was interrupted that night. I might have whispered in a cop's ear that he should do a routine patrol of that lot."

Pestilence and the demons had taken off since their victims had been pretty much used up anyway. The sick bastard.

"Let go of the guilt over what happened that night," Reaver said. "It wasn't you. You and Jillian both needed each other to heal what Pestilence did."

"I needed her. She didn't need me."

"You're wrong," Reaver murmured.

Reseph didn't think so, but he didn't feel like arguing. He had to find a place to live, kill a few more of Pestilence's asshole buddies, and hang out in Jillian's barn like a loser.

Yep, his calendar was full.

Full of suck.

Jillian didn't answer the phone for two days. She'd never ignored Stacey's calls before, but how was she supposed to explain what had happened with Reseph? The situation wasn't exactly your typical breakup.

So . . . my boyfriend killed a lot of people.

No, that didn't have the proper ring to it.

Turns out that my lover murdered millions of people.

Better, but still didn't quite achieve that jaw-dropping horror factor.

Before I found him frozen in a snowdrift, my half-demon lover tortured and slaughtered men, women, and children by the millions.

Perfect. And as Stacey's old Bronco pulled up to the house, Jillian braced herself for the *I-told-you-so*. But first she had to get through the *why-the-hell-haven't-you-answered-the-phone* lecture.

Sure enough, the second Jillian opened the door, Stacey lit into her.

"Why the hell haven't you answered the phone? Do you know how worried I've been? I was sure you were dead in the woods somewhere!" Stacey took a break to breathe, looking Jillian up and down. "And when is the last time you combed your hair or showered or got dressed?"

"Good to see you too, Stace." Jillian stood back to let her friend inside.

Stacey slipped out of her parka as Jillian closed the door. "So. What's going on?" Stacey kicked out of her boots and looked around. "Where's Reseph?"

A lump of emotion clogged Jillian's throat, and she had to swallow a few times before she could talk. "He's not here."

"Good." Stacey started toward the kitchen. "I wanted to talk to you alone." She helped herself to a Sprite from the fridge.

"Why's that?"

Turning to Jillian, Stacey popped the tab on the soda. "I needed to apologize. I was a little hard on you and Reseph. You've had a rough time, and if you need him in your life, I have no right to interfere."

"You were just looking out for me," Jillian said miserably. "If you'd taken in a complete stranger with no background history, I'd have done the same thing." Turned out Stacey was right to be worried, which made this even worse.

Stacey ran her finger along the rim of the can, averting her gaze. "Maybe. But I think I was a little jealous, too. The way he was watching out for you ... it kind of made me feel useless, you know?"

"Oh, Stace." Jillian's voice was toast, her words coming out as a croak. "You could never be useless." She hurried over to her best friend and gave her a big hug, not even realizing until that moment how badly she herself needed one.

Stacey knew, though, and the moment Jillian pulled back, Stacey stiffened. "What's wrong?"

"You should probably sit down."

"Dammit, Jillian, you're scaring me."

Scaring you? Girlfriend, you ain't seen scared yet. Jillian took a seat at the table and gestured for Stacey to sit. "Reseph got his memory back."

Stacey inhaled a harsh breath as she pulled out a chair. "Oh, wow. Is that why he's not here? Where is he? What did he remember?"

"It's bad," Jillian said. "Really unbelievable."

Stacey's fingers tightened on the can. "Do *not* tell me I was right. That he's a drug dealer or serial killer or some shit."

"Worse," she rasped.

"How can it be *worse* than a serial killer?" Stacey shook her head. "Unless he's a genocidal dictator or something."

Jillian's stomach turned over, and she grabbed the soda from her friend, drinking half of it before she could talk again. "You're getting closer."

Stacey stared. "This isn't some kind of sick joke, is it? People with cameras aren't going to pop out of your closet, right?"

"Just think about the last year. About the demons. Entire countries overrun by them."

"And?"

"And someone was behind it. All of it." She'd learned all the whys of it over the last couple of days, thanks to the book one of the Horsemen had left on her bedside table. It was fascinating reading, completely unbelievable if she hadn't experienced the Horsemen and their world herself.

For a long moment, Stacey just sat there. "I know you aren't saying Reseph is that someone," she said slowly.

A chill wrapped around Jillian at the cold truth coming from her friend's lips. It just sounded so real, so much worse when Stacey said it.

"That's what I'm saying. His brothers and sister showed up, and he remembered everything. This is going to sound crazy, but…he's one of the Four Horsemen of the Apocalypse."

Dead silence fell in the house. Jillian was pretty sure Stacey stopped breathing. And then she stood so fast her chair tipped over.

"Knock it off," Stacey snapped. "If this is a joke, it's not funny. And if it's not a joke, I'm going to kill that bastard for messing with your head like this. What the fuck?

Really? He conned you into believing he's some biblical legend?" She sucked in a sharp breath and grabbed Jillian's hand. "Oh my God, did he get you hooked on drugs?"

Jillian pulled away. "No, and I know this sounds insane, but I saw everything with my own eyes. He remembered, and he went crazy. Turns out his Seal had broken, and he turned evil. I guess one of his brothers killed him, and then an angel rescued him from hell, erased his memory, and sent him here so I could nurse him back to health."

Very calmly, Stacey righted the chair and sat down again. "Sweetie, I think maybe we should go to the hospital."

So, this wasn't going very well. "I don't need a hospital. I need you to believe me."

Closing her eyes, Stacey rubbed her lids, looking suddenly very tired. "Okay, let's say I believe you." She opened her eyes and regarded Jillian with concern. "Where is Reseph now?"

"Greece, maybe. It's where Reseph's sister, Limos, took me."

"You... were in Greece." Stacey's voice dripped with disbelief.

Jillian nodded. "We traveled through some sort of gate that lets them be anywhere in seconds. We went to Reseph and Limos's brother Ares's place. Reseph was in bad shape. The memories of what he'd done were haunting him."

"I'd hope so, given that he's responsible for the deaths of millions." Stacey coughed a little. "You know, if it's true."

"It's true. But it wasn't him. It was his evil half, a demon named Pestilence."

"Riiiight." Stacey looked at Jillian like she was sizing

her up for a straightjacket. "Maybe you should come stay with me for a little while. We'll find someone to take care of the animals, and you can get some rest."

"I don't need rest."

"Okay, what if Reseph comes back?"

Clearly, Stacey saw Reseph as a threat, but probably because she thought he'd brainwashed her or drove her insane or got her hooked on drugs.

"I don't know." And that was the problem. She didn't know how she felt about everything that had happened. All she knew was that she loved Reseph, which made what he'd done as Pestilence harder to deal with.

"So you're saying that you can forgive everything his alter ego did? You know how no guy you've dated has turned out to be who you thought they were? Well, if it were a competition, Reseph would win world champion triple-gold medal." Stacey gave Jillian a look that tacked on, *if what you're saying is true*.

The doorbell rang, making both Jillian and Stacey nearly jump out of their skin. Stacey reached automatically for her holster before cursing at its absence.

"Civilian clothes," she muttered. "Let me get the door."

"Don't be silly. I'm not an invalid." She tore open the door and silently cursed.

"Good to see you again," the Aegis guy, Lance, said. He glanced over Jillian's shoulder and gave a curt nod. "Officer Markham."

"Who are you?" Stacey asked, moving next to Jillian. "How do you know my name?"

"We know more than you can imagine." Lance's condescending smile was as annoying as his answer.

"Lance and Juan are from The Aegis," Jillian ground

out, never taking her eyes off Lance. "A demon-hunting organization."

Stacey eyed the men and their truck, her expression guarded. "Are you here about the local killings? There's already been a team from DART here to investigate."

Oh, right. Jillian had forgotten to mention that the DART guys were also involved with the Horsemen. One of them was even married to one. That would have been the nail in Stacey's skepticism coffin.

"We're not here about that," Juan said. "We were wondering if Jillian had seen Reseph lately."

Jillian really did not like the vibe she got from these guys. "I've told you all you need to know."

"Then you won't mind if we set up on your property to keep an eye out for him," Juan said, and it wasn't a question.

"Yes, I do mind."

Stacey shoved past Jillian. "What's this about? If Jillian is in danger—"

"We're all in danger," Lance interrupted. "Every day that Horseman and his kin are loose puts the world at risk." He glared at Jillian. "Or maybe you don't remember all the news coverage of the plagues and massacres. Maybe you don't remember the hordes of evil spawn swarming like locusts across entire continents." His lips peeled back in a sneer. "Maybe you don't remember being attacked by demons, Ms. Cardiff? Harboring one of the Horsemen of the Apocalypse isn't some petty offense. It's a crime against humanity that will earn you a place at the wrong end of an executioner's blade. Remember that. If you see him again, we'll expect a call."

Lance and Juan headed back to their truck, leaving

Jillian spitting mad. How had he found out about her attack? Granted, hospital records probably weren't hard to get hold of, but that meant they'd been digging into her past. And how dare they threaten her?

"What a dick," she muttered as she slammed the door closed. She turned to Stacey, who looked like she'd seen a ghost. "Stace?"

Stacey blinked her glazed eyes. "Oh my God. It's real." She licked her dry lips. "I didn't believe you, but unless the demon experts are on the same drugs you are...oh, holy shit. You were...you were sleeping with one of the Four Horsemen of the fucking *Apocalypse*."

"Um...yeah."

Then Stacey, who had never fainted in her life, passed right on out.

Thirty-three

Limos couldn't stop grinning. She'd smiled for the entire rest of the beach party, and during cleanup, and now that everyone was gone and she and Arik were alone in their house, she was still grinning like a fool.

"I'm glad you got a happy baby-daddy ending," he said, as she came out of the master bathroom. "I still can't belicve Reaver is your father."

"I think he's still in shock, too." She opened up the sliding glass door between the bedroom and the dcck and stepped outside into the warm evening breeze. "Did you see how he looked at Logan after it sunk in that the baby was his grandson?"

Arik followed her out, coming up behind her to cage her against the railing as they looked out over the ocean. "Yeah. He couldn't stop staring." He nuzzled the back of her neck, and pleasant shivers skittered over her skin. She loved when he did that. "It's weird to think of him as a grandpa, though. He looks like he's in his early thirties. Thirty-five at the most. Can't believe he's so ancient. Dinosaur ancient. Like, pre-wheel old."

"Funny, Arik. Very funny." She squirmed around to pop him in the shoulder. "We might be as old as dirt, but that only means we're much wiser than you."

He grinned, and she got all weak-kneed, the way she always did when he smiled. "Whatever you say, old lady."

"Oh, you are *so* not getting any tonight."

"Yeah?"

"Yeah." It was totally an idle threat and he knew it, even laughed when she ducked out from under his arms and stomped into the bedroom.

She was definitely getting him into bed, especially since he'd spent the entire day sneaking up to her at every opportunity to whisper erotic things in her ear. He'd told her what he was going to do to her when they were alone, how he was going to do it, what body part he'd do it with . . . all in excruciating detail. She'd been so worked up by the time the party was over that she'd all but run into the house, dragging him behind.

Then he'd gotten a phone call from Decker, which had allowed her to cool down, but only a little. She switched on the ceiling fan and stripped out of her bikini—slowly, so Arik would be tortured for as long as possible.

She loved the way his eyes darkened and his entire body went taut, and as she stepped out of the bikini bottoms, a low growl rumbled through his chest. With a sassy flip of her hair over her shoulder, she sauntered back into the bathroom and closed the door.

"Told you you weren't getting any," she called out.

She heard the unmistakable zing of a zipper, and then,

"I'm getting some right now." His voice was low and rough, and heat built between her legs at the conjured image of him stroking himself.

Okay, enough teasing. She needed him at her sex. Mouth or cock, she didn't care.

She started to turn the doorknob and then *duh*, remembered the reason she'd come back into the bathroom in the first place. She turned to the toilet . . . and stopped breathing.

"Arik?" she croaked.

He burst through the door, his expression fraught with worry. "What? What is it?"

With a shaking hand, she grabbed the little white stick on the back of the toilet. "It's . . . us." She looked up at him, her entire body trembling now—with joy. "We're going to be parents. I'm pregnant. I'm finally pregnant!"

Arik grabbed her in a huge bear hug and lifted her off the ground, his whoop of laughter ringing in her ear. This was the perfect ending to a perfect day. She'd learned that her father was a man she'd already loved like a dad, and now the man she loved as a husband was going to be a father.

And she finally had everything she'd ever wanted. Five thousand years of waiting had definitely been worth it.

Reseph stood at the tiny gravesite on the island of Steara in Sheoul. He used to visit yearly, but it had been a long time since he'd been here.

Guilt and grief wrapped around his heart like barbed wire, digging in more with every beat.

Reseph was so damned weak. For five thousand years he'd believed he was impervious to pain and emotional entanglements. He'd kept the females at arms' length, and he'd done his best to never let family conversation get too serious. Couldn't let his brothers and sister wallow in misery or loneliness, right? Yep, he'd thought he was doing it for them. To help them.

But then he'd sat in Jillian's barn loft and watched her take care of the animals like some kind of pathetic stalker, and he realized that everything he'd done had been to keep him from having to think too hard on his own feelings.

Because the thing was, the old Reseph would have either shoved Jillian out of his mind by now, or he'd have popped into the barn, all smooth talk and smiles, and charmed his way back into her bed. Not back into her *life*, but her bed.

He'd been such a bastard. He'd hated being alone so much that he'd filled his life with parties and females. So many females. For all the companionship, he'd been cold and alone, just the way Jillian had found him in the snowbank. That had been his life. Reaver had known exactly how to make that clear to him, hadn't he?

But now the only thing Reseph wanted was to gather her in his arms and stop her tears.

Between trips to Sheoul to destroy the demons who had helped Pestilence do so much damage and visits to various disaster relief organizations to make donations, he'd checked in on her three times over the last three days. While he was happy to see that she was as strong as ever, handling the chores and the snow just fine, there was a sadness about her. This morning, when Fang-Doodle followed her out to the barn and cried pitifully from on top of a bale of hay, Jillian had broken into tears.

"You miss Reseph, don't you, buddy?" she'd said to the cat. "Me too. But he once said that when something's gone, it's gone."

Reseph had wanted to pop out of the *khote* and take that back, but he'd sat, paralyzed, as she pulled the little bird he'd carved out of her pocket and broke it in half before tossing it in the trash.

Jillian, who held onto everything, including a ring from a guy who didn't deserve to be breathing, had tossed Reseph's gift.

"Guess that includes people, too," she'd whispered.

She was done with him. Reseph had felt as though his entire body was imploding under the weight of his agony.

How could he have said that? *Because you lived by that rule, asshole.*

It took him several hours to go through his entire life, to find the event that had started it all. It was probably fair to say that there were a lot of events, but one in particular stood out, and it filled him with shame.

The little grave at his feet contained a human who shouldn't have died and who, if Reseph had been more watchful, wouldn't be condemned to eternal suffering in hell.

Sinking to his knees, he bowed his head. "I'm sorry, Ariya. I'm sorry I haven't been here for you. I'm sorry I didn't fight for you the way I should have. I can't make it up to you, but I can make it up to someone else. And I'll never miss your birthday again."

He bent forward and pressed a kiss into the headstone he'd carved himself. A sense of peace fell over him, and he could almost believe that his baby sister had given him her blessing.

He'd failed Ariya, but he wouldn't fail Jillian. He was going to fight for her the way he should have from the beginning.

Thirty-four

Jillian pulled the pickup next to the house, and even before she shut off the engine she became aware of a presence nearby. The hairs on the back of her neck prickled as if she was being watched. If those Aegis assholes were spying on her, they were going to see the business end of her shotgun.

Cursing, she hopped out of the truck and stomped to the front of the house. As she opened the door the fresh scent of fir tree hit her. Light spilled from the living room, a familiar multi-colored glow, and as she stepped inside, she saw the Christmas tree lit up in the corner. Beneath it, piled high, were dozens of wrapped presents.

A lump formed in her throat and butterflies flitted in her belly, and when she sensed movement behind her, the butterflies went crazy. "Reseph," she whispered.

"Merry Christmas," he replied softly. "I know it's early, but we never had the chance to get the tree we talked about."

"Because you got your memory back." She turned slowly,

bracing her heart. Didn't work. The sight of him made the stupid organ jerk painfully against her ribs. God, he was as gorgeous as ever, standing there in jeans and a black thermal Henley, his hair falling in lush blond waves to his shoulders.

"I miss you." He cleared his throat. "I want to make it up to you."

He wanted to make up to her the fact that he didn't want to be tied to her? Not a chance. "I don't want to hear it. I want you gone, and I don't want to see you for another eleven and a half months."

"I'm not leaving." His expression hardened. "Not until I'm finished with what I have to say."

"Then you'll be talking to the wall, because I'm not interested." She started for the bedroom, intent upon shutting him out here, but she hadn't gone two steps when she found herself backed against the front door, Reseph's hands on her shoulders, his mouth on hers. Oh, it felt good to be like this again. So good she wanted to weep with relief . . . and with anger.

"I'll talk to the wall," he said against her lips. "I'll talk to a window, the fireplace; hell, I'll talk to the fucking carpet. But eventually I'll get to you, and you *will* listen."

"I hate you." She thrust her hands into his hair and kissed him back. Hard.

He captured her lower lip in his teeth and then laved the gentle bite with his tongue. "I love you." A buzz of both pleasure and pain at his words and the stinging nip rushed through her.

"You hurt me." She tore open his jeans and took him in her hand. His hard length jerked in her grasp, and he moaned. She loved that sound. Loved that she could make him need her.

"Jillian...stop." He captured her wrist and forced her to stop stroking.

"Dammit," she snapped, shoving at his chest, although it was like trying to move a brick wall. "You said you wanted to make it up to me. This is what I want. You hurt me. You made me love you. You made me promises, that you liked this life and wanted to be with me, and then you yanked it all away."

"I know." He sounded like he'd swallowed sand. "That's why I'm here. But we need to talk first."

"Talk? You? Mr. Who Doesn't Love Casual Sex?" She shoved at him again. And again. As if pushing him was going to bring back all the happiness they'd shared. When he didn't budge, she changed tactics and ripped off her sweatshirt. She went for her jeans, but this time Reseph grabbed both her hands.

A rough sound erupted from his throat. "Jillian, stop it." She looked up and nearly swayed at how his eyes glinted with shards of lust. "I'm on the edge right now. Being here with you is making my sex demon half rage. I want to mount you so bad. Throw you against the wall and pound into you until the roof comes down on top of us."

A powerful punch of arousal made Jillian's body quiver at Reseph's words. "Then what's the problem?"

"I don't want it like this, and neither do you."

"You have no idea what I want," she yelled. With a snarl, she shimmied out of her jeans. "I wanted you to fight for me instead of against me. I wanted you to trust yourself as much as I trusted you. I wanted you to want to be tied down."

A shadow of shame crossed his face, but in an instant it was gone, replaced by that intense, dangerous lust that had always permeated their lovemaking.

"I made mistakes," he growled. "But I'm here now."

"Well, give the man a medal," she ground out, and before she even finished her sentence, he'd hauled her off her feet and braced her high up on the wall. His mouth was on hers in a demanding, almost brutal kiss. A raw, animal noise came out of him as he dug his fingers into her bottom to lift her and lower her onto his erection.

He entered her in a hard, powerful surge, and then he was pounding into her the way he'd said, his hips jack-hammering against her. Ecstasy rolled through her, her orgasm hitting her so fast her mind spun. She thrashed against Reseph, loving how he wasn't sparing her mouth, her back as it scraped against the wall, or her sex as he pumped into her in a ruthless, delicious onslaught.

His pace picked up, but how that was possible she had no idea. He jerked wildly, his body shuddering, and another climax ripped through her as his hot semen splashed inside her. A shout tore from his throat, and they both convulsed, swamped by pleasure.

When the shuddering and panting waned, Jillian's muscles turned to water, and very gently, Reseph eased her feet to the floor.

"Fuck," he muttered, shoving himself away.

She blinked, brain fuzzed out and not functioning yet. "What's wrong?"

He zipped up and then snatched the blanket off the back of the couch and handed it to her. "Condom. Forgot to protect you again. I want to know if you're pregnant."

It was on the tip of her tongue to ask him what he'd do if she were, but she was suddenly too tired to fight. "I'm not from the last time." She'd started her period the day after she'd returned from Greece, and she'd been strangely sad about it. And God, how bizarre was it to think she could have been impregnated by one of the Four Horsemen of the Apocalypse?

He watched her wrap up in the blanket, the lights from the Christmas tree glittering in his eyes. "Are you okay?" His voice was gravelly. "I was too rough with you."

"Honestly, I don't think that would be possible." The air crackled with instant tension as that night in the airport parking lot got between them. Dammit. She quickly pretended she didn't notice the taut strain in the room. "Where have you been staying? I've worried about you."

"In an old hunting cabin in Switzerland."

"So far away," she mused.

Twisting around, he straightened the silver garland wrapped around the tree. "Not when all I have to do is step through a gate to be anywhere in the world in seconds."

"True," she said. "But I thought you hated the snow."

Reseph smiled. "I've learned to like it, I think. Reminds me of you."

A dull ache began to pound in her chest, because she wasn't ready for this "talk" yet. Her emotions were too raw. "But you don't like to be alone."

His shrug was halfhearted. "Without my family and you, I don't want to be with anyone else."

"Your family turned you away?" She'd hoped that with the return of his sanity, his siblings would welcome him back.

"They had no choice, Jillian. If Pestilence returns, I could turn on them."

This again. She gathered the blanket more tightly around her. "That wouldn't happen."

"We can't guarantee that."

She felt like screaming in frustration. "God, Reseph, how can I have faith in you, but you don't?"

Reseph turned away from her, and his voice went low. "I've had to spend a lot of time alone, Jillian. And it turns out that I don't like myself very much. Now I know why I surrounded myself with people. I was shallow and vain, and I couldn't let myself get attached to anyone." He inhaled a shaky breath. "I went to Sheoul today to visit my sister's grave."

Grave? She understood loss far too well, and she drifted closer to him. But was it for his comfort, or hers?

"You have another sister? A Horseman?"

"Human." He kept fiddling with the tree, rearranging ornaments and lights. "My real mother, the sex demon, abandoned me with a human female who raised me as her own. Of course, she wasn't much better than the demon mom. My human mother left me alone to fend for myself so much that I think I was malnourished for the first twelve years of my life. Almost died in a fire once, because there was no one around to save me. I'm still not sure how I got out if it." He shrugged. "Anyway, I didn't know she wasn't my mother until I was an adult."

"That's when you were cursed to be a Horseman, right?"

"Yeah." He moved a red bulb next to a blue one. "My human mother gave birth to a girl a year before our curses." Affection drenched his voice. "Ariya was great. The one thing that really made me happy. I didn't see her as much as I should have . . . I was always out drinking and whoring. And then, after our curses, we all kind of went insane for a while."

She'd read about their killing rampages, the destruction they'd caused everywhere they went. Reseph, having been cursed as Pestilence, had been given the power to inflict plagues on people, animals, and crops, and his swath of death had been widespread.

"When I finally went back home during a period of lucidity, I found that, as usual, my mother had left Ariya alone. I tried to take care of her, but..." His big shoulders rose and fell a few times before he continued. "But I went crazy again, drinking, sexing, killing. It was just two days, but by the time I got back home, Ariya was gone."

"Gone where?"

"A demon took her. I tracked that fucker to Sheoul and made him suffer for days before I killed him."

"And your sister?" Jillian asked weakly.

"She died when the demon took her through the Harrowgate." He swung around, devastation etched into his expression. "Since she died in Sheoul, her soul is trapped there for eternity to be tortured by any demon who can detect souls."

Horror sifted hot and cold through Jillian like dry ice, and she slapped her hand over her mouth. "Oh my God," she mumbled into her palm. "That's..." There was no word for it, so she gave up trying to find one.

"Yeah." He inhaled, taking a very long time. "I buried her in the nicest part of Sheoul, and I didn't leave her for months. I didn't eat. Didn't drink. I slept beside her grave. Limos finally found me and dragged me out of there. But it hurt like hell for so many years. After that, I guess I never wanted to love anyone like that again. I know I never wanted to feel like that again. Easier to be happy and unattached. Take the easy road, as Ares put it."

"But you did get attached again, right?" She swallowed the lump in her throat. "You got attached to me."

He laughed bitterly. "But would my old self have gotten attached? No. I'd have fucked you and left you so fast your head would have spun."

His ugly words drilled a hole in her chest, but she soldiered on, determined to talk some sense into him. "That's what I'm trying to tell you. You aren't that person anymore. And you're not the evil demon who tried to start the Apocalypse." On some level, she still couldn't believe she was saying things like that.

"But I'm not the Reseph you knew, either."

"He's the real you," she insisted in what Reseph had called her *stern frying-pan voice*. "He's the one who came out when there was no history to mold his personality."

"Maybe." He walked over and sat across from her on the coffee table. "Whoever I am, I'm going to fight for you. I want you in my life. I want you to be my mate, and I want you to bear my children."

She blinked. Holy shit, she was going to fall over. When he jumped into something, he jumped all the way into the deep end, didn't he? No testing the waters.

"You don't have to answer now. I'm willing to wait. It's probably best anyway."

Maybe she was still reeling from the mate and children thing, but she was confused as hell about that last bit he'd said. "Wait? It's not that I disagree, but... why is it for the best?"

"Because I'm still not sure I can keep Pestilence at bay. I'm not sure I can patch my head up enough to protect you."

Her heart sank. Plummeted right to her feet. "Then we can't be together," she croaked.

He stiffened. "What do you mean?"

God, how could this be happening? "I can't go through this again. I can't be with you and wonder if someday you're going to leave because you don't have faith in your ability to control Pestilence."

"It won't be like that." He took her hand and squeezed, tugging her closer. "I'll be here for you. I might need time now and then, but I'll be here. It might just be a while before we can settle down with a family."

"How long?"

There was a long silence. "I can't answer that. Not yet."

"Exactly. I'm not waiting around for years, only to have you one day say it can't happen." Her eyes stung, and her vision blurred as she peeled away from him and got to her feet. "I love you more than I've ever loved anyone, and I know I can't live through that pain."

She steeled herself against the hurt in his eyes. The man she loved was in there, but until he realized it himself, she couldn't back down.

"Go, Reseph. I love you, but I can't be with you until you can trust in yourself the way I trust in you. I'm not going to compromise on what I want." She'd done that with every man she'd been with, and her relationships had always ended badly. Reseph, more than any of the others, had the power to destroy her.

Reseph moved to her, but she sidestepped and gestured to the door. "Dammit, Jillian, I won't give up."

"That's your choice," she said. "But know that I won't give in."

The moment the door closed, Jillian sank to the floor in a pool of blankets. She wouldn't cry. Not again.

She told herself that over and over, but the tears came anyway.

Thirty-five

"Is everything in place?"

From inside the *khote*, Gethel looked down on Jillian Cardiff's little farm. "Yes." She turned to Lucifer, who shared the invisible space. "The Aegis believes I've given them the tools to capture and hold the Horsemen. First thing in the morning, their plan kicks off."

Lucifer, his black eyes glinting, smiled. As an angel, he'd been handsome. As the second most powerful fallen angel in Sheoul, he was stunning.

"And our plan kicks off shortly after that."

Gethel shivered with anticipation. By noon tomorrow, a whole bunch of birds were going to go down with one stone. Lucifer would strike a powerful blow to The Aegis, and he'd dole out punishment to the Horsemen like they'd never seen. Reseph had made a huge mistake when he'd sought revenge against those who had sided with Pestilence. Killing Lilith had been the fatal error that sealed his fate.

Lucifer couldn't destroy the Horsemen, but he'd devised a trap of epic proportions. "You're certain your cage will hold them?" she asked.

"Their prison is constructed of hellhound venom, rendered from hundreds of the beasts. The Horsemen merely need to touch the cage walls and they'll be rendered immobile. I'll also have Sheoul's most powerful mages continuously refreshing and renewing the walls so they never weaken or lose potency."

"Excellent." She knew he also planned to hang their cages above roaring fires so the assholes would roast for all eternity. Once imprisoned, even if their biblical Seals broke, they would be helpless to escape or fight on the side of good in the Apocalypse. "Don't forget my payment."

Lucifer inclined his head. "Thanatos's child will be yours to do what you will with him." He reached out and fingered the tip of her wing, and she shivered with both pleasure and fear, an intoxicating combination. "What do you plan for him?"

The child was a perfect, beautiful combination of light and dark, with unusually strong battle angel tendencies as well as a powerful demon half. So much potential there.

"I intend to exploit his demon side and raise him to be an angel assassin."

Lucifer smiled. "Nice."

Hardly. She had no intention of being nice. But then, neither did Lucifer. The story of the horrors he'd inflict on the Horsemen and their loved ones would be written in their blood and passed down through history.

The Horsemen would pay for turning their backs on her. And she was going to love watching them suffer.

Thirty-six

Morning came way too early for Jillian. She hated mornings now that Reseph was gone. She hated waking up alone. Hated feeling the cold side of the mattress. Hated not having anyone to cook breakfast for.

Peeling open her puffy eyes, she crawled out of bed and shuffled to the bathroom. The mirror was not her friend today. She looked like hell.

Had she done the right thing by sending him away? Doubt made her nauscous. Logically, she knew she'd done what she needed to do for her self-esteem, but emotionally, she felt wretched. Was it better to be mostly happy in a relationship filled with uncertainty or filled with self-righteousness but miserable and alone?

Alone had never bothered her. She'd never been miserable.

Until now.

She did her best to not think about Reseph as she

dressed and headed out to the barn. The animals were happy to see her, as always. She scooped a bucketful of cracked corn for the chickens, and just as she got to the coop, the rumble of unfamiliar trucks coming up the driveway stopped her in her tracks.

Two military-style rigs with tented boxy sections in the rear topped the rise, and alarm spiked. There was no good reason for vehicles like that to be at her house, and her first instinct was to dart back inside the barn and grab the shotgun.

When the vehicles ground to a halt and Lance and Juan climbed out of one of the cabs, she wished she'd acted on that instinct.

Lance approached while Juan tromped through deep snow to the rear of one of the trucks.

"Nice to see you again, Ms. Cardiff."

She smiled, but no doubt it looked as fake as it was. "I wish I could say the same. Am I going to have to get a restraining order? You can't seem to leave me alone."

"Don't worry," he said. "After today you won't be seeing us again. We just need you to contact Pestilence." Behind Lance, dozens of men in arctic fatigues filed out of the backs of the trucks, all armed to the teeth.

"Well, that'll be a little difficult, since I've never met Pestilence."

Lance's smile was painfully tolerant. "You know what I mean."

"Then say it." She dropped the bucket, and corn spilled all over the snow. "I won't play your games."

All trace of civility left Lance's expression. "Good. We can get down to business then. Contact Reseph."

"Why?"

His hand lowered to a sheath at his hip, where he caressed the thick handle of some sort of dagger. "Because we need to talk to him."

"If you want to talk business, then I suggest you be straight with me." She kept her tone businesslike, forceful, and prayed her nervousness didn't show. "You don't want to *talk* to him, or you wouldn't have brought a truck and fifty men dressed like they're prepared to do battle with Godzilla."

A dozen of the men surrounded her, and her pulse kicked into high gear. "You want it straight, we'll give it to you straight. The Horseman is dangerous. They all are. We have the means to capture and hold them, and we need your help to do it."

"Why would you want to hold them?"

"Pestilence nearly brought about the end of days. Do you want that to happen again?"

What a stupid question. As if she'd jump up and down and shout, "Yes, I love apocalypses!" What a moron.

"They said it won't. Their Seals can't be broken until the biblical prophecy."

Lance leveled a cold look at her, made much more chilling by the fact that he was smiling. "Some of us don't believe they'll fight on the side of good. And even if they do fight on our team, it could be centuries before it happens. In the meantime, these guys are loose, wreaking havoc."

She shrugged. "I haven't seen any havoc."

"You have no idea what they've done." Lance unsnapped the strap holding the dagger in place, but Jillian refused to acknowledge his menacing actions. "The Horsemen are responsible for the Black Death, the Antonine Plague, the Hundred Years' War—"

"Wow. Busy people." Jillian crossed her arms over her chest. "Were they responsible for the fall of Rome and World War Two? Maybe the eruption of Mount Vesuvius? Hurricane Katrina?"

Lance's hand snapped out to grab her biceps. "Listen to me, you Horseman groupie. I know your kind. You're like one of those pathetic women who defends her abusive husband because deep down *he's really a nice guy.*" He jerked her close, baring his teeth. "You're going to help us. Because your boyfriend *really* isn't a nice guy."

She spit in his face. "Go fuck yourself."

Cursing, Lance shoved her away and gestured to Juan. "Go through her shit. Cell phone, notes, everything. There's got to be a way to contact the Horsemen."

Juan snagged her by the arm before she could even think about fleeing. "And if we don't find anything?"

Lance's voice was pure evil. "Then we torture her until one shows up."

Thirty-seven

Jillian had been terrified more than once in her life. The worst, by far, had been when the demons attacked her in the ATC parking lot.

Until now.

For some reason, these Aegis guys scared her even more. With the demons, she knew what to expect; pain, blood, and death. With Lance and Juan, the unknown was making her sick with fear, and it was a huge shock to realize that humans were, by far, more terrifying than demons.

The men who had climbed out of the trucks had melted into the surrounding forest, and after tearing apart her house, Lance had forced Jillian onto the snow-covered ground. Juan stood behind her, a wicked, S-shaped blade in his hand. Lance squatted down in front of her, her cell phone in hand.

"Your house was a treasure trove of information. I'm guessing that the phone entry Limos is who I think it is?"

Jillian shrugged. "It's a common name here in Nowhere, Colorado."

"Smartass. I wonder," Lance murmured, "if Pestilence cares enough about you to feel your pain." He slammed his fist into her face, knocking her backward into Juan's legs. Agony spiderwebbed through her cheek and jaw, all the way to the top of her skull.

"Stop it," Juan hissed. "She's human."

"She's involved with demons." Lance shot Juan a disgusted glare. "I thought we agreed on this."

"As a last resort."

"If you have a problem with it, maybe you should have gone with Kynan, Val, and Regan and joined their little ragtag agency."

"You know that's not what I want." Juan eased Jillian off his legs. Face throbbing, she fell forward on her knees and spat blood onto the once pristine snow. "But some of Kynan and Val's ideas on how The Aegis should conduct itself were valid. We need people to trust us and not run roughshod over everyone just because we can."

"We do what we have to do. The Apocalypse almost happened because of the 'new, gentler' rules. We won't let that happen again."

Jillian tested one of her teeth with her tongue. "I don't understand." Her words were mushy, spoken through her split lip.

"Some of our colleagues are demon lovers. Kynan fucking married one, and Val's daughter is a vampire. So they wanted to get all buddy-buddy with the freaks instead of killing them. When a demon named Sin came onto the scene, instead of killing her, Kynan let her live, and she started the plague that broke Pestilence's Seal."

Lance snorted. "We should have sent Kynan packing right then and there."

"You won't get any argument from me on that point," Juan said.

"Now," Lance said, as he flipped open a pocketknife. "Your pain doesn't seem to have brought Pestilence around, so let's see if your screams will do it."

Terror flooded her as she scrambled backward, the scream he wanted so badly lodged in her throat. He lunged, catching her by her coat's collar and yanking her toward him as he jammed the tip of the blade beneath her right eye.

Suddenly, from the forest, a snarl rent the air.

Lance smiled. "Looks like your honey has come to rescue you."

A deep male scream joined a chorus of growls and the gruesome wet sounds of tearing flesh. A chill that had nothing to do with the cold slithered down Jillian's spine. She recognized those noises.

"Soulshredder," she rasped. "Oh, shit—"

Two demons burst from the foliage and ran toward them, their gaping maws dripping saliva and blood. Lance and Juan shouted curses and sent weapons hurling at the things as Jillian scrambled to get to the house. But her panic and the icy ground cost her, sent her slipping and sliding.

Even as she was reaching for the snow shovel propped up against the porch, Lance snared her ankle. "You little bitch! Look what your boyfriend sent!"

Reseph hadn't sent the demons and she knew it, but arguing was useless. She kicked at Lance, knocking him away. From all around, the Aegis people ran toward the demons. She grabbed the shovel and swung around, biting off a scream when one of the Soulshredders punched his fist through Juan's chest and ripped his heart and lungs right out of his rib cage.

A jumbled tirade of curses and insults erupted from Lance. He didn't stop yelling even as he sank one end of his S-shaped blade into the creature's back. Jillian swung the shovel, nailing it in the midsection. The demon screamed and spun, slamming its arm down on the wooden handle and breaking it in half. Lance was tossed into the snow in an awkward tangle of limbs. The other Guardians attacked, and although one of the Soulshredders was badly injured, the other wasn't at all slowed.

"Get the bitch in the house," Lance shouted.

One of the Guardians broke away from the battle with the demons to rush her. Wielding the shovel handle like a baseball bat, she prepared to defend herself. And then, from out of nowhere, a huge man in torn jeans and a ratty yellowed T-shirt bowled the Guardian over. Who the hell was that? There was no time to ask questions, though, not when she had both demons and humans after her. She needed help.

As fast as she could, she threw herself onto the porch. The icy deck sent her sprawling, but she somehow managed to claw and crawl her way through the front door and lock it behind her. The Guardians had ransacked her living room...shit! Where was the card with Kynan's number on it?

Someone or some*thing* pounded on the door, putting a crack in the wood. Desperately, she tore through the mess, praying she'd find the card, because if she didn't, she had a feeling she'd soon be praying for death.

Reseph was so not done fighting for Jillian. In fact, the challenge of winning a female, something he'd never really had before, left him energized. He wasn't sure how he was going to accomplish what she wanted, because he wasn't sure he'd ever be able to say, with one hundred percent certainty, that Pestilence was no longer an issue.

He just had to find a way around Jillian's demand, and if anyone could help with that, it was Ares. He'd have to discuss it with him soon. That was, of course, if Reseph wasn't dead.

Right now, he had to make things better for other people he'd hurt, and those people might demand payment in blood.

He stood at the entrance to Than's keep, feeling oddly unsure about entering, even though he'd called everyone to meet him here. He used to walk inside like he owned the place, but now he felt like a complete stranger. An intruder.

An enemy.

Taking a bracing breath, he pushed the door open. Inside, Than, Limos, and Ares were waiting, and surprise, surprise, so were Reaver and Revenant.

Reseph's siblings were armored. Man, that fact hit him like a punch to the gut.

"Thanks for coming," Reseph said.

Than, who had been lounging on the couch, shoved to his feet, his expression stern. "What's this about?"

"I wanted to let you know I got a place to live." At least, for now. He hadn't exactly rented a place. He'd commandeered the run-down cabin he was staying in.

Thanks to the fortune Thanatos had amassed for them by investing gold he'd looted hundreds of years ago, Reseph could have afforded to rent anyplace he wanted. But he didn't care about comfort, and he didn't want to be around anyone.

"You could have left a message," Ares said. "Why gather us here?"

Because I miss you. "I was hoping we could find a way to give Arik's soul back to him." He'd thought about that last night... between bouts of thinking about Jillian and all the ways he'd fucked things up with her.

"Really?" Limos came forward. "You think you can do that?"

"I don't know." He looked at Reaver. His *father*. "Is it possible?"

Revenant answered before Reaver could. "Only Pestilence can do that. Either through his death or by consent." He shot a toothy smile at Limos. "Looks like your human is out of luck. Sad."

"You're such an asshole," Limos bit out.

Total understatement. Reseph really hated their new Watcher. "Okay then, there's only one thing to do," Reseph said to Reaver. "Do you still have Wormwood?"

Very slowly, Reaver nodded.

"You have to kill Pestilence."

Silence fell in the room. A moment later, it erupted in *Whats?* And, *Are you crazys?* Then there was Revenant's *Gladly.*

Reaver strode across the room and stopped a foot away from Reseph. "Do you know what you're saying? Killing him will kill you. Your soul will spend hundreds, maybe thousands, of years in Sheoul-gra being tortured until the biblical Apocalypse. Even then, there's no guarantee that you'll be reincarnated. The Watcher Council has calculated that the chances of good beating evil in the Final Battle are dismal without you."

"I have to make things better, Reaver. I have to repair some of the damage I've done."

"Not like this," he said. "Arik is immortal now. He doesn't need his soul anytime soon. We have time to find another way."

"You said there isn't one."

"Dammit, Reseph." Ares approached, his expression grim. "There *is* another way. You can let Pestilence out and—"

"And what? You ask him nicely? He's not exactly the kind to negotiate. And I won't expose you to him again."

"I'm happy to torture Arik's soul out of him," Than said, with a little too much relish. Not that Reseph could blame him. But God, letting Pestilence out could only lead to bad things.

"What if I can't put him back?" Reseph rasped.

Revenant crossed his arms over his puffed-out, leather-clad chest. "Then Pestilence goes on a rampage and butchers everyone you love."

"No, he wouldn't." Ares stared at Revenant with contempt, his hand hovering over the sword at his hip. "Because we'd have him pinned down with hellhound venom." He glanced over at Reaver. "Since Pestilence no longer has the power of the broken Seal behind him, hellhound poison should work on him, right?"

Reaver didn't answer, which meant it was one of those things he *couldn't* answer because of stupid Watcher rules.

"You'd better hope so," Revenant said, sounding so damned slimy. "Because Reseph will never be able to put him back."

The fallen angel's words went right to Reseph's gut, because that was exactly what Reseph was afraid of.

"I am so sick of your ugly ass," Limos snapped.

Reseph strode to the center of the room, stopping the conversation. "All of this is pointless. It's Arik's decision. We ask him and go from there."

Total silence, because everyone in the room knew exactly what Arik would say.

Kill Pestilence.

"Reseph..." Limos bit down on her lower lip, and Reseph's heart bled for her. She had to support her husband, but at the same time, doing so might mean death for her brother. She was in the worst of all positions.

A phone beeped, and Limos grabbed her cell off the coffee table. "Shit." She listened, her color fading until moments later, she wheeled around to Reseph. "It was Kynan. Jillian called him. She's in trouble. The Aegis. Demons. Ky and Arik are on their way to her house."

Reseph's heart nearly burst out of his chest as he swiped his finger over his armor scar. "I don't have any right to ask you this, but—"

"I'm with you," Ares said.

"Yup." Limos joined Reseph at his side.

Thanatos nodded. "Let's go save your female."

Thirty-eight

Jillian hung up the phone just as the door crashed in. A demon lunged through the doorway, its teeth snapping, its rotten stench making her gag. A startled yelp escaped her as she rolled out of the way of the creature's claws. Suddenly the thing hissed, spitting frothy saliva as it flew backward through the doorway, its eyes wide with shock. The stranger who had arrived before she shut herself in the house stood where the demon had been.

"Stay inside," the man growled at her. He spun around and tackled the demon he'd hauled out of the house, taking it to the deck.

Stay inside. Right. Good plan. Gripping her shovel handle, she started for the bedroom but skidded to a halt at the crash of broken glass and the nasty snarl that followed. A demon pulled itself through the window next to the bed.

Not good. Holy shit, so not good.

Praying Doodle was hiding somewhere safe, she swiped

the snowmobile keys off the floor and bolted out the door. If she could get away from all of this, maybe she had a chance. She leaped off the porch, narrowly missing being grabbed by Lance. A grayish, eyeless demon lumbered in front of the snowmachine, cutting her off. Demons poured into the house, their screeches and clacking teeth joining the shouts and screams of the Guardians engaged in battle all around the farm. She darted toward the barn, but the battle closed in, and suddenly, she was in the thick of it with nothing but a piece of wood and keys for weapons.

Then came the most beautiful sound in the world.

Horse hooves pounded across the clearing from the forest. Four armored riders, Reseph in the lead, stormed toward her in a cloud of churned-up snow. For just a moment, the battle all around Jillian stopped. Reseph's gaze caught hers, and she knew without a doubt that she was safe.

"Shit!" Lance's curse broke the spell that had fallen over the battlefield. Humans and demons exploded into action. An SUV tore up the drive, sideswiping a Soulshredder before spinning out and crunching into one of the Aegis trucks. Arik and Kynan leaped out, weapons flashing and slashing.

Lance hurled a blade at Reseph, who whipped up a crossbow and shot the blade out of the air.

"He's mine," Thanatos roared, cutting between Reseph and Lance.

Jillian didn't understand why, but clearly, the yellow-eyed Horseman harbored a murderous hatred for the Guardian.

"Wraith's gonna be pissed!" Kynan shouted, even as he ducked a swipe from a Soulshredder's claws. "He ordered Lance for dinner."

Thanatos flashed a set of wicked fangs. Fangs? Did Reseph have them, too? "I'll take him a doggie bag of leftovers."

Jillian dove for the ground as Thanatos thundered past, a scythe in his hand. As she rolled in the snow, she caught a glimpse of Thanatos swinging that wicked blade and cleaving Lance's head from his shoulders.

Another Soulshredder burst out of the forest and was on her before she could even scream. Heart pounding, she jerked the shovel handle upward, catching the creature in the ribs. The wood penetrated deep, driving so hard it erupted from the demon's back. It howled, its massive jaws opening in front of her face. She could smell its foul breath and the rank feces-like odor that clung to its skin. A flashback to the night at the ATC parking lot tore through her brain.

She'd been helpless. Terrified.

Yeah, well, she was terrified now, too, but she was *not* helpless.

She wrenched her makeshift stake upward, shoving it toward the thing's heart. It howled again, spraying foul-smelling liquid in her face.

Her stomach heaved, and she scrambled wildly backward, narrowly avoiding having her head bitten off.

Even impaled, the demon lurched at her, its clawed hand raised for a killing blow. An arrow blew through its eye, and it fell backward, landing in a bloody, twitching heap. Reseph leaped off his horse and swept her up like some kind of legendary knight in shining armor.

"Are you okay?"

"Yes—" She broke off, her breath rushing from her lungs as Reseph whipped around and took out two skinny, six-legged demons with a sword that seemed to come from nowhere.

"Stay down!" Reseph shoved her behind him, pinning her between his body and the deck, and then he was a flurry of armor and swords and crossbows that demolished half a dozen demons in a matter of seconds.

Before this, she'd seen only a man...granted, a super sexy, dangerous man. But for the first time she was truly witnessing a warrior in action. The man she loved, one of the Four Horsemen of the Apocalypse, could kick some serious ass.

He was a thing of beauty, a smooth, confident fighter who knew exactly where and how to strike each of his enemies. All of the Horsemen were, actually. She watched in awe and not a small amount of horror as all around her the Horsemen, the stranger, and Kynan and Arik battled the demons and Guardians, and she could only pray that no one had breached the barn to hurt her animals.

Time seemed to slow, becoming a spinning vortex of screams, growls, and blood. Eventually, Reseph kneeled in front of her, his expression concerned and serious.

"It's over. Everything's okay."

"But..." Frowning, she looked around.

With the exception of the stranger, who was twisting a demon's neck so hard she heard a crack, nothing was moving in the clearing. Near the barn, Limos, Ares, and Thanatos had rounded up the surviving Guardians and were holding them at swordpoint. Arik and Kynan were triaging the human survivors and dispatching wounded demons.

The stranger jogged over, but when he reached for Jillian, Reseph grabbed him. "Who the fuck are you?"

He threw the man against the side of the house, and when

the man struck back, lunging for Reseph, Jillian experienced an odd, panicky sensation.

She shoved her hand between the two males, her palm making a metallic clang against Reseph's breastplate. "Reseph, stop!"

"Why?"

The stranger, panting and bleeding, stared at Jillian as if he knew her, which only confused her more. "I don't know," she said honestly. "Who are you?"

He fell to his knees and bowed his head. "Permission?"

Jillian blinked. "What?"

"Permission." The guy flinched as though expecting to be struck. "To speak."

Baffled, she glanced at Reseph, who shrugged. "Um... okay. You have permission to speak. Who are you?"

"I have no name," he said gruffly. "You must give me one."

"Ah, fuck," Reseph breathed. "He's a slave."

"A slave?" Surely not, but Reseph didn't look like he was kidding. "Are you serious?"

"Yep. And apparently, he thinks you're his master." Reseph grabbed the man's jaw and lifted his face, but the *slave*'s eyes remained downcast. "Why are you here? Why do you think Jillian is your master?"

The man looked at Jillian for guidance, just a flicker of a glance that pleaded for an okay to talk, and this was just... sick. "Yes, you can speak. You don't need to ask permission again. You can always speak."

For some reason, her reply seemed to pain him. "My bond was transferred."

"From who?" Reseph asked.

"Harvester."

Reseph tensed and stepped back. "Did you agree to this, Jillian?"

"I-I don't know. I don't think so."

Reseph rounded on the nameless guy. "How did this happen?"

"There would have been blood involved," the man said.

Jillian swore under her breath. "When I agreed to giving you some of my mind, Harvester...she put a drop of blood over my heart."

"Damn her," Reseph breathed. "Why did she do it?"

Nameless guy bowed his head. "There's only one reason she would have done it. She expects to die, and her death would have transferred my bond to her killer."

Reseph scrubbed his hand over his face. "So she was trying to save you from a terrible fate by giving you to someone of her choosing."

"Yes."

Jillian's stomach, already fragile from the bloody battle, lurched hard enough that she had to swallow bile. "This isn't right. Slavery isn't right. I can't do this. I'll set you free."

"You can't," Reseph said. "A blood-bonded slave will die without the bond. If someone kills you, his bond will transfer. If you die of natural causes or in an accident, he'll die shortly after." He looked at the nameless guy, who was still eyeing the ground. "What species are you?"

"Warg."

"Warg?" Jillian glanced at Reseph. "What's that?"

"Humans call them werewolves," Reseph said. "Warg, how old are you?"

"I don't know." The man lifted his face into the icy breeze like a dog with its head out the window. Pure ecstasy lit up his expression, and it was with reluctance that he returned his attention to Reseph. "Under fifty years, I'd guess."

"Excellent." Reseph slid Jillian a smile. "Werewolves live for hundreds of years. The bond will give you his lifespan."

She sucked in a breath. "I—I don't know what to say." This entire morning had been one huge shock after another.

"Please, mistress, can I have a name?"

Uncomfortable lording over him like this, she went down on her heels so they'd be at eye level. "What did Harvester call you?"

"I was Whine."

Jillian winced. What was wrong with people? "Did you have a name before you were a slave?"

"I was given up as an infant." His sandy hair concealed his expression as he looked down at the ground. "I don't remember my name, but I'm told it was Tracker."

He'd been a slave since he was a baby? She wanted to hug him. Instead, she took a deep, bracing breath. "Then that's your name."

Kynan jogged over, gave Tracker a cursory glance, and turned to Reseph and Jillian. "We've got a hell of a mess on our hands here." He made a broad gesture over the battle scene. "What was all of this about?"

Jillian came to her feet. "The Aegis was here to capture Reseph, but the demons... I don't know."

Ares joined them, his expression so thunderous Jillian actually took a step back. "Limos tried to open a gate and couldn't. I tried, same result. Than discovered an invisible barrier around the farm." A growl erupted from his chest. "We can't get out of here. Fuck, Reseph... this was a trap."

Thirty-nine

Alarm rang through Reseph like a bell had rung in his head. "A trap? Set by who?"

A sudden rumbling shook the ground like a magnitude-nine earthquake, felling trees at the edge of Jillian's property. A malevolent undercurrent swirling in the air raised the hairs on the back of Reseph's neck. He whirled in the direction of the source of the vibe, his lungs seizing at the sight of Lucifer standing a hundred yards away. Behind the fallen angel, rising up out of the soil, was an army of demons.

"Oh, that's got to be bad," Arik breathed.

"Aren't you the king of understatements." Reseph shouted to Than and Limos, who were still keeping the surviving Guardians corralled. "Release them! We might need the extra muscle." Not that he expected them to be a huge help against Lucifer, but Reseph had a feeling they would need all the help they could get.

The Guardians scattered, taking defensive positions near the trucks, barn, and in the surrounding forest.

"Reseph?" Jillian tugged at his arm. Her hair was tangled and full of snow, blood streaked her skin and clothes, and although she had every reason to be afraid, she was alert and calm, a warrior even if she didn't know it. "What's going on?"

"Let's get inside." He ushered everyone into Jillian's house, ignoring the amplified sound of Lucifer's laughter.

Tracker was on Jillian's heels, almost as close as Reseph was, and had this been any other situation and any other male, Reseph would have gutted the guy. But the warg was clearly invested in protecting her, and that would only be a good thing.

"Who is this guy?" Ky cast a wary glance at Tracker.

"Jillian's slave." As Ares and Than righted the furniture that had been tumbled by demons, Reseph parked himself next to one of the front windows so he could keep an eye on Lucifer. "Harvester transferred the bond to her."

Thanatos cocked a pale eyebrow at Tracker, who backed himself into a corner near Jillian, head bowed. "Interesting."

"Come out of there, Horsemen." Lucifer's cajoling voice boomed as if from a loudspeaker, "Come see what the lives of hundreds of your pet hellhounds have given me."

The growl that came out of Than rattled his bone plate armor.

Jillian rubbed her arms through her coat. "Is someone going to tell me what's going on?"

Limos, her black hair tied in a high knot on her head, peeked out of one of the windows. "Reseph has been busy killing everyone in the underworld who helped Pestilence, and he's kind of pissed off Lucifer."

"You did your fair share of pissing off Lucifer when you killed his pet angel," Ares pointed out, and Limos blushed.

"Wait. Lucifer?" Jillian's voice vibrated with shock. And terror, which made Reseph want to gate her anywhere but here. Except no place was safe from the fallen angel. "*The* Lucifer? That's who's outside?"

"Yes," Thanatos said, "but he's not Satan, if that's what you're thinking. Lucifer is Satan's second in command, though, so we're talking about a demon who ranks in the top ten on the 'Who's Who of Most Powerful Beings in the Universe' list."

"Oh, God." Jillian hugged herself, and Reseph fought the urge to take her in his arms. He'd brought this down on her, and he doubted she'd welcome anything from him right now. "What does he want?"

"To destroy us," Limos said. "And if anyone has the power to do it, it's him."

"And he won't stop with us," Ares said, his leather armor creaking as he paced. "He'll take out our families, too."

Reseph closed his eyes, guilt pouring out of him in massive waves. "I'm sorry," he croaked. "This is all my fault."

A tense silence fell, and then he felt Jillian's hand twining with his. God, he didn't deserve to be comforted.

"Reseph." Ares's voice cracked loud enough to jolt Reseph's eyes open. "None of this is your fault. What Pestilence did is on *his* shoulders. You've been trying to make things right. You've taken out a fuckton of evil in the last few days, and the truth is that Lucifer was going to come after us eventually anyway."

Thanatos nodded. "A showdown has been coming for a while now."

Limos fingered her sword. "We've just got to figure out how to beat him."

A blast of annoyance came off Arik as he strode across the room to her. "You aren't fighting, Li."

"Of course I am."

Arik cursed. "I fight, you stay in here."

"Hey, man." Ares clapped Arik on the shoulder. "I know you've got a protective streak a mile wide, but you're going overboard with the me-man-you-woman shit."

"See?" Limos said, batting her eyelashes at her husband. "You're being ridiculous."

"You want to tell them or should I?" Arik's voice was sharp.

Reseph went taut. "Tell us what?"

"Dammit, Arik," Limos snapped. "This isn't necessary—"

"She's pregnant," Arik broke in. "No way is she fighting."

It took a second for the news to sink in, and when it did, happiness collided with worry for her and the baby, because sure as shit, this wasn't the ideal place for either one of them.

"Okay, yeah," Than agreed. "Limos doesn't fight."

Limos huffed. "Guys, hellooooo. I'm immortal. I'll be fine."

"You might be immortal, but you aren't immune to injury," Ares reminded her. "And remember what Reaver said about unborn children of immortals when Regan was pregnant? That their mortal status can't be judged until they're born? They're still vulnerable in the womb."

Reseph nodded. "No fighting, Li. And no arguing."

Outside the ground rumbled again. Reseph turned back to the window and abruptly wished he hadn't. "Jesus. There's got to be thousands of demons out there now. And they're closing in."

A hundred curses fell from Ares's lips in as many languages. "We can't stand up to that. Shit. Where the fuck is Reaver? I summoned him an hour ago."

"I'm done waiting, Horsemen." Lucifer's voice rattled what was left of Jillian's windows. "I think I'll send for your mates and children. And then I'll tear their limbs off one by one until you show your cowardly faces. Come out now and spare their lives."

"*Bastard.*" Thanatos raced for the door, Ares on his heels, but Reseph leaped in front of them. They checked up, but barely, their big bodies trembling with the desire to fight for their families.

For the first time, Reseph understood that.

"I'll surrender myself," Reseph said to them. "It's me he wants."

"Reseph, no," Jillian gasped. "You can't."

"Excuse me." Tracker crept forward tentatively, haltingly, as if he expected to be struck for speaking. He pulled a small, clear case from his pocket, and deep inside Reseph, Pestilence stirred. "I have something for Reseph." He held it out, but a booming voice froze them all.

"*Reseph!*" Reaver materialized at Tracker's side. "Do not take that."

"Why not?"

"It's concentrated evil," Reaver said in a commanding tone that shook the entire house. "Merely touching it could set Pestilence free."

Forty

Bile rose up in Reseph's throat as he stared at the crystal case. "I don't understand."

"It's the *malador*." Tracker lifted the lid to reveal a thorny black chain connected to a pulsing obsidian stone. "Harvester said it will give you the power you need to defeat Lucifer."

Reaver palmed Reseph's shoulder, and he felt the angel's heat through the metal. "Don't take it. Don't even *think* about taking it. That's what Lucifer tortured Harvester for, and if Lucifer wants it, it's gotta be plutonium-grade evil."

Reseph understood Reaver's concern. Hell, Reseph had the same concern. But this might be the only shot they had at beating Lucifer. Then again, if Pestilence came out... shit.

"Look outside, Reaver. We can't defeat Lucifer." Deep inside Reseph, Pestilence laughed. The fucker. "Not without help. If I can keep control of Pestilence, this could work."

"It's risky," Thanatos said. "*Too* risky." Souls swirled

all around him as he paced in front of the door, his rage barely contained. Ares wasn't much better off, his hand opening and closing over the pommel of his sword.

"Reaver, can't you help?" Arik asked. "You're an angel. Angels are supposed to fight demons, right?"

"If Lucifer was attacking humans, yes. But this is a demon matter. No civilian humans are involved. Your mates don't count because they've been altered in some way. We can't interfere." Reaver's eyes glittered. "Well, other angels can't. I won't let my children suffer."

"What about your Watcher rules?" Reseph asked.

"Fuck it," Reaver said with a shrug. "I've broken rules before."

Reseph looked at each person in the room, ending with Jillian. He'd caused everyone so much pain, had never shown a bit of mercy. Now he could spare them more pain. No one would fight, and Reaver wouldn't break any rules.

"I'm going alone."

There was a chorus of *bullshit*s and *fuck you*s from everyone, including, surprisingly, Arik.

Reseph cut them all off with a curse of his own. "I swear to you, I'll control Pestilence, but for this to work, Lucifer has to believe he's in charge and I've turned my back on you."

"My minions are outside Ares's mansion." Lucifer called out. "You have two minutes before I order an attack." As his voice faded away, a war chant started up, a guttural oath in Sheoulic that spoke of breaking bones, spilled innards, and skull-fucking.

Yeah, Reseph was going to end this. None of those hellspawn were going to lay a hand—or anything worse—on Jillian's skull.

Taking a deep breath, Reseph took the case from Tracker's hand. The moment he did, a dark, oily evil hit him like a fist. It was a punch to the head with a follow-up strike to the gut. His stomach rolled, and deep inside him, the container holding Pestilence developed a massive new crack.

Yes, yes, yes! The voice was a whisper in Reseph's mind, a whisper, and yet somehow it was way too loud. *Put it on. We'll rule the world.*

"Shut the fuck up," Reseph muttered.

"Reseph?" Jillian's sweet voice came from behind him.

His throat clogged as he turned to her. "It'll be okay." If he had to make a deal with the devil—literally—he would. "I just hope you don't hate me after this."

"Never," she whispered, but he doubted that.

Reseph dipped his head so his lips grazed the shell of her ear. "Thank you for giving me the happiest days of my life."

Before she could say anything, he kissed her. Kissed her with as much passion as he could put into it. And then, before he could change his mind, he broke away from her.

Fisting the chain, he slipped it over his head. Pestilence roared to the surface, victory exploding from his very essence.

Join with Lucifer. Destroy our siblings! Fuck your little whore until she's dead!

"No!" Reseph fell to his knees, struggling to keep Pestilence from completely escaping the vessel and throwing off the hands that came down to help him. Pestilence wasn't going to play nice. Reseph had to find another way. Get his cooperation. He looked out at the army of demons. "We want that army for ourselves. If we destroy Lucifer, *we* can be Satan's right hand. We can assure ourselves a place at his side when the biblical Apocalypse begins."

Yes... yes, I like that. Lucifer was always such an asshole.

It was dangerous to work with Pestilence, and Reseph knew it. The joy Pestilence took in killing would fill Reseph like a drug and cloud his judgment. But he had no choice. He just had to hope no one in the house believed what he'd just said out loud in his conversation with his evil half.

Shoving to his feet, he staggered to the doorway, refusing to meet anyone's gaze. Especially not Jillian's. Get it together ... get it together ...

He breathed deeply, giving himself a moment to draw on Pestilence's malignant energy and fill himself with strength. Power sizzled over the surface of his skin and his muscles juiced up, turning his body into a giant battery of evil.

That's it. We are invincible.

Palming his sword, Reseph strode out of the house and across the clearing. The first ten demons who tried to strike him down found out how powerful a tiny piece of evil could make a Horseman. The eleventh, a Cruentus male who had served Pestilence, recognized his master and fell to his knees in awesome supplication.

After that, the crowd parted like the Red Sea before Moses.

Reseph approached Lucifer, employing his trademark cocky confidence and Pestilence's arrogance. "Hey, Lucy."

The fallen angel, currently dressed as a leather-clad biker with waist-length black hair, gave him a nasty smile. All around him, the wind shrieked as if it were being tortured, but not a single snowflake touched Lucifer. Even Mother Nature kept a respectful distance from the evil monster.

"I'm going to cut that loose tongue right out of your head, you pompous cock."

"Aw." Reseph feigned a pout. "You're sad that Lilith's tongue no longer services that tiny dick of yours."

Lucifer hissed. He'd never had much of a sense of humor. "Let the pain begin." He raised his hand, and his minions readied their weapons.

"Hold!" Reseph's voice carried on the wind, amplified by Pestilence's resonance. "We're ready to strike a deal."

Deal? No deal! Pestilence beat at the walls of Reseph's skull.

"I'll serve you. I'll be your lackey, your whipping boy, your . . . whatever. Willingly." God, he nearly threw up at the words. Pestilence had been at Lilith's with Lucifer enough to know what peculiar tastes the male had. But Reseph would do whatever Lucifer wanted for all eternity if it meant his family would be safe. "Leave my family alone, and I'll do whatever you want."

This is a trick, yes? We'll crush him in his own house. Reseph ignored Pestilence.

"No deal, asshole. You'll do all of that anyway. *After* I crush everyone and everything you hold dear."

Lucifer, in a massive surge of power, snared Reseph by the throat and lifted him into the air. Reseph strained in his grip, managing to strike out with his fist, but Reseph's blows barely made the demon flinch. Lucifer squeezed, digging his fingers into Reseph's skin so hard he heard popping noises and felt blood spurt. Pain shot down his spine—hot, molten—and he swore his muscles were peeling off the bones.

Impotent fury pounded in Reseph's veins, and pressure constricted his lungs, filling them with fire instead of air.

"This," Lucifer growled, "is for Lilith."

He hurled Reseph across the clearing as easily as if he'd thrown a ball for a dog. Reseph smashed through the side of Jillian's house and landed in a crumpled heap of pain, broken bones, and failure.

Forty-one

Reaver beat everyone to Reseph, who was lying dazed on the floor behind Jillian's couch. "Reseph? Can you hear me?" As Jillian kneeled at Reseph's side Reaver channeled healing power into the Horseman, and within seconds, Reseph's bones knitted back together.

"Got my immortal ass kicked," he muttered. He looked up and snarled. "What's Revenant doing here?"

Reaver glared at his evil counterpart. "He showed up a minute ago."

"I'm here to keep Reaver in line," Revenant said. "Can't have any broken rules now, can we?"

Outside, the chanting started again. Rising up above the chants were thunderous footsteps. Coming close. Too close, too fast.

Reaver moved from Reseph to Kynan in the blink of a human eye. Being an angel was awesome sometimes. "I need you to do something that's going to rebel against your every instinct."

Ky narrowed his eyes. "What?"

"Do you trust me?"

"Yeah." Kynan inclined his head in a slow, serious nod. "There's no one I trust more."

Reaver prepared himself for something he never thought he'd say. Something that could put Heaven in the worst kind of danger. Something that would go down as either a brilliant strategy—or the most disastrous move in history. "Give Heofon to Reseph."

"What?" Kynan backed up so fast he bumped into Revenant, who hissed like the bad-tempered ass he was. "Heofon won't give him the charmed protection I have. Why would you want him to have it?"

"Heofon," Ares rumbled. "It's a piece of Heaven, isn't it?"

Reaver nodded. "A couple of years ago, a fallen angel used it to try to open a gate between Sheoul and Heaven. We stopped him before that could happen, and Ky was given Heofon to guard. With it, Reseph can draw on the powers of Heaven."

Reseph linked one hand with Jillian's and toyed with the chain around his neck with the other. "And combined with the powers of Sheoul I'm drawing with this amulet, I'd be all but invincible." His voice vibrated with self-loathing. "And so would Pestilence. I can't risk it. I'm already fighting him. If he overpowers me…fuck. He'd be able to open that gate…"

"And lead a demonic invasion into Heaven," Kynan finished.

Revenant grinned like a vampire in a blood bank.

"No." Shaking his head, Reseph stood, backing away from Jillian and continuing his momentum until his spine cracked against the wall. "I'm not strong enough for this."

"Yes, you are." Jillian approached him cautiously, as if he were a flighty foal she didn't want to startle. "I've seen how strong you are. I know you can do this."

Reseph's eyes were wild. "Can't."

Jillian took his hand. "I promise you, you can."

"Reaver." Thanatos moved forward. "What are our options if Pestilence opens a gate? Can we stop him?"

"He won't be as strong as he was when his Seal was broken, but he'll have a demon army behind him."

"With no prophecy to help you pathetic losers along with this," Revenant chimed in, "you're kind of screwed."

"That's so helpful," Limos muttered.

Reseph turned to Reaver. "What about Wormwood?"

Everyone got quiet...except Jillian. "What's Wormwood?"

"It's the only weapon that can kill Pestilence," Reaver said.

"But...won't that kill Reseph, too?" Jillian plastered herself to Reseph's side. "No. You can't do that."

Turning, Reseph drove his fingers into Jillian's hair on either side of her head and drew her close enough that their foreheads almost touched. The intimacy left Reaver touched with an odd sense of longing. Why, he wasn't sure. He'd long ago decided bachelorhood was the best fit for him.

Then again, so had Reseph. "It might be the only way," Reseph murmured to Jillian. "I can't live as Pestilence again."

"But you'll *die*."

"Pestilence will die. I'm just collateral damage."

Kynan closed his eyes, and when he opened them again, they drilled into Reaver. "You sure about this?"

"I am." Reaver looked over at Reseph. "My son is

stronger than he thinks. I've always known that. And I suspect his brothers and sister know that, too."

Taking his time and with the greatest of care, Kynan handed the necklace to Jillian. Reaver didn't miss the way Revenant's eyes glittered. No doubt the evil bastard would give his very soul to gain possession of such a powerful object.

"This is a real piece of Heaven, huh?" Jillian's voice was barely a whisper. She turned to Reseph. "You can do this. It's up to you now. You'll save us. I know you will."

He swallowed. "No pressure, right?"

"No pressure," Jillian answered.

Reseph tugged her hard against him and kissed her. Out of respect, Reaver turned away, giving them a moment of privacy.

When Reaver had first taken the job of Watcher, Harvester had told him about Reseph's past. Given the flighty playboy Horseman's history, Reaver hadn't expected to see him ever fall for any one person. But clearly, he'd found his match in Jillian. They'd healed each other.

Hopefully, Jillian would be enough of an anchor for him to fight his evil half.

He turned back to the couple as they pulled apart. Reseph ducked his head, and Jillian slipped the necklace over it.

And then all hell broke loose.

Forty-two

Reseph fucking exploded out of his armor. As if a nuclear bomb had gone off on the surface of his skin, his armor blasted off his body, blowing through the living room like shrapnel.

Fucking. Awesome.

Completely naked, his skin glowing, Reseph looked through Pestilence's eyes on his family, some of whom had taken damage. Ares was wrenching a shard of metal out of his thigh. Thanatos was bleeding from a gash in his cheek. Limos and Arik were untouched, as was Kynan.

Jillian!

Reseph spun to where she'd been standing, ignoring Pestilence's cackling laughter. Blood splattered the floor, but Jillian was okay. Reaver must have shoved her behind him. The angel, on the other hand, was clutching his belly, from which a dinner plate–sized piece of metal jutted.

Funny.

Reseph wanted to help. Wanted to say he was sorry. But Pestilence had taken away his voice. He felt like a spectator as his own hand reached out in a *come to Papa* gesture, and suddenly, all of his armor ripped free of the walls, the furniture, from bodies, and snapped back into place.

We are so strong, Pestilence shouted. *We can rule the heavens now!*

First things first, Reseph reminded him. *We need to destroy Lucifer.*

The power-hungry demon purred his approval. *And with the two amulets and Lucifer's blood, we can break the barrier between Heaven and Sheoul.*

The container that had housed Pestilence was wide open and empty. Reseph knew, without a doubt, that when the battle with Lucifer was over, the battle for freedom would begin. One of them would return to the container.

Reluctantly, Reseph let Pestilence take over. Pestilence's pure evil vibe would give them an advantage, and they needed every extra edge they could get.

But Reseph refused to go too deep, terrified that if he buried himself too heavily under Pestilence, he'd never be able to claw his way back out.

At the living room door, Pestilence, that bastard, halted. Very slowly he turned to Jillian, and Reseph felt Pestilence's twisted lust heat his groin.

The parking lot incident flashed through Reseph's head—Jillian's screams, her terror, Pestilence's sick anticipation. The things he had planned to do to her after the Soulshredders were done...

"No!" Reseph lurched toward her, but someone shoved him outside the house, and Pestilence took over, laughing his fucking ass off.

They cut a swath through the army of demons, kicking at the ones who didn't bow deeply enough and beheading the ones who didn't bow at all.

Lucifer, standing atop the shallow rise at the rear of the army, grinned as they approached. "Back for more? Or are you here to surrender?"

"Neither." The voice coming from Reseph's mouth was smoky and harsh, singing with power, and Lucifer's expression fell.

"Pestilence." Lucifer narrowed his eyes. "What trick is this? I feel power around you."

"Trick?" Pestilence's and Reseph's speech and thoughts were in perfect sync, and for the first time, Reseph realized how intertwined they really were. "We're here to bleed you dry, you prick."

Lucifer didn't hesitate. He shed his human skin and morphed into a massive, veiny beast, its wingspan nearing thirty feet, its horns jutting out of its skull like the world's largest bull. With a lightning-quick wave of his clawed hand, a bolt of lava-hot electricity shot through Reseph's armor. Pain ripped through him, but it was dull, as if divided between Pestilence and him.

"You silly fuck." Again, Reseph and Pestilence were in sync. "We have the power of Heaven behind us, as well as the power of hell." He cocked his head at Lucifer. "You die now."

Reseph launched at Lucifer, punching through one of the demon's leathery wings, crushing bones, shredding skin. Lucifer roared in fury, raking his serrated claws across Reseph's face and flaying open his cheek. He healed almost instantly, which was super cool.

The pendants around his neck vibrated and began

to glow bright enough to cast light deep into the forest beyond. Lucifer's gaze dropped to the stones, and with a hiss, he stumbled backward.

"*Heofon.*" Lucifer's voice quivered, and Pestilence nearly came at the fear and envy mingling in Lucifer's words. "Give it to me."

"As if." Reseph snorted. "Do you think we can deal now?"

Pestilence laughed, aware that Reseph was fucking with the demon.

"Heofon for the lives of your families," Lucifer said.

"I have a better idea." Pestilence thrust his sword through Lucifer's abdomen. "Your death for a gate between Heaven and Sheoul."

No! Reseph screamed, helpless to stop Pestilence. Blood splashed onto the amulets and sudden power sang through Reseph like a tuning fork, the rush of unlimited strength filling his body. It was like a drug...a damned-near orgasmic drug that stroked every one of Reseph's pleasure centers. Not just stroked them, but sucked them off and swallowed.

Ah...damn...so...good.

Pestilence rose up, taking full control. As if in a fog—a fog of euphoria—Reseph watched his sword hack apart Lucifer. The fallen angel wasn't going to die from blows alone...hell, nothing Pestilence could do would actually kill Lucifer.

But Pestilence wouldn't have to.

The very air surrounding them warped, turning everything outside their bubble of normalcy into contorted reflections from funhouse mirrors. A churning wind spun up, swirling around them like a tornado. It shot upward, piercing the sky and stretching toward the heavens. Beneath their feet, the ground fell away, leaving them hovering over a black hole that plunged straight into hell.

The gate. Holy fuck, the gate!

Lucifer screamed as the whirling tornado snatched him, bit by bit, pulling him apart and sucking pieces of his body into the maelstrom. Red streaks discolored the translucent vortex as his blood spun higher and higher.

The last chunk of Lucifer, a section of his skull, disappeared into the wind. It would be only minutes until the gate was fully opened, and hordes from hell could swarm into Heaven.

"Stop!" Reseph clawed at Pestilence, hammered at his mind, but it was like trying to wake from a nightmare. This was a repeat of being helpless as Pestilence committed atrocities for an entire year. He couldn't go through that again. The difference was that during the year Pestilence had been at the helm Reseph hadn't been this close to the surface. Reseph also hadn't believed he had so much to fight for.

Now he did. He had brothers and a sister, in-laws, a nephew, and another niece or nephew on the way. A father. A mate—if Jillian would have him, anyway. He couldn't lose any of those people.

If he could just ... force ... Pestilence—

"Reseph!"

Jillian?

In excruciatingly slow motion, Reseph turned around. Jillian stood outside the vortex, her hair blowing wildly, her eyes shot wide with terror. And yet, she stood strong, a warrior facing almost certain death.

Pestilence smiled. "We're going to kill you, human whore."

Shut up!

Pestilence didn't listen. "Your screams will be the theme music for the demon march to Heaven."

Jillian held out her hand. "Take me then. Finish what you started."

Jillian, no!

Reseph watched in horror as Pestilence reached out and yanked Jillian into the vortex.

Jillian had thought she was prepared to do this. To face down the thing that terrified her the most in hopes of helping Reseph fight to defeat Pestilence.

But as Pestilence tugged her against him, his cold grin sending shivers down her spine, she knew she was in way over her head.

"Reseph," she cried, "I know you're in there."

"Oh, he's in here." Pestilence twined her hair in his fist and yanked her head back, nearly snapping her neck. "And he doesn't care what I do to you."

Reaver had warned her that Pestilence would lie to her, try to hurt her any way he could, and clearly, the angel had been right. She hadn't needed the warning though; she knew Reseph too well.

"Fight, Reseph—"

Pestilence jerked her head viciously to the side, exposing her throat, and then he exposed her chest when he tore open her shirt.

"We're going to have some fun, Jillian."

"Reseph!"

A godawful roar erupted from Pestilence, and the evil glow in his eyes dimmed. Reseph. It was Reseph!

"Baby," he croaked. "Get out…get…*out*." He shoved her, but she hooked her leg around his and clung to his arm with all her strength. Awkwardly, she reached up and swept her fingers over his armor scar the way Limos had told her to do.

In less time than it took for Sam to stomp his big foot, Reseph's armor disappeared, and he looked down, confused. He seemed to be a mix of Reseph and Pestilence now, as if they were sharing equal power. She took advantage, snatching Wormwood from the waistband of her jeans and bringing it up to Reseph's chest.

She'd sworn to Reseph's siblings that she'd destroy Pestilence if she had to, but dammit, she knew it wouldn't come to that. She had faith that Reseph would beat that bastard himself.

"Bitch!" Pestilence hissed. Bitterly cold breath stung her cheeks as he leaned in. "I'm going to flay you—" His head snapped to the side as if he'd been struck.

Reseph broke through, wrapping his hand around Jillian's. "Do it," he croaked. "Please." Jillian struggled, but she was no match for his strength as he pressed in, and the tip of the blade penetrated his skin.

Reseph's expression contorted, his eyes alternating between glowing malevolence and the intense cleverness that always glittered in Reseph's gaze. The internal battle raged, and even though Jillian was plastered to his body, she was somehow in the middle of the struggle, sometimes her grip on the dagger being peeled away, and sometimes being forced tighter.

"Arik's soul," Reseph bit out. "Release Arik's soul and I'll ditch the dagger."

Pestilence must have refused. The dagger in her hand sliced forward, plunging deep into Reseph's flesh.

"No!" She tried to pull Wormwood free, but Reseph was holding it steady. Sweat dampened his pale skin, and his teeth were clenched hard.

"Fuck you, Pestilence." Reseph smiled down at Jillian, although it was really more of a grimace. "Another centimeter in and we're both done. You know I'll do it. Release Arik's soul *now*."

Reseph's body went slack, but only for a heartbeat. In another heartbeat, she was thrown clear of the vortex, landing hard on the sheet of ice that had formed in a thirty-yard circle around them. The demon army had long since disappeared, sucked away when the freaky tornado had taken form. Instead, Thanatos, Limos, Ares, Arik, Kynan, Tracker, and the two Watchers were standing nearby.

They ran toward her, but her focus was on Reseph, who was still inside the cyclone. Something seemed to be wrong, though...or maybe right?

He was twisting in what looked like agony, grabbing his head and tearing at his hair. He yanked Wormwood out of his chest with a bellow of victory, and then the dagger was spinning up into the sky. Shrill screeches, like a million crows cawing, erupted from deep below the ground.

Revenant laughed. "Satan's forces are coming. The gate is open!"

"Reseph!" she screamed.

Reseph threw himself against the wall of the tornado, over and over, clutching his head as the noises grew louder.

"Please! You can do this." Jillian's voice was a sob now as despair squeezed her in its grip.

Throwing back his head, Reseph roared. The vortex wobbled, just a little. Another roar, and the wobble moved the entire thing several feet. Sections of it began to disintegrate, and the wobbling grew more violent.

Jillian shoved to her feet. "Reseph?"

He hurled himself out, landing in front of her, his body bruised and bloody. Groaning, he twisted around to look at her.

With Pestilence's eyes.

Swallowing her fear, Jillian framed his face in her hands. "I love you. Come back to me." Without thinking, she kissed him.

Startled, he pulled back, but she didn't let him go. She kept her mouth on his, kissing him hard, kissing him in a frenzied, last-ditch effort to bring back the Horseman she loved.

For a beautiful moment, he kissed her back, his lips tender, his tongue a fleeting brush against hers. Elation warmed her, fed into her hope that this was it. This was Reseph winning—

Stinging pain seared her mouth. He'd bitten her lip. She tasted blood, felt her world crash down around her.

"*Jillian.*" Reseph's voice dripped with agony. He reared back, a snarl tearing from his throat. "You. Will. Not. Win!"

Reaching up, he gripped the two chains around his neck and yanked them hard enough to snap the links.

As if the air had been let out of a giant balloon, everything went still and eerily quiet. The tornado disappeared as if it had never been, the gate closed, and Reseph collapsed onto the ice.

"Reseph?" She brushed his hair away from his face, willing him to open his eyes. "Are you okay? Talk to me."

When he didn't move, she put her ear to his chest. What if Wormwood *had* worked? *Please don't be dead... please don't be dead...*

He had a heartbeat. Thank God, he was alive, but why wasn't he moving? "Reseph!" She shook his shoulders, and his eyes popped open.

An exhausted smile curved his lips. "Hey, babe."

She threw herself at him. Covered his body with hers and just held on. "Please tell me it's over. Please."

His arms came around her. "It's over," he rasped. "I beat the bastard. It was like mental arm wrestling, but I did it."

"Are you sure?" Thanatos crouched a few feet away, the broken chain belonging to the evil stone dangling from his hand. "Pestilence is contained?"

"Yeah. I repaired the vessel."

Jillian's breath trembled out of her. "Vessel?"

"Long story." Reseph looked up at Jillian, his gaze so tender it brought tears to her eyes. "It was you, Jillian. I honestly don't know if I'd have had the strength to overcome him, but I couldn't let him hurt you. And I couldn't let what he'd done keep haunting me and cracking the container."

She buried her face in his neck, not caring about any strange container. What mattered was that he'd won. "I knew you could do it. I never doubted you."

"Arik, you got your soul back." Reseph smoothed his palm up and down her back. "I know it doesn't make up for everything—"

"Hey." Arik cut off Reseph. "I think it's time we all start over."

"I agree," Jillian murmured. "I'm ready for a fresh

start." She pushed up and looked down at her blood-streaked skin and torn shirt. "And a shower."

Reseph grinned. "I'm in."

"Jesus," Ares muttered. "A whopping two minutes have passed since you nearly started a war between Heaven and Sheoul and you're already getting frisky?"

"It wasn't me who nearly started the war," Reseph said. "It was Pestilence."

Jillian tightened her arms around him, relief settling over her in the first pure, warm peace she'd felt in a long time. This was truly the first time he'd acknowledged that Pestilence had been the source of evil in every event. Yes, she knew he'd always harbor guilt for everything that had happened, but the victory today had gone a long way toward healing a devastating wound.

"And," Reseph continued, "Do you even know me? Hellooo...I'm naked, with a drop-dead gorgeous female lying on top of me. I'm not made of stone, you know."

Jillian's cheeks heated as a chorus of groans came from all sides.

"Yeah...that's our cue to leave," Limos said. She smiled down at Jillian and Reseph. "Thanks, Jillian. We all owe you. And Reseph? Good to have you back."

They all offered some sort of thanks and acknowledgment that Reseph was back...except Revenant. He looked like he'd swallowed a rotten egg as he flashed away with a snarl.

Reaver went down on his heels, taking the *malador* from Thanatos and tossing Heofon to Kynan. "I'm proud of you, Reseph." The angel squeezed Reseph's shoulder and brushed the pads of his fingers over Jillian's cheek. "Take care."

And then he was gone, flashing away in a burst of golden light.

"I hate it when he takes off like that," Kynan muttered. He gestured toward Jillian's house. "I'll handle the Aegis situation and arrange for repairs to your house. You two... get a room for the night somewhere. You deserve it."

He tucked Heofon in his coat pocket and strode away. Tracker inched closer, but kept his gaze averted. "Mistress, I can take care of the animals and bed down in the barn."

"That's not necessary—"

"Please."

Reseph tapped on Jillian's shoulder, and when she caught his eye, he nodded. She sighed. "Okay, Tracker. For tonight. Tomorrow we'll work something else out." Looking like she'd given him a reprieve from death, he took off at a run. "What was that about?"

"He doesn't know anything else," Reseph explained. "Slaves in Sheoul don't know kindness. When they get it, it's always followed by pain. He's not used to being treated well, and it's making him uncomfortable."

"That's horrible." And familiar. She stared after the werewolf, thinking about how she'd been wary when men were charming and nice, because inevitably, she'd get hurt. It had taken Reseph to change that, and somehow, she'd show Tracker that kindness didn't have to hurt.

Sighing, she looked down at Reseph. His eyes were liquid, and on her back, his hands quivered. Alarm rang through her. "Hey, what's wrong?"

"Nothing," he whispered. "Everything's right. So right."

"Because of your family? Because they're welcoming you back?"

"Yeah." Caging her in his strong arms, he rolled her onto her back, his muscled weight a welcome indulgence. The chill of the ice barely registered as he settled himself between her legs. "And because of you. A few days ago I had nothing but revenge to keep my heart beating. Now I have my family back, and I have you." He paused. "I do have you, right?"

"Oh, yes." She trailed her fingers over his jaw, loving the way he rubbed against them. "I said I wanted the Reseph I found in the snowbank, and here you are."

"But I'm not exactly him," he said, an emotional warble in his voice revealing his fear. "So much has happened since then—"

"Shh." She silenced him with a finger against his lips. "Yes, so much has happened. You learned you were strong enough to keep Pestilence at bay, and I learned that the man I love is willing to fight demons for me. You have me." She gave him a sultry smile and slid her hand between their bodies to palm his erection. "And you can have me anytime."

"God, I love you," he groaned. The next thing she knew, she was in his arms, cradled against his chest, and he was opening a Harrowgate. "First, we're stopping at Ares's place for a hot shower and clothes. Then I'm taking you to the most luxurious hotel in the Bahamas."

"Sounds decadent." Even as exhausted as she was, she could imagine all the ways they could enjoy each other. In both places.

He hugged her tight. "This is just the beginning for us, and I can't wait to get started."

Neither could she.

Forty-three

Reaver didn't bother to ask permission to enter Archangel Hall. He strode inside with an I-don't-give-a-shit attitude and a smug expression to match.

Maybe at some point in his life he'd been in awe of the giant gold columns that pierced the endless azure sky and of the crystal rivers that wound through lush grass that went on forever. But not now.

Now he just wanted answers.

An angel dressed in some sort of obnoxious crimson medieval garb came from out of nowhere and blocked Reaver's path. "Who are you, and why are you here?"

"I'm Reaver. I need to see an archangel."

The male smiled. "Then go through the proper channels with your request."

"It's not a request, and I can't wait years for this."

Crimson Angel Guy narrowed his eyes. "Go away—"

"Hold." A tall black-haired male materialized like

something out of a *Star Trek* transporter, all gold and silver sparkles. His Greek-style robe was cinched at the waist with a simple brown rope, and his leather boots were nothing to write home about, but somehow this angel exuded power and royalty. His raven wings, shot through with gold, were probably the envy of everyone he came into contact with.

Reaver included.

The newcomer, definitely an archangel, waved his hand, and the angel in the crimson getup flashed away in a huff.

"Well, well," the archangel said. "Reaver. Still not one for following rules, I see."

"Since you seem to know so much about me, how about some reciprocation?"

The male's smile was cold. "Raphael. Now, why are you here?"

Straight to it, then. Good, because Reaver wasn't in the mood to mess around. "I want to know why my memory was taken."

"I'm sure you do."

Alrighty then. "I know who I am," Reaver ground out. "I know my given name is Yenrieth, so I might as well have my memories back."

The chilly smile fell off Raphael's face. "That is... unexpected." He wheeled away, only to pace in a wide circle before stopping in front of Reaver again. "But it makes no difference. You don't get your memory back."

"Damn you—"

Reaver didn't get to finish his sentence. Pain like a million lightning bolts crackling through him sent him crumpling to the ground, blinded and groaning like a green soldier who'd taken his first wound. When he could see again…felt like a year later…Raphael was looking down at him, his silver eyes flashing like blades.

"You do not speak like that to me, nor do you question my decisions."

By some miracle, Reaver didn't groan again as he staggered to his feet. "So memory loss it is." His head throbbed like he'd been clobbered by his own halo. "Maybe you can tell me why my daughter and sons have a new evil Watcher. Do you know what rule Harvester broke?"

For a long time, Raphael merely stared, his expression blank. Just as Reaver's archangel-acute migraine started to ease, Raphael said, "She didn't break any rules. She was taken for espionage. For helping the wrong side."

"Helping the wrong side? You mean *us*?" Raphael had to be mistaken. "How?"

"By manipulating events."

Now it was Reaver's turn to stare. "I don't…I don't understand. She's the one who wrote the note that The Aegis found…the one that Pestilence believed would break Than's Seal."

The archangel inclined his head in a slight nod. "She did it knowing sex wouldn't break Than's Seal. She did it so a child would be conceived. A child who could end the Apocalypse if all went well, and she had faith that the Horsemen would figure out how to stop Pestilence."

Reaver's head spun, which didn't help the throbbing. "Why would she do that?"

"Because she was a spy."

"A…spy?" Reaver asked, incredulous. "For how long?"

"Since the beginning." Raphael said it so easily, as if everyone should have been aware of this information. "We fabricated a story about how she'd begun to kill humans for fun, leading to her fall, but in truth, she fell in order to infiltrate the highest orders in Sheoul and earn her way to become Watcher."

"But why? Why would she give up so much to become a fallen angel?"

Raphael's shake of his head and rolling eyes told Reaver what the archangel thought of Harvester's reasons. "She'd been watching over your children since before they were Horsemen. She even saved Reseph from a fire that would have killed him. She loved them."

This kept getting more and more unbelievable. "Where was I?" Reaver demanded. "Why wasn't *I* watching over my children?"

"It doesn't matter," Raphael said, his tone making it clear that Reaver wasn't going to get any answers about his past. "What matters is that Harvester was a spy, and she's done the world a great service."

Reaver threw his hand out to catch himself on a pillar before he fell over. "Why didn't she tell me? Why didn't *someone* tell me about her?"

"We couldn't risk anyone knowing. Any slip could have been dangerous." Raphael's expression became clouded with anger, and a menacing growl rose up in his chest. "Look what happened with Gethel."

The time he'd caught Gethel working Harvester over with *treclan* spikes came back to him, and his breath hitched. "Gethel tortured Harvester. She suspected, didn't she?"

"Most likely," Raphael said. "I'm almost certain it was Gethel who ratted Harvester out to the forces of Sheoul."

Ah, damn. Harvester had tried to warn Reaver, had said that Gethel wasn't right. She didn't mean that Gethel was *wrong*. She'd meant that Gethel was *mental*, and maybe playing for the wrong side, if she was torturing Harvester for proof that Harvester was a good guy.

But had Gethel spoken the truth about *anything*?

"Gethel told me Harvester was Satan's consort and she fell from Heaven to be with him. How does that play into any of this?"

Raphael's eyebrows shot up. "That's what she told you? Gethel loved messing with your head, didn't she?"

"She wouldn't need to mess with my head if I had my memories," Reaver growled. "So Harvester wasn't secretly sleeping around with Satan?"

Raphael laughed. Actually *laughed*. "I should hope not. He's her father."

Father? Holy... shit. Reaver's voice was slightly strangled when he spoke. "So what do we do now?"

"We hunt Gethel down and destroy her."

Gladly. "And Harvester?"

"She is lost to us."

An unexpected stab of guilt lanced Reaver in the chest. "She's dead?"

Raphael shrugged. "We lost contact with her when she was dragged to Sheoul. No doubt she'll be tortured for some time."

"Won't Satan protect her?"

Another burst of laughter from Raphael set Reaver's nerves on edge. "The only thing Satan hates more than a traitor is a traitor in his family. You should have seen what was left of one of his sons after he sided with another fallen angel in an argument between the angel and Satan." Raphael shook his head. "No, Harvester will suffer like no one ever has for this."

"Then we need to rescue her."

Raphael waved his hand in dismissal. "She knew the risks when she volunteered for the assignment. She understood that it was a one-way trip and that if she was caught, we would disavow all knowledge of her actions."

Reaver's jaw nearly hit the ground. "Are you kidding me? We can't leave her there!"

"Any attempt at rescue would be an admission of our involvement. They can't know that we arranged for two agents of good to be assigned to the Horsemen. It could start another war between Heaven and Hell. Even if it were possible to get her out, she won't be the same innocent young angel who fell. To survive Sheoul and earn a place as Watcher, she had to do things that hardened her heart and blackened her soul. Her sacrifice is one of the greatest in angelic history, but she is lost to us."

"There has to be a way."

"Let it go, Yenrieth." Raphael's voice deepened, became a booming thunder. "Hear me now. You will not make any attempt to rescue her. If you do, I'll tear off your wings myself and toss you into the darkest pit in Sheoul. Do you understand?"

Reaver understood, all right. He understood that Raphael was a massive douchebag.

"I'm also taking you off Watcher duty."

A bone-deep fury welled up in Reaver, scouring his veins as if they ran with steam instead of blood. "You can't do that."

Raphael's calm was maddening. "I can do anything I please. You are the Horsemen's father, and that knowledge means you can no longer be a neutral party."

"*Neutral?* Harvester wasn't neutral, either, if she was a spy, you piece of—"

"I wouldn't finish that sentence," Raphael warned. "You're getting off lightly, given all the rules you've broken recently. Releasing Reseph from Sheoul-gra? Keeping Wormwood from Thanatos? Giving Heofon to Pestilence? Shall I go on?"

"The *rules* are bullshit. You broke the biggest of all by sending Harvester to infiltrate hell. How dare you accuse *me* of breaking rules, you overgrown vulture."

"One more word," Raphael said slowly, "and you will lose what little memory you have, and I'll wipe you from your children's minds as well."

Trembling with the kind of rage Reaver rarely experienced, he spun and headed toward the exit. As he reached it, he flared his wings high and violently, a big, fat, *fuck you* to the angel watching him leave.

It was about time for a vacation, and Reaver had heard that Sheoul was nice this time of year.

Forty-four

Reseph finished scooping grain into a bucket and popped the lid onto the bin. Impatient snorts told him he was moving too slow as he hauled the feed to the stalls at the end of the barn, where Sammy and Conquest waited. The two horses had struck a friendship that, to be honest, baffled Reseph. Conquest wasn't the nicest of stallions, but he'd taken to the gelding and liked to hang out in the barn with him.

"You two are goofballs," Reseph muttered as he poured grain into their troughs.

He headed back to the house, casting a quick look toward the clearing where, just beyond, they were building a cabin for Tracker. The warg refused to live any farther away, and despite Jillian's desire to have him stay in the guest bedroom while the cabin was being constructed, he preferred to sleep in the barn.

Reseph stomped the snow off his boots on the porch

and went inside the house, where Jillian was waiting, curled up on the couch under a blanket, two steaming cups of hot cocoa on the table in front of her.

"Critters are all fed and happy." He glanced over at Fang-Doodle, who was dozing in his usual spot in front of the fire. "Some of them are a little fatter and happier than others."

Jillian narrowed her eyes at him. "I hope you aren't talking about me."

Grinning, Reseph sank down on the couch, straddling her on all fours. "What, you aren't happy?"

"Jerk." She gave him a playful swat on the shoulder, but a frown followed on its heels. "Are you sure *you'll* be happy here? It's in the middle of nowhere, not much to keep you busy, and we get tons of snow—"

"Shh." He brushed his lips over hers. Emotion welled up in him, filling him so completely that he could barely breathe, let alone speak. "I'm sure. I spent so much time keeping busy and being empty. But out here, with you, I don't need to be busy. I feel like I'm finally whole. I'm five thousand years old," he rasped. "But the day you found me in the woods, that's when my life started."

Jillian gripped his collar and tugged him down on top of her. "I spent so much time worrying that no man would ever be what he appeared to be that I didn't realize being more isn't always bad."

"So you're glad I'm not the man you found in the snowbank?"

"Oh, you are that man. But you're so much more, too." She rolled her bottom lip between her teeth and gave him a hesitant glance. "I feel terrible though ... I haven't had time to get you anything for Christmas."

"Are you kidding me? You've given me everything. I even have my family back because of you."

Now that everyone was sure Reseph could control Pestilence, he and Jillian were welcome at his siblings' houses, and they'd all popped over here as well. Thanatos had even allowed Reseph to hold Logan. They still had to work on getting the hellhounds to come around, but Reseph figured there was plenty of time for that.

"Speaking of which," she said, "we're invited to Than's place for Christmas dinner tomorrow. They said if Tracker is back from his pack by then to bring him, too." She sighed. "I'll bet he's never celebrated Christmas."

Seriously doubtful. Few human holidays were celebrated in Sheoul. "Let's pick up something for him tomorrow. I know a great electronics store in Tokyo."

"See?" Her hands traveled slowly down his back, massaging as they went. "That's what I mean about being so much more than the man I found in a snowbank. Who else can take me shopping in another country in a matter of seconds?"

He nuzzled her neck. "Wanna know what else I can do in a matter of seconds?"

Shifting so he settled between her thighs, she arched under him, and her voice went deep and husky. "Oh, I'm very well aware of that."

"Yeah?"

"Yeah. And I think I do know what to give you for Christmas." She gave him a naughty smile. "But first, you have to unwrap me."

Oh, how Reseph loved presents. "And then you unwrap me?"

"Mmm. Very, very slowly."

Jillian followed up on the slowly thing. After he was naked, she spent an hour worshipping his body and doing wicked things with one of the candy canes on the tree.

As Reseph lay sated and exhausted, tangled with her in front of the fire, he could only think that hundreds of Christmases and thousands of presents had come and gone for him, but this one, above all others, was the best. The Apocalypse was over, his entire family was whole and happy, and he'd been given the greatest gift of all.

Love.

Turn the page for an excerpt of

PLEASURE UNBOUND

the first in Larissa Ione's
fantastic Demonica series

ONE

❧

> **The demon is a prince of the air and can
> transform himself into several shapes, delude
> our senses for a time; but his power is determined,
> he may terrify us but not hurt.**
> **– Robert Burton, *Anatomy of Melancholy***

Had Eidolon been anywhere but the hospital, he would have killed the guy pleading for his life before him.

As it was, he'd have to save the bastard.

'Sometimes, being a doctor blows,' he muttered, and jabbed the demon in a human suit with a syringe full of hemoxacin.

The patient screamed as the needle passed through mangled thigh tissue, releasing blood sterilization medication into the wound.

'You didn't numb him first?'

Eidolon snorted at his younger brother's words. 'The Haven spell keeps me from killing him. It doesn't prevent me from dispensing a little justice during treatment.'

'Can't escape your old job, huh?' Shade pushed aside the curtain separating two of the three ER cubicles and stepped fully inside. 'The son of a bitch eats babies. Let me wheel him outside and waste his sorry ass.'

'Wraith already offered.'

'Wraith offers to waste all the patients.'

Eidolon grunted. 'Probably a good thing our little brother didn't go the doctor route.'

'Neither did I.'

'You had different reasons.'

Shade hadn't wanted to spend that much time in school, especially since his healing gift was better suited to his chosen field, paramedicine. He was all about scraping patients off the street and keeping them alive long enough for the Underworld General staff to fix them.

Blood dripped to the obsidian floor as Eidolon probed the patient's most serious wound. A female Umber demon, the same species as Shade's mother, had caught the patient sneaking into her nursery, and had somehow impaled him – several times – with a toilet brush.

Then again, Umber demons were remarkably strong for their petite size. The females were especially so. Eidolon had, on several occasions, enjoyed the application of that strength in bed. In fact, when he could no longer resist the final maturation cycle his body had entered, he planned to make an Umber female his first *infadre*. Umbers made good mothers, and only rarely did they kill the unwanted offspring of a Seminus demon.

Putting aside the thoughts that plagued him more frequently as The Change progressed, Eidolon glanced at the patient's face. The skin that should have been a deep reddish-brown was now pale with pain and blood loss. 'What's your name?'

The patient groaned. 'Derc.'

'Listen, Derc. I'm going to repair this unsightly hole, but it's going to hurt. A lot. Try not to move. Or scream like a cowering little imp.'

'Give me something for the pain, you fucking parasite,' he snarled.

'*Doctor* parasite.' Eidolon nodded at the equipment tray, and Paige, one of their few human nurses, handed him clamps.

'Derc, buddy, did you eat any of the Umber's young before she caught you?'

Hatred rolled off Shade's body as Derc shook his head, sharp teeth bared, eyes glowing orange.

'Today isn't your lucky day then. Didn't get a meal, and you aren't getting anything for the pain, either.'

Allowing himself a grim smile, Eidolon clamped the damaged artery in two places as Derc screamed vile curses and struggled against the restraints that held him on the metal table.

'Scalpel.'

Paige handed him the instrument, and he expertly sliced between the clamps. Shade crowded close, watching as he shaved away the shredded artery tissue and then held the newly clean ends together. A warm tingle wound its way down his right arm along his dermal markings to the tips of his gloved fingers, and the artery fused. The baby-eater would no longer have to worry about bleeding out. From the expression on Shade's face, however, he would have to worry about surviving more than two steps outside the hospital.

It wouldn't be the first time he'd saved a life only to have it taken once the patient had been released.

'BP's dropping.' Shade's gaze focused on the bedside monitor. 'Could be shock.'

'There's another bleed somewhere. Bring up his pressure.'

Reluctantly, Shade placed his large palm over the bony ridges in Derc's forehead. The numbers on the monitor dipped, raised, and then stabilized, but the change would be temporary. Shade's powers couldn't sustain life that wasn't there, and if Eidolon couldn't find the problem, nothing Shade did would make a difference.

A rapid assessment of the other wounds revealed nothing to explain the drop in vitals. Then, just below the patient's twelfth rib, a fresh scar. Beneath the razor-straight mark, something bubbled.

'Shade.'

'Hell's fires,' Shade breathed. His gaze snapped up as he raked his fingers through nearly black hair that, at shoulder-length, was longer than but identical in color to Eidolon's. 'It might be nothing. It might not be Ghouls.'

Ghouls. Not the cannibalistic monsters of human lore, but the term for those who carved up demons to sell their parts on the underworld black market.

Hoping his brother was right but not ripped from the womb yesterday, Eidolon pressed softly on the scar.

'Derc, what happened here?'

'Cut myself.'

'This is a surgical scar.'

UG was the only medical facility in the world that performed surgery on their kind, and Derc hadn't been treated here before.

Eidolon caught the pungent stink of fear. 'No. It was an accident.' Derc clenched his fists, his lidless eyes wild. 'You must believe me.'

'Derc, calm down. Derc?'

Monitor alarms beeped, and the baby-eater convulsed.

'Paige, grab the crash cart. Shade, keep his vitals up.'

An eerie wail seemed to leak from every pore in Derc's skin, and a stench like rotting bacon and licorice filled the small space. Paige lost her lunch in the garbage can.

The heart monitor flatlined. Shade removed his hand from the patient's forehead.

'I hate it when they do that.' Wondering what had frightened Derc so badly he'd felt the need to stop his own bodily functions, Eidolon opened the scar with a smooth slash of a scalpel, knowing what he'd find, but needing to see for sure.

Shade dug through his uniform shirt pocket and pulled out his ever-present pack of bubble gum. 'What's missing?'

'The Pan Tai sac. It processes digestive waste and returns it to the body so his species never has to urinate or defecate.'

'Handy,' Shade murmured. 'What would someone want with it?'

Paige dabbed her mouth with a surgical sponge, her complexion still greenish, though the patient's death stench had largely dissipated. 'The contents are used in some voodoo curses that affect bowel movements.'

Shade shook his head and passed the nurse a stick of gum. 'Is nothing sacred anymore?' He turned to Eidolon. 'Why didn't they kill him? They've killed the others.'

'He was worth more alive. His species can grow another organ in a matter of weeks.'

'Which they could harvest.' Shade let out a string of curses that included some Eidolon hadn't heard in his hundred years of life. 'It's gotta be The Aegis. Sick bastards.'

Whoever the bastards were, they'd been busy. Medics had brought in twelve mutilated bodies over the last two weeks, and the violence had escalated. Some of the victims showed evidence of having been carved up while still alive – and awake.

Worse, demons as a whole couldn't care less, and those who did wouldn't cooperate with other species' Councils in order to organize an investigation. Eidolon cared, not only because someone with medical knowledge was involved, but because it was only a matter of time before the butchers nabbed someone he knew.

'Paige, have the morgue fetch the body and let them know I want a copy of the autopsy report. I'm going to find out who these assholes are.'

☙

'Doc E!' Eidolon hadn't taken more than a dozen steps when Nancy, a vampire who'd been a nurse since before she was turned thirty years ago, shouted from where she sat behind the triage desk. 'Skulk called, said she's bringing in a Cruentus. ETA two minutes.'

Eidolon nearly groaned. Cruenti lived to kill, their desire to slaughter so uncontrollable that even while mating they sometimes tore each other apart. Their last Cruentus patient had broken free of his bonds and destroyed half the hospital before he could be sedated.

'Prepare ER two with the gold restraints, and page Dr. Yuri. He likes Cruenti.'

'She also said she's bringing a surprise patient.'

This time he did groan. Skulk's last surprise turned out to be a dog struck by a car. A dog he'd had to take home with him because releasing it outside the ER would have meant a fresh meal for any number of staff members. Now the damned mutt had eaten three pairs of shoes and taken over his apartment.

Shade seemed torn between wanting to be irritable with Skulk, his Umber sister, and wanting to flirt with Nancy, whom he'd already bedded twice that Eidolon knew about.

'I'm going to kill her.' Clearly, irritability won out.

'Not if I get to her first.'

'She's off-limits to you.'

'You never said I can't kill her,' Eidolon pointed out. 'Just that I can't sleep with her.'

'True.' Shade shrugged. 'You kill her, then. My mom would never forgive me.'

Shade had that right. Though Eidolon, Wraith, and Shade were purebred Seminus demons with the same long-dead sire, their mothers were all of different species, and of them, Shade's was the most maternal and protective.

Red halogen beacons rotated in their ceiling mountings, signaling the ambulance's approach. The light splashed crimson around the room, bringing out the writing on the gray walls. The drab shade hadn't been Eidolon's first choice, but it held spells better than any other color, and in a hospital where everyone was someone's mortal enemy, every advantage was critical. Because of that, the symbols and incantations had been modified to increase their protective powers.

Instead of paint, they'd been written in blood.

The ambulance pulled into the subterranean facility's bay, and Eidolon's adrenaline shot hotly into his veins. He loved this job. Loved managing his own little piece of hell that was as close to heaven as he'd ever get.

The hospital, located beneath New York City's bustling streets and hidden by sorcery right under the clueless humans' noses, was his baby. More than that, it was his promise to demonkind – whether they lived in the bowels of the earth or above ground with the humans – that they would be treated without discrimination, that their race was not forsaken by all.

The sliding ER doors whooshed open, and Skulk's paramedic partner, a werewolf who hated everyone and everything, wheeled in a bloodied Cruentus demon that had been securely strapped to the stretcher. Eidolon and Shade fell into step with Luc, and though they both topped six feet three, the were's extra three inches and thick build dwarfed them.

'Cruentus,' Luc growled, because he never made any other noises even while in human form, as he was now. 'Found unconscious. Open tib-fib fracture to the right leg. Crush wound to the back of the skull. Both injuries are sealing. Nonsealing deep lacerations to the abdomen and throat.'

Eidolon raised an eyebrow at that last. Only gold or magically enhanced weapons could have caused nonsealing wounds. All other injuries closed up on their own as the Cruentus regenerated.

'Who summoned help?'

'Some vamp found them. The Cruentus and—' he cocked one long-nailed thumb back toward the ambulance, where Skulk had rolled out the secondary stretcher '—that.'

Eidolon halted in his tracks, Shade with him. For a moment, they both stared at the unconscious humanoid female. One of the medics had cut away her red leather clothes that lay like flayed flesh beneath her. She now wore only restraints, matching black panties and bra, and a variety of weapons sheaths around her ankles and forearms.

A chill went up his double-jointed spine, and fuck no, this would not happen. 'You brought an Aegis slayer into my ER? What in all that's unholy were you thinking?'

Skulk huffed, looked up at him with flashing gunmetal eyes that matched her ashen skin and hair. 'What else was I supposed to do with her? Her partner is rat chow.'

'The Cruentus took out an Aegi?' Shade asked, and when his sister nodded, he raked his gaze over the injured human. Average humans posed little threat to demons, but those who belonged to The Aegis, a warrior guild sworn to slay them, weren't average. 'Never thought I'd thank a Cruentus. You should have turned this one into rat chow too.'

'Her injuries might do the job for us.' Skulk rattled off the list of wounds, all of which were serious, but the worst, the punctured lung, had the potential to kill the fastest. Skulk had performed a needle decompression, and for now, the slayer was stable, her color good. 'And,' she added, 'her aura is weak, thin. She hasn't been well for a long time.'

Paige drifted toward them, her hazel eyes gleaming with something close to awe. 'Never seen a Buffy before. Not a live one, anyway.'

'I have. Several.' Wraith's gravelly voice came from somewhere behind Eidolon. 'But they didn't stay alive for long.' Wraith, nearly identical to his brothers except for his blue eyes and shoulder-length, bleached blond hair, took control of the stretcher. 'I'll take her outside and dispose of her.'

Dispose of her. It was the right thing to do. After all, it was what The Aegis had done to their brother, Roag, a loss Eidolon still felt like a hole in the soul. 'No,' he said, grinding his teeth at his own decision. 'Wait.'

As tempting as it was to let Wraith have his way, only three types of beings could be turned away at UG, according to the charter he himself drafted, and Aegis butchers weren't among those listed, an oversight he intended to correct. Granted, as the equivalent to a human hospital's chief of staff, he had the final say, could send the woman to her death, but they'd just been handed a rare opportunity. His personal feelings about slayers would have to be put aside.

'Take her to ER one.'

'E,' Shade said in a voice that had gone low with disapproval, 'catch and release in this case is a bad idea. What if it's a trap? What if she's wearing some sort of tracking device?'

Wraith looked around as though he expected Aegis slayers – 'Guardians,' they called themselves – to pop in from nowhere.

'We're protected by the Haven spell.'

'Only if they attack from the inside. If they find out where we are, they could go Bin Laden on the building.'

'We'll fix her and worry about the rest later.' Eidolon wheeled the human into the prepared room, both paranoid brothers and Paige on his heels. 'We have an opportunity to learn about them. The knowledge we could gain outweighs the dangers.'

He removed the restraints and lifted her left hand. The silver and black ring on her pinky finger looked innocent enough, but when he removed it, the Aegis shield engraved on the inside of the band confirmed her identity and sent a chill through his heart. If the rumors were true, any jewelry bearing the shield was imbued with powers that bestowed slayers with night vision, resistance to certain spells, the ability to see through invisibility mantles, and gods knew what else.

'You'd better know what you're doing, E.' Wraith whipped the curtain closed to shut out the gawking staff.

Judging by the number of onlookers, they'd probably been paged. *Come see the Buffy, the nightmare that lurks in our closets.*

'Not so scary now, are you, little killer?' Eidolon murmured as he gloved up.

Her upper lip curled as though she'd heard him, and he

suddenly knew he wouldn't lose this patient. Death despised strength and stubbornness, qualities that radiated from her in waves. Unsure if her survival would be a good thing or a bad one, he cut away her bra and inspected the chest lacerations. Shade, who had been hanging around while waiting for his medic shift to start, managed her vitals, his gifted touch easing her labored, gurgling breaths.

'Paige, type her blood and get me some human O while we're waiting.'

The nurse set to work, and Eidolon widened the slayer's most serious wound with a scalpel. Blood and air bubbled through damaged lung and chest wall tissue as he inserted his fingers and held the ragged edges together for fusion.

Wraith folded his thick arms over his chest, his biceps twitching as if they wanted to lead the charge to kill the slayer. 'This is going to bite us in the ass, and you two are too stupid and arrogant to see it.'

'Ironic, isn't it,' Eidolon said flatly, 'that *you* would lecture *us* on arrogance and stupidity.'

Wraith flipped him the bird, and Shade laughed. 'Someone got up on the wrong side of the crypt. You jonesing for a fix, bro? I saw a tasty-looking junkie topside. Why don't you go eat him?'

'Screw you.'

'Shut up,' Eidolon snapped. 'Both of you. Something isn't right. Shade, look at this.' He adjusted the overhead light. 'I haven't been to med school in decades, but I've treated enough humans to know this isn't normal.'

Shade peered at the woman's organs, at the tangled mass of veins and arteries, at the strange ropes of nerve tissue that wove in and out of muscle and spongy lung. 'Looks like a bomb went off in there. What is all that?'

'No idea.' He'd never seen anything like the mess that had scrambled the slayer's insides. 'Check this out.' He pointed to a blackened blob that resembled a blood clot. A pulsing, morphing blood clot that, as they watched, swallowed healthy tissue. 'It's like it's taking over.'

Eidolon peeled back the gelled mass. His breath caught, and he rocked back on his heels.

'Hell's rings,' Shade breathed. 'She's a fucking demon.'

'*We're* fucking demons. She's some other species.'

For the first time, Eidolon allowed himself a frank, unhurried look at the nearly naked woman, from her black-painted toes to matted hair the color of red wine. Smooth skin stretched over curves and lean muscle that even in unconsciousness conveyed coiled, deadly strength. Probably in her midtwenties, she was in her prime, and if she weren't a murderous fiend, she'd be hot. He fingered her ruined clothing. He'd always been a sucker for women in leather. Preferably, short leather skirts, but tight pants would do.

Wraith tipped the woman's chin back and inspected her face. 'I thought Aegi were human. She looks human. Smells human.' His fangs flashed as his tongue swiped at the bloody punctures in her throat. 'Tastes human.'

Eidolon probed a peculiar valve bisecting the transverse colon. 'What did I say about tasting patients?'

'What?' Wraith asked innocently. 'We had to know if she's human.'

'She is. Aegi are human.' Shade shook his head, making his stud earring glint in the light from the overhead. 'Something's wrong here. It's like she's infected with a demon mutation. Maybe a virus.'

'No, she was born this way. She's got a demon parent. Look.' Eidolon showed his brother the genetic proof, the organs that had formed from a human-demon union, something that occurred more frequently than most knew, but that human doctors diagnosed as certain 'syndromes.' 'Her physical abnormalities could be a birth defect. Or maybe these two species aren't compatible genetically. She was probably born with some unusual traits, ones she's been hiding or that haven't been blatantly noticeable. Like better-than-average eyesight. Or telepathy. But I'll bet my stethoscope this is causing problems now.'

'Like what?'

'Could be anything. Maybe she's losing her hearing or pissing herself in public.' Excited, because this kind of thing made his corner of hell interesting, he glanced up at Shade, who palmed her forehead and closed his eyes.

'I can feel it,' he said, his voice rough with the effort he expended to go deep into her body at the cellular level. 'Some of her DNA feels fragmented. We can fuse it. We could—'

Wraith let out a disgusted snort. 'Don't even think about it. If you fix her, you could turn her into some sort of uber assassin. That's all we need hunting us.'

'He's right,' Shade agreed, the glossy black of his eyes going flat. 'Depending on the species, it's possible that we could turn her damn near immortal.'

Sedating and medicating could also prove difficult, given the unidentified demon DNA. Something as seemingly innocent as aspirin could kill her.

Eidolon studied her for a moment, thinking. 'We'll take care of her immediate injuries, and deal with the rest later. She should have the choice about whether or not she wants the demon half to be integrated.'

'Choice?' Wraith scoffed. 'You think she gives her victims a choice? You think Roag had a choice?'

Though Eidolon often thought about their fallen brother, hearing his name out loud was a punch to the gut. 'Do you give your victims a choice?' he asked softly.

'I have to feed.'

'You need to drink blood. You don't need to kill.'

Wraith pushed away from the wall. 'You're an asshole.' Lashing out with one arm, he sent a tray full of surgical instruments flying and swept out of the room.

Shade crouched to help Paige pick up the mess. 'You shouldn't provoke him.'

'You're the one who brought up the junkie.'

'He knows I was yanking his chain. He's been clean for months.'

Eidolon wished he could share Shade's certainty. Wraith liked to escape his life now and then, but since their species was immune to drug and alcohol highs unless the substances had been processed through human blood, eating a human druggie was Wraith's only path to blotto.

'I'm tired of coddling him,' Eidolon said, pulling another tray of instruments to him. 'Let alone constantly yanking his ass out of trouble.'

'He needs time.'

'Ninety-eight years isn't enough time? Shade, in two years he's going to go through his transition. He's not ready. He'll get us all killed.'

Shade said nothing, probably because there was nothing to say. Their brother was out of control, and as the only Seminus demon in history to have been conceived by a vampire female, he was alone and had no idea how to handle his urges and instincts. As a male who had been tortured in the most heinous ways imaginable by the vampires who'd raised him, he had no idea how to live life at all.

Not that Eidolon had room to judge. He'd spent the last half-century concentrating on nothing but medicine, but unless he found a mate, in a few months his focus would shift and narrow until he became a mindless beast that functioned on instinct alone.

Maybe he should let the Buffy kill him now and get it over with.

He looked down at her, at the deceptively innocent face, and wondered just how easily and remorselessly she'd take him down.

Before she could do that, though, he'd have to fix her.

'Paige, scalpel.'

൭

Awareness came slowly, in a haze of black blotches punctuated by points of light. Warm, elastic darkness tugged at Tayla, luring her toward slumber, but pain prodded her into consciousness. Every inch of her body ached, and her head felt heavy, too large for her neck to support. Groaning, she opened her eyes.

Fuzzy, shadowy images swirled and pulsed in front of her. Gradually, her vision came into focus, and whoa . . . she must be in another realm, because the dark-haired man staring down at her was a god. His lips, glistening sensuously as if he'd just licked them, were moving, but the buzz in her ears drowned out his words.

She narrowed her eyes and concentrated on his mouth. Name. He wanted her name. She had to think about it for a second before she remembered. Great. She must have hit her head. Which, duh, explained the headache.

'Tayla,' she croaked, and wondered why her throat hurt so much. 'Tayla Mancuso. I think. Does that sound right to you?'

He smiled, and if she weren't dying on some type of table, she'd have appreciated the sexy curve of his mouth and the flash of very white teeth. The guy must have a fab dentist.

'Tayla? Can you hear me?'

She could, but the buzzing lingered. 'Uh-huh.'

'Good.' He put a hand on her forehead, allowing her a glimpse of one muscular arm adorned by intricate, swirling tribal tattoos. 'You're at a hospital. Is there anything I need to know? Allergies? Medical conditions? Parentage?'

She blinked. Had he said 'parentage'? And could eyelashes hurt? Because hers did.

'This is a waste of time.' The new speaker, an exotic-looking man, Middle Eastern, maybe, glared down at her.

'Go handle your own patients, Yuri.' The hot doctor with the espresso eyes shoved Yuri aside. 'Can you answer my question, Tayla?'

Right. Allergies, parentage, medical conditions. 'Um, no. No allergies.' No parents, either. And her medical condition wasn't something she could share.

'Okay then. I'm going to give you something to help you sleep, and if it doesn't kill you, when you wake up you'll feel better.'

Better would be good. Because if she felt a little less like she'd been run over by a truck, she could jump on Dr. Hottie.

The very fact that she wanted to jump Dr. Hottie told her more about the state of her head trauma than anything else, but what the hell. The pretty nurse had just injected her with something that totally rocked, and if she wanted to think about boinking a bronzed, tattooed, impossibly handsome doctor who was so far out of her league she needed a telescope to see him, then screw it.

Screw him. Over and over.

'I'll bet you could make a woman throw out all her toys.' Had she said that out loud? The cocky grin on his face told her that yes, she'd verbalized her runaway thoughts. 'Drugs talking. Don't get excited.'

'Paige, push another milligram,' he said, in his rich, smooth doctor voice.

A warm, burning sensation washed through her veins from the IV line in the back of her hand. 'Mmm, trying to get rid of me, huh?'

'That's already been discussed.'

Damn, this guy was saying some weird shit. Not that it mattered. Her eyes wouldn't open anymore, and her body wouldn't work. Only her ears still seemed to function, and as she drifted off, she heard one last thing.

'Wraith, I already told you. You can't kill her.'

Aww. Her hot doctor was protecting her. She'd have smiled if her face hadn't frozen. And clearly, her hearing had gone, too, because he couldn't have tacked on what she thought he tacked on.

'Yet.'

DESIRE UNCHAINED

Runa Wagner never meant to fall in love with the sexy stranger but she couldn't resist the unbelievable passion that burned between them . . . a passion that died when she discovered his betrayal and found herself forever changed. Now, determined to make Shade pay for the transformation that haunts her, Runa searches for him – but ends up prisoner to his darkest enemy.

A Seminus Demon with a love-curse that threatens him with eternal torment, Shade hoped he'd seen the last of Runa and her irresistible charm. But when he wakes up in a dank dungeon chained next to a mysteriously powerful Runa, he realises that her effect on him is more dangerous than ever. As their captor casts a spell that bonds them as lifemates, Shade and Runa must fight for their lives and their hearts – or succumb to a madman's evil plans.

978-0-7499-5567-0

PASSION UNLEASHED

Serena Kelley is an archaeologist and treasure hunter – and a woman with a secret. Since she was seven, she's been a keeper of a powerful charm that grants her health and immortality . . . as long as she stays a virgin. But Serena isn't all that innocent. And when a dangerously handsome stranger brings her to the brink of ecstasy, she wonders if she's finally met the one man she cannot resist.

Wraith is a Seminus demon with a death wish. But when an old enemy poisons him, he must find Serena and persuade her to give him the only known antidote in the universe – her charm. Yet, as she begins to surrender to his seductions and Wraith senses the cure is within his grasp, he realises a horrible truth: he's falling for the woman whose life he must take in order to save his own.

978-0-7499-5572-4

ECSTASY UNVEILED

Lore, a Seminus half-breed demon, has been forced to act as his master's assassin. Now to earn his freedom and save his sister's life, he must complete one last kill. Powerful and ruthless, he'll stop at nothing to carry out this deadly mission.

Idess is an earthbound angel sworn to protect the human Lore is targeting. She's determined to thwart her wickedly handsome adversary by any means necessary. But what begins as a simple seduction soon turns into all-consuming passion. Torn between duty and desire, Lore and Idess must join forces as they battle their attraction for each other. Because an enemy from the past is rising again – one hell-bent on vengeance and unthinkable destruction.

978-0-7499-5577-9

SIN UNDONE

As the only female Seminus demon ever born, master assassin
Sinead Donnelly is used to being treated like an outcast. She spent
decades enslaved, and now vows she'll die before she'll relinquish
her freedom again. Then Sin's innate ability to kill her enemies
goes awry: she creates a lethal new werewolf virus that sparks
a firestorm of panic and violence.

Half-werewolf, half-vampire Conall Dearghul is charged with bringing in Sin to face punishment for the plague. And she's no stranger:
he's bound to her by blood, and the one sexual encounter they shared
has left him hungering for her raw sensuality. Worse, Sin is the underworld's most wanted and Con soon learns he's the only one who can
help her . . . and that saving her life might mean sacrificing his own.

978-0-7499-5582-3